# Chanting Denied Shores

- The Komagata Maru Narratives -

A Novel by

# Tariq Malik

BAYEUX

To all hyphenated Canadians




And three remarkable teachers
*Sadhu Binning, Hugh Johnston and Sultan Somjee*

CHANTING DENIED SHORES
© 2010 Bayeux Arts
119 Stratton Cres. SW.
Calgary, Canada T3H 1T7

www.bayeux.com

Cover illustration and book's design and layout: Hadi Farahani

First printing: November 2010

Library and Archives Canada Cataloguing in Publication


Malik, Tariq, 1951-
    Chanting Denied Shores : Komagata Maru Narratives / Tariq Malik.

ISBN 978-1-897411-16-2


1. Komagata Maru Incident, 1914--Fiction. I. Title.

PS8626.A44C43 2010              C813'.6
C2010-907151-4

Printed in Canada

Books published by Bayeux Arts are available at special quantity discounts
to use as premiums and sales promotions, or for use in corporate training
programs. For more information, please write to Special Sales, Bayeux Arts,
Inc., 119 Stratton Crescent SW, Calgary, Canada T3H 1T7.

The ongoing publishing activities of Bayeux Arts, under its "Bayeux" and
"Gondolier" imprints, are supported by the Canada Council for the Arts, the
Alberta Foundation for the Arts, and the Government of Canada through the
Book Publishing Industry Development Program.

21 May 1914


Approaching the final quarter of the night all onboard human activity finally ceases. The ship's cavernous hull now begins to reverberate in response to a deep and sonorous wailing rising from the depths.
The singsong drowns the throb and hiss of the steamship's bellows and lapses into silence.

Whalesong! Informs my agitated mind as I try to pad silently up the clanging metal stairs.

No. A call to prayer! Murmurs my heart; this is a muffled call to prayer coming from a submerged, dislocated minaret;
a call to morning chanting.

## PROLOGUE

## 19TH MAY 1914

## BASHIR AND *THE LAST BEST WEST*

If my journey has a beginning at all it is here, with the moneylender tenderly stroking his battered briefcase and uttering the cryptic mantra under his breath - *Free Land, Free Land for the million in Kanada* - as if the deed to the Promised Land was already his to give. And, upon seeing that he has piqued my interest, his hand reaches reverentially into the briefcase to extract a large folded poster.

It feels refreshingly cool to the touch.

Until this pivotal moment in my life, every brochure I have seen promoting immigration to Canada has, oh so solicitously and compellingly, instructed me to *Head West, Head WEST!* Multi-hued profiles of heroic figures with chiseled, Teutonic features have perched atop mountain peaks, and pointed to the right half of these posters, as if urging one and all to discard the baggage of their past lives and launch themselves towards an earthly paradise. No one has yet been able to explain to me why this tantalizing future has always been touted as being as close to me as the nearest western horizon, perhaps lying just beyond the reassuring sweep of those muscular arms. In these heady times, it has seemed that this unabashed campaign to direct me westwards with the veritable slogan of *The Last Best West* has been proclaimed from every page that I have turned to. And, the bright, multi-hued, lithographic promotion slipped so gratuitously into my hand, its corners already partially disintegrated from multiple handlings, has been no different.

Here, don't just take my word for it, let me show it to you, or at least what is left of it with me. I know its contents by heart by now. You see, it has traveled with me all the way to Canada and then back. Twice.

Here, let me read it to you.

You see this large washed out body of text at the top. It once read:

*FREE FARMS FOR THE MILLION*
*Free farms of 160 acres given to every male adult of 18 years and over,*
*in the green fertile belt of Manitoba, Canadian Northwest and British Columbia.*
*100 to 200 acres are offered in other parts of Canada*
*Climate the healthiest in the world*
*The Department of the Interior - High Commissioner for Canada*

And further down the page, right here amidst this jumble of smaller text and images, is an endorsement by the Canadian Pacific Railway for immigration to these farmlands. Here is a series of illustrations of what appear to be a number of farms. Just look at how neatly organized, bustling, prosperous and modern these farms appear to be. Now, if one were to believe the self-congratulatory claims being made here by the officious sounding Dominion of Canada, these farms were apparently just lying in wait for millions of men like me to walk in and stake their claim.

You will obviously have seen similar posters floating around in other parts of eastern Asia. I couldn't possibly have known it at the time as assuredly as I do now, but these must originally have been targeted at someone other than myself, perhaps someone traveling west from Europe? And, how these beguiling summons made their way into the hands of our astute village moneylender merely goes to show his resourcefulness.

However, this pertinent bit of geographical detail will only be challenged much later, when I am freshly delivered so close to the Canadian shore by conversely having traveled solely eastwards. I will then begin to wonder why had I - Bashir Ali Lopoke, a 28 years old Punjabi farmer's son turned teacher, and an 'Easterner' compelled to travel even further east - been so prompt to shed the burden of my 'past lives'. Why had I been so eager to shed this skin and assume others in order to launch myself towards an unfamiliar shore, and an even more unsecured future?

Was it this celestial hand that had finally nudged me east, and planted the original notion that my future lay somewhere beyond the eastern horizon?

There will be time later to ponder each of these motivations.

For now, with our vessel continuing to drift eastwards in the Pacific penumbral light, the universe is held in breathless thrall of its own re-creation. And, I am sufficiently attuned to this phenomenon to realize that this very ordinary and innocent pre-dawn world has suddenly become full of tangential possibilities.

Much later in life, whenever Jean remembered the time of the twin tragedies, she would also recall how the new house had greeted them. Its heady and unwelcome whiff of unfamiliar odours. The mingling of fresh paint, the tingle of cut cardboard, the homely odour of wallpaper glue and the astringent bite of cedar wood shavings that continued to linger for months no matter how much the house was aired.

Barely seven at the time, Jean could still recall in minute detail the initial bout of disorientation that would heighten the nostalgia for her former Denman street neighbourhood. She missed its heady brew of frequent street brawls, dogs barking at passing streetcars and the waterfront whistles of steamships, ferries and tugboats. Whenever an autumn fog rolled onto their street the lighthouse foghorn would begin moaning early in the evening, the sidewalk planks whispering with the delicate nocturnal scampering of deer and racoons.

Whenever the nine-o'clock-gun went off in the nearby Stanley Park to announce the nightly hour for locals and ships at sea, her meticulous father, 'Hopi' to her, and Mr. Hopkinson to everyone else, would animatedly raise his arms in the air as if he were tracing out an ethereal sphere to inform our visitors: "This boom will now be heard at Granville and Hastings at exactly five seconds after nine. It will reach the neighbourhood of Marpole thirty seconds later, and distant New Westminster a full minute after nine. Folks in far off Mission claim they can hear it at three minutes after nine."

Obviously her father took an inordinate pride in sharing such trivia.

Jean would particularly miss the personal history embedded into every feature of their abandoned, scruffy home – the aroma of rising sourdough and the permanent whiff of pipe tobacco smoke that they had somehow inherited, even though no one in their family had ever smoked. Even the smouldering sawdust in the kitchen burner had added an ingrained residue of smoked resin into the draperies and every piece of furniture.

At the time of relocating to their new Kitsilano house over the previous summer, most of their personal belongings still remained unpacked and scattered about the porch. However, her tow-headed sister, Connie, barely two at time, had already made herself at home, crawling and scrambling over the unpacked luggage and repeatedly getting tangled underfoot. During those first cluttered days, their mum, Nellie, would often have to extricate and carry Connie upstairs, having either caught her intently licking on the square-headed nails hammered into the exposed tarpaper, or attempting to push open the outer door. It was as if she, too, wanted to get as far away as possible from the new home.

But what the new house lacked in charm, the world outdoors amply made up for the two sisters. The neighbourhood of Kitsilano on the outskirts of Vancouver was still considered new and remote enough that Jean's mother had a hard time convincing downtown merchants to make commercial deliveries. And, Jean had been quick to discover that, located as the house was on a slight plateau of land bounded by Sixth and Vine on one side and Balsam and Fourth Avenue on the other, it was only a short two blocks from all the shiny candy stores, the bustling traffic of noisy back-firing and exhaust spewing automobiles, bicyclists, horse drawn carts, and even the occasional lone horse-rider. Unlike Denman, the trolley line here ran smack down the middle of Fourth Avenue where the tar macadam was at its driest and firmest.

During the long summer days, with the household chores all completed, the two sisters had already begun to head out into the street where Jean's friends would eagerly gather to play. And, by the end of their first month of move, she had realized that this street, too, was equally magical as any. Here fanciful pageants unfolded daily before their windows while an endless parade of eccentric men and women plied their trades from house to house. Gradually, the once familiar world of Denman was to become too laid back and staid for their newly acquired freedom and tastes.

Since the front road to their house slopes downwards on either side of the house, enterprising salesmen have a hard time making it all the way to their doorstep. Minding Connie in front of the house, Jean watches intent native Indians and Chinese washerwomen stomp quietly by, while other working women rattle off on bicycles to offices with their skirts hitched above their ankles with garters and rubber bands. Later in the morning, heavy-set tradesmen patiently labour up the slope, often having to alight from their carriages to walk besides their horses, muttering to them softly in their guttural east European accents or humming snippets from their stock of folk songs.

A simple set of delivery instructions posted inside the front windows of the houses has the power to summon a host of these men to appear at every doorstep.

The first of these to venture up to the Hopkinson's street on summer mornings is usually the ice deliveryman. Even though each block of ice with its floating pool of opacity is Jean's height, this brute of a man is capable of swinging it gracefully like a pendulum over the carriage top and onto the sidewalk. He then rapidly splits up each chunk with an ice pick - not a single motion wasted in his race against time, evaporation and heat. If the sisters are lucky they will be offered slivers of ice to chew before the ice disappears under its jute sack.

A Chinaman delivers live fish wrapped in moistened leaves that are crammed into two ceramic bowls slung over his shoulder. On the rare occasions that Nellie buys fish from him, he will squat at their doorstep to dress the fish by chopping its head off with a single blow of a large cleaver. Near Christmastime, he will also deliver tiny baskets of mandarin oranges that are individually wrapped in tissue paper, the only time of the year when you would actually got to see these.

When the knife sharpener makes his rounds he will invite the neighbourhood to bring out their dull knives, scissors, garden shears, and axe blades. He will then raise his bike onto its stand and peddling furiously with one foot send a comet of sparks flying everywhere, his skilled hands barely touching the whirring surface of the sander.

However, the most intriguing and entertaining of all these visitors to their street will turn out to be the bearded men from the nearby mills and lumber yards who deliver loose cords of firewood. Jean's father has taught the sisters that these men are not 'Hindoos', as everyone else calls them, but Sikhs who belong to an Indian religion, and are easily recognized by their turbans and beards as they make their deliveries from hand-pulled wooden carts. Unlike all the other hawkers no one has ever seen them use a horse for this purpose.

Then, one day, a strange thing happens. While Jean is out playing in the front yard she notices three Sikhs crossing the street and heading straight for their doorstep. They stand there squinting wordlessly for some time as if expecting someone to greet them. Eventually, one of them pulls out a pocket watch and examines it closely. Thinking the visitors are here to make a delivery Jean points to the side of the house where the chutes for coal, firewood and sawdust were located. She has seen Nellie do this countless times.

It is only then that she notices that they do not have a cart or firewood with them.

Seeing her puzzled expression, all three break into grins simultaneously, the tallest one stepping forward and explaining gently, his eyes twinkling with amusement at her naïve assumption. "No, no, *bibi sahiba, na*. We are coming here looking for mister Hopkins *saab*. Tell us, is he home?"

This is to be her first introduction to the three kindly but odd men whom she will later come to know so fondly as her three teddy bear uncles – Bela, Baboo and Ganga. Whenever they arrive at the doorstep it will always be with the same request to see Hopi. And, once they get to know her better – as Nellie is never inclined to talk to any of them directly when Hopi is away – Jean is always sent out to receive their messages.

Besides, she has already learnt how amused the visitors will be whenever she calls her father 'Hopi', and she never lets an opportunity go by to show off. She has grown up hearing her uncle Wally call her father Bill, but Nellie has always addressed him as Hopi, and that has settled the matter for Jean. For a while Jean had even experimented with calling her mum 'Nell', even though she was pointedly ignored. The matter had come to a head with Nell finally losing all patience and blurting out, "Young girl, you are no tramp. You will always address me properly as Nellie, or mother, or even mum if you must. But I never expect to hear you call me by my maiden name when in polite company."

William Charles Hopkinson, British Columbia's Head Inspector of Immigration, has been expecting the men all Sunday afternoon, even though aware of their uncertain and tardy routines. On hearing them chattering like a flock of birds settling onto his backyard, he must now make a determined effort to tone down his irritation with them. Bela's unmistakable sonorous growl is already rising above his daughter's dulcet squeals of delight. There is no keeping this girl from attention, he thinks, hurrying up the stairs, and blinking rapidly in the strikingly bright sunlight.

The three men are peering down with presumptuous familiarity at his little girl while prattling on with one voice. Seeing her father approaching, Jean is suddenly self-conscious and vanishes abruptly indoors.

"Bela, Baboo, ah! Ganga Ram. Good, good. Yes, you all are finally here," Hopkinson nods in establishing eye contact with each one in greeting. As usual, Ganga's eyes remain averted.

"So, what urgency brings you here on a Sunday afternoon? Do you have something new to report?" Hopkinson is careful to address Bela directly.

"Sar, they will be here soon."

"Soon, how soon is soon?"

"I don't know exactly, sar." Bela steps closer to Hopkinson so that the others have to strain to overhear them.

"Well, have you found out who is leading them?" Hopkinson demands.

"They say it is one named Gurdit," offers Bela diffidently.

"One? Who is One?" asks Ganga abruptly, sheepishly waking up to find himself in the midst of their dialogue.

*"Teri maa da yaar."* Bela whispers under his breath, spinning around gracefully on the balls of his feet, and winking as he lays a large hairy paw on Ganga's diminutive shoulder. All the while he keeps an eye on Hopkinson to see if his brief flash of insolence has registered their internal friction.

To Hopkinson he now reveals: "Sar, one named Gurdit Singh Sarhadi or Sarhali or something similar? A friend of the Canadian high commissioner in Hong Kong. An educated and very rich man from Singapore by all accounts."

"Hmm. Yes, yes, but what else do you know about him? What does he intend to do here in Canada? And, more importantly, does he have any links to anyone on our watch list? Any close friends or relatives here in Canada?"

"They say that he is such a successful businessman that he wants to challenge the Empire."

"Challenge the Empire? How does he intend to do that?" Hopkinson is at pains to keep his irritation in check.

"By gathering a group of dissatisfied Hindus and sailing with them to Canada."

"When are they expected to make shore?"

"No one seems to know that for sure, sar. I have been getting all kinds of answers. According to Hari, they should be here in a week or two."

"Well that narrows it down then, doesn't it? They could be here tomorrow or the next month? Bela, I have told you time and time again to keep an eye on that Hardayal. You can't always rely merely on what he chooses to pass on to you. All this is hearsay to me, and what have I repeatedly told you about such gossip?"

Bela is momentarily stumped for a response. "It is hard to be accurate in these matters, sar," he offers lamely while stubbornly holding his gaze. "They say different things. I don't think even they know the exact date. Perhaps, we could get on the radio and try to find out for ourselves before they do. And then set up a very warm reception for them, huh?"

"Only if the ship too has a radio," quips Hopkinson.

"It would if it were heading into open water and planning a secret Pacific crossing."

"Well, we can't be sure of that, either. Can we?" Hopkinson is now beginning to openly show his exasperation with all the wild-eyed conjecturing that is being offered to him as reliable information.

The brief silence that follows is the cue for Ganga Ram to offer his report.

"I have heard that one Balwant Singh arrived from Moji by steamer yesterday and spoke to a meeting in the Victoria *gurdwara*. He also brought an advertisement for Gurdit's mission. By evening he reached Vancouver and claims to have spoken to Gurdit himself and to those aboard the ship."

"Is that our temple *granthi* Balwant Singh? I thought he was still in Hong Kong."

"No, sar. He is now here. And I even have with me the advertisement he brought along. You can see how Gurdit has been using this to recruit men for his voyage."

The four men crowd around him to examine the paper Ganga Ram holds out.

"There is this one other thing that I have to report, sar." This time it is the unassuming Baboo Singh who has remained sullen and withdrawn till now.

"What is it?" Hopkinson is livid that he has had to wait so long to hear from him.

"I have heard something about the ship now heading for the port of Alberni on Vancouver Island."

"Port Alberni? Why there? It is so far inland, nearly half the way across the island. Maybe Mr. Gurdit intends to dump his passengers and cargo there in a remote location and thus circumvent the authorities," Hopkinson finds himself speculating.

"I say we should take the lead from the Shore Committee to show us the way to the ship," Bela, is now quick to point out, realizing that the conversation is slipping away from him and scrambling to regain a perceived loss of face. He searches Hopkinson's face for clues to a possible outcome.

"Yes, the Shore Committee. Bela, I understand some of the local chaps are already going around Vancouver gathering food and funds for Gurdit and his men. If that is true then they already know more about these new arrivals than us. I want you and your men to dig a little deeper. I need names. Personal histories. Something concrete. Enough of this letting the Shore Committee solve the mystery for us. We should be anticipating their every move instead of letting them lead us by the nose."

Hopkinson searches their faces for signs of disquiet, wondering if there was something useful they were still withholding, before he abruptly turns to Bela. "My friend, I think the stage is now set for our Narain *bhai* to make an appearance."

Bela's only acknowledgement to this is to snicker inwardly, twirling a strand of his whiskers, and, noting that he has been dismissed, hustles his men out of the gate.

Jean, the men notice, has still not emerged from her cocoon.

By late Sunday morning when the rain finally lets up, the two Sikh deliverymen follow a circuitous uphill route of freshly laid tarmac, lugging a cart overflowing with odd cords of firewood and storage boxes of sawdust.

In trundling up the classy Shaughnessy Heights' newly minted estates, their path lies in spotty patches of shade from the odd mature cedar or maple that has been spared the original cull, a handful of spindly six-year old oaks, and the exuberance of blossoming Japanese cherries and apples. As they pass the well-trimmed croquet, badminton and tennis courts, their attention wanders to the fanciful ornamental topiaries that are tended by gardeners armed with palm-sized clippers. Other men are busy watering the patchwork of sprawling lawns hugging each nook of this ordered sloping contour of the land.

This exclusive and rambling enclave rising in south Vancouver, named after the Canadian Pacific Railway's president and budding scion, Sir Thomas Shaughnessy, has become the west coast's equivalent of Montreal's elite Square Mile. Nearly all of Shaughnessy Heights' 243 discriminating households are listed in the Vancouver social register, from which Jews and Orientals have been solicitously excluded by a decree of the city council. And, to those who have thus been disqualified, life on these hillsides seems to be an endless summer filled with rounds of afternoon teas and picnics, yacht parties and charity balls.

Safely ensconced in their widely spaced houses, amidst their clutter of accumulated knickknacks, and shielded from the hectic world scurrying barely a city block away along the Granville Street, Vancouver's elite could be forgiven for indulging in the delicious delusion that it really is summer forever here in Paradise. The two enterprising mill hands are bewildered to discover that so much of the surrounding opulence has been left unoccupied - the residing maharajas are conspicuous by their leisured absence from their properties.

When these men initially began their firewood enterprise for the single day off from work at the lumber mill, their instructions had been simple: "*Yaaro*, all you need to learn is to count change in English and to shout out the words 'firewood' and 'sawdust'. Mind you, you will be competing against coal gas, bunker fuel and piped gas that burn cleaner. However, what you also need to bear in mind is that there will always be a demand for our good old firewood. Nothing can ever replace the fireplace."

Or so they have optimistically been led to believe by their well-meaning friends.

Tall and bulky Mewa, and his stolid roommate Raghvir, are now headed for one of the crown jewels of this exclusive enclave, the Glen Brae. This spectacularly towering mansion belongs to the retired lumber baron William Lamont Tait and they are guided to the estate by its prominent twin copulas soaring over the surroundings. These peculiar hemispheres have already become the butt of several rude jokes amongst the local rubes, with some even considering this, in spite of the pretensions of its current owner, to be the ugliest house in Vancouver. The deliverymen stare at the twin protuberances hovering above them and Raghvir momentarily lets go of the cart to reach heavenwards with open arms. They grin back at each other.

In the owner's absence on personal business on the Continent, his dignified Indian cook, Nirmal *Khansama*, now manages the estate. It was he who had sent for the men during a trip downtown. Beaming with obvious pride in his freshly acquired stature, and resplendent in an extravagant gold silk jacket, complete with epaulets, tightly wound starched green turban, silk cummerbund and spotless white gloves, he now greets the firewood-hawkers at the back gate. During an extended visit to Delhi, Mr. Lamont Tait had somehow overheard that the man leading an Indian marching band was also an exquisite master of North Indian cuisine. And, Lamont's discerning eye had immediately plucked Nirmal out of the band, briskly made the acquisitions and transfers, and then proceeded to patiently coach him on each of the requisite social protocols at the Glen Brae. The inspired gold braided uniform is a constant reminder of that fortunate event. Surprised to learn that his Indian chef was not familiar with a favorite South Indian soup, Tait had good-naturedly instructed him on the Canadian version of Mulligatawny, one that substituted scrawny Indian chicken with brawny Alberta beef.

The deliverymen have also been lured so far from their beaten path by Nirmal's promise of a grand tour of the interior of the mansion. And, after the deliveries have been made, he asks the visitors to remove their shoes at the door - pointedly not removing his own. He now leads them through the backdoor into two adjacent rooms that, the visitors are startled to learn, both serve as kitchens.

"We only use the smaller of these two rooms as our spice kitchen," he ostentatiously points out. Led up to Vancouver's first residential elevator the visitors note that the room reeks vaguely of disinfectant.

Alighting on the third floor, Nirmal pauses to point reverentially at the floor. "Look here, just feel this floor! See, even though this is hardwood it feels as soft as a silk carpet." Sliding his hand across the shiny surface Mewa is astonished to find the floorboards giving way to his gentle touch.

"This room was especially designed for dances and these floorboards have been thoughtfully laid over a bed of seaweed to ease stress on dancing feet." Noting the visitors now gingerly stepping over the yielding floor, he directs their attention to the two identical Victrola machines that are positioned at opposite corners of the room. Encased in their individual glass casings, each gleaming machine is equipped with a neat stack of bakelite Edison records. He resists the temptation to play a snippet of operatic music to further impress his guests, and then steers them towards a ten-foot wide stained glass window that occupies most of the opposite wall. They now peer down into the front yard at an ornate cast-iron gate that faces the front of the house.

"Can you guess how much money was spent by Mr. Lamont Tait to obtain this gate?" he asks with undisguised pride and obvious unwillingness to wait for their response.

"Incredible as it may sound, this one piece of metal-ware cost Mr. Tait more than $10,000, and it was shipped here all the way from distant Glasgow. It took a dozen men just to unpack and install it."

Gratified by the fitting response on the visitors' faces, Nirmal hustles them to ride the elevator back to the lower floor. Here they pause briefly to explore a hallway, where Nirmal dramatically opens and closes several doors to reveal a series of cluttered and elaborate bedrooms, libraries and offices.

The tour ends all too soon on the ground floor with the revelation of a secret doorway that has been skillfully blended entirely into the wallpaper.

"See, Mr. Lamont Tait has thought of everything. There are similar hidden passages and stairways built into the walls of the entire house. These have been specially designed for servicemen to hurry about their business without intruding upon the inhabitants of the manor." Noting their look of bafflement, Nirmal's smugness stretches to an even deeper level.

With the payments for the firewood completed, the visitors now head home with their empty cart. And, once the two are safely out of hearing distance of the garish and patronizing Nirmal, it is Mewa who is first to break their silence.

"First head band master, now head *khansama!* Our Nirmal seems to have come a long way from Hindustan," Mewa snickers.

"And, this spice kitchen? Raghu, remind me again, yaar, what's a spice kitchen?"

"I think it is a place where Mister Shonsy-Hites chews spices," Raghvir offers.

"Hahn," Mewa nods distractedly. "Do you also notice how seamlessly each lawn spills from one property to another. Not a hedge, stone or brick to define their boundary. It is as if the owners were saying to us that our lot in life may have been an accident of birth but now this entire world is our estate. *Waheguru!*"

"Hahn, yaar," Raghvir responds equally despondently. "Our entire living quarters could fit into that space identified for us as the 'spice kitchen'. Mewa, do you think any of these people realize how fortunate they are?"

And, thus, chastened and overwhelmed by the surrounding opulence, they fall silent again; their minds filled with images of rabbit-sized servants scurrying through secret passageways fitted into the walls. Neither of them is yet able to comprehend the fact that the lifesavings they carry buried in the folds of their turbans have already made them wealthier than the average Vancouverite.

The momentum of the cart gently nudges them downhill.

# BASHIR, ADRIFT

# FINAL QUARTER OF THE NIGHT
## 21 May 1914

Approaching the final quarter of the night all onboard human activity finally ceases. The ship's cavernous hull now begins to reverberate in response to a deep and sonorous wailing surfacing up from the depths. The singsong peaks over the metronomic thrum and hiss of the steamship's bellows before subsiding into silence.

*Whalesong!* Informs my agitated mind as I try to pad silently up the clanging metal stairs.

*No. A call to prayer!* Murmurs my untethered heart; this is a muted call to prayer coming from a submerged and dislocated minaret; a call to morning chanting.

My legs are the oars of a boat rowed in opposite directions by its several occupants. And, I am only aware of the urgent fact that it is precisely this fleeting interlude of light between night and day - *when a naked eye can first distinguish a black thread from a white one* - a clearly defined instant prescribed for Morning Prayer by my thirteen-century-old scripture, the Quran. I imagine the sphere of this world spinning under the rising sun, the millions of inhabitants of each new land aligning themselves wave upon wave to offer their shared harmonies.

But there is also an insistent, albeit consciously suppressed, voice already tugging at my sleeve to redirect my attention elsewhere. It claims this as the *Amrit Vela* - that ambrosial pause when the Guru's blessings descend upon all those who seek them - *In the Amrit Vela, chant the True Name, and contemplate His Glorious Greatness. The devotees of the Lord plant the seed of the Lord's wealth in the ambrosial hours; they eat it, and spend it, but it is never exhausted.*

A half hour later, my state of indecision finds me hovering close to the railing with the rolled prayer mat still tucked tightly under my arm.

Every prayer is its own reward. Or so I have been led to believe till now.

But I keep losing myself in the petty details of that first voyage, and must now somehow clear up the issue of how I got to be onboard a ship heading for the western coast of Canada.

A long time before this onboard personal spiritual crisis there was a visit to the moneylender's house in my central Punjab hometown of Lopoke. On that fateful late summer afternoon my personal desperation had finally led me to the doorstep from which my would-be benefactor the moneylender-turned-travel-financer, Bansi Lal, ran his business.

A young boy not quite of age to attend school had ushered me into a dark, adjacent room. And, during the next half hour I sweated out my anxiety amidst the sparse furnishings of the room. The boy had stood staring back at me from the doorsill while slurping noisily on a stick of last winter's sugarcane, its juices flowing down his chin and onto the ground.

In total silence the boy spits out the pulp onto the freshly layered earthen floor, and a halo of flies immediately begins to form at his feet. He remains oddly reticent in casually deflecting my every attempt to engage him in conversation. In the starkness of the unfurnished room with its two sagging, stringed cots, and the only available light pouring in through the open door, I recall noting dryly to myself: Only our Jatt and goldsmith families are richer than our moneylender, yet, is this really how sumptuously he lives?

I am jolted out of my reverie by the boy slinking out of the door to the sound of a man loudly clearing his throat upon entering the courtyard. A moment later, Bansi's generous frame has totally filled the doorway, blocking all light to the room. He seems characteristically flustered and out of breath, sweat oozing from every pore of his shiny, puffed body, the leather briefcase clutched tightly under one sweaty armpit.

"*Hai Ram*, this heat", he finally sighs witheringly to himself before casting an indignant look in my direction. He eases himself onto the spare cot and I watch the frayed fabric stretch taut beneath him. Having thus spent all his energy on seating himself comfortably, he continues to fan his naked upper torso with his shoulder cloth, the ample shiny folds of his upper arms wiggling hypnotically. I have to force myself to look away.

"*Aray, wah, wah! Aray babu,*" Bansi chides me. "What do we have here? Are my eyes deceiving me? Is that really you, *Bashir?*" He shakes his head in mock disbelief. "What could possibly have compelled you to come crawling to my doorstep?"

While he sniffs nervously at the flies buzzing excitedly over the dessicated cane, I wave the poster nervously in his face, taken aback by this unexpected reception. I take this hostility as my cue.

"I came here to see you about this..," I begin holding out the poster but then unsure of how to broach the subject I unexpectedly fall silent.

"I know. Calm down, I know exactly why you are here. You are here for the same reason that the rest of your friends have been here with their tails between your legs. Am I right?"

This time Bansi does not wait for my response.

"Well, now that you are finally here, I want you to clear up something for me. Can you tell me what else you miserable, and indebted Lopoke-wallahs have left to lose? Just look at how the Angrez has whittled away ever larger chunks of your land, then appropriated your harvests, and finally left you burdened with a new set of taxes. What more can you beg for?"

His cynicism is obvious, for having spent all his energy on the opening gambit he now pauses momentarily, breathing noisily through his mouth, and stares belligerently at me in genuine displeasure. He is still agitated enough to rise up and begin pacing before me.

Several minutes later, when his breathing gradually returns to normal he seats himself opposite me, his limpid eyes reflecting the doorway. He blinks rapidly and looks up at me in alarm as if seeing me afresh. He holds up an index finger as if to draw attention to a point he is about to make.

"Look, Bashir bhai let me begin this anew. Let me start by informing you how fully I understand the pickle you and your friends have got yourselves in. I can actually tell you exactly, to the last cowry, how much of a fortune you are currently earning here as our elementary schoolmaster. I know reliably that this amounts to barely three rupiyas, and some loose change. But wait. Let me be more precise," he pauses theatrically as if deciphering the etchings across the ceiling's tangled reed work, before resuming: "Let me make that three rupiyas and one and half anna a month. Am I right? Am I right? Huh?"

He chortles at my obvious discomfort.

"So, Bashir-ji, now consider my next words even more carefully. Your entire monthly salary today amounts to roughly one Amriki dallar! Just one whole dallar!"

Up comes the index finger again for emphasis, only this time it is pointed at my face.

"Now you tell me, master-ji, how much do you think a hard workingman in Kanada or Amrika can earn in the course of just a single working day?"

"Ten dollars?" I offer with faint optimism, yet squirming in the face of such a candid evaluation of the net worth of my day's work. I am left wondering how the government pay scale had become public knowledge?

"*Hah*! Ten dallar? *Wah, wah!*" He cackles animated with obvious comic relief. He even claps his hands silently in applause before clutching his briefcase close to his body.

29

"The time for jokes, my little babu, is long since past. But, seriously, can you imagine being able to save as much as three dallar in the course of just one day. See, for you, bhai Bashir, just one day of employment in Kanada will be worth more than a month of misery in the Punjab."

He now leans back, contentedly stretching his arms backwards and surveys a suspiciously dark corner of the room once more. This makes me even more nervous. Was someone hiding in there listening to our every word? Were there to be other witnesses to this humiliation?

After a few moments of further silence during which he picks at the greasy thread looped over his shoulder, he returns his gaze towards me. This time his tone is almost solemn.

"Now, I do know for a fact that as of today your one Amriki dallar is equal to three of our Indian rupiyas. Given this exchange rate, can you even begin to comprehend how much more you will be able to earn within a month, and how easily you could multiply these savings in just a single year?"

I am now aware that we are entering familiar territory that has been expounded over upon several such visits. While I ponder how to curtail the ensuing monologue, a part of me is still recoiling in humiliation, and the realization of how paltry my net worth must seem to everyone.

Meanwhile, Bansi has been droning on and on.

"Do you recall how your neighbor Karim bhai was able to toil away at a meager wage of only two dollars a day in a Vancouver mill, yet he managed to save over one thousand dallars in no time at all, ... what a fortune for such a simple-minded farmer. And, to think that only three years ago he was as dirt poor as any one of your friends..."

The torrent does not stop at this.

"...And besides this, unlike the rest of these rough men, you are educated. You have an excellent command of English, Arabic, Urdu, Farsi *and* Punjabi. Surely, relying on these skills you will have no problem in finding office work or a teaching post in Kanada. You may never have to toil in the lumber mills or farms, or even dirty your hands; just hire others to work your land for you. I am sure you will have read somewhere what our scholar Swami-ji Ram Tirth has to say recommending America as a second home. How different can it possibly be in Kanada?"

However, what our facilitating Bansi Lal does not know during this exchange is that I have a more compelling argument in favor of my decision to relocate, an ulterior motive that has more to do with my personal safety then personal gain. But I must leave that revelation for later as I seem to be leaping ahead of myself.

Given as we are here in Lopoke to exaggeration, I cannot definitely claim to have been the first Indian to have ventured out to

Canada, or 'Kanada' as that great land has been locally known to us; there was already a sizeable Indian community of about two thousand of us eking out a living of sorts in Canada before me. And, though our bhai Gurdit-ji will protest vehemently over this, let me also put to rest any lingering notion that we ventured out of India overflowing with revolutionary fervor to overthrow the British and gain independence for our India, or that anyone of us fully anticipated or prepared for what lay in wait for us across the Pacific. In fact, my case was typical of the rest of us onboard. Simply stated, I just wanted a better life than the one I had been cornered into in India.

Like me, some of the other farmers still owned small parcels of land that we often celebrated as the most fertile lands in the world, a land that had yielded two crops a year since anyone could remember. However, as the ruling British continued to siphon off food grains and raw materials to keep their own folks back home securely employed and well fed, whole rural regions of India were still being devastated by a series of crippling famines.

I had read comments on this from no less illustrious and insightful figures than Karl Marx who had stated nearly half a century earlier, and I quote from the booklet that has survived my travels: *'If we knew nothing of the past history of Hindostan, would there not be the one great and incontestable fact, that even at this moment India is held in English thraldom by an Indian army maintained at the cost of India? The question, therefore, is not whether the English had a right to conquer India, but whether we are to prefer India conquered by the Turk, by the Persian, by the Russian, to India conquered by the Briton. England has to fulfill a double mission in India: one destructive, the other regenerating the annihilation of old Asiatic society, and laying the material foundations of Western society in Asia.'*

Realistically speaking, there were now really only two options left open to the males of farming families like mine: join the Indian British army or immigrate to some undeveloped far-flung corner of the British Empire. As Indian Punjabis we had all seen our inherited lands reduced by subdivisions into smaller and smaller plots shared among the male siblings of the family. And, discontentment, as the American scholar Benjamin Franklin has pointed out, makes even a rich man poor. Given my recent murky personal past, recruitment into the British army was not even a remote prospect. And since all other popular destinations of South Africa, Australia and New Zealand were busy introducing restrictive legislation to keep out any new immigrants, moving to Canada seemed to be the only option out of my current predicament.

At the time, immigration to any of Britain's dominions had continued to become an ever daunting challenge. Sardar Bhavan, a college classmate, had already returned from an unsuccessful attempt to enter Australia after failing his literacy dictation. Implemented under the country's new Immigration Restriction Act, it required would-be immigrants to take a 50-word test in a 'European language'. Seeing that Bhavan was fluent in English he was administered the test in Dutch.

Now, if there was one country left that still offered hope it was Canada. And, if it were to be Canada, then Vancouver would have to be the point of entry. Besides, for almost a decade the Punjabis had looked upon this distant Canadian city of Vancouver, or 'One-Couver', in a manner that New York had long been viewed in the imagination of early east European immigrants: the land of immense wealth, hope and equal opportunity. For over a decade we had been inundated by glorified accounts of the vacant Canadian farmlands just waiting to be claimed, and of the endless wild and rolling prairie lands that seemed so suited to the cultivation of our familiar wheat. These oft-repeated legends from the mouths of those who had seen these wonders first-hand, had acquired the drone of a mantra, one that begun to sound as if the vacant land itself was repeating to farmers half way across the world.

While all these dark thoughts have been tumbling in rapid succession through my head, Bansi's voice has continued to whine on:

"... in Kanada and Amrika, unlike here, the factory owners and farmers reward their laborers very handsomely. And if you continue to work hard, you can easily earn six to nine rupiyas every single day. And, by continuing to live frugally and saving, you will amass a fortune in no time at all. And, ...."

I notice that having excitedly counted off each argument and supporting figures on his stubby fingertips, he does not require a response from me. Meanwhile, the room has continued to get more cramped and stuffier by the minute, and I realize I will now have to somehow hurry this one-sided bargaining on to its logical conclusion.

Eventually, he falls silent and opening his palms wide as if to say that he has nothing else left to reveal. He declares: "I shall lend you all the money you need to reach your destination in Kanada. And, once you have made a better life there for yourself, you can begin repaying me the little that you still owe me. Surely, anything you earn over there will be an improvement over what you have going on here."

At this he glances slyly at me. "You have seen the posters. It is none other than the Kanada sarkar itself that has issued them. It is Kanada sarkar that is promising you this free land, and all I am guaranteeing is to get you to this piece of land for a small fee."

"But, Bansi, how can I be sure that there are no local farmers pining to snap up these generous offers?" I feel a strong compulsion to get this matter out of the way.

"Hmmm!" He exhales loudly, seemingly uncomfortable for the

first time under my probing gaze, and returns to toying with the thread, sending tremors down the folds of his exposed flesh. Out comes that chastising index finger again, but this time it is no longer being wagged in my direction.

"Master-ji, you are indeed crafty, always teasing out the underlying motivations with your jokes. I should have known immediately what a rough diamond your father was polishing when he borrowed money to send you off to that university in Lahore. Come; let us see if we can work something out that is of mutual benefit."

And, thus, thinking soberly about my financial state, the amounts in question begin not to seem so princely. The baniya will charge a $65 fee for the opportunity to reach Canada and a further fee of $5 per month for every hundred on the outstanding balance.

For the next half hour the banter of the thrust and parry of our bargaining will continue unabated until the young boy reappears at the door, summoned by an unseen signal. This time he is carrying two clattering cups of chai that have overflowed into their chipped saucers. He slips out quietly after placing them at our feet.

The moneylender promptly begins cooling the chai in his cup his cup by pouring it into the saucer, blowing on it rapidly and then slurping it down noisily, while his limpid eyes continue to stare back at me. Then he leans back, and clearing his throat noisily and then wiping his mouth with the back of his hand, he inverts the empty cup over the saucer. I can sense that we are about to conclude our business.

"Now, I am finally going to have the obvious and immense satisfaction of not having to listen to your daily gripes. All these are now common knowledge, and I fully understand your predicament." He pauses for me to add further to this list.

"However, there is one other vital issue you must address before you set out. Do not overlook the little matter of the two hundred dallar head tax that you need to pay to the Kanada sarkar. It would have been a lot cheaper if you had made up your mind earlier as this amount was only twenty-five dallars at the time, but never mind that now. Just remember that once you land in One-Couver, should you wish to do so, you can just as easily continue to travel on to Amrika. It's close by. And I have heard it said that it is all just one big country out there. And, also when you have established yourself over there and struck it rich, you can begin paying me back the little you still owe me."

He follows this with a murmured afterthought: "Topped by a small commission, of course."

"Yes, of course," I concede, "the small commission. And what a 'small commission' it is," I tease, inverting the empty cup over the saucer, thus sealing our agreement. He grins back obligingly, his single gold tooth now gleaming against the dark of his face and the darker interior of the room.

He proceeds to wipe his hands on his tunic, while I tuck the poster away one final time.

Now, with the actual landmass of Canada so close at hand to me, I impulsively reach for this poster to hold up for comparison against a shoreline that I am sure will soon emerge out of this dawn light.

A free farm in Canada!

A *Free Farm* to one who has never farmed in his life or worked outside the classroom, is a *Free Farm* nevertheless to the aspirations of a farmer's son. It will be the pursuit of this reward that after a month of mid-summer's protracted days and compacted nights, I will find myself here, onboard the chartered Japanese vessel, the Komagata Maru, amidst the enveloping expanse of brine that will have swallowed my every familiar horizon.

# LOCATING TRUE NORTH

After gingerly clutching the railing for nearly an hour and relishing the early dawn rush of moist air across my face, I am still sheepishly trying to look past my unresolved dilemmas, the prayer mat under one arm.

As a devout Muslim, I must first locate myself accurately in time and space before I offering my prayers. And, after determining the correct time for the Morning Prayer, I must now also ensure that I am facing in the correct direction of the *qibla* – the shortest distance between Arabia's Mecca and myself. Historically, it was this exigency of locating oneself precisely in time and place that once inspired early Muslims to elaborate and perfect the navigational astrolabe. With the sun marking off the hours dedicated to prayer, and the cycles of the moon counting off my monthly calendar, the night sky would have simply identified this direction for me. However, onboard a moving vessel, so utterly complete has been my state of dislocation and disorientation that all familiar horizons have now become transient.

And, adding to this dislocation is the fact at some point in our northeastwards journey the ship has crossed over a threshold, where the purported shortest distance to Mecca must have shifted from its familiar westward location to somewhere closer to the stationary North Pole star.

For brevity's sake, I must also record here that it is not as if determining my position relative to Mecca has been the only impasse: within the space of a fortnight the nights with their onset of sudden chills have rapidly shortened as the warm days have lengthened; there is the disconcerting awareness that at this instance nightfall is settling over the landmass of India, while I am staring at the first signs of a new dawn rise before me over the North American continent. It is as if every reliable and steadfast axis of my spiritual and physical world has not only begun to progressively unravel, but has tilted tortuously directly overhead - causing me to momentarily loose my balance. I feel as if I have been spun around rapidly and then set free to the mercy of a dizzying vortex.

Unable to thus locate the true direction of a receding stone square in a distant and fading continent, I must now rely on my spiritual training: a lifelong practicing Muslim learns to trust the lodestone of his heart to locate his true North. I now repeatedly examine an unfamiliar sky, hesitantly facing one direction before turning and facing another, waves of self-doubt washing over me, and in seeking a familiar true North I can no longer find anything in response to anchor me firmly to earth.

The rest of the twenty-three fellow Muslims onboard who could be of assistance to me, have chosen to sleep blissfully past sunrise on a day that may well be the last of our journey together. Accompanying our insignificant group of Muslims, there are also a dozen Hindus amidst this congregation of three hundred and forty of Guru Nanak's followers. I can already hear the Sikhs gather for their morning *kirtan,* the swell of their verses drifting upwards through the open arms of the metal doors as a spiritual testimony. A disoriented and conflicted part of me, aware that this fleeting hiatus is also the *Amrit Vela,* the time of nectar, wants to descend the stairs and seek the reassurance and comfort of these familiar chants. But, here too, there are spiritual quandaries that I must be careful to skirt around for the sake of my personal safety. Even if the fiery chants that I once composed to set hearts aflame have been doused, I must now learn to assume different voices, and chant other verses. If today it is my confusion over the choice of morning chants that exposes me, then how far back will this uncertainty take me tomorrow?

The fact that we Muslims are a relatively small minority onboard has recently been brought brusquely home to me. When, amidst much rejoicing and backslapping, this ship was renamed 'Nanak Jahaz' in honor of the founder of the Sikh faith, my suggestions to call it 'Freedom India' were mockingly brushed aside by all.

This is what I had said in voicing my concerns: Is it not enough that the uninvited intruder camped in our midst for over a century has already splintered our social fabric by defining us first along religious lines and then cultural ones? If to them our secular identities are colored by our individual faiths as Hindus, Muslims and Sikhs, and then further shades of regionalism of our being Punjabis, Pushtuns, Sindhis, Bengalis - why have we been so quick to apply these colonial strategies to ourselves? Have we not each in our own personal manner chosen to risk all we possess in participating as equal partners in this journey of eighteen long days and nights since our last port of call at Yokohama?

But mine had been a lone dissenting voice, and I had been intimidated into silence.

As we steam full speed ahead towards the shoreline in the dim light, I can sense the riveted metal plates of the ship's prow straining as they slice vertically through the massed wall of opposing seawater. The collected pools of rainwater trapped around the bridge house ripple in tune to the engines' throb; mastheads strain against under their tether of ropes and chains, and the deck heaves and falls off imperceptibly to a gentle, inner cadence.

I notice that the stars have already begun to fade into the ruddy complexion of a new day's awakening. Everywhere I look now along the faint murky horizon the shoreline is enveloped in swirling wisps of smoke that is punctuated with the occasional bright spark of flames;

and at every close approach streaks of ash begin to rain down upon us. However, wherever the shore is untouched by fire, it is carpeted with towering timbers that stretch all the way to the water's edge. Occasionally, the tree line gives way to the odd log cabin of whitewashed boards, batten walls and rusted roof. Massive interlocked log booms culled from the surrounding forests and set adrift now cling tenuously to these cabins; giant smoke stacks tower over sawmills perched atop stilts as if stretching their feet across the water, and neat rows of cannery sheds crowd the quiet inlets - and nowhere yet the sight of local men.

I have also not yet seen a single farm, a tilled field or tended orchard. There have only been endless, featureless stretches of forest that seem as unproductive and untamed as the Indian jungle, and I am curious as to how the inhabitants feed themselves. If this soil-poor country is indeed the fabled farmland we have been promised, then we will have to resign ourselves to expending years of labor in clearing and leveling large tracts of encroaching bush to make it suitable for farming.

This final leg of our disquieting approach to land may have been marked by apprehension, but wherever the fires have not yet touched it, we have also watched the undulating shorelines transformed into exotic prayer mats that have come to life. Wholly unfamiliar menageries of patch-worked calico creatures now tumble out of these shores towards us: stately birds swoop out of the sky in striking tawny patches of pale and dark feathers; V-shaped flights of giant geese with masked faces take wing; giant ebony fish arc out of water, their dorsal fins etched with pale saddle-like markings; gray and white dolphins frolic in the ship's froth, and above us there is a constant, raucous scrimmage of diving seagulls. I cannot help but wonder: surely a continent whose shores are so richly teeming with such imposing creatures cannot possibly be any less majestic.

With the Canadian shoreline once again so clearly revealed and the forests directly before us imploding in flame, the wind now carries with it an unmistakable aroma of roasted nuts. I watch spellbound as giant trees explode and crackle, spraying the surrounding ones with burning resin. And with ash once again beginning to drift in with the shifting wind, the ship finally turns away from the shore for safety, and heading due south to our destination.

Bracing myself against the iodine-laden, ozone-charged sea breeze, I feel its faint sizzle against my exposed skin and all along the delicate lining of my pharynx; even my forearms have begun to tingle. Layered over this aspirant moistness is the faint but distinctly lingering trace of familiarity that immediately transports me back to my early childhood.

When I was much younger, our entire extended family of five

households would huddle together for warmth in order to ward off the winter night chill, thronging around the simmering coals of a dozen braziers. In this habitually amicable, sometimes fractious company, our conversation would flow freely like a warm liquid being poured from one vessel into another; all the while, our nimble fingers would be snapping the delicate but crisp warm, hard shells of pine nuts between the teeth, and then sliding the reward of the waxen nut down the throat. The discarded pine shells would then be tossed back into the coals to launch brief spurts of smoky flame.

Having stood so close to a blazing forest, I realize now with a flood of unexpected nostalgia that it has been this faint yet distinct scent of pine nuts roasting over coals that has traversed the waters. Somehow, it has managed to surface through layered accretion of memories. Why, of course, I realize that the shoreline forests must consist of the familiar pine, the analytical part of my mind immediately seizing upon this as a reassuring personal omen.

I am suddenly very conscious of all the other jubilant passengers thronging the deck.

# INTO THE PATH OF RIPTIDES
## 22 May 1914

Out of the fifteen odd Japanese seamen operating the Komagata Maru, there is only one with whom I have been able to establish any form of personal rapport and communication. I will discover later that his name is Nakajima Hirosuke, but for now as fortnight old acquaintances we have had to rely on a crude line of communication. Since we both understand so little of each other's tongues, we have had to regress to a form of sign language that has an unchanging primal script of exclamations and grunts that to an outsider may seem as comical as they are earnest.

Upon seeing each other daily for the first time at dawn when I appear on deck for my morning prayers, and he is either coming off night duty or going in to day shift or merely hanging around the deck dressed casually in a kimono, I usually initiate the first exchange with a cursory wave of my hand. Then, as a matter of routine, I will point in the general direction of what I presume to be the eastern horizon.

"Vancouver?" I query. To this his invariable response has so far been a wide grin accompanied by a sideways shake of his head.

"Nah!" He retorts.

And when I counter with: "Canada?"

"Nah Kan-nada, nah One-Couver," comes the prompt response. "Ten-couver. Ten!"

*Ten-couver*, as you may have surmised means ten days to our destination. We have thus ritualistically tolled off the countdown on our fingers.

With today probably being our final day on board, I am surprised on greeting him in the morning to note that he does not seem his usual cheerful self. However, in response to my cursory wave across the deck he hastily holds up an index finger, feebly pantomiming the word: "*One-Couver!*"

Much later that same day it is almost nine and the sun is nowhere near its setting point; there is sufficient light to sit on deck and read a newspaper. The three Canadian immigration officials who have been placed onboard at Victoria to ensure that we do not stray from our designated path are already ensconced in the bridge house.

By now we have also been offered further tantalizing glimpses of a southern shore that is beginning to emerge in the early morning light. It wavers through the lingering wisps of fog as flocks of seagulls head out for the open ocean behind us. The water here is extremely turbulent as it races on ahead of us with the incoming tide, ceaselessly churning through the narrow passageways reminiscent of a giant unassembled jigsaw puzzle that has been randomly sprinkled before us. Each strip of land is lined with wind-inclined trees that I will soon learn to identify as cypresses, fir, hemlock or cedar, each sickle island similar in its curving pattern of shorelines, with the salty surf riding the plume, and leaching greedily at the limestone and sand rock. A wisp of a snow-shrouded volcano hovers ethereally across the southern horizon, but my attention is diverted by the two lighthouses that dot the nearest craggy cliffs.

With most of the passengers already crowding the deck, our beaming, stocky captain, Yamamoto, has finally appeared on deck. He is in a jovial mood, informing us in his clipped English that one of the large lighthouse positioned so tantalizingly close to us is actually that of Cape Flattery, and that the American shoreline at this point is merely ten miles away, and thus closer to us than the Canadian.

"You can deduce from the convoluted outline of these shores," he indicates with a seaward wave of his hand, his eyes crinkled against the brisk sea air "that these are indeed very treacherous waters. Though the west coast of Vancouver Island has only about two hundred and fifty miles of shoreline," he continues, "the water seems relatively calm at this time of the day. However, during ebb tide this stretch of water can be as treacherous as any I have known." He knows we are all listening raptly to his words, with someone even translating into Punjabi.

Seeing that he has piqued our interest, he resumes after a brief pause: "There are narrow passages along this route that do not permit you to turn the vessel around and you have to travel some of them in reverse; in times of fog when the shores are not visible we sound the whistle to hear its echo. During a storm I have seen high tidal waters strike the ship at stern with such an impact from each passing wave that it is deflected through the entire length of the vessel - a very unpleasant twisting and rolling motion. Very often, at this point in the journey, all onboard will fall sick. At such times we try to duck behind an island's sheltered waters to see out a storm. You gentlemen have been very lucky."

However, in pointing out the salient features of the distant horizon he also appears to be somewhat distracted from his lecture. His eyes keep roving back towards his gathered crewmembers, who are agitatedly leaning over the deck railing. One of them is actually dangling his feet precariously in the air. I realize with a surprise that this is none other than my acquaintance Nakajima, who has also spotted the distant American lighthouse. His face is set in a vacant look. I notice that he is also wearing a lifejacket over the same kimono he has been seen in while off-duty. As his captain approaches closer to him, I can sense the tension between them rising; their exchanges in Japanese are at first curt and brief, with Nakajima's agitation rising with each exchange.

The rest of the passengers on deck have also suddenly become aware of the heightening human drama unfolding before them.

There comes a point in this altercation when the captain makes a sudden lunge to grab his errant crewman, and before any of us has realized what is happening, Nakajima has swiftly cleared the deck and the railing and leapt directly into the water. Peering overboard we can see his head rapidly disappear behind the whitecaps, his bright orange jacket is only glimpsed briefly before the waves rise over him. Barely a minute later, with the wind now whipping the tops of the waves and sending plumes of froth into the air, and the ship rapidly receding from him, Nakajima is partially hidden from view. By the time the ship finally come to a stop, the tiny speck of a human head is being buffeted randomly amidst the churning waves, before it disappears entirely from our view.

We watch the stunned captain's face turn livid as other crewmen rush to the railing to apprise themselves of the situation. They attend to their captain who is continuing his tirade, hurling abuses after the receding figure.

Much later we catch fleeting glimpses of the bobbing figure flailing helplessly in the turbulence. The three Canadian Immigration officers onboard have witnessed the whole episode dispassionately.

Nearly half an hour later, with the skipper still feeble but gesticulating wildly, the silent crewmembers lead him below deck and the ship resumes its eastwards journey. Our elation at having finally been allowed to proceed from Vancouver Island's southern port of Victoria to Vancouver has evaporated in the confusion of this event.

# THE REAL INDIANS
## 23 May 1914

Throughout this voyage our curiosity about our destination and its surrounding environment has been piqued by endless rounds of stirring legends from those who have seen it all before us. And the most eloquent and imaginative of these accounts has come from my restive friend and bunkmate, Puran. By his portrayal, whatever merits or demerits Vancouver may have as a city, none is more striking than its natural setting and the surrounding mountains. He claims that under certain light conditions, and when viewed from certain angles – conveniently forgetting to mention is that when fueled by the ripened imagination of those who have been too long at sea - these slopes, peaks and ridges are transformed into the evocative shapes of giant maidens sleeping in the midst of resting prides of lions. With the narrowing shores of our passageway beginning to emerge before us in the flooding light, each one of us has eagerly taken to scanning the horizon for these illusive creatures.

The stretch of water ahead of us narrows into a heavily silted passageway where the water miraculously surges ahead of us as if moving uphill in the grip of an incoming tide. The narrow channel directly before us is now speckled with schools of wild salmon that are intent on outpacing each other in desperately leaping to escape from some unseen underwater danger. From our vantage point above the surface we can see several dark, balloon shaped heads bobbing up behind the fish. As each of these pursuing creatures disappears beneath the surface, dozens of arm-length salmon leap diagonally out of their path, skipping and dimpling the water in bright silvery flashes. What we are witnessing are seals hunting their favorite prey. Within minutes, just as suddenly as it began the turmoil in the water dies off with the prey and its predators heading ahead of us into the sheltered inner waters. I notice a pair of triangular dark fins also darting behind the salmon and the seals, and I turn to Puran to ask: "What are those? Sharks?"

"Nah. Killer whales," he murmurs appreciatively. He is returning to Vancouver after a sojourn of nearly a year, and has been excitedly commenting on how the salmon migration this year appears to be back up in numbers after having been severely depleted the previous year. However, the dramatic life and death struggle in the water ahead does not easily distract him for long; he has waited too long to point out for our benefit the looming mythical women and the slumbering lions.

"Any minute now," he beams excitedly, drawing our attention to a series of surrounding northern ridges.

"Look closely at that first peak, and then that gently rounded rise next to it over there, … and over there, and tell me if it is not the profile of a woman asleep. And those two smooth bumps next to that sharp ridge over there, are they not that of another sleeping maiden? Does it not seem to you from this distance as if she were almost alive and breathing. Just look at how real they all seem." He is incredulous as a child at the zoo.

"Where, where?" I ask flummoxed at the realization that though I have been at sea for exactly the same number of days as him, yet I am still unable to tease even the vaguest of familiar patterns from the mountain ridges and peaks before us. But he is too excited to pause and listen to me.

A moment later, when another group of viewers begins gesticulating excitedly at some other part of the same ridge, and muttering *"tigers, tigers"*, I turn my attention back to the tidal bay waters directly before us. The blue of the sea inlet is now mingling rapidly with the muddy river water. And a silting river water can only mean eroding soil, and farmlands somewhere up ahead.

The ship now grinds to a halt as a launch carrying the local harbor pilot approaches, and we resume the last brief leg of our remaining journey.

Noticing that Puran is somewhat calmer now and idly resting his elbows on the railing I poke him lightly in the ribs. "Perhaps my imagination is not yet ripe enough to transform a random geological feature into any semblance of living forms, human or non-human. Maybe later on I'll learn to see what you see in these hillsides, huh?"

He ignores my jibe, seemingly more composed and pensive, now that the initial excitement of having shown off the mythical creatures has worn off. Seeing that this is a form of homecoming for him, I wonder whether he should be more excited about the destination rather than the hypothetical creatures hidden in its terrain?

I direct his attention towards the opposite shore at a native village of elongated log houses as it glides past. I notice that he has also spotted a dugout canoe with six occupants as it heads towards us. The canoe, with an elaborate carved wooden figurehead fixed to its stern, is traveling faster than us. With each occupant rowing vigorously, the sight of our ship looming in their path is somehow unable to distract them from their pursuit of the fish.

I turn to Puran and ask: "Are these the local Indians known as Red Indians that I have been reading about in books?"

"Oh, them. Yes, these are the local Indians," he offers off-handedly.

"Indians? Indians?" Someone close by snorts. "Nah! You tell

me, if these are Indians, then who are we?"

"We, too, are Indians – but we are the *original* Indians. We are the *real* Indians," snaps Puran.

"Indians, huh? If they are Indians then they must also be from India, nah?"

"Not that I know of. Unless, of course, they somehow rowed here ahead of us."

"Them and us, *nah yaar*, we can't all be Indians," comes the disgruntled answer. I notice our three-way dialogue has now gathered an attentive audience, the prospect of mountain-sized women consorting with wild animals having lost all its potential appeal.

"Yes, I know that we can't all be Indians," Puran concedes with a note of irritation. "However, the locals make no such distinction."

Seeing that Puran is unwilling to elaborate on this subject the conversation ends and the men drift away. However, I have another question for him on this subject.

"But this doesn't make any sense to me, either. Doesn't this mix-up lead to endless confusions?" I ask in exasperation, "...and then once this mix-up has been discovered... shouldn't it have become obvious to the people who pride themselves on precisely labeling everything, whether animate or inanimate, and then correctly placing everything exactly where it belongs in the grand scheme of things?"

"Indians, locals, natives, red or brown, Hindus, Hindustanis! What do they care? All they know is that we are not one of them, and of course, as you can plainly see, we are not white. Even more significantly that we are not of English descent. Why do you think it is that they persist in labeling all Indians as Hindus?" Puran reluctantly spits out these words as if they were being forcefully drawn out of him.

"This one I do know," I offer, wading in to his rescue. "You see, before coming here, I have been reading accounts from around the world on the British colonialism. I think it probably began when the first of our people landed here, and when asked where they had come from, they stated in their local language the name of their homeland as *Hindustan*, the land of Hindus. So, you see, it is all perfectly logical for the locals to think we are all Hindus."

"Yaar, I know that part of the explanation. But, you will find that all such labels are fine distinctions that matter only to us. All of us on this ship have already been lumped together as Hindus. Or *HinDoos* as they are so fond of labeling us. So, the sooner you learn this simple lesson the easier it will be for you to live in harmony here in Canada." Puran makes this final pronouncement and is silent.

"But I am certainly not a Hindu!" I persist, somehow unable to leave the matter alone.

"Yes, I am fully aware of that, my friend Bashir, but you are from Hindustan, aren't you? So by the British definition you have already become a Hindu." He is glaring openly at me by now; leaving me wondering when I had struck a raw nerve in him during our exchange.

Ramdas from our neighboring bunk, who has also been following our dialogue, and has been regularly butting into most of our exchanges, interjects: "…and speaking of the British, have you noticed that in dealing with us as local inhabitants of India, how devious and subtle is their peculiar tactic of defining us by our faiths. I am a Hindu, you are Muslim, and they are all Sikhs. And if you take the crew of this ship into account, they are all probably Buddhists? So, in a blink of an eye we are all so very different from each other. How easily we are made to forget that we are all Indians, whereas all English, Scotsmen, Irishmen and Welshmen on Indian soil, regardless of their faith and their home region, can still stand before us united as Britishers. By this same logic I suppose lumping us all together as *Hindus* doesn't seem like such a bad idea to me."

None of us has an appropriate response to his tirade. By now the ship is carving a wide starboard curve in turning southwards for its final approach to the docks.

"You see that green piece of headland over there?" Puran asks. "That is called Stanley Park." He gesticulates towards a tiny island to our right that we have been circumnavigating. It is covered with stands of spindly trees. He has obviously been trying to steer our conversation away from a topic he is not fully comfortable with at this time. He points to the body of water directly in our path, and reminds us all once again that he once saw a pod of a dozen killer whales cavorting here last summer at about this time.

"They must have been following the salmon run just like the seals we saw today. If we are lucky we might see them again today," he offers, returning to familiar territory.

Located at the farthest end of the calm body of water opening up before us is what appears to be a very busy harbor, and beyond it stretching as far as we can see, is our first sighting of a tumble of buildings crowding the waterfront. The fact that this is a relatively new town being carved out of the surrounding low-lying slopes is made evident by the widespread rash of irregular tree stubs. This, I realize with a sudden intake of breath, is our final destination.

"*One-couver,*" we exclaim in unison, a mixture of relief and collective disbelief.

Having visited similar cities in other parts of the empire this one seems unremarkable by any standard. Beyond the foreground activity at the waterfront of sheds swarming with cargo barges, sailboats and tugboats, there stretch rows of beige and gray buildings that crowd the waterfront like eager spectators elbowing each other at a sporting event. Arrayed behind them are further rows of buildings, each lined with its banks of rectangular windows. A solitary slim gray tower rises above the wind-whipped smoke streams of chimneys. We can also spot church spires, and the masts and rigging of several steam cranes as they arch their angled necks over the gabled rooftops.

I can already visualize how at that ground level some of these streets will be monopolized on either sides of pavement by the posturing of exaggerated facades. Shops will be lined with colorful awnings, windows crammed with displays, garish signboards vying for attention, and since it is morning time, housewives hunting for bargains, their shopping baskets laden with ingredients for the dinner table. There will also be hordes of pedestrians getting in each other's way amidst street trolleys, horse drawn carriages and buggies waiting at every corner. Later in the day pubs and saloons will be crowded with sojourning travelers, and sailors and soldiers on furlough.

Essentially, the bustle of any waterfront town is no different in the fact that transport is its major commerce. And, this town, with its swarming waterfront dwarfed by its hillsides, is still very much a work in progress. This conclusion can only lead to a feeling of disappointment and I try hard to fight it, while a part of me is already wondering what was so special about this one little muddle of bricks and mortar. And, with what lofty pretensions will this remote outpost of the empire greet our unannounced arrival?

Sometimes, my cynicism gets the better of me. I must have been smirking, for Puran, who has still remained immune to the contagious excitement of our arrival, has more to reveal than I am willing to listen to at this pivotal moment.

"Bashir bhai, I can fully understand your enthusiasm at having made it this far. But, believe me when I say this that it won't be such a great tragedy if the locals do not let you touch their precious land, or whether they offer you *a Free Farm*, or not. Even though our numbers amongst them remain like salt in the dough, it is not as if they are busy spreading out the welcoming mat for us."

I had earlier on questioned Puran about the types of jobs that would be available to someone like myself. Perhaps, I had speculated, I could teach English to our own people.

"Hah, a farmer's son who no longer wants to farm but instead wants to teach Angrezi to his humble compatriots," he had sneered at me. "Sorry, master-ji, no one has time to study anything here, unless it is on Sundays. The rest of the weekdays are dedicated from dawn to dusk to work. And, you should not even contemplate finding any sort of office work. The locals have already secured all that. You could try your hand at working as a translator with the immigration department but those well-paid jobs have also been monopolized by a number of our men who are close to the immigration officers. Or they are all related to each other in some way. So, I guess that leaves the lumberyards and the farms still open to you and me."

"What about fishing? I could work on a fishing vessel. On the way I here I saw dozens of fishing vessels at sea." But I could gather from his expression that I was merely clutching at straws.

"Come on, be realistic for once, Bashir. I know that throughout the voyage we have been swapping tall fishing stories with the best of them, but, honestly, when have you ever fished from a real vessel?" I realized he was poking fun at my increasing alarm and resulting discomfort. "Fishing is a wholly different industry here, and the Japanese dominate it completely. You could work at one of the several canneries on the fishing wharfs at Richmond. But there again you would be up against the local Indians, and the Chinese and the Japanese hands. However, there are other jobs that the locals will not do themselves, and for these they will always need us. And, yet though they are unwilling to soil their hands at these jobs they will only pay you a fraction of what they would have paid to one of their own."

He stares at me witheringly. "Furthermore, if these realities are not a hurdle in themselves, you will have to quickly learn to be mindful of who you are, and also learn to read the constant reminders that you do not belong here. There will be times when you are out walking on a narrow sidewalk and happen to approach one of them. Very often, they will cross over to the other side of the street rather than brush past you at such close quarters. And, if by some miracle you do manage to somehow touch land, you will have to put up with all such abuses on a daily basis." He is quiet for a moment before summing it up for my benefit. "There, I have said it all. I had wanted to ease you into this reality but you just keep goading me on."

This depressing conversation had taken place much earlier while we were still at sea and idling on our bunks, waiting for the noon heat to ease. And I remember that all I could offer in countering his argument had been: "Well, if this treatment is such an onerous behavior to you, then you tell me how is it any different from the times when the proud Brahman pundit in our Lopoke, on noticing my humble shadow sully his frame, must immediately rush back to his house and bathe himself all over again?"

This time it had been nosey Ramdas once again who had broken out in chuckles, and in peering down at us decided to join our discussion. "Consider this, you two: how is this phenomenon any different from the time when my mother set out to look for a girl for me to wed. The only condition she laid down for all prospective girls was that my mate must be tall and very fair… she wouldn't stop gloating that when my daughter-in-law will drink water you will be able to see every drop descend down her transparent throat. However, as far as you can all plainly see, she has no such demands of her own son."

I recall that at the time these trifle distractions had not eased Puran's personal frustrations and he had gone on to elaborate: "You know, a while back I read somewhere that in defending his country's political stand against letting Hindus into Canada, the Canadian Prime Minister had famously gone so far as to proclaim that '*this land is not suited to the Hindu*'. I would very much like to have questioned him how well India was suited to the British character, after all haven't they been camped there for nearly a century and half. What I do know is how well they appear to be suited for the luxurious lifestyle that they have adopted in India. Could they have ever dreamt of such a regal lifestyle in their own land?"

I had learnt by then to keep my mouth shut whenever he got off on one of these habitual rants.

And, yet, nothing can alter the fact that we are now here, safe and sound in the Vancouver harbour, the destination finally within shouting distance.

# DRESS REHEARSAL
## 11:00 A.M., 23 May 1914

By mid morning Vancouver harbor pilot Barney Johnson has securely anchored the Komagata Maru about two hundred yards off Number Two berth. Though the engines are turned off and the heartbeat of the ship is silenced, steam continues to escape from the funnel in anticipation, perhaps, of a final berthing closer to the shore.

The voyage is finally over.

No sooner have we entered the harbour that we are surrounded by an odd flotilla of scows, launches and tugboats from which curious onlookers gawk at us. Some of them wave, or shout inaudible instructions, gesturing for us to strike heroic postures or wave back for the benefit of their cameras.

How can I fully convey the novelty of that first morning inside the Vancouver harbour, the sun having cleared the backdrop of mountains before six on a clear and cloudless day, the spectacular smoky, blue-forested mountains descending all the way to the inlet shores?

Here we all are, milling about excited as children at a carnival, showing off our new clothes. Gurdit is resplendent in his best silken white three-piece suit that matches his luxuriant beard and turban, and is in sharp contrast to all the dark-suited men surrounding him. Even his young and precocious seven-year-old son Balwant, peering disarmingly and self-consciously back from the shadows, is equally spick and span in his fitted jacket, pants and an adult sized turban perched atop his tiny head. Standing next to Gurdit in suit and tie is his secretary, Daljit Singh, and other members of the Komagata Committee – Amar Singh, Harnam Singh, Sunder Singh and Vir Singh. Next to them stand the two students here for further studies, Puran Singh Jauhal and Gurmukh Singh Lalton. Others pose stiffly around them, squinting at the camera in the bright sunlight.

It seems this colourful regiment has been preparing for muster for weeks. Several military uniforms that have been saved for just such an occasion are also on display – the coats are buttoned down, brass glinting in the sun, and festooned with victory medals. Everyone looks polished and buffed, each head crowned with crisply folded and freshly starched turban. In fact, turbans of all colours festoon the entire deck: black, or blue, a few even in ochre, and some in regimental colours, wound over meticulously combed hair. Seeing that all of my Muslim brethren have donned their scarlet fezzes I dash below deck to fetch mine, a boxed present from Maulavi Barakat Ullah. Like others I place it at a rakish angle, imagining a residual shadow of Maulavi saab's undisguised look of disapproval following me everywhere.

In the initial excitement of having finally reached our destination I have forgotten to mention that there are some members of our community on board who have not entirely been awed by the prospect of entering Canada. About a dozen of these men have not even bothered to dress up formally for this occasion or participate in any of the rituals of the new arrivals. I have noticed that they have even hauled up their luggage and are now gathered near the gangway in preparation for disembarking. No formalities here. Obviously, they have been here before and are familiar with the immigration protocols.

One of the passengers is so overcome by the enormity of the occasion that he turns to one of the onboard immigration officers and announces ominously: "This ship now belongs to the whole of India, this is a symbol of the honour of India and if this is detained, there will be mutiny in the armies."

When a launch carrying a local reporter approaches adjacent to the ship and begins shouting questions, Gurdit's secretary, Daljit, lowers a prepared message that is attached to the end of a turban.

The message states: "The main objective of coming is to let the British government know how they can maintain their rule in India, as the Indian government is in danger nowadays. We can absolutely state how the British government will last in India forever."

Our anticipation comes to a head when we see the launch carrying the immigration officials approaching us. The harbour pilot, impatient to disembark after having ensured that the ship was safely anchored, also seems to share our state of anxiety. Gurdit's repeated inquiries of him as to why we are not approaching one of the off-loading wharfs have all been met with stony silence. When Gurdit will not let him off the hook, he offers: "Sir, I only have orders to secure the ship away from the main shipping lanes and at an approachable distance from the immigration offices. This is all I can reveal to you. You should take up the matter personally with Mr. Reid, the Chief Immigration Officer, when he comes onboard shortly."

When the immigration scow 'Sea Lion' is securely tied up starboard, there is a surge of the passengers towards the lowered gangway. And, as soon as the harbor pilot has stepped off, three members of the immigration staff gingerly ascend up to the deck.

The first to clamber clumsily aboard is greeted with a round of whispers. This is none other than the infamous William C. Hopkinson, the province's head immigration inspector. Lanky, long-legged, Hopkinson hastily straightens his tunic and adjusts the angle of his gold embroidered cap, and stretching fully to his imposing six and a half feet, steps nervously onto the deck. I have heard so much about this two-headed snake - the *do-mui* - that hybrid creature able to speak dual languages. Seeing him thus coming onboard suddenly makes my stomach turn with anxiety and I have to hastily step away from the railing. I have traveled an ocean to escape this predator and the instant I hear his rasping high-pitched whine I know that I am already in a pickle. Would my cover pass muster before these trained, prying eyes? Would I be found out and exposed for who I really am, right here in front of all these men who only know me as just another farmer's son who has been restrained of manner during most of the voyage and is only now showing signs of interest in the outcome of this endeavor? In hindsight, I know I should have come better prepared for this inevitable confrontation with my nemesis, and after the initial wave of nausea passes I begin to feel calmer. I remind myself that there is no way Hopkinson or anyone in his employ will ever be able to link me to my past an that I have put myself through the most stringent wringer to be here and have made every effort to come out clean at the other end. I remind myself that so many years have passed since our last encounter and no one has yet made the slightest revelation of my other alter ego.

Hopkinson now finds himself peering into the bulldog set face of Gurdit Singh hovering balefully before him. "What is the meaning of this? Why are we not pulling in to the open berths at the wharfs?" Gurdit's broad face is made larger by the frame of his white beard, the message delivered in a gruff, clipped English by way of greeting.

There is obvious relief on the head immigration official's face at this exchange - there will now be no need for translators. Momentarily overcome by the enormity of the message he has to deliver, Hopkinson can only stammer in greeting: "I am the Canadian Government's Chief Immigration Inspector... my name is ...", he pauses briefly trying to recollect his thoughts. "I am Hopkinson," he finally manages.

By this time, two of his assistants, Gwyther the interpreter and Baboo Singh have also elbowed their way to his side, and are busying themselves in making the formal introductions, first in Punjabi and then in English.

"This is Hopkinson sahib, the Canadian Head Inspector of immigration," the interpreter informs Gurdit who nods, absent-mindedly wrinkling his nose, his eyes twinkling briefly in reluctant recognition.

"I know, I know who this man is," Gurdit whispers back hoarsely. He had earlier on raised his right hand impulsively in greeting before thinking the better of it and retreating, choosing merely to nod curtly, uncomfortable for once in the full glare of the dozens of eyes following his every gesture. How he behaves here may well determine their immediate fate. Both he and Hopkinson have been honing their reactions in anticipation of these formalities, and both are conscious and nervous in their mutual awareness of the historical significance of this moment. Hopkinson straightens himself until he is no longer slouching, and standing fully erect signals the 'all clear' to the remaining men in the launch below with a wave of his hand.

The rest of the immigration party now warily ascends the walkway. The next person to be introduced is a burly, mustachioed, immaculately dressed official who also towers above most of us, the visor of his gold braided cap and the brass buttons of his tunic gleaming brightly in the sunlight. He is introduced as the British Columbian Immigration Chief, Malcolm J. Reid. Reid is quickly followed by the equally stocky but more compact British Columbian Member of Parliament, Harry H. Stevens, who is seen clutching his fawn hat firmly against the sea breeze whipping at his trench coat, his face set in a determined grimace. Like Reid, he too has the steely, lock-jawed look of a determined gatekeeper, his jowls bulging briefly. He does not meet Gurdit's gaze, choosing instead to look out over the harbor.

The rest of the lead-footed procession follows Gurdit below deck where several desks have been setup for this purpose.

An hour later, the official parties emerge on deck with Reid now addressing Gurdit directly: "Sir, having examined the ship's manifest I can see that even though all the passengers on this ship are citizens of India, this ship did not sail to Canada directly *from* India. The records indicate that the origin of your voyage was in Hong Kong. You are thus in violation of Section 23 of the Immigration Act. Furthermore, federal Orders In Council PC 23 and PC 24 of 1914 and PC 2642 of 1913 do not permit artisans or labourers skilled or unskilled to enter Canada." He pauses dramatically to see what form of response will be offered, and seeing that there is none, continues:

"It is my duty to inform you that the provincial government of British Columbia as well as the federal government of the dominion of Canada cannot permit all the passengers of this vessel to land."

This is Gurdit's cue to state his opposition. He waves expansively in the general direction of Stanley Park and the northern shore beyond it with the intent of including the longhouses he has seen lining its shores. "And, it is my duty to inform you, sir, that this is *not* your land, and *you* cannot impose your laws on it. It belongs to people who were here long before you arrived on the scene."

Seeing that Reid is taken aback by his unexpected response, Gurdit now presses home his advantage. "The rights for access to these lands are not yours to grant. Not here, nor anywhere else in Canada. I assure you, sir, within my lifetime we shall see the Empire crumble and collapse upon itself from its excesses. You can send us back but after us there will be other ships come to challenge your shores. How long can your dominion hold out against this flood, how many of us will you turn away?" One day our tide will overwhelm you!"

A stalemate follows as both parties realize how far apart their positions are, and that both may well have been staking out positions that were meant for consumption by the press, as well as to reassure their own followers.

An hour after the first official meeting, another such scrimmage takes place on the deck. Seeing that local and foreign journalists have gathered here not only from Vancouver, but Montreal, Seattle, and from as far as San Francisco, the developments of the day are recapped for their benefit. This second assembly is for the benefit of the press and it takes place before the deckhouse. A number of reporters and cameramen from The Province and Vancouver World have are eagerly waiting with their notepads and flashes. As the cameramen frame the scene, the dwarfed figure of the Parliamentarian H. H. Stevens stands heatedly debating, a finger raised in emphasis. Meanwhile, Reid, as usual, has characteristically positioned himself strategically so that he is in center stage directly facing the cameraman. Hopkinson stands to Stevens' left, languidly leaning back into his wiry frame and observing the proceedings, one hand in his trouser pocket, his watch chain glinting in the sun.

"The province cannot," Harry Stevens stresses wagging an index finger at the camera, "allow these passengers entry into British Columbia as they have not met the requirements of the orders in council. As far as we are concerned, this is now a shut case. Since most of the passengers do not meet the requisite conditions stipulated by the legislation of the Province as well as those of the Dominion, they will be sent back to where they have come from. The ship has violated the extant immigration regulations, in particular the so-called 'Continuous Passage' clause and two Orders of the Council, as well as Section 23 of the Canadian Immigration Act. According to the ship's manifesto only twenty of its passengers are residents returning to Vancouver, and these will be permitted to land. The rest will not be allowed to leave this ship. Immigration boats with armed guards will now circle the Komagata Maru twenty-four hours and no one will be permitted to go ashore and no one will be permitted to come in contact with those onboard."

Stevens now glances briefly at Gurdit's agitated face before hurriedly adding: "No one onboard will be allowed to conduct any business onshore, nor will any supplies be permitted to be brought in."

This is too much for Gurdit to bear in silence and raising his voice at an even higher tone he announces: "We are all British subjects and we all have valid British passports. You cannot legally detain us like this. You cannot deny us access to any part of the British Empire. Your very own king has guaranteed us these rights. And as far as I know, the last time I checked he was still the ruler."

He looks around at the silenced men gathered around him, the reporters' pencils busy transcribing his every word. "You should also note that I am a merchant and there is no law that prevents a merchant from going ashore to pursue his business. You can detain the passengers, but not me. And, let me also remind you, sir, that you are responsible for any damages that your restrictions may incur."

With the official confrontation and formalities now over, a photographer instructs all the men gathered on deck to stand before him in neat rows so that they are carefully aligned for the benefit of the camera. The taller ones are nudged to the periphery or to the rear to stand stiffly, glaring back at the camera. Gurdit, as befitting his status, is singled out and positioned in the forefront. The sizzle and smoke of flashes briefly lights up the shadows making everyone squint in the late morning light. As soon as the photographer is ready for the next shot, Gurdit moves out of his assigned position, and stretches out his hand to his son. Balwant has been watching all the excitement from behind the bridge house and now comes over to stand next to him. For a while there is total silence again on the sun-drenched deck. Gurdit, peering imperiously at the cameramen, is aware that the formal brilliance of this moment, now captured for posterity, will never fade.

Much later in the day, he will even pose precariously leaning out from a lifeboat while swinging a pair of binoculars.

For now, he holds back the tears of joy at his accomplishment, his eyes mere pinpricks scanning the distant shore. Nagging doubts about his enterprise that had plagued him throughout the journey have now been exposed as bitter realities.

Earlier in the day upon his arrival he had asked a visitor about the onshore men chanting with one vociferous voice. He had been conveyed the words to the litany of *Whiteman's Canada*. Now that he has had time to digest the racist overtones of these lyrics, he reflects: "I have never been able to fathom the rationale behind these belligerent chants or peer into their dark hearts. This thing they keep taunting us with, this unholy slogan of a 'white Canada'. For their benefit I would like to state that wasn't this once a red Canada? And now that it is white, is it not logical that if this persecution continues might it not one day become a yellow or even a brown Canada?"

Also, later in the day there will be interviews with pressmen who have been denied access, but never-the-less approach alongside the ship. Here, Gurdit will be sensational in his triumph and pronouncements, expounding on his struggles against all odds to reach this shore. He will even repeat his earlier bold proclamations: "We are British citizens and we consider we have a right to visit any part of the Empire. We are determined to make this a test case and if we are refused entrance into your country, the matter will not end here. What is done with this shipload of my people will determine whether we shall have peace in all parts of the Empire."

With the upper deck humming with activity, the immigration formalities and medical examinations are well underway in the rest of the ship. While two of his assistants are busy with interviews and translations of the statements of the prospective immigrants, Hopkinson briskly flips through the pages of the ship's passenger manifest. The seven pages of neat columns are itemized by Date, Name, Age, City, Available Funds, Embarkation - each column entry tabulated with the florid unfurling of the fountain pen. Hopkinson's index finger scrolls rapidly down the column listing 'City'. On page three it comes to rest against one entry: *Lopoke*. Date of Embarkation: 04/04/14, Name: Bashir Ali, Age: 28, Village: Lopoke, Available Funds: $200.00, Port of Embarkation: Hong Kong.

*City: Lopoke!*

"Got you!" Hopkinson mutters under his breath, tapping the page and looking up abruptly from the table, his thoughts outpacing his heartbeat.

"Hah! All the way here in our Vancouver harbour from sorry little Lopoke! As if I did not already know what Bashir was doing here thousands of miles away from home."

Elated at the discovery, Hopkinson ascends to the deck with the open manifest flapping in his hands, and the sunlight momentarily blinding him. Stumbling onto the deck he refocuses his attention on a number of men clustered around the staircase in the anticipation of their names being called out for a favourable resolution. For them the frustrating hours waiting for a formal review have continued to tumble all morning into mid afternoon, and only seventeen names have been called out so far. Now the men scatter before him in unison like a flock of birds startled by his sudden appearance in their midst, the mounting tension evident on their faces.

"Which one of this sorry lot is it going to be?" Hopkinson wonders as he scans each face, registering every feature against a catalogue of particulars filed in his memory. In his mind he is already goading himself on, betting that unaided he will be able to pick Bashir Ali out of this crowd. "One look and you are done for, Mr. Bashir!" He mutters, smirking to himself.

Clearing his throat loudly for attention and holding up the registry he announces: "Is there anybody here named Bashir? Ali, Bashir? Anyone here from Lopoke, district Amritsar?"

The only responses are evasive, nervous snickers.

He wonders why the suspect has not made any attempt to hide

the name of his hometown? LOPOKE. There it is for all to see clear and bright in indelible ink.

He approaches yet another group of men milling about like cattle yet unwilling to engage him in dialogue.

"Bashir?"

He surveys the nervous dark eyes narrowed to pinpricks against the bright light. On seeing that there is no response, the scratchy tone of his voice rises and his impatience begins to surface.

"Lopoke, huh? Bashir?" Only impassivity and the reluctance to meet his direct gaze. He points to one tall man wearing a red fez cocked comically at an odd angle over his head.

"Are you Bashir?"

"Na, sar. Hopkins saab, I am Fakir Mahmud. I come... I come from Kolkuta," comes the nervous response.

Hopkinson tries others: "Name, age, village, district, is this your first visit to Canada, where are you coming from, man, where did you get on this ship from, how much money do you have on you? When were you born? What is your grandfather's name, who is the nambardar of your village, where is the nearest thanna to your village? Quick, hurry up and tell me, my man... where, who, when? I need names, dates... *jaldi, jaldi! Kya naam hai tumhara? Bolo!*"

The responses do not vary by much. "I am Bagga Singh. I am Inder, I am Jeevan, I am Mewa, I am Puran. We are from Dhudike."

The litany rolls on. The faces are now alarmed each time he appears before them, each face flushed in the rapid-fire barrage of his interrogation. Hopkinson is unable to disguise his rising disappointment, impatient with himself as much as this grovelling mass before him. Not one man has had the spine to stand up to bear the brunt of this belligerence - each cringing back to stammer: "I am ... from Amritsar ... from Delhi ... Sialkot... Ludhiana." There are a couple from Lahore, but most are from the district of Ferozepur. "I have this dallar..." each one claiming he has come directly from India... and also owns the requisite funds for landing... which went to show that someone had already coached them on the stipulations of the continuous journey. He has also begun musing over the realization that just because Bashir happens to be a Muslim name it could not be inferred that the actual person would also be a Muslim from his outward appearance. Yet, there must be other pertinent clues that could reveal the true identity. That shifty Husain Rahim who claims to head the local Shore Committee carries a Muslim name yet everyone knows him to be a Hindu? And, if the person's faith is not made obvious by the name and external pretense then perhaps Hopkinson should be looking for more than mere physical signs. Could it be a shaved mustache with a full beard that was currently being supported by Muslims all over India? A red, green or even black fez instead of a turban, a trimmed beard, a callus at mid forehead?

The feet!

Hopkinson is sure he could recognize a devout Muslim's faith by just a glimpse of their feet. The attitudes of five daily prayers will leave a recognizable pattern of calluses on the supplicant's feet. But at twenty-eight would this etching be that obvious? Would it be visible on Bashir's feet as well? Realizing that he is now closer to making the kill Hopkinson can feel his confidence seeping back.

Finally, after having grilled over twenty men in close proximity, someone points out a tall man who is in conversation with another passenger and leaning against the distant railing.

"Bashir?" Hopkinson seeks confirmation, then excitedly scrambles over the tangled mass of moorings, wires and ropes, while cautiously approaching the two men at the railing.

I note that this is the first time he has moved away from the safety of the bridge house. From the moment he stepped onboard I have nervously been following his progress and I can now see him heading in my direction. The dreaded moment has finally arrived. Maybe I should have gone below deck, or leapt overboard instead of just loitering, seemingly unconcerned above deck and in plain view of everyone.

Barely a few moments ago my friend Puran had been pointing out the waterfront Hastings sawmill before which several men were squatting on the beach. Some of these men even appearred to be waving back at us. Puran had noted that several of our men work at this mill and there are similar mills scattered up and down the downtown waterfront area.

But, I notice that Hopkinson does not approach us directly, choosing instead to observe silently about a dozen feet from us, perched between two coils of rope. Perhaps he is waiting for me to take the initiative and offer him some clue to my identity. Perhaps I have not yet been found out and there is yet hope for me.

I have anticipated and dreaded this encounter for some time, knowing that Hopkinson would in all probability show up to greet this particular ship once it was in his harbor. The real question before me is whether he will be able to uncover my real identity? I am suddenly aware that the hair at the back of my neck are standing on end, and my mouth is suddenly dry. Why would I have been singled out if not for my compromising past? Had someone been watching my every movement and anticipated my arrival in Canada? And, if so, then who tipped the immigration authorities to my true identity? Was it someone onboard? If I was able to recognize Hopkinson so easily after all these years, would he also recognize me as the younger Kartar Singh without my unkempt beard and locks, my shorn turban, my wet loincloth and my wrists fettered in metal cuffs?

After what seems an eternity Hopkinson takes the final step to come closer: *"Thum, Bashir ho? Thum Lopoke se ho?"*

I nod, all the while watching him intently and anticipating the violence that is sure to follow. Now would be the time to leap into the water and make for the shore. Or, maybe I should lunge at him and silence him before he can reveal me. Maybe, I should...

*"Thum Angrezi boltay ho?"* He asks.

"Yes," I nod, unsure yet of his intentions.

"Yes. Well, is this your first visit to Canada?"

"Yes."

"Let me ask you this again. Are you really Bashir Ali of Lopoke?"

"Yes! I am Bashir Ali Lopoke. I just told you that."

"And do you personally possess the requisite $200 head fee?"

"Yes, I do."

I hear the words being uttered but my mind is racing on ahead. How could I have I been identified so easily?

"Is your father's name Qudarat Ali Lopoke?"

"Yes."

"Is he deceased or alive?"

"What kind of a question is that? What does this have to do with who I am? Or why I wish to settle in Canada?"

"We'll come to that later. For now I need to confirm that you are indeed whom I have been looking for a very long time." With the comfort of his suspicions now confirmed, Hopkinson has been wondering: "So this is what death looks like. This slithering, evasive, bewildered, clueless creature before me. What will he do next when he is cornered? Will he lunge at me? Or, will he leap and make an attempt to swim for the shore? Does he have accomplices onshore waiting to spirit him away? Are there other accomplices onboard? What if, what if, what if?"

"What is the purpose of your visit to Canada?"

"I am here to make a living."

"Ah, yes, yes. And, what will you make your living at?"

"As a farmer or a laborer." I hesitate and then add: "...or as a teacher".

"An educated farmer, I see. However, what I would really like to know is who has sent you here? And, whether you know anything about the rebellion?"

"What rebellion? I think you have mistaken me for someone else. I am from Lopoke, yes. But I know nothing of the rebellion. I think you are confusing me with someone else."

"Is that so? Do you honestly think I do not know who you really are or why you have been sent here? Do you take me for a fool?" I notice that Hopkinson's face is drained of all colour and his voice is further strained as he scratches at his starched collar.

"Do you think you can sneak up on me so easily? Come on, my man; tell me who you really are? Come on, out with it?"

"I am Bashir Ali of Lopoke. I am here to make a living as a farmer or as a laborer. I do not see why that should be cause for suspicion."

"Of course you are. But see, I have you in my control now. A word from me and you are back in Lopoke. Just like that. Don't you think I already know of the schemes you hatch against me, and against the Dominion? Rest assured they shall all come to no avail. And if you are thinking of swimming for the shore I already have guards posted all around the ship. Look, there and there."

He points at the two tugboats hovering at a short distance.

"See," he gloats. "See, I, too can read your mind."

For the next several minutes Hopkinson keeps me close to him shielding me from the rest of the passengers as if I were in mortal danger from them. He continues to talk incessantly, now beseeching, now cajoling, all bluster and bluff, and now pleading.

And me equally desperate in trying to make sense of what is happening, sounding indignant: "I do not know what you want from me, Hopkinson saab, or what you ask of me? Will you at least tell me what I am guilty of?"

"Tell me, tell me where will it be, how will it end... who are you here to kill?"

"I know nothing of what you are asking me, Hopkinson. I know nothing of the rebellion, or the killings you speak of."

"Yes, yes, I know that you do. But, you, Mister Bashir, and I, as your folks have a way of saying, 'have locked our horns till death'."

Realizing that the moment now calls for decisive action Hopkinson raises a hand above his head and snaps his fingers. A uniformed guard immediately rushes forward. Before I have the time to realize what is happening, he slips a pair of handcuffs on me, with Hopkinson moving in to shield me from any hostility from the men beginning to crowd around us.

During our brief exchange the alarm of my having been singled out has spread rapidly across the deck, concern spreading on their faces, the whispers already beginning to make the rounds.

"*Ay* bhai Bashir, what have you been up to this time?" An unidentifiable voice asks.

Another queries: "Why you, why not me?"

Hopkinson abruptly grabs hold of my arm and leads me away

from the throng. As we approach closer to the railing he signals to the waiting tugboat below to draw near.

But, before we can descend, a few of my shipmates come closer to bid farewell, sure that I had somehow been blessed with the privilege of being allowed to land. Hands thump my back.

"*Wah* Bashir. It's you again. You are turning out to be a *chhuppa Rustum*."

This comment is in reference to an earlier incident at Yokohama when a fez-toting visitor named Maulavi Barkatullah had asked for me and then taken me ashore for several hours.

Someone else asks in husky Punjabi: "So, tell us what was it that you revealed to him? Is it a mantar, or a magic phrase that will set us free, too? How much money is he asking for?"

But the raw words that I will recall forever are still to be uttered by someone closer to me.

"*Wah*, Bashir bhai, who could have suspected that you would turn out to be one of them. All this *natak* of becoming a fisherman one day, or finding a teaching job. And none of us had the slightest inkling of who you really were."

These taunts are heaped on me by none other than my friend Puran who follows us as far as the guards will allow him. One of these guards now tosses a blanket over my head. Through a tiny gap in this cloth I watch my unsteady feet descend the sloped gangway. There is a flash of green light from the approaching edge of the water. Unseen hands push me roughly onto the patrol boat, and on the heaving deck I feel myself lurching out of control, the water finally within reach.

As I reach a hand out to touch the surface something cold and brittle strikes the back of my head.

When I come to, it is nearly dark. I find myself lying on the floor of a large wood-paneled room. There are several armed men standing around me. They take no interest in me. My head hurts terribly and when I touch my hair above the left ear it is matted with blood.

While still lying prone I peer out of a window and notice that a lifebuoy tacked to the deck has the words SEA LION stenciled on it. A tall, familiar looking uniformed man clutching a gold braided cap is standing close by whispering to another. I can only gather a smattering of their conversation.

"… this way you can always keep an eye on him. Where can he go with the police boats surrounding the ship all day and night?"

"I need him safely locked in a cell where I can keep a closer eye. I need him for further questioning. This man knows…"

"No, no. My instructions to you are final. You cannot take him ashore. …what if he were somehow able to escape, or came to harm?

Imagine the ruckus that would create. Ottawa is already looking for any opportunity to come breathing down our necks."

"But what he knows is vital to... he may be the Kartar Singh I have been pursuing all the way from India. I am convinced he has been sent here on a mission and I need to know what that is. This could be more important than the arrival of the ship. There is even a possibility that the entire manifest is made up of revolutionaries. All I need to do is take a peek at his feet."

They hear me moaning and are silent.

This time when I regain consciousness I am being prodded to a standing position. As I shakily rise up, a dark blanket is once again draped over my head and I am led up a flight of rickety stairs and then left alone. I can hear a babble of excited, incoherent voices around me. Several helping hands receive me back on the deck. There are shouts of outrage as the blanket is removed.

Moments later I can hear Gurdit's sonorous rumbling voice calling out my name.

# SHORE WATCHERS

By late Saturday afternoon there are only a handful of men still left squatting facing the ship and the north shore. The distant, clattering of the Fraser Mill where most of them work, interrupts their reveries with the hum of its mechanical routines of shift changeovers and the whining of mechanical saws, the hissing of steam marking the passage of the hours. The whistles of squat tugs hustling wet tree trunks into manageable booms match these blasts in the midst of the shouted instructions from within the hulls of waiting ships.

These men have trickled down to this shore several times through out the morning and noon, leaving work briefly to confirm and unravel the swirl of rumors circulating in the mill since early morning.

The ship, the ship, the ship with a fresh boatload of their fellow countrymen will be here in Vancouver. They have waited for so long for it, and now it is finally here, it is fast approaching the harbor, it will be berthed any minute now. This is followed by the dramatic news that it has now anchored offshore and the immigration authorities have gone aboard. And now, so late in the day, the men can easily identify a launch hired by the Shore Committee as it warily circles the ship. It soon becomes apparent that the launch is engaged in a cat and mouse game with the immigration department, in which their every approach close to the ship has been foiled by urgent whistles and angry mega phoned instructions from the harbor authorities.

Amidst all this activity, the initial excitement at actually seeing the dark bulk of the Nanak Jahaz silhouetted against the deep green of the Vancouver harbor, has now evaporated and the watching men have grown quieter with each passing hour. By late afternoon, the ship has still remained firmly anchored at a considerable distance from the landing docks - a single persistent rumor returning to plague them: the new comers have not been allowed to disembark. However, despite the uncertainty, they have clung adamantly to the slim hope that whatever is preventing the passengers from disembarking will turn out to be a minor technicality, and the men will then be able to go down to the wharfs and greet each of the newcomers with open arms. They have anticipated their every step and plotted it on imaginary maps and eagerly prepared for this for so long, surely no one can now deny them this.

From this distance, the ship's outline appears to waver over the water, the single funnel continuing to belch out sporadic plumes of smoke that linger close to the water, and through it all they can clearly see that the decks are swarming with passengers.

By now, the shadows of the crouched figures have begun to

stretch far across the wet sand. A cool breeze caresses the open water with gentle wavelets that endlessly crackle and re-arrange the powdered seashells and pebbles at their feet. The sound is deceptively similar to that of human sighing.

Crouching on his haunches with his friends, a worried Mewa Singh of Lopoke, also stares pensively at the downtown Vancouver buildings crest over the entire western horizon and stretch all the way down to the waterfront. In the middle distance a smattering of scrawny firs mark the eastern limit of Stanley Park. In between this backdrop of uneven trees and much closer to their left are three steamers moored around the Pier One. Two of these steam ships are the Empress of Japan and Empress of Asia, and they are berthed on opposite sides of the larger of the two wharfs, their infrequent plumes of smoke drifting down onto the decks. Here hundreds of new arrivals are descending from the gangways. As their twin funnels billow furiously in preparation for the return voyage the two ships are also taking on fresh supplies and passengers. Mewa notices that most of the disembarking newcomers are weighed down with rolled bundles of personal belongings.

In contrast to these, far out in the middle of the bay, though easily dwarfed by either one of these two passenger ships in the inlet, is a distinctive single-funnelled bulk contrasting sharply against the dull background of the water, its white lettering vaguely legible from even this distance: KOMAGATA MARU, renamed the NANAK JAHAZ, the Guru's ship. This looming vessel has continued to remain anchored in the middle of the Burrard Inlet at some distance off Pier Two since eleven in the morning, the minuscule boats of the immigration officials tethered to one side. And, though they have continued to watch it closely well into the late afternoon. None of passengers of this ship have yet disembarked, nor has any of its cargo been offloaded.

As Mewa watches intently, the deck suddenly erupts in a flurry of activity, with people milling about the decks, first gathering at one railing amidships before relocating to the other side. Perhaps, like them they have been stirred up by a fresh round of rumours, with each relay of words resulting in brief spurts of activity. Keenly observing this, the men gathered around Mewa have begun to speculate that any moment now the Shore Committee will be allowed to clamber aboard and greet the enterprising passengers and the charterer of the vessel, our hero Bagga Gurdit Sarhali, himself. They can even spy the outline of a passenger waving a pair of hand-held flags with red and yellow squares.

"They have signalling flags and are calling out to us," someone yells excitedly before the signaller disappears in the onboard confusion.

A full hour later they watch elatedly as the first of the passengers is actually seen heading down the gangway, their belongings slung over their heads. Each descending passenger is eagerly counted. Seventeen! Seventeen and the trickle of passengers comes to a stop. Just seventeen? What about the rest? And, already the officials are departing one by one in their boats, the stairway has been slung onboard, and only two patrol boats have been left behind to police the ship.

With this development the rumour mills begin to churn afresh.

From the first whisper nearly a month ago that a large group of Indians was collectively heading out to Vancouver, to this scene in the harbor, these men have eagerly followed each step of the ship's perilous journey from Hong Kong to Shanghai to Yokohama to Moji to Kobe to Yokohama, before it headed out east and disappearing into the open Pacific. At that moment the Komagata Maru could just as well have fallen off the edge of the world and none would have been wiser. There was to be no further contact till yesterday when it showed up William's Head near Victoria.

Gurbaksh, who is the only one amongst them following the local newspapers on a regular basis, has joined the group with fresh copies of the evening's two papers. But Mewa knows that tucked inside one of his pockets is an earlier edition of Times Colonist. He recites it repeatedly to them as if it were a favourite quote, scanning it repeatedly for some hidden message.

Under the headline: *Mystery Surrounds Movements Of Ship*, the fortnight old newspaper states - *Much interest is evinced in immigration and shipping circles concerning the movements of the mysterious ship Komagata Maru, which, for some time past, has been reported on passage from the Orient with an unusually large complement of Hindus aboard for British Columbia. For a long time it has been known that the Hindus have had under consideration the charter of a steamer, by which means they could comply with the previous immigration order which completely barred and influx of Indian natives, unless they could prove to the authorities on this side that direct passage had been made from the land of birth. Since that time, however, a more drastic order has been drafted, which effectively prevents all labourers, skilled and unskilled, and artisans from entering the Dominion until the end of September. Speculation was rife, whether, under these circumstances, the Hindus would go to the expense of chartering a steamer to carry a large number of turbaned men across the broad expanse of the Pacific, when it was known that serious complications would arise upon the ship reaching her destination.*

And, then late last evening the electrifying rumour made the rounds of all the sawmills that the ship had already made it into the Canadian waters. This led to further speculation over whether it would first be allowed to dock at Victoria before heading for Vancouver. Later in the evening this rumour was quickly followed by another that instead of aiming for Vancouver directly the ship would now be heading for Port Alberni, and everyone had chuckled over this bold tactic. They had learnt earlier that the Shore Committee, formed to facilitate Komagata Maru's arrival, had, with the aid of their legal counsel, stumbled upon a loophole in the local immigration regulations. These listed the inland port of Port Alberni, located at the end of a deep estuary in the middle of Vancouver Island, as an entry port at which the extant regulations forbidding entrance of incoming labourers into British Columbia, and hence to Canada, did not apply. This discovery led to the widespread belief that, if, somehow the new arrivals could be diverted to this destination, then they would find safe passage into Canada and escape prosecution under the Continuous Journey clause. Yet, right before their disbelieving eyes, having rounded the First Narrows and circled Stanley Park in the late morning the beleaguered ship and its eager passengers have now been miraculously delivered at their doorstep. They have come to rest at some distance from them in mid bay, barely a few hundred yards from the bustling local wharfs.

Gurbaksh, chooses this opportune moment to hold up a copy of the Vancouver Province for them all to examine.

"Look here", he announces dramatically reading off the headlines:

*'Boat Loads of Hindus on Way to Vancouver and Hindu Invasion of Canada.* They are now officially calling it an invasion of Canada!" This piece of news is greeted by another round of boisterous applause.

"It says here: *Hindu invaders now in the city harbor on Komagata Maru.* Look, they even have a photo of the ship here. But, can any of you see an invader onboard the Nanak Jahaz?" He asks pointing in the general direction of the ship.

"I'll show you *invaders* if you can spot any *HinDoo* on board?" This is Indar stressing the 'D' in an anglicized imitation of the word 'Hindoo', glancing slyly at Sundar, and poking him in the ribs. Both of them collapse in laughter.

"Read some more, yaar. Come on read on; tell us more when this invasion will take place. Where are these so called *invaders*, and is there any *Ravan* or *Halaku* or even a Changez Khan amongst them?"

"Nah, yaar, first tell us more about these so-called *HinDooos!* And, why are they are so bent on invading this peaceful Dominion of Canada," comes the rejoinder from Shergill.

*'The vessel arrived here this morning before daybreak – Excited crowds of Hindus assemble on the waterfront –* that's us they are talking about, yaaro. *Newcomers seem assured of being admitted. Gungeet Singh,* who is this Gungeet Singh? Gurbaksh pauses, puzzled by the misprint. Do they mean our Bagga, our *'babar sher'* Gurdit Singh Serhali? Is he also supposed to be one of these invaders?"

"Anyway, later on in the same article he is also referred to as

Gundit Singh. *Gundit Singh issues statement containing veiled threat.* Veiled indeed."

As Gurbaksh translates more of the day's sensational news, the listeners' mirth can only be sustained for just so long, the sobering reality lying before them in mid-water quashing any further speculation that the affair will be resolved favourably any time soon.

It is now Mewa's sombre friend Bishan's turn to wade into the discussion. "Bhai, I have also been following this breaking news very nervously and have come to the conclusion that if the passengers of Nanak Jahaz are destined to land at all in Canada, it will have to be within this week, or never."

"And how did you figure that out all by yourself?" Queries an irritated Gurbaksh.

"I understand that by the time this week is out, our people are probably going to find out how hopelessly entangled they have become in yet another bureaucratic technicality. They will never fully understand the implications of what has come to pass here today. Look, just because the passengers of Panama Maru were eventually allowed to land here on a technicality, now it will now be tougher to get the next batch of our people off so lightly? The goras are not going to leave this precious loophole, as well as others, open any longer for us to exploit." Falling silent his gaze wanders off towards the water.

Shergill, who is also staring silently out at the water, turns to Bishan to ask: "I wonder why did they not just head out for Port Alberni as they were instructed to by the committee's lawyer, Bird? This way they would have avoided the inevitable malaise of a direct confrontation."

"Perhaps the Shore Committee was not able to get the message to them on time," Bishan offers.

"Or, perhaps, they were somehow prevented from doing so. And, in order to prevent them from doing so, you would first have to uncover this secret ploy. If we have only been discussing these matters amongst ourselves at the temple, then how could the authorities learn about it unless they were informed?"

An uncomfortable silence follows during which everyone turns to stare at the constant churning of the crushed seashells at their feet.

Just before hunger and anxiety finally drives them all homewards, someone brings out a snuffbox with a mirror top, and they take turns reflecting the lowering sun towards the stationary ship. At this distance there is no means of verifying whether they have received a response from the quiet and suddenly deserted decks.

Harnam chooses this moment to walk over to where Mewa is squatting. "Bhai, this is it for me. That hawk-eyed headmaster Reid is not going to let them off so easily, and will probably do anything and everything he can to keep this lot where he can keep a closer eye on their every move. In no way is he letting this one sneak by on his watch. You see, after the black eye of his bungling of the Panama Maru incident, he has a personal reputation to repair, and, more importantly, he has a lesson to teach us Indians. With his career now riding upon how he plays his cards this time around, he has to find a sure way to land this one very slippery fish in his very own backyard."

He stares morosely at the water for a while and yawns, expansively stretching his arms upwards, drawling: "*Chal yaar* Mewa, it is time to head for home. There's nothing more to do here for now. At least we know the ship will still be here in the morning. Come; let us see what our *khansama* Ramu has concocted to challenge our appetites today."

It now seems almost an age since Hopkinson sneaked on board to whisk me off the ship. Earlier on, someone else had also came on board the Komagata Maru with a premeditated mission for me. At the time we had been docked for three days at Yokohama to take on the last batch of passengers. On the evening of the second day of our stay we were surprised to hear that the venerable Maulavi Barakat Ullah Bhopali was coming onboard to visit us.

From his outer appearance, Maulavi Sahib was to be nothing that I had expected from his manifestos. Instead of the dowdy, professorial gentleman I had been expecting from his writings, he was extremely well groomed and immaculate in white shirt, gray tie and jacket, his full lips pursed in an unselfconscious half smile that was half hidden behind a full moustache, the circular rimmed glasses flashed in time with the swish of the tassels of his red fez. I observed that whenever he was in deep thought he was prone to removing and polishing these glasses using a handkerchief retrieved with a flourish from a breast pocket, squinting in bright light, the bridge of his nose pinched where the frames had rested. But it was the delivery of his speech that continued to hold my attention long after the visit; every word of his erudition exposing my ignorance and naiveté.

It has been my good fortune all my life to come under the spell of men whom I have considered to be larger than real life. Before this meeting with Maulavi sahib, I had formed a warm rapport with the principal of the Victoria Diamond Jubilee Hindu Technical Institute that I had attended at Lahore. From professor Puran Singh-ji I had imbibed the first seeds of political consciousness. Other contemporary influences, like the reformer Sir Syed Ahmed Khan, novelist Maulavi Nazir Ahmad, and the ardent educationist Munshi Zaka Ullah, were each instrumental in channeling my growing disillusion with the British, which eventually led me to abandon some of my naïve pacifism.

I had been following the career of Maulavi Barakatullah from afar through the pursuits of my college teachers. Of Maulavi Sahib, I already knew that barely three years ago he had been to Constantinople and Petrograd to promote his peculiar message. He then returned to his teaching post at Tokyo to teach Hindi, and to publish a popular article referring to the advent of a great pan-Islamic Alliance that would also include Afghanistan, which he expected to become 'the future Japan of Central Asia'. In Japan he was able to convert to Islam his teaching assistant and the assistant's wife, and her father, thus making the first such conversions in Japan. Meanwhile, his vociferous and dissident tone was becoming more anti-British with every outing. In his paper the *Christian Combination Against Islam*, Maulavi Sahib had singled out the Emperor William of Germany as the one man *'who holds the peace of the world as well as the war in the hollow of his hand: it is the duty of the Muslims to be united, to stand by the Khalif; with their life and property, and to side with Germany.'*

Quoting a Roman poet, Maulavi Barakat Ullah reminded his readers that the Anglo-Saxons had once been sea wolves, living on the pillage of the world. The difference in modern times was the 'refinement of hypocrisy which sharpens the edge of brutality.' The paper was hastily condemned and prohibited by the authorities, both in India and Japan. Meanwhile, copies of another paper called *El Islam* began to appear in India, continuing his political propaganda until its eventual suppression. This was soon followed by a lithographed Urdu pamphlet, *The Sword is the last Resort*, which was modelled on the style of the publications of the Ghadar party of San Francisco. And, finally by the end of March this year, the Japanese authorities had terminated his teaching appointment.

The company of such great men in my life had always had the effect of making me feel, at least momentarily, more cosmopolitan and well informed in my worldview. Yet, I had initially not taken easily to adopting personal teachers. More than once a spiritual guide had delivered to me the old chestnut: *a teacher shatters the statue the student builds of him.* Professor-ji, observing that my impatience with the pace of his teaching was stunting my intellectual growth, had only obliquely countered my reticence with: *you can perform first aid by putting a bandage on a wound, but you cannot operate on yourself.*

Accompanying Maulavi Sahib on this visit onboard the Komagata Maru was his faithful disciple, the firebrand fugitive, temple preacher and *granthi*, Bhagwan Singh Jakh, alias Natha Singh, whose name I had heard mentioned several times onboard and in the Punjab. With his flowing dark beard and piercing eyes, Bhagwan Singh was the perfect counterfoil to Maulavi Sahib's detached elegance.

Beneath the welcoming cheers that greeted the arrival of these extraordinary men in our midst there was also a vicious undercurrent of rumors. Since both these visitors were known to be vociferous opponents of the British occupation of India, their presence in our midst carried about it an undeniable whiff of disrepute. This mainly centered on Maulavi Sahib's recent termination as professor of the Hindi language at the Tokyo University for his strident, and increasingly militant, pan-Islamist views. Bhagwan, the natural showman, wearing the mantle of notoriety with ease, was rumored to be 'the most wanted rebel' by the British and was being hunted down on account of his seditious activities on two continents. These activities had secured his dismissal from the post of *granthi* at the Sikh temples at Penang and then at Hong Kong.

He had been deported from Victoria on the Empress of Japan barely a year ago for having illegally entered Canada. Rumor had it that once the Empress of Japan had made the ocean crossing, Bhagwan had promptly jumped ship at Yokohama. Now, here he was before us, just itching to get his feet planted back on the American continent, and yet for all his bravado seemingly reluctant to throw in his lot in with us. Today, his original bluster appears to have been blunted behind those fierce, beady eyes, but I could tell that the repressed manic energy was barely contained.

In order to deliver their particular message forcefully across to us, the two men had also brought with them several Urdu and Gurmukhi copies of their shared manifesto, 'Ghadar', the official paper of the Indian Rebellion. However, by that time I was already thoroughly familiar with both their works after having written several revolutionary poems of my own. Some of them were printed in *Ghadar Ki Goonj* and widely quoted and recirculated around the world.

I noticed that the garish covers of the new Ghadar magazines were still adorned with black, white and red collages of angry fists raised diagonally at the sky, shattered chains swinging in the air and fluttering red flags rising out of the flames. All this was as familiar a territory as were Bhagwan's showcased inflammatory poems. Each of these verses had once been a fiery missive hurled into the enemy camp, easily able to tap into a receptive audience eager to lap up each word, the venomous potency of each verse multiplying with their transfer from mouths to other ears.

These men had come onboard claiming to forewarn us of what possible fate may await us at the end of our journey. It was Bhagwan, the seasoned preacher most at ease before a large congregation, who first introduced us to their unwelcome message. Once we were all gathered before him, he addressed his words directly to the lion amongst us, the ship's charterer Gurdit Singh, and yet I realized that his remarks were also meant to enlighten the rest of us.

After adjusting his black turban several times and then clearing his throat to draw attention, he begins his sermon of revolt by nervously stroking his dark flowing beard: "Maulavi sahib and I have information…," there is a moment of hesitation before he continues, "…we have reliable information that the Canadian government will do everything within its power to prevent you from setting foot on their land."

These words are delivered with such conviction they have the desired effect, instantly silencing our murmuring and focusing our attention on the speakers. He holds up an index finger for emphasis and squinting his eyes tightly he repeats: "Mark my words as those delivered by a man who has personally been there and seen it all with his own two eyes. They will *not* let you land!"

And now, into this sea of open hostilities steps Maulavi sahib, one hand raised for attention, taking up the thread of the message in a similar vein; the silken tassels of his bright fez agitated with every move of his head.

"Just one moment here," he says holding up an open palm for silence, "first hear us out before you pass judgment. I, too, have come to warn you of this very serious matter, whether you realize it or not at this juncture in your journey. At this very moment the Canadian government is busy cooking up new regulations specifically tailored to discourage any 'new settlers'; and by 'new settlers' they mean people like you and me who are heading there indirectly from India. Your claim that this makes a sham of the emperor's claim that all British subjects in all his many dominions are equal and free to visit and settle where-ever they please to, holds a different meaning when implemented in the colonial realities across the empire. This imperial concession was never intended for the colonized natives to be able to relocate.

There is total silence and even our normally pensive Gurdit seems taken aback by their message.

Maulavi sahib continues. "Now, as far as I can see from your uniforms, some of you have also been active in the British army, and I especially empathize with you. Nevertheless, even though you may rightfully claim to be loyal subjects of the British Empire, the Canadian authorities do not see you as such and will never permit you to touch their land."

I notice that his fez is slightly askew. I can also sense that he had not planned initially to join in so early into this discourse, or much less launch off into a personal rant on his favorite peeve. But Bhagwan had already disingenuously launched them in that direction.

"Now, after having informed you of this unwelcome turn of events…," he continues in a mellower tone, his broad round face softening into a smile, "…let me and bhai Bhagwan, also be the first ones to congratulate you on your audacity and your resolve to challenge all such types of discriminatory legislation."

With these words of re-assurance, he and Bhai Bhagwan now raise their fists and lead us through a few faint-hearted rounds of slogans of sacrifice '*Dukhi parja; Hai nai Karja; Inqualab Zindabad*'. This is followed by a reading of some hyperbolic material from the front pages of the current issue of the Ghadar.

The first issue of the Ghadar had appeared in Urdu out of North America last November and in Punjabi a few weeks later. It was published at the Yugantar Ashram in San Francisco. The popularity of the paper soon became such that it was being distributed to regions across the globe where significant numbers of Indians resided - first in the United States and Canada, then Phillipines, Fiji, Sumatra, Japan, Shanghai, Hong Kong, Java, Singapore, Malaya, Siam, Burma, all of India and even in distant shores of East Africa.

Maulavi Sahib proceeded to read a quotation to us from the first issue of the Ghadar:

*'Today, there begins in foreign lands, but in our own country's tongue, a war against the English Raj.... What is our name? Mutiny What is our work? Mutiny. Where will the mutiny break out? In India. The time will soon come when rifles and blood will take the place of pen and ink. Brave men and worthy sons of India, be ready with bullets and shots. Soon the fate of tyrants will be decided on the battlefield, and days of happiness and glory will dawn for India.'*

This issue of the Ghadar would be followed by others that would occasionally also publish the following incendiary advertisement:

*Wanted: Enthusiastic and heroic soldiers for organizing Ghadar in Hindustan*
*Remuneration: Death / Reward: Martyrdom / Pension: Freedom*
*Field of work: Hindustan.*
*What do we want?*
*Freedom!*
*What is our motto?*
*Rebellion!*
*What is our reward?*
*Death!*

Once again this is familiar territory for some even though none of us has openly espoused to it, at least not just yet. I have read watered down versions of similar material in the copies of the *Thundering Dawn* published nearly a decade ago from Lahore by my college principal, Professor Puran Singh. However, just as then, none of it bore any relevance to the adventure we were currently embarked upon. Similar Ghadarite literature had been entering our Punjab for several years from the American shores with impunity and the thrust of all these periodicals remained unchanged: to rid India of the colonizing British.

This would also be an excellent opportunity for me to reveal a little bit more about myself. I, too, have been involved with the Ghadarites, though in a limited role. Working under the assumed name of Kartar Singh, I have published some of the most inflammatory of these slogans. But Bhagwan Singh had out done us all in his writings. He was the one who first proposed taking the battle to the shores of Britain.

In one of the issues of Ghadar he had gone so far as to proclaim:

> *Burn them where you find them*
> *Blood shall flow…*

If there was any solace or hope offered by these words, its affect on us lasted for only a few brief moments; and when the visitors left the deck to confer with Gurdit in private, our anxieties began to plague us. It was as if their blistering declarations of moral support had been proffered to us as stones tossed into a cauldron that momentarily quelled the chaos.

After the speeches and the ensuing arguments, someone followed me down to my bunk to ask if I would like to join Maulavi Barakatullah and Bhagwan Singh for a short while on the shore. With the ship not due to sail for another three days we had ample time to explore this part of Japan. It was already late evening, and while some of my fellow passengers ventured into the massage parlours and were shooed out of one establishment after another while continuing to get drunk at every such encounter, Barakat Ullah sensing my sobriety invited me to join him for a walk. He ended up guiding me through the narrow streets that lead to a stretch of beach not far from where our ship was moored. I soon learnt that one of the reasons for Maulavi sahib's coming onboard was also to meet me, for he had received a letter of appeal from my former principal, to dissuade me from my foolishness, and redirect my energies elsewhere.

Professor-ji had suggested that I join Maulavi sahib instead in his work at the Tokyo University. Seeing that his teaching post no longer existed I could see no threat in talking further to Maulavi sahib about my reasons for the ensuing voyage.

As we moved further away from the port, I could see hundreds of pale crabs scampering ahead of us and wading night birds took wing in alarm. The city lights soon began to waver in the distance; the water seeming to glow faintly so that we could easily discern the outline of the beach stretching before us. Some of the sandy beach before us was strewn with gill nets spread out to dry. Barely a day ago I had watched from the ship as fishermen went about cleaning and repairing these very same nets.

I could tell Maulavi sahib was at ease walking in the sand. "If this were Tokyo I would have invited you to a dinner at my humble abode or at one of my Japanese students' residences. You know, I have been successful in converting at least two of them. And as Muslims, let me tell you that their allegiance to the faith makes our dedications seem remiss."

When I mentioned that our Japanese vessel had been renamed Nanak Jahaz by the Sikhs onboard he had seemed to wince at my words, but I misunderstood his reasons until he placed a paternal hand on my shoulder.

"Bashir, I know you are young and still have a lot to learn, but you have to grow up fast into this world, and leave behind such petty parochial concerns and peevishness. Whether you like to admit to it or not, from this day on you must never forget that every step of your journey, and your choice of actions, will represent every other Muslim on the Indian subcontinent; you are now a part of a much bigger fraternity that now stretches far beyond India."

He did not look directly at me while conferring this honor on me, but continued in a low soothing voice, his footsteps marking the cadence of his voice. For some odd reason I felt compelled at this moment to show him the neatly creased flyer that had launched me on this journey.

"You must consider this opportunity as a special mission; something that bhai Puran and I have both assigned to you." He proceeded to lead me further from the cluster of houses and shops crowding the waterfront, further revealing to me that he would soon be traveling to San Francisco with bhai Bhagwan and that a massive sea change was about to overcome our corner of the world.

"Perhaps, we shall overtake you during our Pacific crossing. But wherever you end up traveling, I want you to write to me about all you see, and the things that interest you and that affect you, and through your eyes we shall all also bear witness to history."

When we paused briefly we were still out of reach of the waves, and I was alarmed to see him removing his shoes and socks and gesturing towards me to do the same.

"Come on," he gestured, carefully rolling up the cuffs of his trouser and placing his shoes out of reach of the tide. "I want you to remember this moment when you make it across the ocean. Do you know what these waters are called?"

"The Pacific!" I was quick to answer.

"Yes, of course. Where we stand now is the western shore of the Pacific Ocean. And you are headed for its eastern shore. Just look at the vast distances you have already traversed and where Allah Kareem has brought you. All the way from tiny Lopoke to this beach, and now you are headed out there." At this point he gestured with both arms to include the whole of the eastern horizon, the stretch of water before us and the canopy of stars.

"Inshallah, one day you will reach your destination at the other end of your journey - the place you have chosen to make your living.

If Vancouver is not to be that destination then for the purposes of your mission it may just as well be Astoria, Stockton, Los Angeles, or San Francisco, or even Mexico. Only Allah knows best. Perhaps, you may even choose to settle in distant Brazil. But wherever you do finally choose to settle down, remember this that you are an Indian first. Never forget the socio-political compulsions that have led you to abandon the hometown of your extended family and to risk all for your personal survival.

"How long can the inhabitants of one proportionally miniscule, windy, fog-shrouded island of stones and rolling hills be presumptuous enough to claim the world as their manifest destiny, or its children own it as their natural birthright? Have they learnt nothing from history or from the fate of empires? Even we as Muslims, whose Empire in its heyday stretched from Qurtoba to Rangoon, have been humbled so that we can only call the states of Turkey, Arabia, Persia and Afghanistan as our own. Barely four nations with less than fifty million people to call our own. Do you see how an empire that was destined to endure forever has been undone in less than two centuries?

"Let me give you a more homely example. Do you remember as children used to fight over the burnt caramelized rice at the bottom of the pot? It was always the best part of the dish? Was it not? Now, do you recall what it was called?"

"I think we used to call it *krori*." I am now wondering where this conversation is leading unless there was a culinary tip buried in this advice.

"Yes, that prized *krori*. Bashir, after you have gone through the fire and have been tempered by it you will have become this prized *krori*. It is no ordinary opponent your companions have chosen to tackle. This is the British Empire, a kingdom that they so often boast stretches from one end of the world to the other, and the most widespread empire that has ever existed. In actuality, now, with the underwater trans-continental cable completed from Vancouver to Sidney, Australia, the electronic arms of the Empire have physically encircled the entire globe in its stifling embrace.

"Neither the Egyptians, the Greeks, nor the Romans contemplated that their reach could spread so far, knew such extravagance, or held such a range of subjugated populations and their attended wealth in their hands. In other words, no one else in their most feverish dreams has stretched their greedy fingers so far into the far reaches of the world for tasty morsels. Neither Sikander-e-Azam nor Halaku could have dreamt of such conquests. And your handful lot is questioning this empire's right to govern you in your in own land wherever and however it chooses.

"Look at how our own Punjabis have been ignored in the allocation of educational funds. As a teacher you should know that to a local unlettered Punjabi villager Urdu now sounds as alien as Bengali or Gujrati and must be translated for him to be understood."

Even though my wet feet have grown chilled and wrinkled I am reluctant to interrupt this torrent of words and images.

"The British reluctantly learnt two lessons from the trauma of the first rebellion of 1857: the imperative of commanding a strong army, and having effective communications. And ever since then they have moved onto a global scale by applying these two simple lessons. They have been maneuvering, posturing and forming alliances across the shifting loyalties in The Great Game with Russia and Germany. India is absolutely vital to the British to counter these perceived threats.

"What our bhai Gurdit-ji is attempting to tackle is nothing less than taking on an unforgiving jinn that does not tolerate nuisances lightly. Take it from me as an established fact that they will not let you land in Canada. But in attempting to do so you will prove a point for the rest of the world, and bear witness to the fallacy of the British statement that the ruled are free to move about and relocate wherever they want within the empire."

Suddenly, I could not resist the temptation to put forth the other side of this argument.

"Surely, Maulavi Sahib, the British have been of *some* benefit to us? How can you say that in the process of governing India the British have made India a better place for the average citizen? Didn't they, perhaps, educate us; modernized our cities, built irrigation canals to make the land more productive? Surely the preservation of ancient monuments and antiquities deserves praise?"

He looks amazed to hear me say this.

"Well, my naïve friend, let's examine each of these claims in more detail. This is a debilitating illusion fostered by our rulers. Taking our own community only in this context, before the British annexed India and destroyed the fabric our society, ordinary Muslims attended the madrassa where they learnt - in addition to the Koran and Hadith - basic mathametics, and their local Hindi. They also learned a smattering of classical languages, such as Persian and Arabic. Today, the British papers report that the literacy rate in British India is only about five percent. Now how is this five percent literacy an improvement over the usurped popularity of the madrassa. And, of course, you have to keep in mind that, of these fortunate few that comprise the educated, five percent belong mostly to the well-to-do. The average citizen has already been abandoned to make do with his personal means.

"The record for girls is even more appalling. If it weren't for the efforts of your SIR Syed…," he stresses the honorary designation with an audible hiss of emphasis, such that I can sense a point of friction in the divergent social viewpoints of these two influential men, "…there would have been no available education for these girls under the British, their claims to the contrary not withstanding.

"As for the establishment of codes for the protection of our prized antiquities, are you aware of the British plans to dismantle the Taj Mahal and sell off the building materials to developers. The only reason these plans came to naught was the absence of any prospect for profit.

"Westerners who claim to having a civilizing mission in India have forever been trying to impose their social values on us. How many cultures do they know that would have welcomed those early Jews who arrived in Kerala in the first century, or the Persian Parsi refugees when they came to our shores?

"Whether it is irrigation or agricultural development the pitiful state roads, tanks and canals which the Muslim and Hindu administrators originally constructed have all been allowed to fall into disrepair. In Bengal I have seen the canals, which are the lifeblood of the peasantry are now becoming silted from neglect leading to increased flooding and has probably caused more famines than their bureaucratic bungling.

"Life expectancy has fallen dramatically since the British took administration into their hands. For the past four decades our population has grown at an average rate of twenty percent, but during this same period England and Wales' population has grown three times as fast by nearly sixty percent.

"Famines that were a rarity before the Raj, have increased triple-fold perhaps causing over 20 million deaths. That is one-tenth the current total Indian population. And yet, what is even more exasperating is the fact that exports of food grains have increased fourfold during this same period. I have even heard it said that former slave-owners from America have been permitted to set up plantations here. And don't get me started on Lytton, our poet emperor who so adroitly under-estimated the collateral damage from 'managed' famines both in Ireland and later here in India.

"Mark my words, Bashir, colonial greed made the Empire's capitalistic glories possible and spurred its Industrial Revolution, and colonial greed will be its undoing.

"Come on; let us get back to the shore as it is getting late; you have a ship to catch. The water is getting cold. I am sure it would come as a great surprise to all my readers if they saw me like this dabbling in such sentimentality. But, as you see, I, too, am a bit of a pagan at heart and take immense pleasure in performing these peculiar rituals. Inshallah, soon I shall cross this great ocean, and when I touch down at the other end, I shall also dip my feet and repeat this ritual.

"Promise me, Bashir, you will do the same at the other end of this great ocean. I hear that the water is warmer there; it is clearer and more welcoming even if the locals are not."

With this exchange we head back to the waiting ship.

In parting he presented me with a special gift: a red fez with black silken tassels like the one he has worn all his adult life. While nearly everyone onboard has worn some form of headgear - the Sikhs their obligatory colorful turbans, and my Muslim brethren their red fezzes - I had left my head uncovered except for prayer times.

What do grown men do when they are trapped and have nothing better to look forward to from day to day?

They argue amongst themselves, and they obsessively watch their surroundings for the minutest signs of change. The shifting hues of the surrounding hills, the patterns of smoke arising from distant fires, the precision and bone-rattling explosion each evening from the nine-o'clock-gun in Stanley Park, the clutter of marine traffic, and especially the sight of other immigrants alighting from other ships; these now fill their hours.

Their daily routines have now come to include gathering on the deck in groups of threes and fours to argue and speculate on the status and fate of their immigration proceedings onshore. With the initial excitement of the first day and the visit of the immigration officials over, the flash of the pressmen's cameras has been washed out of our eyes. The next moment of equal optimism will only arise two weeks later when someone spies a boat in the middle distance charting a course straight towards our ship.

Standing tall and erect at the helm of a small scow is an aged gentleman in a rumpled dark suit, white hat and a tie flapping in the breeze. The man in the suit turns out to be the one appointed by the Shore Committee to fight for our safe landing. Even from a distance he appears to be impatient to cover the intervening distance, and once the vessel has come in contact with the larger ship, the lawyer stretches himself up to his full length and clasps the edge of the ship's hull. Since Mr. Reid he has not permitted him to come aboard, he peers anxiously up at the rusting metal plates and the rows of anxious faces peering down at him. He asks for 'Mr. Gurdit Singh, the charterer of the Komagata Maru'.

Gurdit, having already recognized the lawyer, has now come to squat close to the railing in order to greet the visitor. The two men gaze at each other rather self-consciously on finding themselves suddenly at such close quarters, and aware of the throng of faces around them.

"Edward Bird, Barrister," he announces breathlessly by way of introduction. "Mr. Gurdit Singh, sir, I would like to welcome you and the rest of the passengers of Komagata Maru to Canada", he states briskly, tiptoeing and stretching precariously from his boat, and holding out his right hand for Gurdit to shake. Other hands reach out eagerly towards him as he steadies himself with the free left hand; an awkward balancing act as the two vessels rise and fall in unsynchronized motion.

"I can see, sir, that you have had quite an eventful voyage," he smiles broadly, relishing the occasion and the challenge the situation presents to him, not only in its legality but the mere physicality of holding onto the edge of a gently swaying ship deck while his own smaller vessel is buffeted by the breeze.

Gurdit pumps the proffered hand and smiles back.

He notices that Edward Bird is tall, dapper, eyes crinkled with deepening crow's feet, a man who is not easy to humour. Today like every other day of official business he is dressed in a cotton suit that has that comfortable lived-in look, the cuffs faintly stained, the trousers legs and the back of his coat drooping and yet somehow carried gracefully throughout the day. On sweaty afternoons he will fan himself with his hat, drawing out a handkerchief to wipe his forehead and cheeks and then hastily tucking it away. With age and experience has come a body that is now breathless upon every exertion, but balancing himself so perilously close to the water, nothing can dampen his moral outrage.

"Mr. Malcolm Reid, the Immigration Chief for British Columbia, has informed Mr. Ramdas of the Shore Committee and me that you are in violation of the Continuous Journey clause. I have been told that based on this and other pertinent facts you have not been allowed to enter Canada."

Gurdit squats at ease while listening attentively, nodding and cocking his head sideways, and bringing the knuckles of his left hand under his chin for support.

"Sir, for all our sakes, I had sincerely hoped you would have made it to Port Alberni. Once there, no one would have challenged your right to land in Canada. Anyway, contrary to what some of our locals will have you believe, all is not lost. We need to take a closer look at the challenge on our hands and evaluate how to best deal with the issues before us."

Gurdit is diffident, and spreading his palms wide open he states. "Mr. Bird, we really had no way of obtaining this vital piece of information when we needed it most. Do you think there is another port we can head out for from here and still meet the requirements of the immigration regulations?"

"No, I am afraid not. It's too late for that. They pretty much have you locked out of everywhere else at this point. However, like I said, all is not lost yet. There are several venues still open to us for exploration. And explore each one we shall," sounding a great deal as he does on an average day in court. "But first of all, we need to prepare carefully for the challenge that lies directly ahead of us.

"You are all British subjects and have the legal right to travel freely to any part of the Empire, and we shall go to the highest court to challenge your right to do so. I will consult with my colleagues and the Shore Committee and inform you of our plan of action. I am absolutely convinced that the immigration department cannot legally keep you and the passengers of this ship here for long."

In this moment of silence his mind is already mapping the legal strategies that he needs to bring to the court battle. The first move will be to challenge the two Orders of the Council - Section 23 of the Immigration Act, and then quote the petition for habeas corpus that was recently upheld by the Supreme Court and accepted by Chief Justice Hunter, holding both the Orders in the Council beyond the application of the Immigration Act.

It is precisely his insistence on taking on this kind of moral challenges that has lead to personal threats so that his professional insurance has been jeopardized by his insistence on staying the course and being less circumspect in his selection of court cases. A man's chosen lifework must sustain him physically as well as spiritually, he muses to himself. We leave traces of ourselves in our toils, in our mental obsessions and our daily preoccupations. After all, he muses, at the end of the day you have to justify all your exertions to yourselves as well as to your God.

"Mr. Singh," he finally sighs, "we need to be watchful of the true intentions of our adversaries lest we find ourselves in a pickle from which we may not be able to extricate ourselves. Truth, as I am sure you are aware, can be a slippery slope. And, the truth of this matter is that you have come to our shores in all good faith. Sadly good faith does not hold much water these days."

He steps back, carefully letting go of the railing and waves as the tugboat begins to pull away to head for shore. Gurdit can only nod his quiet assent as the lone outline of the lawyer preoccupied in thought remains visible at the helm, a figure still staring intently back at him, the jacket and tie whipped by the wind and the tug disappears into the gathering gloom.

# THE NARRATIVES OF HOPKINSON

## VICTORIA DAY CELEBRATIONS
## MONDAY, MAY 25TH, 1914

With the Komagata Maru and its pleading and helpless passengers completely isolated in midstream, the attention of the Vancouverites has been easily diverted to celebrations of a more auspicious occasion. The daily *Sun* effusively reminds its readers:

'Yesterday, May 24 being Sunday, today will be the national holiday when all the subjects of the British Empire will remember the name and fame of Victoria the Good, under whose wise and fortunate rule, the empire rose to proportions of grandeur and power excelled by no other empire since the beginning of the world. So long as the fame of the British Empire remains, the name of Victoria the Good must be indissolubly connected to it.' It reminds them that 'upon her death when the question was raised 'should Victoria Day be made a permanent institution in the empire or should its significance be transferred to the birthday of Edward VII?' The King declared that the subjects of his throne would best declare their loyalty to him by signifying their gratitude to his mother. For over three generations the subjects of the British throne have been accustomed to look upon the 'May 24th' as the official opening of the games and recreations of the summer season. On that day all plans, which have been formulated during the tedious winter season, bear fruition in a hysterical desire for out-of-door sports. Today in Vancouver, the old customs, which have been established institutions for so long, will be well observed and countless parties will disport themselves upon the numerous playgrounds, national and artificial, which the coast possesses. Games of all descriptions will mark the passing of the day and no doubt those who participate in them will remember the gracious personality of the great queen to whom they are indebted for their holiday.'

In preparation for this special day, several public announcements have been made over the past fortnight. Above an inch-wide banner: 'God Save the King', a BC Electric streetcar service advertisement in the *Sun* lists 'Where To Go On Victoria Day Attractions'. There are to be extended services to transport the citizens to all the main events. A multitude of choices to suit every taste: Boxing contests at the Steveston

Arena, Minto Cup match of Lacrosse at New Westminster's Queen Park, Hunt Club races held on Lulu Island with special ferries direct to the race ground, two games of baseball at Athletic Park with Vancouver taking on Spokane; and picnic parties at the English Bay and Kitsilano. Lacrosse at New Westminster's Queens Park, Horse races at Richmond's Minoru Park, special train services for special occasions. For those seeking a less rough and tumble form of enlightened entertainment, there is the Orpheus Male Choir performance at Stanley Park bandstand arranged by the Park Board, 'The Versatiles' by the popular Pierrot Troupe will launch the new season with performances at 3 and 8 p.m. at the English Bay Beach. 'Free Moving Pictures' at the Arena Rink featuring the Photo Drama of Creation will also follow the same timings with no collection or admission charge. Topping the entertainment list is the one for Sells-Floto Circus street parade at 10:20 p.m.: Performances near Main and Prior Streets at 2 and 8 p.m.

By late afternoon, William C. Hopkinson's entire family is gathered in front of a series of large wall-sized posters. For Hopkinson, this occasion has come as a welcome relief from the malaise and anxieties of the last few days.

"Look, Connie, the other Indians!" Seven-year-old Jean Hopkinson points at a wall high poster under the watchful gaze of their parents. Hopkinson is proud to note her astute observation that these are 'the other Indians' and different from those that routinely visit their Kitsilano home.

"And, look, here is another stagecoach loaded with women and children," Jean squeals with obvious delight and for the benefit of her younger sister. "And here are cowboys firing at the Indians on horseback. Look, you can actually see the arrows and bullets flying through the air."

Seeking further approval from her parents Jean is unable to resist the temptation to show off her precocious reading abilities: 'BUFFALO BILL'S WILD WEST AND CONGRESS OF ROUGH RIDERS OF THE WORLD'.

"Hopi, what's a congress?" She turns to her father only to discover that he has drifted away. Jean's mother, Nellie Hopkinson, steps in to pat her daughter's shoulder in proud acknowledgement.

The children's attention is now drawn to another striking poster. This one has a bright blue foreground of a smoke-filled sky, beneath which a set of six carriage horses are in full flight, the frightened occupants of the carriage staring wide-eyed out of the windows while four other men riding on the roof set off their firearms. The plight of these desperate riders is further heightened by their pursuit by hordes of horseback riding Indians that stretches far into the fading horizon.

Further up the wall is another poster that shows Buffalo Bill dressed as an Indian scout and surrounded by the eight chiefs that are part of his entourage; each image of the chief is labelled with an evocative title lifted from the pages of current popular western literature: Brave Chief, Eagle Chief, Knife Chief, Young Chief, standing to Bill's right, while to his left stand American Horse, Rocky Bear, Flies Above, Long Wolf. Cody, alias Buffalo Bill, Nellie is surprised to note, is the only one of the group who is armed, his hands resting on a favourite front muzzle-loader. While the Indians are dressed in overflowing feathered headdresses and leather tunics, Cody poses in thigh length riding boots, army scout tassels, the outsized rim of his hat tipped rakishly over his lanky ponytail.

To Nellie's dismay, Hopkinson has wandered off again, distracted by the flash of camera flares that briefly light up a group of men. He is quick to spot that the person who is causing the most stir is no other than the legendary Buffalo Bill himself, his goateed, southern gentlemanly demeanour a shabby resemblance to that of the advertised *'most recognizable face in America'*. The staginess of his costume does nothing to disguise his face's increasing resemblance to the weatherworn hide of the creatures whose numbers he has so skilfully decimated to the brink of extinction. Hopkinson has seen the legend portrayed in several promotional films, perhaps best captured in the film of the Sioux fire dance. Beyond these artefacts has been the phenomenon of the American public's insatiable nostalgia for the tranquil life of the disappearing frontier.

Now, surrounded by a throng of pressmen armed with cameras and fawning circus-goers, Buffalo Bill Cody attempts to stand out against a background that is not too busy or too loud, preferably one that will not clash too much with the pastel shade of his velvet suit. He finally settles for the blank wall of a circus tent. A natural showman, he has been careful enough to always face the cameras directly, leaning theatrically on a hefty rifle that has not been fired for over three decades. The camera flashes are promptly loaded, set and fired, before the barrage of routine questions is unleashed.

And, after the usual inquiries of the special features in the current show, a thoughtful reporter pauses long enough to ask Cody for his views on the current state of affairs and the direction the world seems to be taking in its heady pursuit of modern times. But Cody is dismissive of the inquiry, brushing it aside with a wave of his hand. Another reporter, sensing Cody's reticence, and the interview deteriorating into maudlin sentiment, steers it towards familiar territory.

"Sir, will you be building an Indian camp within the arena?"

Lately, Cody has often been questioned a great deal on this subject. The onstage assembly of an actual Indian camp complete with wigwams has been a regular feature of every Buffalo Bill's Wild West Shows, but this showpiece that he has so painstakingly choreographed is now under threat from fickle audiences.

Fully aware that his words must now reflect not only his innermost beliefs, but also what the public has come to expect of him as one who has single-handedly represents the disappearing frontier, Cody clears his throat and takes a few deep breaths. He then removes his bifocals, carefully polishing and then returning them to his pocket. He has become vain enough in public not to put these on after having seen several printed images of himself where his eyes have been entirely washed out by the reflection. Would posterity remember him thus as a man whose gaze appeared to be averted and thus one who could not be trusted? He now peers myopically into the blurry mass of a distant stand of quivering aspen and watches it disappear under a cloud of dust kicked up by the parade. He pauses long enough for the roughness in his throat to settle.

At such times a grave sombreness begins to creep into his southern drawl, as if he were deliberating over each uttered word, aware that what he says here may well survive to be all that posterity shall remember him by.

"The building of an Indian camp within our arena," he begins, his southern drawl now heavy with solemnity, "takes about one full hour of show time. This short period is the actual time it takes to build an Indian camp in real life. However, I am noticing these days that our audiences are growing restless in this relatively brief stretch of time. It seems to me as if they have less and less time and patience for this type of verisimilitude. I suspect, folks, it has been the negative influence of other forms of entertainment. I do believe it is these moving pictures that can take a whole day's slice of our lives and pare it down to a few seconds for a viewer's focused attention."

By the end of this monologue he feels his gravelly voice beginning to sound rasping again, and he removes a white silk handkerchief from an inside pocket to dab at his forehead. He swallows rapidly so that his Adam's apple rubs against the hard edge of his spotless shirt, the pink tip of the tongue momentarily visible as he moistens his lips.

"Now, it seems to me that you folks apparently do not have the patience any more to sit through even a single hour of spectacle unless it is somehow speeded up for your convenience. An onscreen journey that in reality would take weeks to make can now be completed within the space of a few seconds. Whereas, as you folks have witnessed, in all my shows verisimilitude still rules. Just as in reality there can be no hurrying up the pace of life to suit our altered tastes, I will not condescend to compressing a real event into a convenient parcel of time so that you can be home in time for your Sunday steak. Gentlemen, sadly, after today's show we will no longer continue to present this majestic spectacle of nature and I have reluctantly had to forgo this event completely from our touring itinerary. The spectacle of the original Indians engaged in an authentic struggle for survival will now end up going the way of the prairie native himself; disappearing altogether from the face of this earth with the buffalo. I call upon you today to admire the Indian in all his glory, and all his peculiar survival skills in the face of certain exploitation. He will soon become nothing but a shadow on our walls, a mere flickering flame, much like his images projected on our theatre screens. Mark my words. Very soon the only residue left behind of the Indian will be his artefacts in museums and history books, and of course, shows like ours. So folks, take time to enjoy this majestic spectacle while it lasts. I assure you what we are presenting today in collaboration with the Sells-Floto Circus is going to be the greatest show you have ever witnessed."

However, most of Cody's comments appear repetitious and provide scant new material for the newsmen to print. One of them is now inspired to point towards the waterfront and ask, "And, what about the Indians in the water? Sir, as a champion of the Indian will you be saving them, too?"

This elicits a round of guffaws.

"Hah! Those are none of my concern. All my interests still lie here with the West…," and lest he seem outdated and irrelevant to the day's audiences, Cody quickly adds, "…the modern West."

By the time of this last remark, Hopkinson's family has rejoined him, eager for the rest of the day's entertainment.

At this moment an agitated reporter sends out a cry of alarm from one of the many kiosks lining the circus tents like barnacles. He has just finished talking to a fortune-teller named *Madam Shakira*, named after the heroine of the Indian adventure column serialized in the local daily *Sun*. And, what she has had to confide in him has alarmed him sufficiently to draw the attention of the rest of the reporters.

*Madam Shakira* now seizes the moment to announce theatrically, "In the course of my work I have peered into the palms of thousands of brash young men who have stumbled into my booth. And, I am deeply concerned for their welfare. I am beginning to notice that so many of them have their lifelines prematurely severed at the middle stage of their young lives. I wonder what we are heading into at this time? What new calamity awaits us?"

Unfortunately, amidst the daily posturings and grandstanding on the belligerent European political stage of the summer of 1914, her concerns and comments would not make it into the following day's papers.

*The men who built up this country, who hewed homes out of the forest, were men of first class, A1 stock, and the responsibility they left us is great. The sentiment expressed in the proud phrase, Civis Ramanus sum, becomes the citizen of Canada as well as it became the citizen of Rome. A race of men who cannot appreciate our mode of life, our mode of education, all that goes out to make up Canadian citizenship, are not fit immigrants of this country.'*

- R.G. MacPherson, Liberal Member of Parliament for Vancouver, at a public meeting convened in 1906 to protest Indian immigration.

*'I have no ill-feeling against people coming from Asia personally but I reaffirm that the national life of Canada will not permit any large degree of immigration from Asia . . .*
*I intend to stand up absolutely on all occasions on this one great principle - of a white country and a white British Columbia.'*

— British Columbian Member of Parliament, Harry H. Stevens, 1907.

*'What we face in British Columbia and in Canada today is this - whether or not the civilization which finds its highest exemplification in Anglo-Saxon British rule shall or shall not prevail in the Dominion of Canada ... I am absolutely convinced ... that we cannot allow indiscriminate immigration from the Orient and hope to build up a Nation in Canada on the foundations upon which we have commenced our national life ... I hold that no immigration can be successful where it is impossible to assimilate the immigrant'*

- British Columbian Member of Parliament, Harry H. Stevens, 1913.

*'The transfer of any people from a tropical climate to a northern one, which for months in winter is damp and cold, must of necessity result in much physical suffering and danger to health.'*

- W.D. Scott, federal superintendent of immigration in 1906.

*'It was clearly recognized in regard to emigration from India to Canada that the native of India is not a person suited to this country, that, accustomed as many of them are to the conditions of a tropical climate and possessing manners and customs so unlike those of our own people, their inability to readily adapt themselves to*

*surroundings entirely different could not do other than entail an amount of privation and suffering which render a discontinuance of such immigration most desirable in the interests of the Indians themselves.'*

-Federal Deputy Minister of Labour, later to become Prime Minister of Canada, in his 1908 report on the causes of the anti-Oriental riots of 1907.

*'Such land is good for the energetic man. It is also not so bad for the loafer... I have come six thousand miles to study the Hindoo problem. I have seen all Hindoos in many places and they are the same all over except that here they seem to be more timid and weak than is their wont.... the time is coming when you will have to choose between the desired reinforcements of your own stock and blood, and the undesired races to whom you are strangers, whose speech you do not understand, and from whose instincts and traditions you are separated by thousands of years.'*

Rudyard Kipling on British Columbia Vancouver, October 7, 1907.

*'Since the Komagata Maru started on her wanderings with her emigrants various religious rites have been a great feature of life aboard. Prayers have been said in great abundance and the blessing of the Sikh saints have been invoked daily. The Sikh guru and his holy men have run through the rituals of their religion, which is one of the fifty-seven varieties of Buddhism, every day. Buddha asks no sacrifice of living things in the practice of his faith, but expressly forbids it. But the Hindus aboard the ship are worshippers of Shiva and Vishnu who demand chickens. Yesterday the last of the sacrificial fowls on board were assassinated with appropriate ceremonies, and the proper amount of sanctification.'*

The Sun, June 6, 1914.

Records of several conversations held at the Vancouver Immigration Office during the period from May to June, 1914:

Present: HH Stevens, JRB Reid, WC Hopkinson
Location: JRB Reid's office

By the time Hopkinson finally arrives at his office building the meeting is already in full swing. Malcolm Reid, the port chief, and Hopkinson's direct supervisor, is already tracing circles around his desk, his shoes squeaking at every step across the hardwood floor, his cigar shedding fresh ash with every move.

"Oh, Lord, not another one of his rants," Hopkinson groans inwardly in observing the scene; the pent up resentments against his direct manager beginning to tumble like rough stones through his ragged mind. "And, now with Harry, 'The People's Dick' in their midst, these two will be at till nightfall like foghorns sounding off from opposite shores. No one will get out of here alive."

Acknowledging Hopkinson's presence with a nod in his direction, Reid fixes him with a steely look. "What are you snickering at, Hopkinson? I was just telling Harry here how some wild ideas are like embers that will not keep by themselves. They need constant tending. The fury of this fire is a contamination that needs constant refuelling. Believe me when I say this that there is no lack of succour from our southern friends, always meddling in our affairs and challenging our faith in monarchies with their own grand delusions of democratic institutions."

Reid marches on, spiralling closer to the desk with each delivered bout of anxiety, all the while nodding to himself. Hopkinson is already familiar with this brand of ideas and his mind is left free to wander about the room, safe in the knowledge that as long as he nods occasionally he will not be asked to respond. The Dominion's Chief Immigration Inspector extraordinaire, is fully in his element!

It was not long ago that in this very same office his chief had revealed to Hopkinson his deepest and personal aspirations of his perception of what his adoring public expected from this high office.

"Hopkinson," he had said while staring out the window, "the tyrant in his lifetime builds monuments commemorating his achievements, but for the truly egalitarians, their subjects express their adoration and gratitude by building their own commemorative statues. Perhaps, some of our enlightened Vancouverites will someday celebrate our role in this affair in a similar manner."

Ever the schoolteacher, Reid is now driving home his point, each such occasion an opportunity for him to shed the benefit of his personal ruminations.

"… this raggedy bunch of people are somehow united under a single presumption, misconstrued as it maybe, that they have equal rights to settle in any part of the Empire of their choosing."

He turns to face Harry. "Just try and imagine a sea of these fierce olive men gathered in one place, each one similarly bearded and turbaned, mind you, hundreds of thousands of them, each with the same surname – SinG!"

He lingers harshly over the final consonant, making Hopkinson wince inwardly.

"…all this single-minded and headstrong mass of humanity swarming together and banging their fists at our frontiers and shores, attempting, no, demanding, to be let in to share in the just reward that is the sweat of our brows.

"In reality, what they really want are the just rewards and the fruits of the toils of others. Now that the wilderness has been trampled and tamed into submission, and the forests cleared, the swamps drained, and the Lord's given fertile land made ready for tilling, they show up claiming that this bounty is as much theirs as ours. Imagine the nerve. Do you follow what I am saying? Do you see where I am going with this, Harry?"

He snorts, sniffing the air nervously before continuing in this vein, the subtle nudge totally lost on him.

"If you let in this scruffy lot, who is going to deny the next horde that hops aboard a tramp ship and is deposited at our shores for us to feed, clothe and house. Imagine this scene if you can, and you will begin to see the challenge of separating this fierce lot into identifiable individuals.

"You are never going to get peaches out of acorns," he finally concludes, abruptly posing in mid-step, and subduing his errant moustache into submission by twirling it between forefinger and thumb. Like most moralistic men who hold repugnant in others what they detest most within themselves, he is a pathological talker and he will not pause long enough to listen; quick to pronounce judgment on the slightest infraction of an imagined moral boundary.

In the heat of the moment Reid eases himself behind the desk, disingenuously stretching his shoes across the desk so that they are pointing at his audience.

Meanwhile, Hopkinson has had time to reflect that this cramped office that now serves as Reid's centre of operations is comparatively modest; the room floodlit like a stage by two north-facing windows overlooking the harbour, and the expanse of water stretching all the way to Stanley Park with the pale mountains forming the background. The large, green felt-covered oak desk has been placed here in the middle of the room to face the door instead of the distractions from the windows. A glass inkwell, a pair of fountain pens, an array of rubber stamps and a pad, a blotter, several ledgers, and a shiny metal cigar holder and lighter are all neatly arranged around the periphery, leaving the welcoming central workspace spotless for now.

The rough frayed edges of this desk give the impression that this was once a heavily used working area; actually, it has been commandeered from the immigration interviewing area for Arrivals. Its presence in this confined space still resonates with the power its former occupants once wielded in deciding the fate of an endless stream of hopeful immigrants, of passports being examined, of eager and anxious faces being discreetly and briefly appraised, the entire family circling the patriarch, as the officer flips through the passport pages. Here is one opinion that he shares with his supervisor: That the initial examination of potential immigrants should be carried out with the air of solemnity that announces 'No one will move past this desk until its current occupant has fully satisfied himself with your net worth and suitability for the privilege of entry into our Dominion'.

Behind the desk hangs the ubiquitous framed photo of the royal monarch, and one of the Dominion's prime ministers, and the red, blue and white of a union Jack fills the rest of the office wall. A smaller version of Canada's red ensign defaced with the arms of the four original provinces, stirs imperceptibly from the desk with every movement in the room.

Occupying a prominent place on the wall between the two windows is an ornately framed, translucent pigskin. In the elaborate swirl and flourish of Roman script it reads:

*'Any man can work when every stroke of his hands brings down the fruit from the tree, but to labour in season and out of season, under every discouragement requires a heroism that is transcendent'.*

Beneath this quotation, in fine italic etching is the legend:
*Henry Ward Beecher (1813 - 1887).*

The words of the US abolitionist and clergyman hold a personal resonance for the occupant of this room. Indeed, they have become a lifelong obsession with him, and he is often given to quoting verbatim and uncalled for terse snippets from Reverend Beecher's repository of human knowledge. These may take the form of admonishments, such as: 'Never forget what a man says to you when he is angry', or, 'You never know till you try to reach them how accessible men are; but you must approach each man by the right door'.

Cigar smoke now drifts through the light poring in through a partially open window, and layered over the trapped sweaty aroma of this sleepy interior lingers a faint hint of barbershop talc and shoe polish. Bill Reid is known by all to be as meticulous of dress as he is un-circumspect of manner. From his brass buttoned coat and dark official jacket, judiciously let out annually by a visiting tailor, Reid has always been fully cognizant of his place at the top of bureaucratic ticking represented by this maze of offices and warehouse sized waterfront buildings.

The three men now huddle around the desk in a semi circle, seemingly unaware of the claustrophobia in the muggy interior.

This is a historic moment, a fact that Mr. Reid has been quick to belabour more than once. Should the occasion arise to take notes or issue an official statement, a stenographer has also been summoned to wait in an adjacent office. The only woman in the offices at the time, she sits demurely sorting through the personal correspondence, intelligence reports and multiple clippings from recent papers. These are to be sorted by subject matter for Mr. Reid's personal records. Glancing briefly at the heap of the papers before her selects one sent out by a Shanghai exchange. It states that 'the Japanese steamer Komagata Maru has sailed for British Columbia from Shanghai on April 16, 1914, with a complement of between 500 and 600 Hindus aboard'.

Other far ranging messages also littering the desk are of a more frantic nature, these are exchanges between Ottawa, Vancouver, Hong Kong, and the India office. Even distant, remote and overbearing London has weighed in on the matter in response to alarmed appeals from those being accused. One such report penned in 1910 by Hopkinson is a record of a meeting between Teja Singh and a South African lawyer of Indian descent, Mohandas Gandhi. The surveillance report states: *'Gandhi is a prominent man in South Africa and is purported to be connected with some Hindu trouble in that country, and from what I can learn is at present in jail serving a sentence'.*

In addition to these confidential intelligence reports, there are letters from several grateful Vancouverites, each commending the immigration officer for his dedicated efforts on their behalf.

One from Dec. 3rd 1913, is signed by the Secretary Ward 7, Ratepayers Association, Mr. W. J. Pascoe: *'At a meeting held at our association rooms last night, a resolution was passed heartily endorsing the drastic steps taken by yourself in the ejection of unsuitable subjects from our shores, and they spoke particularly of the steps taken by yourself in the recent affair in Victoria by your ejection of the Hindu priest'.*

The letter ends with: *'Now, dear Sir, we hope you will be as fearless in the future as you have in the past and act as you have on your good judgment to exclude any and all such unworthy subjects from our shores'.*

Another letter from one H. H. Davies attempts to address the 'Hindoo Question' by stating:

*'I have for the past year watched with great admiration your untiring efforts to effect a proper regulation of the Oriental Immigration to British Columbia.*

*I have lived for eight years in southern India and I am one of your strongest backers in the determination that you are displaying to eliminate entirely the immigration of the Hindoo. He is an undesirable and one of the most dangerous weapons to have in our midst in connection with Empire matters and especially do I refer to the Indian Empire.*

*I sincerely hope you are successful in stopping immigration of the Hindoo into Canada'.*

And, there is even a copy of a correspondence from Mr. Reid to W. D. Scott, Superintendent of Immigration, Ottawa, Ontario, recommending that *'Messrs. Gwyther and Munnings as competent interpreters who are equally anxious for the appointment as 'Assistant Hindu Interpreters', given Mr. Hopkinson's extended periods of leave from office on business and increasing work load'.*

Meanwhile, in the adjacent office she can hear Mr. Reid's baritone echoing through the walls.

Hopkinson has been compelled to lean against a wall to contain both his weariness and impatience with the proceedings. Examining Reid closely once again during the course of this meeting he is struck once again by the man's handsome demeanour – his carriage and deportment strongly demonstrating Reid's oft stated belief that good grooming is always more important than mere good looks. To this end Reid always carries two tiny combs in his breast pocket: one for grooming his waxed moustache, and the other for his full head of hair. Hopkinson also knows that stored in one of the lower drawers of this desk is a tin that bears the label *Athlete Cigarettes Have No Rivals*. It contains a sable brush to maintain the sheen on Reid's calf-length leather boots. His left jacket pocket holds a jewelled snuffbox that rests adjacent to a cigarette case. His meticulously waxed walrus moustache that at first glance appears to be a plump bicycle handle is actually twirled outwards at both ends. It needs constant grooming by deft twirling upwards as it tends to droop by the end of the day, and, under certain light, as now, gives his broad moon face the garish look of a sneer.

Now, Harry is nodding in agreement with Reid, "Bill, I whole-heartedly concur," in recognizing that the thrust of Reid's arguments neatly dovetails into his own Lutheran moral conservatism.

But Reid is now a steamroller that cannot be stopped.

"Now that we know what their intentions are, the question is how do we get them out of here, and once they are out of our harbor, how do we ensure that they stay out? What next? Today it is a piece of our land they want, tomorrow it will be our jobs. These are harsh times, just look around you. We have honest, hard-working miners who have now been reduced to begging from house to house. If there were any jobs to be had wouldn't they have found them? I tell you, I have just had my fingers burnt earlier with that rowdy lot, and I am not about to repeat that experience."

Hopkinson wishes to intercede and recommend prudence, letting tempers cool down, but he already knows that neither Reid nor Harry will hear him out. He knows that the usual response to his suggestions will be: "Hopkinson, there you go off again confounding the issue with too many details. You know me well enough by now. I believe that if you keep the central issue in focus, everything else in the periphery will take care of itself. Keep it simple and don't confuse me with too many facts."

At this point Harry interjects, directing his remarks to Hopkinson:

"You have to remember, my boy, the basic urge that drives the basest of these men is the opportunity to seize what they have not earned through the sweat of their own brow."

He too waves his cigar expansively, strewing ash all over the green desktop felt.

"And now this scruffy lot is here to test our mettle all over again. Why don't they ever learn? I know well the likes of these men, having lived with them in China as well as India. I even have a theory on why they get that way. Such men have grown up scrounging for a better part of their lives, and would think nothing of stealing or cheating or lying to get their way. They will readily adopt the way of the jungle. I call them 'self-maximizers'. They would think nothing of stealing whatever they could lay their hands on, or lying and cheating their way into any place denied to them.

"That pettifogger hired by the Shore Committee to make their case has repeatedly proclaimed that the Hindus are all British citizens and they should thus be allowed into Canada. But, Section 95 of the BNA Act, especially Section 3 of the Immigration Act, gives Canada and not Britain, full control of immigration to our dominion, and this act could apply to any nationality, and classes of British subjects. We can allow or withhold entry to potential immigrants who are insane, diseased, crippled, criminal, or vagrant even if they are British. I wonder if our litigious Gurdit has been informed of this."

"Perhaps, he should be made aware of it," offers Reid. "Somehow we have to find ways to dampen this fire in their bellies with some other form of obsession. And damn Ottawa this time if they choose to intervene or challenge us. Perhaps, we could offer these men something more base, a less noble and endearing goal, such as the pursuit of food or drink."

Reid continues to pace back-and-forth restlessly in the tiny clearance between the desk and the door, deep in thought and yet excited at the manner in which the task ahead of him seems to be shaping up. His pupils are dilated to pin pricks.

Seeing how Hopkinson is fully distracted from their conversation with his attention wandering across the room, Harry turns to him once again to muster support.

"Hopkinson, I am sure you have actually had the opportunity to see first-hand how they choose to live in their swarming warrens, two dozen to a single room; whether it is Victoria or Vancouver's Chinatown, whether it is Peking, Shanghai or Hong Kong. And because they choose to live in this manner their needs are few. They buy none of our produce or services. They choose not to use our banks; instead carrying all their wages and savings on themselves, squirreled away in their headgear. And if they want none of what this great country has to offer them, then I say keep them out."

Reid, who has been angling for a break in this monologue, noticing Harry preoccupied with removing a handkerchief to polish his eyeglasses, hastily steps in.

"Perhaps, something as basic as food, or even water, can be made into the focus of their current preoccupation. All we have to do is delay the delivery of vital supplies to the ship without being seen to have deliberately taken a step in this direction. Keep a man hungry and thirsty for a few days, and he will eventually sell his own soul. Fortunately for us, they are over there, surrounded by nothing, but salt, water and air. Now that our patrol boats have ensured that no sustenance will reach them, what are they going to eat, seagulls?"

Harry once again: "Bill, I tell you, Ottawa has to be made to understand that there will be riots in Vancouver if this lot is permitted to land, and this time, it will not be restricted to Vancouver but all across the province. Our vigilante mobs have been known to take such affairs into their own hands, and begin massing at the city hall and the mayor's residence. They have been demanding for along time to be armed in order to settle this Hindu matter promptly rather than wait for bureaucracy to work its way through to misguided resolutions."

Both Harry and Reid have expressed their annoyance that the story of the city's struggle to extradite the unwelcome guests has not only made the front page of all the local papers, but the major ones in the dominion as well. Hordes of reporters have descended on Vancouver after having traveled from up and down the west coast, from Oregon, Washington, California, and one has even made it here from as far east as New York. And, there is general agreement in this room that all provincial immigration officials involved in the matter will be condemned by one and all as having been spineless in their response.

"These people!" Harry finally mutters under his breath, giving voice to their underlying frustrations, and shaking his head in consternation, his lips pursed tight.

"I can't believe them. I have said it a thousand times before and I will never tire of saying it again, Bill, you and I are like the bedrock upon which these importune and unceasing waves will crash and shatter. That old boy Kipling said it best during his last visit here. Wife and I went to hear him, and I still recall his words well: '*Were I an intending immigrant I would risk a great deal of discomfort to get on the land in British Columbia, and were I rich, with no attachments outside England, I would swiftly buy me a farm or a house in that country for the mere joy of it'*. Now, who would not be tempted by such an endorsement from such an illustrious voice?"

Hopkinson recalls that barely six years ago when he had first reported to this office for duty, Reid had formally introduced him to his gathered staff with the words: "Ladies and gentlemen, the cavalry has arrived."

Barely a year later, the dry formality of their perfunctory exchanges had given way to a series of guarded exchanges on his part and an unwelcome familiarity on Reid's part. And, in the ensuing weeks there was to occur another such opportunity in the presence of some visiting Ottawa bigwigs; Reid, perhaps unable to resist some inner resentment, had taken a few lethal verbal jibes at Hopkinson.

Seeing that he had gained everyone's undivided attention, he had introduced the newest member of his staff with the remarks: "Now, tell me, what was the name of this place where you began your training and career as a civil servant, this place called *'La .., La…'* something," he had stammered, feigning a momentary lapse of memory. This had prompted Hopkinson into stepping in ingenuously to snap at the bait:

*"Lahore!"* He had promptly offered; realizing too late what had just happened.

*"La-hore!"* Reid had repeated, a little louder this time for the benefit of the audience. "Now what kind of whore town is this? No better than *'Allah-bad'*, I suppose."

"… but wait, there is more," Reid had parroted, unable to resist offering another morsel. "And what is the name of this other place where some of these *HinDoos* are coming from, this place called *'Low Poke'* that you appear to be so obsessed with?"

*"Lo-Pokay,"* Hopkinson had promptly stepped in to correct his tormenter and a round of renewed guffaws.

The humiliation is renewed afresh as the room around him continues to grow narrower with each passing minute.

# HOPKINSON RECALLS LOPOKE

On such slack days as today, with Hopkinson isolated and immersed in some bureaucratic formality amidst the Immigration department's labyrinth of broad green felt desks and uncomfortable rigid chairs, the afternoons begin to stretch before him languid as a pliant rubber band. Though his body is pre-occupied with the monotonous task at hand that requires barely a fraction of his mind to be present, the certain slant of sunlight falling at just the right angle allows for his conscious thoughts to disassociate freely. He escapes readily into another world, a landscape far removed from Vancouver harbour, one that stretches several years into his past; unbidden genies have suddenly been dredged up from a nether land to be explored in the light of the present day. Increasingly, these scenes have surfaced at certain unguarded moments in his life, as raw and immediate as the initial experience.

Hopkinson is also aware of another corollary to this retreat - that there can be no further resolution of any of his unresolved personal dilemmas at this juncture.

One such afternoon had taken place almost seven years ago on his visit to an Indian village police station during the Punjabi post-monsoon season.

Hopkinson had once observed to the interrogation of a young Sikh captive in the Lahore jail. Captured during a night raid at one of the huts surrounding Lahore's myriad printing presses that made up the Urdu Bazaar, the culprit had been brought blindfolded into the police compound. A police informant had identified him as a prominent writer for the Ghadarites whose fiery poetry was beginning to inspire other men towards seditious activities. The young man had voluntarily given his name as Kartar or Sardar or something – another one of those Singhs whose surname is associated with the name of village of origin – and, for this unfortunate man it had been 'Lopoke'!

Having seen similar cases handled before him, Hopkinson had watched the familiar scenario unfold with the foreknowledge that the wretched man's fate had been all but sealed the moment he was singled out by the informant. Yet, the chief inspector, …Hopkinson is unable to recall the name at the moment no matter how much he now tries, his recollection of it blocked by some unresolved conflict with the man… Anyhow, given the severity of the alleged crime, this inspector had insisted that the suspect be brought before another witness to corroborate the initial identification. This second witness was under arrest for his own protection and now being held in the Lopoke jail.

"Men," the inspector had cautioned in stating the obvious, "it is not so much that we need to confirm this man's real identity, but to ensure that we do not leave the real culprit out there to inflict more damage."

What the chief had left out of the briefing was the fact that an arrest of this significance would eventually lead to a major promotion for anyone even remotely held accountable for it.

Though only wearing a thin waistcloth, blindfolded and handcuffed, Hopkinson noticed that the culprit's hair was thoroughly drenched, and he was shivering uncontrollably. Whether this was from the morning chill or anxiety, it was hard to say. Yet, within minutes of the search party's return to the police compound, the subedar had begun to administer what could euphemistically be termed as *the third degree*.

Before nightfall, the culprit was fitted with a pair of heavy leg-manacles and transferred to his hometown jail.

But that is not all Hopkinson can now recall of that place and time.

At the morning briefing he had learnt that this prisoner as well as the second witness had somehow managed to escape from the jail before first light. Hopkinson was now assigned a dozen men to head out to Lopoke, retrieve the other witness for further questioning, and somehow hunt down the escaped culprit and bring him back.

The trip from the Lahore station to Lopoke over a rutted and slippery road took over an hour, with the village turning out to be completely surrounded by flooded paddy fields readied for the transplanting of rice seedlings. Vapour rose from the stagnant water in blankets of mist that from a distant made the mirage-like horizon quiver in the breeze. The sweet stench of decaying vegetation pervaded everywhere.

The policemen began their search by noisily entering the village from opposite sides. As a matter of routine, the police began their search by thoroughly ransacking the entire village and questioning everyone they could lay their hands on. And, by the time they finished, the sun was rapidly approaching the midpoint - the day was headed for another scorcher. Hopkinson had decided by then to pay a visit to the local thanna to see if the policemen would be of any help.

Pulling up before the freshly whitewashed walls, it immediately struck Hopkinson as peculiar that the police post was set so far back from the main road. The austere cement rectangle with a wide front veranda appeared to be in an advanced state of collapse, a massive pipal tree looming over the front room in such a manner that it had already dismantled the outer wall of the compound. As heat arose in waves, Hopkinson couldn't help noticing the limp and motionless foliage of the pipal tree.

Somewhere within the compound a goat bleated pitiably. I could see a mongrel fast asleep on the steps with its muzzle resting on its front paws, presumably guarding the outer gate. It now suddenly awoke and began barking. A ragged flock of crows that had excitedly been teasing something in the bushes adjacent to the wall also arose noisily.

It was much cooler inside the main cement building, though it reeked of urine and decaying fruit. A pile of shrivelled mango peels and watermelon rinds were heaped in one corner of the front room where fruit flies droned in circular patterns.

As the visitors entered the building, the constables on duty had made no movement to greet them or fetch their officer in command. That there had been a good reason for this Hopkinson soon discovered once they had proceeded inside. A pot-bellied station officer was fast asleep at his cluttered desk, the racket of the barking dog and the noisy flock of crows having failed to rouse him. Two other constables also slouched on separate benches on either side of the desk, and they also seemed similarly unperturbed by the presence of the visitors in their midst.

Instead of alerting anyone else, Hopkinson had decided on immediately setting out to inspect the two adjacent lockups. These appeared to be unoccupied. Hopkinson noticed several pairs of leg irons and handcuffs hanging limply on one grimy lime-washed wall; there were stains of paan spittle, appearing oddly like clotted blood, dotting every corner of these rooms.

After satisfying himself of the desperate state of affairs, Hopkinson had approached the desk and slammed his palm hard against the flat surface close enough to the officer's head to cause the poor man to leap into the air with a start. Hopkinson had let him straighten his tunic with one hand while he ran the other hand through his oily matted locks.

"I am here to interrogate the two political prisoners you arrested last night under the sedition ordinance. Where are they? *Jaldi, jaldi*, take me to them." Hopkinson had demanded.

At this the stationmaster had risen unsteadily to his feet, eyeing Hopkinson's epaulets, and muttering: "Sar... sar, this way. I have him safe in the innermost lockups, saab."

"Him? What do you mean ...have him? I was informed there were two men you were to hold for positive identification..."

"Yes, sar but I had to let the other two go on the recommendations of our chowkidar."

"You did what? You set the two culprits free?" Hopkinson had been exasperated and yet reluctant to admit that he had been expecting

102

something of this sort to occur.

"I had to," the stationmaster had sputtered. "You see, they were both connected to the family of our sarpanch."

The lone inmate that Hopkinson was eventually shown sat forlornly clutching the bars of his cell for support to prop up his beaten body. His turban had come loose and hung partially over his face so that it was impossible to get a good look at his face. He, too, was sound asleep snoring loudly; his hair Hopkinson had noted was matted with blood.

Though the British had modelled the administration of the Indian police on the Royal Irish Constabulary and included the ancient 'village watch' in their administration of the local police forces, the role of the *chowkidar*, the local village watchman, often a member of the criminal class, at these police thannas had always been an ambiguous one. Nominated by the *lambardar*, the headman of the village, the *chowkidar's* duties would have included keeping watch at night, uncovering all the arrivals and departures, observing strangers and reporting all suspicious activities to the *lambardar* and the police stationmaster. More often than not, he would have informed the *lambardar* first and the police only at his own discretion. The assumption by the organizers of employing indigenous police, the *chowkidars*, usually a hereditary position, put in place before the Mughals and readily adopted by the British, had been that the man being a local, unlike the other police employees, was more likely to notice anything suspicious. Sometimes, he would be held accountable for any thefts, thus having to make up the loss from his own resources. However, with such an open conflict of loyalties, the *chowkidar* often became a liability for bringing the criminals to justice under the civil governments. If at any time the *lambardar* had wanted any prisoner freed he would definitely have used the *chowkidar* to do so.

Hopkinson had thus been sure that in this case a similar conflict of interest must have taken place. And, the men they had travelled so far to fetch had vacated the region.

For the next six months the district police were to continue to search in vain for Kartar Singh until an Amritsari informant offered up a tantalizing end to their speculation and search. It turned out that the informant Bela Singh, a man who towered over Hopkinson's lanky frame, had let it be known that he had reliable information that Kartar Singh had crossed the ocean and joined his other Ghadarite friends on the American west coast.

This piece of information fitted in neatly with a familiar emerging pattern that security forces across India had been observing, and Hopkinson had reluctantly accepted the fact that in spite of the official line, the Ghadarites were no longer just a handful of disgruntled farmers who had been led to believe that their lives would be dramatically altered by overthrowing the British in India. These men were now beginning to foment political unrest all the way across the eastern Pacific coast. In fact, recent intelligence reports were focusing more often on the subversive activities coalescing around the Ghadarites, thus indicating that a new rebellion was being plotted with immunity from across the Pacific. And, Kartar Singh Lopoke and his companions had to be party to such an insurgency. Having once slipped through the Indian security net they would now be harder to catch, and the arms of the British investigators were not long enough to pluck these men from across the water. Given his vast experience in Punjab and facility with Punjabi language, Hopkinson would eventually be appointed to Vancouver as a direct response to this threat. At the time it had seemed to Hopkinson that it was the illusive Kartar Singh who was leading him and the entire Indian security forces on a wild goose chase.

It was also arranged that once both of them had arrived separately in British Columbia the stalwart Bela Singh would also be stationed with Hopkinson. At earlier times, with the knowledge that the hub of all Indian sedition was based in the Vancouver temple, Indian security men had been sent to Canada disguised as temple priests called *garanthis*. However, with an irascible person like Bela it would have been a hopeless task – he would have blown their cover within a day of his landing. It was decided that Bela would go in the guise of a lumberyard hand and only then team up with Hopkinson once the two men were in Vancouver.

Yet it had continued to amaze Hopkinson that no one else had had the vision or will to see the pattern or the full scale of the political unrest developing on the Pacific coast. His warnings to this effect were to go unheeded for months, until the day the seditionists began taunting the British from afar with their malicious literature. Whether it was printed in Astoria, Stockton or Frisco or Victoria, their fiery words found their way back to the Indian soil. Border security forces would seize bales of it buried in grain shipments and paper rolls, or carried in with passenger luggage.

Hence, the employment of William C. Hopkinson, British Columbia's Head Immigration Inspector, and the deployment of his alias, Narain Singh, to scour the north American west coast.

As my Teddy Bear uncles got to know us better they took to bringing us fragile, intricate toys that had been patiently carved out of wood cords. First a sailboat, then a cloth doll sewn out of canvas and decorated with colourful buttons and seashells. Later, when they discovered my weakness for jaggery, I was assured a constant supply of slivers of it delivered to me wrapped in packets of silver foil or coloured kite paper. Of course, I had to be careful not to be discovered with it by Nellie. I knew she would never let me bring any of these gifts into the house, and after heaping endless scorn on our heads she would have made me toss them out into the garbage. Whenever I indulged in this guilty pleasure, I could already hear her nagging me: "The shame, the shame of it. Accepting presents from complete strangers! Where are your manners, girl? Honestly, you become more like you father each day."

I quickly learnt to hide the dewy, resinous chips amongst my collection of knick-knacks and keepsakes in a biscuit tin and would secretly nibble on them when alone at night. When she did catch me chewing on a piece of jaggery, she scolded me loudly enough to snap Hopi out of his daydreams: "Girl, how can you possibly put such a vile thing into your mouth. Have you any idea how many hands have touched it? Let me see you toss it away right now before you catch something nasty from it."

Later, there was to follow another such occasion when she thought I was gnashing my teeth again and I had to suffer the reprimand: "Will you stop that noise immediately, or you will end up grinding your teeth down to stubs like that O'Reilly's kid, and then not be able to chew anything for the rest of your life."

What I also remember from that time is a very special Christmas eve present when the Sikhs brought me a tiny rocking cradle for my favourite doll, the one with the ceramic head and eyes that closed when you laid her down.

Even though receiving these unexpected and exuberant presents from men who worked for Hopi, it was also a time of rampant joblessness in the region. Several coal miners had gone on strike, and these men now beginning to show up in the impromptu shanty towns that were rising up under the bridges or deep inside the forests.

Hopi would repeatedly remind us how lucky he was to have a job with a steady income, and would wonder how long his good fortune would last. Other employers were routinely cutting salaries everywhere in order to retain jobs. Mr. Spenser, who was our neighbour to the left, also owned a shoe factory that employed over a dozen men. He, too, would articulate the same fear every time he visited us. "To me this has all the makings of another depression. Mark my words, Bill, any day now the banks we will throw us all out of our homes."

At the same time, dusty, ragged strangers in threadbare clothes began showing up unannounced at our door. They would usually appear shouldering their entire belongings in gunnysacks on their backs, and have newspapers stuffed in their shoes for warmth. They would knock gently and then nervously look away in silence when the door was opened; very politely asking for a bowl of soup or a chunk of bread, muttering something about work for food, their eyes averted in the shame and indignity of starvation. During such times, each act of fresh unrest up north or in the interior would set off new waves of misery rapidly spreading through the web of food chains. And, the end result would always be the same with the most vulnerable the first to go under.

This reminded my uncle Wally of an incident he had recently witnessed somewhere at a farm in the interior of BC. After the harvest was safely in and the fields had been left fallow, a series of gleaners and clodhoppers descended onto the field to compete with the opportune wildfowl. They began by first sweeping the deserted field clean of any grain that had been carelessly spilled or overlooked by the last batch of searching fingers and watchful eyes. As Wally had watched a family of three working together in a small harvested field, they first scraped a fingernail thick slice of the topsoil. This filled up four guinea sacks.

Later on, he came upon them at the back of a shed. They were cautiously puffing away at the chaff and then sifting the soil through a loosely woven scarf. All their efforts resulted in three cupfuls of recovered grain.

Such were the times that Hopi grew sufficiently alarmed at the parade of these strangers showing up unannounced at our doorstep at all hours of day and night that he bought a collie and kept it tied all day at the front gate. Yet the traffic of itinerants continued unabated at our door even though our neighbours remained unvisited. This remained a mystery to us until we discovered that one grateful visitor, who had been provided with a warm meal on a particularly freezing day, had upon departing scrawled an 'x' on our fence gate. Others in similar predicament following his footsteps were also thus assured of the benefit of our perceived largesse and generosity. The next time we entertained or fed one of these transients, Nellie made sure afterwards that I immediately went out and erased any new markings that I could find on the side of our house facing the street.

It's not that we were poor or mean or anything like that, but Hopi did not know whether to trust these men. And, though there was never an incident where they harmed or threatened anyone in the neighbourhood, he had decided to be cautious.

The large collie we had acquired to serve as our protector slept all day and barked all night at imaginary raccoons, before it finally decided to call it quits and ran away as none of the adults seemed the least bit inclined to care for it.

"Never forget that this is a man's world, Jean," an anxious Nellie took to reminding Connie and me. "And they expect us to stay put in the kitchen and take care of them. Seeing the alarm on my face she had softened her tone.

"Its can't be easy for you to understand this now, but only enterprising women without husbands or fathers to support them have been able to openly enter the work force, or become domestics. And, look, what this approach has resulted in. We are bound to the hearth. Even the jobs left traditionally to women are now being taken over by men. Out there, the very instant a man wants a particular job held by a woman she is turned out on the street. I have even seen men applying for jobs as stenographers. And, in order to compete with the desperation of these men you will have to be ten times smarter than them as well as excel at everything you do."

Fortunately for us, in spite of the tough times, Hopi was able to hold onto his job and mum did not have to return and work for as long as Hopi was there for us.

And, then sadly, as fate would have it, after he was gone she would have to return to her old job as stenographer at the immigration department.

I think it was around this chaotic time that Wally moved in to live with us. But long before doing so, we had only known him simply as Uncle Wally, someone whom Hopi had befriended when he was still single and lodging in a rooming house in downtown Vancouver. All Nellie knew about him was that Wally had lived forever by himself in a rundown shack located in the woods at some distance from our Denman home. And, the details handed to us of his life there were as legendary and far-fetched as those of the hermit who lived in a tree stump in east Vancouver.

Wally was never known to wear socks, and seemingly impervious to the elements, wore a threadbare outer cotton jacket over a woolen shirt and undershirt, all winter and summer. As a result of this his forearms were as freckled as the patches of skull visible beneath his sparse reddish hair. I noticed that he also had a permanent grimace across his face, as if he was bracing from a stiff drink, or something in the air was disagreeing with him. I would later discover that this was due to his aching arthritic joints. Squat and slim-waisted, he walked with a practiced slouch, and a leftwards lurch which I knew was due to the fact he could not bend his right knee without considerable discomfort. What I also learnt later was that Wally had suffered a stroke in midlife that had left him paralyzed for several years. Even now, when there was a chill in the air, he would have bouts of partial loss of mobility in the weaker side of his body, and his tongue would begin to twist and flop about like a stranded fish, his words would emerge distorted and lisped out of one side of his mouth.

But for the better part of that time he was also remarkably proficient with his hands. He continued to build miniature and intricate birdhouses for us. I recall him telling Hopi that the openings to the birdhouses must always be less than a digit wide or the finches wouldn't feel safe enough to inhabit them. "By the end of spring you will have them all fully occupied," he predicted correctly.

As the rows of newer, cramped houses had gone up all around him he had clung even more tenaciously on to his collapsing hovel, unable to repair it himself and too poor to have it repaired by someone else. By then he had already begun to threaten us with every visit that he would not only immolate himself and the forsaken shack but also the surrounding properties if the logging in his vicinity was not stopped. I remember the heated exchanges of those rare visits to his place with Hopi, and how the interior of his single dank room was strewn everywhere with spud halves into which pieces of tallow had been clumsily stuffed. Where flaps of tarpaper had come loose they had been clumsily tacked over with faded newspapers.

There is one other thing that I do recall clearly from that time. During every visit I would receive a sand-dollar from him, and he even showed me a large jar full of these seashells that he kept under his bed.

The fact that something far greater was wrong with Wally than his obvious personal isolation dawned on me one night on overhearing my parents arguing loudly until they probably sensed that I was listening in to their heated exchange, their exchange took on a more muted tone. However, I was able to surmise that they were now unable to bear how forgetful and erratic Wally was getting in his old age, and that eventually he would have to move into our new house with us.

The basement that had till then served as our year-round coal and sawdust bin and cold storage in summer, was hastily cleared out, scrubbed clean, and fully repainted. Somehow, my parents then managed to persuade uncle Wally to move in to this room. And, even after he moved in with us and was bathing regularly, he never lost that peculiar smell of spuds gone bad. But, back then everyone else also smelled of sweat, lumbago ointments, smokes or something or the other.

The first time Wally visited us at the new house Hopi had proudly shown him the electric light bulbs in each room, which we had proudly left on during the first few weeks. Even the gas piping was proudly pointed out to him, knocked and commented upon and duly admired.

"No more topping up with water like the old gas meters," Hopi boasted. And though banished to the basement, I would find Wally up and about at odd hours shuffling about the rest of the house. I asked him once what he was searching for during these excursions.

"Where do I top up the water on these gas meters?" He had asked in genuine confusion.

During those days, by descending the fifteen steps to the basement I was always assured of being privy to Wally's remarkable inner life. Since he spent most of the winter afternoons in his room, I was able talk to him in a manner I would never dare to talk to either of my parents. And, much later on when he was ailing, I would be able to run errands for him or sit by his bedside and hold still his unsteady hands.

Also, around this time certain doubts regarding the Sunday church school teachings were beginning to stir up in me. I would often barge down the stairs to see Wally while proudly yelling the verses:

> *Onward, Christian soldiers, marching as to war,*
> *With the cross of Jesus going on before.*
> *Christ, the royal Master, leads against the foe;*
> *Forward into battle see His banners go!*

"So, I see you have been attending Sunday school," Wally had observed. For some reason, his comment reminded me of Mrs. Johnson, our Sunday school teacher, who, holding a finger across her mouth and whispering through pursed lips had once cautioned me: "Jean Constance Hopkinson, you will keep your eyes and ears open and your lips sealed. The good lord gave us two ears and one mouth so that we would hear twice as much as speak."

I knew Wally would have laughed heartily at this had I repeated it to him.

When I innocently questioned him as to why he never attended church like the rest of my relatives, he chuckled, and wheezed himself into a coughing fit. When he regained his breath he looked at me incredulously.

"Little Jean, do you mean to ask me why I do not show up at the church in my Sunday best with the rest of your family? I bet our Father Sullivan would also like to know the answer to that. Nineteen hundred and fourteen years of concentrated religious thought and the crap of the Sunday sermon is the best he can come up with? Child, for me the risk is not that a distracted God will not deign to answer my desperate pleas, but that when He finally does, I will be so overwhelmed by the act that I may not survive it. I can see from your expression that you are puzzled.

Don't worry; it will all make more sense to you when you are older. Next time you see the pastor chap insist on his pointing out to you where it is that God has been hiding in his church."

I couldn't wait for Sunday to come.

With Wally for company, I continued to revel amongst the skunk cabbage blooms and the creatures of the swamps, eagerly dragging home creepy, slimy things in jam and pickle jars and milk bottles. Uncharacteristically, these discoveries never seemed to faze my parents. The weirder I thought the specimens to be the greater enthusiasm they showed at my exploits, murmuring "Ooh! Look what our Jean has dragged home today?"

And, the disarray in our backyard continued to reflect our own domestic turmoil; all of Nellie's efforts to grow tomatoes in the backyard had been sabotaged by tenacious armies of slugs and mites and Wally refused to offer any solution for this.

By late summer a pair of migrant swallows began building a nest on half an inch of a horizontal metal ledge protected by the porch awning. Over a period of three weeks we watched the pair anchor a thimble sized base of clay and build the rest of their nest, the female preening itself endlessly as it slid into the clay teacup while the male perched close by. One day we awoke to the sound of uproar from our tenacious, uninvited tenants, to find three shiny porcelain eggs deposited in the middle of the palletized concavity. Constance loved to be held up to view them while Nellie worried daily about the mess the swallows were making on her entrance porch. Eventually, only two of the eggs hatched, with one of the babies falling off prematurely from the nest, and the remaining one actually making it into the sky. The nest was then vacated and Nellie was relieved to scrape the last traces of it from the wall and porch.

Wally had also built several bird feeders for us and we had placed them close to our kitchen window, until the day a hawk also discovered their bounty. It quickly learnt to swoop down when the feeders were busiest and panic the feeding birds, which would then crash into the glass panes and fall down stunned. The feeders were promptly stationed further from the windows.

Wally now adopted this hawk's strategy to terrorize my friends as they reached for the last of the remaining shrivelled blackberries on the thorn bushes near our home. He would shoo them away with: "Scram! The songbirds need them more than you do to survive the coming winter."

He also taught us to make bug-lights by trapping glow-worms in glass jars, with the promise that we would set them free within the hour.

During an idle muggy afternoon in the Denman house with the

rain restricting my activities indoors, Wally snoring in the basement, and Nellie in a scratchy mood from one of her frequent migraines - having locked herself in her room with Connie, I often indulged in my favourite indoor pastime. I would spend the entire afternoon exploring the numerous hallway cupboards and shelves, opening unpacked suitcases that were still strewn all over the three-story house and peering into out-of-reach closets. Each space was an unexplored continent to me.

On this particular day, I had stumbled upon a large sized hatbox that I had never seen before. As I gingerly lifted the cardboard lid my heart skipped a beat. Inside it were a beige length of rough cotton yarn, a curled thick bundle of coarse black hair, and beneath these a coil of soft, sky blue cotton that occupied the rest of the box. The cloth turned out to be several yards long. And, tied to one corner of it was a tin of oily mud. I was unable to decide whether this was boot polish or something else since the dented tin was unmarked. The artefacts made me sneeze.

All summer the dress and the accompanying accessories played into my imagination so that I could vividly conjure up a magical genie that had discarded its beard and the beige and blue dress inside the closet and then vanished from sight. I had to wait till the next Christmas dinner for this mystery to be finally resolved.

This particular Christmas, the last as it would turned out to be that the entire family would spend together, would also be the first time I would witness one of Wally's 'episodes' that had caused such alarm and discord amongst my parents.

This was the time when Hopi had just finished entertaining us with another Christmas ritual that was billed as 'The Hopkinson Indian Magic Rope Trick'. In addition to uncle Wally, we also had aunt Martha who had come to stay with us from California, and our neighbors living kitty corner from us, the Fergusons and their two boys. Incidentally, they always introduced themselves as the *Foigussons*, and to them dessert was *dezoit*, and turkey was *toiky*, while I was 'the *goil-nexdo*'.

During the previous night, I had watched Wally help Hopi unscrew three wooden panels off a bedroom closet and had seen them carried downstairs into the parlor. These had been placed on two large vertically placed steamer suitcases and then suitably covered over with mom's prized lace tablecloth. In addition to the dining table we could thus seat four more adults around this large makeshift table. The children ate at the tiny kitchen table. I remember that the Christmas dinner that year for the first time consisted of a large turkey with cranberry sauce, baked potatoes, and celery on side and the usual Yorkshire pudding. Later on there were to be treats of sweet Mandarin oranges, striped peppermints, and hard sweet and sour candy. However, Nellie always spoiled these feasts for me by insisting I finish my helping of – yuck - Brussels sprouts!

111

With the house full of guests, we were even allowed to stay up well past our bedtime to observe a rare display Hopi's playful side. With a bed sheet draped over the doorway to separate the parlour from the dimly lit kitchen, a makeshift stage had been assembled using a crate. I always had the honour of drawing the curtain to reveal Hopi seated cross-legged, and dressed as an Indian beggar, his garb complete with a beard, beige cotton tunic and sky blue turban wound tightly over his head. He was also holding a thin reed like pipe in his hands as if pretending to be playing the flute. The beard, I should note was the same one I had stumbled upon earlier. Though I knew that Hopi had spent some of his past life in India, any mention of it had long been banished from our household; no correspondence, exotic spices or mantelpiece ornaments from that region were ever allowed into the house. Yet, with the stage props and exotic dress in place, all we had to do was wait and watch, knowing that my father would now become an entirely different human being.

Humming loudly to himself, Hopi would twirl the end of the pipe in circular patterns, and miraculously a curled ribbon placed on the floor before him would begin to rise towards the ceiling as if it were being tugged upward by an invisible force. The first time auntie Martha saw this performance she nearly fainted while Wally sitting next to her cackled smugly through the entire performance. When about three or four yards of the ribbon had thus been suspended close to the ceiling, Hopi would suddenly stop playing, and would reach out with one hand and snap his fingers while mouthing the word 'chhoo mantar'. The ribbon would instantly collapse onto the floor. I was never able to figure out how Hopi, with or without Wally's assistance, was able to pull off the entire show. Whatever Nellie thought of these theatrics she kept to herself, I guess having seen the trick performed too many times. She would continue bustling about noisily, scraping and then washing the dishes behind Hopi as the performance went on, and then laying out the desserts, tea, coffee and the treats. Of course, as a family tradition, unlike the rest of my friends the opening of our presents would have to wait till New Year's Eve. And, I never let in on this with my Sikh uncles.

It was at the culmination of the final such performance that Uncle Wally arose stiffly from his seat and proceeded outside the backdoor into the garden. He then reappeared outside our kitchen window. My mother who had been watching out of the window for signs of snow, suddenly let out a stunned "Oh my God" that made us think that Hopi had also cast some spell on her, or that Hopi had finally managed to levitate himself as he often threatened to do. Her scream was followed by the sound of a china dish crashing to the floor.

As we all rushed to her aid, we could clearly see Wally standing

112

outside the windowpane in plain view of everyone inside. As we watched in rising shock, Wally proceeded to unbutton his pants and pushing then them down to his knees began to pee on top of Nellie's sleeping flowerbeds.

This Christmas dinner debacle was only to be the first in a series of similarly bizarre episodes that would lead to Wally's final unraveling during the following summer. I began to notice how in the middle of a certain task he would sometimes forget what he was doing or where he was at. And, though this was a source of endless amusement to all my school friends, it greatly vexed everyone close to him.

Later on, he took to bowing in prayer to the sight of the first crocuses peeking out of the snow; then it was the first of the returning spring swallows that drew his adulation; even the scruffy ravens on our backyard hemlock became cause for veneration. At other times Wally would be so choked for words by the sight of the first snowflakes that tears would roll down his face, and he would even end up prostrating himself, face down into the glistening mud. All the neighbors who witnessed this found it endlessly amusing, while my friends gleefully retold embellished versions of it at school.

There were several times when Hopi had to go and fetch Wally back from the edge of a stream that ran nearby our house. One time he found him kneeling in the water, cooing encouragement to the migrating salmon as they squirmed out of the sea and up the stream.

"Every creature, rich or poor alike," he once announced unexpectedly at the dinner table, "comes into this life condemned to a sentence of a lifetime of labor. And, no one gets out alive."

There were real tears welling up in his rheumy eyes when he said this. And, though I didn't understand his chain of thought at the time, Hopi had countered it with: "Wally, if you have been condemned to a life of labor like the rest of us, then where's the fruit of *your* labor? Ever since I have known you, all you have done is live the life of a vagabond."

Even I could sense that their good-natured ribbing that had once filled the house had now become fractious.

On sunny mornings when I was not attending school, Wally and I gravitated out to the backyard. When he was lifting me up into the swing one morning Wally surprised me with the remark: "You know, Jean, you are lucky to have parents who did not put you to work like mine did.

"Grandma came here from Liverpool with my dad and a widowed sister with her three children. When she landed in Montreal and heard all the French being spoken around her she thought she was in a foreign land, and wanted to get back on the ship and immediately head back to England. Luckily, the train depot was right next to the shipyard, and a week later she had reached Vancouver. My dad had grown up in England in a single parent home and went to school where you paid by working at the school. He had chores to do all day, scrubbing the cobblestones of the dining room and the school stairs. They lived in a depressed area of Lancashire where the cotton mills had shut down as a result of an American embargo. It was Grandma who had some inheritance and paid for all their tickets.

"When I was growing up in these parts, there were coyotes, bears, deer, skunks, raccoons, cougar, loons, and even some moose. And plenty of those pesky '*skitters*' and black flies that drove mad all manner of men and beast. '*Varmint*', they called them. There would be immense swarms of migrating fowl, vast clouds in a flurry of feathers that would darken the earth for miles for an entire day, the whir of their collective wings audible as a hum, and their droppings speckling the ground beneath them with curlicue pellets of white compacted chalk. And in the water there were spots where one need only dip a pail overboard and it would come up alive with darting fingerlings and smelts. In certain spots fish were so plentiful you couldn't help but touch them. Sadly, all that has disappeared within the space of a single generation."

In the silence that follows this interruption of the natural silence, a wood dove sounds it's fluted murmur from a stand of elms; lithe crickets leap a yard above the blades of grass and crash clumsily back. A million specialized multi-toothed mouths chomp, nibble, and gnaw at the frail green offerings of the morning; the moist earth heaves in the churning of slithering bodies as they blindly bludgeon their way through soil, sandstone and chalk. Their progress underground is marked by deposits of neat whorls of smooth dribbled mud. A red-breasted robin alights at the base of the hemlock, hopping on stick feet from one fallen leaf to another, teasing and scooping up offerings of unwary worms caught topside.

Dewdrops deposited before dawn are washed down the ribbed veins of broadleaves and redirected towards the stem and roots, and when left stationary and exposed to sunlight, shrivel and evaporate. A breeze rustles through the pines, its passage marked by the shedding of needles onto the matted ground still left unclaimed by crab grass.

Further south of the garden, where the coarse grass merges into the marshland of a seasonal stream trickling down to the waterfront, the patches of stagnant water are slick with washed down resin at this time of the year. It is here that the skunk cabbage sends forth its solitary brilliant blooms. Amidst this broadleaf forest raccoons stake out their claims to this patch of bog, their random progress unmarked from above except for a telltale quiver of a leaf stalk or bloom. Sounds of hissing accompany their furtive snarls and bared fangs, rivalries are swiftly resolved and the troupe scampers onwards on padded feet, the infants huddled in the middle, the nursing mothers bringing up the rear.

In a hollowed out tree trunk a lone coyote sleeps patiently awaiting dusk.

A solitary spotted woodpecker, its ratcheted crest at rest like a folded Japanese paper fan, begins to pick at the chimney stonework, oblivious of the smoke and heat, the racket of its hammering activity ringing down the chute and rattling the occupants.

How do I know all this? It was Wally who taught me where to look, and, more importantly, to pay attention to what I was hearing.

Beyond the attentive observation of nature, Wally had other lessons to impart to me in those final days:

Life continues to flash all around us like a surging river flowing uninterrupted and unaware of our presence.

A pair of swallows chooses the half inch rusted extension of a wall frame outside our main door to build their nest, raise a family and then migrate elsewhere. A neighbor's favorite cat disappears and returns nearly a fortnight later with a litter that she had hidden in between the walls of her owner's home. The poor lady has been tapping on the walls to locate where the mewling was loudest in order to locate the blind kittens.

And the slugs in our garden have ravenously nibbled on anything and everything they can lay their teeth on.

From the safety of a second story window, Hopi has been watching Wally and me sitting quietly together on the grass. Our silence puzzles him. Wally has a broad grin plastered on his face and I look at him from the corner of my eye and wish I could read every thought and every emotion that was fleeting through his mind at this very moment. If the antics of a ragtag band of ravens swarming into our backyard to examine yesterday's discarded scraps can give him so much pleasure, then I too want to possess such a sensibility. I wonder what he sees in the scene to keep him so keenly amused for so long.

As the ravens dart down from the rooftop awnings their coarse, matted feathers flash in rainbow hues. One of them settles on the grass and then cocks his head sideways as if scratching himself in deep thought, minutely examining objects with one eye before taking flight at the sound of distant barking. The band scatters momentarily, only to alight raggedly on separate branches of the hemlock, their beaks teasing morsels from the crannies and crevices, still skittish at the slightest flurry of activity. I suppose they like our backyard a lot as three of them have taken up permanent daytime residence on the hemlock, flying in at dawn, exploring the neighborhood all day and then flying out at dusk. In a way they remind me of a lot of our neighbors who commute daily to work, heading out each morning and then returning in the evening.

One summer evening, while we were out walking towards the shoreline, Wally had happened to glance up across the water at the downtown buildings, and a look of revulsion suddenly settled over him.

"Mark my words, Jean, by the time you are my age, concrete and tarmac will have undone all that the Creator so graciously once gifted to us. This gray rain of cement will come crashing down upon us and flood us entirely out of his green world. We are being buried in concrete tombs even as we speak, and yet, we willingly embrace it as the price for modern times. Look out for those giant beehive burners and chimneys that hover over every sawmill and factory spew smog, soot and ash in the name of progress. I can already taste this colorless, texture-less world heading towards us. And, thanks to the steam shovel, the roller, the pickaxe, and the thousand toothed saw, our natural bounty is being torn apart right before our eyes. We pour these poisons day and night into the bloodstream and lungs of our world, and in a single generation we have already unmade what nature took thousands of years to perfect. When you are older, my dear, you will understand what I mean by all this."

By then we had reached the edge of the water, the industry-lined shores of False Creek filling our entire horizon. I could sense that Wally's tirade was not fully spent.

"I remember a time when this entire region was a primal forest except where the local Indians were camped out. All this has got the way it is just so you and I can own papers, tables, chairs, houses and other comforts. Trees are very much like our lungs, with the difference being that they can take in our smog and breathe out pure air. But for how much longer can they continue to do this? Now, each morning I wake up coughing. Every metal fixture in the new house is already begun corroding. Even the mirror is clouded. We are like a blight upon this land, a rapidly spreading disease that has stained the hills, plains and valleys, and even the drained marshes. And, our appetites to feed our ravenous lot knows no bounds.

"I have watched thousands of fish dying annually at this spot where we stand. And yet, all that the municipality can do by way of remedy is to conjure up one hare-brained scheme after another.

"And, look! For all of last month every Vancouver beach was declared out of bounds to swimmers for fear of polio infection."

We had come up against a damp log that had freshly escaped from its boom, the dryer part of the log resting halfway out of the water. We settled down on this. Before us stretched a web of smokestacks, railway spurs, and tramway lines, each street dotted with telephone and telegraph poles. We could see elongated plumes of steam escaping from hundreds of towering and stained chimneys. Dogs barked in the distance, and a horse snorted somewhere close by. Further in the distance we could hear the staccato heartbeat of pile drivers and donkey pumps, and see harbor steamships elbowing tall sail ships to head for berth.

To our east lay the Kitsilano municipality of public servants, small businesses and tradesmen, its houses arrayed in a grid that stretched down all the way to the waterfront and its sprawling local Indian reserve. A railway depot connected diagonally to downtown by a trestle over the creek. Tucked close to the Indian Reserve, the railway yards and the waterfront was the communal center of all Hindu activity in our area, the Sikh temple. Clustered around this temple was a small community of South Indians, the Indian Mission, and the area collectively known as Hindutown. These days, with all the turmoil and general malaise heaped against its inhabitants, Hindutown was strictly out of bounds to neighbourhood children. I had heard it said that the men there lived in crowded boarding houses, sometimes hundred to a building, with most of them working in the nearby lumber mills along the False Creek waterfront.

I asked Wally if Hopi had chosen to live in this area so that he could be closer to his work with the Sikhs, but he was still lost too in deep thought to respond immediately.

"Jean, try to think of these men as similar to all the introduced creatures that you see around you here in Canada."

"What introduced creatures?" I wondered aloud.

"Well, name me a few animals that you think have always existed here in British Columbia. I have seen a few foxes around here. So, let's say fox for one."

"That's easy. There are the deer in Stanley Park and around our house, and grey squirrels running up the park trees and benches, and then there are swans in the ponds, and rabbits, horses, dogs, cats everywhere..." I offered eagerly.

"Well, aren't you an observant girl. Yet, I am sorry to disappoint you, but none of these are local creatures. They have all tumbled out of your English storybooks, or, like the wild turkeys, were brought here for sport or by homesick immigrants. It seems to me that if there was one mandate that we all seemed to have brought with us, it must have been to make every place that we stumbled upon 'a fair England'.

"Now, if you were to ask me my absolute favourite of these introduced species, it would have to be the ringed pheasant. You have to see it in full flight on a sunny afternoon to appreciate its full glory. But, you should also know that like all these good creatures, we, too, were introduced here from other lands. And, in our case that happens to be Europe.

"And, in their case," he pointed back at the Sikh Temple and

Mission, "…from India. Now, if like these transplanted rabbits, horses, dogs and cats we can all call this place our home so far from the original homelands, why can't they?"

After these words he fell silent for some time as we watched the waves rock our tree trunk gently, testing our precarious hold.

And with that conversation our time together came to a final end.


By fall, Wally had drowned while trying to swim with the spawning salmon that he loved so much. Perhaps, in his own way, he too, was trying to complete his circle of return.

And, it was to be Hopi who would discover the body.

And, after the body was discovered, with the police suspecting foul play due to the mysterious circumstances of discovery, there were all manner of speculation as to what had actually happened to Wally in his last hours.

I tried to be useful in solving the mystery by offering an explanation of what probably transpired.

"I think I know what he was doing when he drowned," I tried explaining afterwards to Hopi. Obviously Hopi was alarmed to hear this coming from me.

"Doing what?"

"Swimming! He was trying to swim with the salmon. He had often said he wished he could go back home with them," I offered, as yet unwilling to reveal too much of Wally's deeper obsessions and inner demons or further details of our time together.

"Did you actually see him swimming with these salmon?" Hopi asked.

"Yes."

"Why didn't you warn me about this? I may have been able to help the crazy coot."

I kept silent. I never liked it when Hopi described him in this manner.

"How often did he do this? Did he encourage you to do the same?" Hopi wanted to know.

"Never."

"Jean?"

"Never!"

On that idle rainy afternoon when Jean stumbled upon a neatly starched muslin turban, a stage-prop beard, and a pair of worn leather sandals, she did not yet know that these accoutrements actually belonged to her father.

Whenever the state of Hopkinson's inquiries call for such desperate measures he will disappear from the house for days, living secretly in a south Vancouver waterfront shack as an itinerant Hindu labourer named Narain Singh. Unlike Hopkinson's dour and cagey public persona, Narain is a different beast: a sinewy, swarthy, opaque creature unafraid of the light. Gregarious and voluble, he seeks out the new arrivals and the disgruntled, playing on their gullibility, offering sympathy, shelter and solutions to their every dilemma.

As Narain, Hopkinson's language now undergoes a transformation, Hindustani sloughing off his tongue almost as a natural element even when colloquial Punjabi continues to elude him. He has long since realized that in his desire to anglicize his Punjabi, which he pronounces 'Poon-jabi' instead of 'Punj-aabi', that Punjabi's illusive consonants will evade him until he overcomes his innate aversion of polluting his colloquial English.

For those slippery Indian proverbs that his illusive prey uses to confound Narain and his army of translators, he must consult with a secret weapon, his sole possession from a lifetime in India. It is a quaintly titled yet painstakingly researched booklet:

*A Dictionary of Hindustani Proverbs, Including many Marwari, Panjabi, Maggah, Bhojpuri and Tirhutti Proverbs, Saying, emblems, aphorisms, maxims and similes. By the late S.W. Fallon, Ph. D., Halle. Edited and Revised by Capt. R. C. Temple, Bengal Staff Corps, Assisted by Lala Faqir Chand, 1st Urdu Assistant Translator to the government of Bengal. Printed at the Medical Hall Press, Benares,*
*May be had for cash only. 1886.*

This book of lovingly compiled expressions opens with the helpful words: *'There has been a great, but unavoidable delay, in finally producing this work. It is hoped, however, that it will be found to have been carefully compiled to this end.'*

Purchased for a princely sum of ten rupees it has been worth every *paisa*. There was time once inside the Sikh temple, when the worshippers discovered that Narain was amongst them in the congregation, the priestly Balwant Singh had thrown him off by using the expression: *our enemies will become like a 'puran gudi'.*

Once back at the shack it takes Narain barely a minute to discover the true meaning of the phrase: *helter skelter!*

The shack is actually a flimsy clapboard lean-to affair located in a shady part of town on the northern banks of the Fraser River. And from its state of disrepair, it is obvious that it can only be used during milder weather. It is ever in danger of toppling over or collapsing under the next rainstorm or the odd snowfall. If a vagabond were to break into it he would find nothing of value to take away.

Having diligently eliminated all traces of his past life in India from his social life, once he is safely ensconced in this spare shack, Hopkinson's dramatic transformation with the simple costume change into Narain now allows him to relive a vicarious life. The process of sloughing off one skin and slipping into another, once again sets him free to indulge in his fondness for turmeric, fried onions and roasted garlic - personal preferences he assiduously keeps in check when in polite company. Now he openly cavorts in the company of his otherwise aloof and reticent informants, his personal vulnerability momentarily suspended. He is now a creature with an ear out on every street and back-alley, becoming privy to idle gossip. Whether it is mill workers leaning idly against a shaded factory wall during a break to puff on their crushed cigarettes, or the modulated dialogue of farm workers scrutinizing their neatly tilled furrows and ditches for weeds, each becomes grist for his reports.

Conversely, the transformation of their leader also alters the behaviors of his web of cohorts. Emboldened by his presence in their midst, they now carry with them the aura of official formality, of a power that lies beyond their mundane selves. This occurs in response to their own residual past lives in India where even the most powerful and influential learns to respect officialdom and its attendant bureaucracy, its insidious reach and influence digging deep into the petty details of their daily lives. The terse day-to-day exchange of shared information will now be carefully examined and reviewed for the reliability of its sources. In the cocoon of this easy camaraderie the burly Bela will out-drink everyone else under the table, and where Baboo will openly boast of his conquests amongst the native Indian women along the downtown waterfront.

Hopkinson has often been left wondering who had actually coined the term 'three-headed beast' to describe his inner web of cohorts?

He now muses: It should actually be the 'four-headed beast' - Bela Singh Jain, Baboo Singh, Ganga Ram, and finally William Charles Hopkinson - after all they have become as much a part of him, as he is of them. Each has become a lord in his little den. And, he wonders, why is it that he still keeps sorting them out not only by their height, bulk and age, but also by their degrees of introversion and accessibility.

And, let us not overlook the value of their support team, the underlings and hirelings who actually get their hands dirty. He pauses to see if he can register each one for the record: There is Bela's right hand man, the ever-subservient Herman Singh; the others are Arjan Singh, Bhagat Singh Haripura, Serva Singh Numane, and finally, last but not least, outspoken Naina Singh Kadhola. What a handful bunch they are, each tugging in a different direction, with Hopkinson pulling the reins tight to keep them focused on the narrow path ahead.

But, it has always been the towering presence of Bela that easily prevails over them all, having quickly learnt from Hopkinson how to selectively reward each with his compliment of attention. Once portrayed in the local press as a 'Hindu Adonis', he is jovial in company, and when sullen, he will tug at his upper lip, twirling his sparse whiskers absent-mindedly, his eyes dense, vacant and opaque as ink. Never far from the bottle these days, Hopkinson has noted, he shows up for work still flushed and tipsy from last night's hangover. Taller and heavy-set, as an opportunist he has a chameleon's ability to blend into any crowd and situation.

However, not all is well with this man whom Hopkinson has openly declared in Punjabi hyperbole to be his 'right arm'. He also possesses a very fickle temperament, almost primal in his self-righteous urge to settle every imagined insult, yet seemingly able to bully or goad others to greater risks. "Who will find us out in this our great king's domain, who will challenge us, huh? No one!" he proclaims haughtily and frequently.

Reporting directly to Bela is Baboo Singh, a peaceful beast amongst these savages. Immaculate, from starched turban to tightly knotted tie, creased trousers, beard netting and all; he has been ragged at every opportunity for having once carried an ivory handled walking stick before joining the service. Slight of build, he brings a subdued sanity and finesse that the beast lacks when left to its devices; his opinions are often over shadowed when on a feeding frenzy, his counterpoints and voice of reason buried in the banter and bluff. But when he prevails they all heed his warnings. "Listen to me," he cautions in moments of crisis, "let us not be so hasty in our decision-making; what can we do now that we will all wish tomorrow we had done yesterday; sleep on it now and the conflict will resolve itself."

The shorter one of the three, the chimney on fire, endlessly rolling his bidis and then sucking on the rolled tobacco leaf glued to his lip, withdrawn during every free moment of his life, is the cagey Ganga

Ram. He has this deceptive, self-deprecating grin buried somewhere in his full beard and whiskers at all times. Routinely nonchalant, he is non-confrontational, and handles conflict the way he does strangers – obliquely, avoiding eye contact and blinking rapidly with nervousness. Even this early in the morning when reporting for duty his shirt collar is already rumpled, wisps of hair escaping onto his forehead from the blue sagging turban. His rumpled cotton shirt, the coat and trouser are perennially uncreased, and by the end of the day his state of dishevelment will have run its full course. And, in addition to his preference for hand rolled smokes and chewing tobacco, he also carries a snuffbox.

Yet, each one of these beasts has made a personal mark for himself by working as a translator of official documents and has been privy to personal details which would have been unavailable by any other means. For a small fee their clientele relies on them to facilitate the oiling of the solemn grinding of bureaucracy; their skill is in making unstuck what has become stuck. Each has sworn loyalty to the British crown, and has become a misfit in his own society, and unwelcome in others. Hopkinson's network has embraced them all into its folds; and though theirs is not so secret a society they still wield an immense influence that stretches well beyond their assigned roles and boundaries. Everything Hopkinson has learnt in his CID training at Lahore and Calcutta has gone into channelling their individual strengths, and focusing their propensity for attention to the incidental detail.

Hopkinson is also aware that operating under their guise of official translators, they have also been siphoning unsolicited tolls and bribes for their illicit operations; and have easy access to forged documents, contraband, and privileged information that can later be exchanged for further payments or bribes. He also knows that without him these men can easily become good-for-nothing louts who show up unannounced at his backdoor at all hours of the day and night with what they presume are urgent messages, always outwardly respectful, mind you, sar this sar that, and demanding to know where Hopkins sahib was and when would he please be back home. It is as if *he* was ever at their beck and call.

And, Hopkinson's little ones ever so eager to please and so readily adopting these three men as their long-lost uncles, and blabbing to them about the most trivial matters of their lives, even going so far as to recite nursery rhymes to their gathered applause. With the others of the gang unable to be equally expressive or unable to overcome their natural formality and shyness, the sly, rascal Bela, boldly exploring the limits of familiarity at every opportunity, holding the tiny hands of Hopkinson's daughters or lifting them onto the swing beneath the hemlock. Watch out for these louts, Hopkinson keeps reminding himself; this multi-headed beast is a double-edged sword that cuts both ways.

But Narain is also cautious by nature, having learnt from that one time in Frisco when he had been momentarily inattentive during an assignment. During an evening of celebratory drinking he had let down his guard, and had been identified and then resiliently followed through the dark steeply inclined streets. The impact of the shots fired at him that night had swiftly carried the news of his presumed death over the borders and into Vancouver, where, he had later been informed, there were premature celebrations and sighs of relief among the Indian community chafing under his unrelenting scrutiny.

Among the several intelligence reports prepared for today Narain's review is one by Baboo. He must read it before Reid's arrival at the shack in the evening.

It reads:

On Powell St. about 3 o'clock on the 8th July 1914, conversation took place between H. Rahim, Sohan Lal & Mohamed Akbar.

| | |
|---|---|
| M. Akbar. | What you think about Mr. Reid & Hopkinson? |
| Sohan Lal. | Both of these persons are great robbers. All our hopes and works we intend to do are ruined. |
| Rahim. | It is a shame for us, there are so many Hindoos here. If two or three will die for them it will not be a bad thing to do. |
| M. Akbar. | We ought to talk this matter over in the committee, and I will get someone ready for this work; but that man is too greedy. |
| Rahim. | Then we can pay him two or three thousand dollars by the collections. You can get that man ready. |
| M. Akbar. | Very well, I will try for this. |
| Sohan Lal. | I think I will try to get one man ready. We ought to tell about this in Committee. |
| Rahim. | Be careful, don't let anyone hear about it. |
| M. Akbar. | I think we ought to speak to Bhag Singh first privately, and then discuss in committee. |
| Rahim. | What you think about this, Sohan Lal? |
| Sohan Lal. | As you say. |
| Rahim. | We will see Monday, and also arrange for price on Monday. |
| Sohan Lal. | Don't you think Mammed Akbar Shah will do this work? |
| Rahim. | No, he can't, but we will get some whiteman from Socialist Party. I will see and let you know if I can get some. |

M. Akbar.         Well, I am going. See you Monday.
                  Bande Matram.

What is Narain expected to do with such trivia? Idle gossip? Idle boasts by bored, or worse, drunken men aware that they were being overheard? Everyone knows by now that Baboo works for Hopkinson. Why should they be so careless as to reveal their covert plans so openly unless it was a trap? At such times Narain knows that almost every trivial exchange will be leant gravity merely by the act of it being recorded on paper.

Even now when some of the men of the Indian community openly scoff at him: "Who is this *nautanki-walla*, this stage actor really fooling by dressing up in that ridiculous costume?" Narain is able to continue to go about undetected in screening all newcomers. He attends temple meetings, shuffling out under a shawl before *langar* is served, attending religious festivals and meetings by blending into the throngs. He now reminds himself that it is not as if he is the only one in this south Asian community to be living under an assumed nickname. "Did not Bhagwan Singh, the *granthi* of the Sikh temple at Hong Kong, also go by an adopted alias of convenience: a Natha Singh? And, what of Hussein Rahim? Don't tell me this musalman is not known by any other name?"

Narain now comforts himself by repeating the mantra that has become his life's mission:

"We are like termites gnawing at your tenuous foothold on this continent. Our interlinked arms coil surreptitiously into your every one of your social establishments. We hear the tickle of every gossip exchanging hands, and not once has anyone stood up to openly identify us or confront us.

"I am a chameleon in my ability to blend into this background while the treacherous whirlpools of incriminating gossip and speculation agitates around me like so many dust motes churning in a sunlit beam.

"I weave unseen, a shadow passing through your lives, I become one of you at a whim. I wind my turban meticulously like you over my head, rolling my beard into the hair net, slipping the *kirpan* into its sheath and sliding the *kurha* onto my wrist; I worship with you, and eat at the *langar* with you, I eavesdrop on your every conversation. I'm invisible and invincible as a scrumptious rumour. There is an inevitability to my schemes, each straight as a launched arrow. As a planted thought I move through your collective minds, a residue of memory, as slippery and close to you as your shadow, always invisible even though I am right beneath your noses. I have enmeshed myself into your fatalistic rituals of fealty, faith, and allegiance, and the muddled accounts of the history of the ten saints.

"After the black eye of the Mutiny in 1857, the wary and paranoid Indian government can barely look at an Indian and not flinch, and only I am able to tell them apart; whom they can trust and whom they should incarcerate."

There are certain sleepless nights on which Hopi will toss this way and that, unable to find a comfortable position, mumbling to himself in a feverish delirium, the travails of his day not allowing him to sleep until early dawn. His mind will now dredge up residues of the day's verbal exchanges.

"We are troubled. We are laying our head on the pillow but we do not sleep," someone had remarked during the day.

Another had noted: "Their heart is in one place and their tongues in another."

"Who had it been?" Hopkinson now wonders.

"Was it that devious Randhir, ever ingratiating himself with *Maharaj, prabhu ki kirpa hai* - suddenly willing to cooperate and pay any amount to stay his expulsion from Canada?

"Or was it one of the members of 'the beast'? Perhaps, Babu? But Babu is too circumspect and polished for his own good, and would never utter such a thing. Was it Bela, then? Why would Bela say such a thing? When was the last time he had heard of Bela troubled by a profound thought?

"What had this person meant by "we are laying our head but we are not sleeping? What was keeping him awake? "

Everywhere Hopkinson looks he finds clues left by his assassin.

It is just before daybreak. As if waiting for him in repose, out of the murky world of this insomnia there now emerges before him a face he cannot yet clearly distinguish. It appears as if being viewed underwater. Yet, peering directly at this face he can find nothing distinctive about it in order to anchor it to any recollection from the labyrinths of memory. And yet this splintered montage of features is vaguely familiar, perhaps only because it has surfaced from a recurring nightmare. This face could well be that of an assassin, a composite of several illusive and shifty characters that has been his lot to pursue through his working days. A part of his mind is aware that in the grip of this nightmare he can only repeat certain acts that he has already performed in real life, and that there will be no unexpected outcomes or further resolutions to his dilemmas. However, the thought continues to linger below the threshold of his consciousness that if the face before him is an amalgamation of all that is familiar then his presence here in this space, too, is a sole construct of his own mind.

Yet the voice in his ears insists:

*I am here. Waiting.*

Who are you? For whom are you waiting? asks Hopkinson.

*I am your twin, comes the reply.*

I have no twin, announces Hopkinson.

*We are twins. No matter how you deny it today we were bonded at birth, coming into this world only so that we could destroy each other.*

Why won't you show yourself to me? Let me identify you once and for all and get this over with.

*You don't need to look far to find me. I am the sinuous liquid of the shadow pouring behind you down every path you descend.*

*If you want me, seek me in your shadow.*

*I am the wolf at your door waiting with bated breath, pawing at the doorsill of this locked door that is your soul.*

*We are here only to set each other free of our life's mission.*

And, what mission is that?

*The only way this can end for either one of us, is in the fire, there is no other way…*

*If you value all you have wrought in this life then run.*

Run?

*Run! But run where and to whom will you run to?*

Why should I run?

*Run anywhere. Just don't let me find you out.*

I will not let you pull me down. I will not let you undo the webs I have woven so assiduously. Such care and precision has gone into them, for so long have I toiled at it, and all at such an exorbitant personal price.

*Run!*

But run where?

*From me there is no safe haven, no assurance other than the one I give that I shall find you. Even in the darkest hell I will seek you out.*

But I have so much yet to do, so many webs as yet unwoven and awaiting my undivided attention.

*The wolf at your door can wait no more.*

*Even when he waits with bated breath, his paws are rasping on the doorsill, his tongue slithering past the bared fangs. The wolf at your door has a warm, feathery breath, his eyes seeing through your pulsating heart, knocking and resounding loudly in your ribcage. He pricks his ears at the sound of blood coursing in your vein; his razor claws shear your doormat.*

*Your days are like brittle bones his sharp teeth have picked bare, at nights he snaps at your heels and barely misses, he is here in the synchronized, diurnal pulse, asleep and awake, in motion and at rest, he draws nourishment from your fears and gnaws patiently on the chicken bone you have offer up to him.*

*Have you not felt the rasp of its bark-like texture against your teeth and under your tongue; felt it alive in the air you breathed.*

*I am like the hawk you once watched panicking feeding birds.*

*All your life we have both turned in unison at every point of flux, graceful as a dancer's repose, leaning gracefully into the curves, spending the light of your allotted suns in countering the weighted stone suspended in the birdcage of your ribs; in counter-balance it is a bird lifting off and alighting, yet unable to free itself from the tether of your gravity.*

*Can you not hear the bellows of your laboring lungs, the block hammer of your heart, or feel the fever on your brain? Can you not hear my angry thoughts coursing through these rusted wires?*

I will not let you stop me or destroy what I have built.

*And I will not let you go any further. You and I were braided together at birth, and now only death can untangle us.*

I never had any true friends, but then tell me, just who does? And me, neither my father's pasty white, nor my mother's wheat-brown. Orphaned, disowned and distrusted by both sides. And just look at me now, an orphan with no mentor to guide me or protect me, no family connections to speak of, no birthright, no claims to nobility, nor the distinct advantage of an Eton, Ludgrove, Sandhurst or Wetherby education, and yet here I am now with the world grovelling at my feet and licking my boots, hanging on every word I utter. Daily I decide the fate of hundreds, no, hundreds of thousands, of these unwashed beige men, women and children teeming at this gateway with their dewy dreams of a new paradise. On a whim I can make or destroy any one of them.

*Self-pity does not become you, Hopkins. But my decision is not based on a whim. My intent has forever been premeditated.*

And you tell me that I cannot do as I please; that I cannot continue to do what I do so well. There are countless others who depend upon my services. The fate of three majestic and towering nations hangs in balance on the surveillance reports and inside scoops, not to mention juicy gossip that I provide them...

*... And now there are countless others like me who need me to do the necessary. Our will cannot be dismissed so easily.*

*And should I fail, there are lakhs of us still willing to follow in my footsteps. They will hunt you down? But why then should I fail. I have the blessings of the Gurus. Too long have you toyed with the lives of our people and denied us a better life; too long have you been divisive and have split us apart, this rift in the Khalsa must be healed, and we as a people made whole again. The peace of our gurdwaras is at stake here. I will see to it that this shall come to pass through my hands. May the Guru accept my sacrifice.*

*We both came out of the same region of Punjab; we are both 34 years of age.*

*We have lived barely fifty miles apart, peering over the banks of the same sluggish muddy River Ravi and wondering simultaneously about the future awaiting us across its waters.*

*Which of your mothers will you then beseech when I come looking for you. Which British mother of convenience will you conjure up for comfort at that moment, Hopkins Saab?*

*Tell me, tell me, tell me!*

*Jaldi, jaldi, jaldi. Isn't that how you conduct your interrogations?*

Why is there curry spilled everywhere?

Why have all the clocks in the house come to a stop?

What kind of a is it movement that I see outside the house?

Is that someone peering into the windows?

I see horse's hoof slicing through the air.

I see Kartar Singh loose again somewhere out there seeking my jugular.

Everywhere I look I see signs…

An insomniac Hopkinson pads about the house during all hours, sleep walking or awake at odd hours, winding and rewinding clocks in the house, opening and closing closet doors and cabinet drawers. He re-examines his costume meticulously for ticks, repeatedly airing out the indigo-dyed turban the colour of sky. He fidgets with locks and latches on doors and windows, adjusting curtains when dark to prevent any light from escaping and informing anyone watching on the outside of the activities of the inhabitants. There have been a number of attacks recently on Indians living in his neighborhood. In one incident a bomb was tossed into a house through a glass window. And, neighborhood children had already been discouraged from wandering into the Hindutown. Could it happen here so close to the Indian Mission, in this house, if the men outside knew he or his family were still inside?

In the grip of one nightmare Hopkinson finds himself in an unoccupied room, the only feature of which is a spiral staircase rising all the way up to the ceiling from the middle of the floor. The door clangs shut behind him as if swept in a draft. He notices several clocks with unmoving hands lining the opposite wall. He is able to register the individual ticking of each clock. He recognizes one of these clocks as that from his living room. It has no hands even though the pendulum continues to swing.

Through the only window in the room he can see a crisscrossed path of black and white ceramic tiles stretching far off in to the distance, the monotony of the horizon broken only by a river that crosses his path of sight. He notices that the chessboard pattern of tiles continues on the opposite side of the river.

It is only when he turns his gaze back into the room that he realizes that beneath his feet stretches a carpet of weed-choked grass. And, in the diffused light what he has taken to be his shadow is actually a wall mirror. Across this mirror is an image of him.

*Run*, the image mouths the word silently.

In this recurring nightmare there will be nothing distinctive feature to define one particular face from another.

Who are you?

*I shall be present forever in your shadow…*

A hand is gently shaking his shoulder.

"Hopi, Hopi, you are muttering your sleep again. Who is this twin you keep speaking to. You have no twin." Nellie rolls over and returns to sleep.

"My turban," Hopkinson's disjointed voice murmurs, "I have to wash the turban… it reeks of curry."

"Yes, I know. I meant to ask you about that. I soaked it overnight after rinsing it twice and yet … honestly, what is it that you really do out there all alone at the shack? Why is there curry spilled over everything?"

"Remind me in the morning to wind up the living room clock."

"All right, all right. Now get back to sleep, you have a busy day ahead of you. The court proceedings wait for no one."

"Direct to me, me, me, me, me, only me, the instructions have flown from London, and from Ottawa, and from Washington, and even royal Delhi, and see how promptly my coveted badge has arrived in a formal and reluctant recognition of my vital role in the preservation of the Dominion."

*We are both arrows launched from the same bow, our destinies inextricably locked. How long will it be before we collide? My brothers are as numerous as the waves that wash upon your shores, massing somewhere offshore, challenging rip tides, circumventing obstacles, heading for this shore.*

"I revel in the fact that the fates of four mighty governments depend upon what I choose to reveal to them, my allegiance tested by each, distrusting my ulterior motives when they are not aligned with theirs. My own web of informers keeps me in the eye of the hurricane, fingering out those who are even now merely mumbling their resentments, or have past lives to hide.

"The young Canadian Dominion is innocent to the simmering threat residing within its borders, washing up on its western shores from overseas and from the south, from Portland, Sacramento, San Francisco, and as far as South America. The agents of change are already chipping away at its borders like termites chewing at the foundation of this edifice with every bite.

"You are still mumbling," Nellie's voice swims out of the fog.

"Where will they escape from me, Nellie? I have always

remembered their faces, even a beard and turban cannot hide the finer details of the angled slant of the jaw in reference to the arc of the lips; the proportions of the brow to the space between the eyes, no two have ever been the same. Show me a face just once and I am able to recall it years later, and its variance from the norm. And this one I know and have seen before, though age and life has distorted it now. Was it in a Lahore jail a decade ago when I was still a novice at my job?

"Was it the face of the man in a dark Frisco street?

"I know this man from somewhere."

The moisture trapped inside the Hopkinson house condenses on the windowpanes, fades the mirrors, bleaches out the colour from fabrics, peels paint off the walls and ceilings, and stains the kitchen sink. Spores proliferate in the presence of this moisture and the absence of light, and wherever the spores land they breed further stains.

Nellie, moving a moistened rag in circular motions over these stains further smears the grimy pane of the uneven glass before her, redistributing the spores she has observed flourishing in her kitchen. And, as the pane becomes clearer under her ministrations and more light enters the room, she is able to see the outside world emerge into view.

Having moved here with her large family so far and so long ago from London's Highgate, Nellie constantly dreams of settling in a sunnier, dryer place. A place that is far and deep into the south, farther away from foggy London, and even further away from all the moisture surrounding her here in Vancouver.

This evening she greets Hopkinson at the door with the stained grey rag in hand. She holds it close to his face, and demands:

"Do you see this? Do you now see what I am confronted with every single day of my life here? Hopi, for once get your head out of the fog. Look at this," she waves the rag once again as evidence. "No matter how much I scrub and clean Heaven only knows from where this keeps coming back to taunt me."

"Hopi," she has frequently chided him, "Hopi, you have already seen all that this place has to offer. Let's pack up and leave while we can. The girls are still young. They will grow up in a cosmopolitan city, attend better schools and meet a better class of companions. With the conditions in Vancouver being what they are, everyone else we know is moving out and heading south. Come on, you remember how cosy it was over there last winter."

And Hopkinson absent-mindedly nods consent, already recoiling at what is sure to follow next.

"… and then we shall finally be far from this ceaseless rain. You know what they say about the rain here. 'If you can see the mountains it is about to rain, if you cannot see them then it is already raining'. Tell me, who would want to live in such a place?"

Hopkinson can see that the constant downpour, characteristic of the northwest coast, has finally overwhelmed his Nell's serenity and resolve.

"This unrelenting sluice has already claimed a hundred and ninety days so far this year alone. And, I really don't see how your insistence on staying here is of benefit to anyone?" she continues to berate him.

"Come on, Nell. You know well enough that all my contacts are located right here. What am I going to do in California?"

"Probably make much more money than the pittance Reid has to offer you, and be a whole lot safer."

"It maybe so," he counters, half teasing and half attentive to the massive cloud cover gathering overhead. "Or, maybe, I should become an umbrella salesman. I bet that would be an improvement over surveillance. Ever question why we don't see any of them around here?" he wonders aloud.

"Perhaps, everyone who really needs an umbrella already has more than four," comes the rejoinder.

"Maybe I could open an umbrella store. I could then call it 'Hopi's Brollies'? Better than calling it 'Nellie's Brollies', huh?" he waits for her response, and seeing Nellie's set expression rumbles on. "There has to be a huge demand for brollies in a town like this, where, my fair Nell has duly noted it pours every second day. Maybe, I should set up my shop closer to an entry point into the city. At the central station, for instance. Or, if somehow I could rent a space near my office at the immigration building, I could hop over there in between stints at my regular work."

But his attempt at humour is wasted on Nellie, who impatiently taps her fingers on the sink. She knows him well enough. There can be no talking to Hopi when he is carrying on this way, and the only way to end such a monologue is to join him in it.

"And, maybe, you could try selling those new Parasolettes for automobiles. They come in all the staple colours and fold neatly into their wooden frame cases. I see more and more motorcars equipped with these passing by our windows. Every open car will surely need one of our Parasolettes."

"Our Parasolettes?" "Yes, Ours. For once try to keep up with me. Honestly, Hopi I have no idea where you are at half the time."

"All right, all right then. This is all very well, but how easily you forget what happened to me the last time I headed down to California." Hopkinson is referring again to the street shooting; the mention of this near fatal incident is where this argument has always ended in the past. Down south on official business, someone had followed Hopkinson and sent a bullet grazing his head. A week later, with his head now wrapped in a bandage, Hopkinson had re-appeared in Vancouver and to put a damper on the premature celebrations in Hindutown.

# THE NARRATIVES OF BASHIR

# MEWA'S ARREST AT SUMAS

## WEEKLY REPORT OF THE DIRECTOR OF CRIMINAL INTELLIGENCE
### July 1914.

"Several attempts have been made in Victoria, Vancouver, and a few adjacent towns, to purchase wholesale supplies of small arms and ammunition, with the object of furnishing them in those on board the Komagata Maru so that they should be in a position to offer armed resistance to the Immigration officials and the officers of the law. About three weeks ago, two Hindu residents of Victoria, B.C., named respectively Harnam Singh and Hookum Singh, made an attempt to purchase 25 automatic revolvers and ammunition in that city. The hardware people refused to sell the arms and ammunition, where-upon Harnam Singh stated to the salesman that they could easily procure their wants at Port Angeles, Washington, where a countryman, named Taraknath Das, had made arrangements to assist them in their purchases. On the 17th July Harnam Singh took with him three other Hindus, named Bhag Singh, Balwant Singh and Mewa Singh, and proceeded by electric train to Huntingdon, B.C., where they were interviewed  by the United States Immigration Inspector in charge, Mr. Jenkins, and stated that they had come to meet some friends in Sumas and wished to have an hour or two in their company. Unfortunately Mr. Jenkins was not aware of the fact that Bhag Singh, Balwant Singh and Harnam Singh had been debarred from entering the United States and granted their request. Some hours afterwards the Provincial Police in Abbotsford, a short distance from the United States territory, arrested the Hindu named Mewa Singh. On searching him we found in his possession two automatic revolvers and 500 rounds of ammunition, which he said he had purchased in Sumas. This clue led to the discovery that Bhag Singh, Balwant Singh and Harnam Singh were still in Sumas, and our Immigration Officer at Huntingdon was instructed to refuse them entry into Canada on their return. Inspector Jenkins, to whom the information was communicated, soon traced these three men and found that they had been in conference with Taraknath Das. It was also found that besides Taraknath Das, there were three other Hindus from the United States who were implicated,

137

one of these being Bhagwan Singh. On Inspector Jenkins talking these three men were taken into custody, it was discovered that they were each armed with automatic revolvers and ammunition.

"Balwant Singh was a member of the recent deputation from the Sikhs in Canada to His Excellency the Viceroy. Bhag Singh and Harnam Singh are well known to us as leaders of the seditious movement in British Columbia. Bhagwan Singh, who was deported from Canada for preaching sedition and Taraknath Das, Har Dayal's lieutenant, are too well known to need description.

"There is reason to believe that the attempts to smuggle arms on board were not altogether unsuccessful, as it is reported that during the fight with the police in Vancouver harbor two or three shots were fired from the ship."

The police interrogation room is deliberately sparse. It is equipped with a sturdy functional table, and two chairs that have been placed in the middle of the floor. A single feeble gaslight floods the tabletop. Even feebler than the gas fixture is the natural light that pours down from a rectangular opening placed high on the wall opposite the door. The table is strewn with a number of official looking documents, registers, notebooks, and court records that appear to have been left open randomly.

On one of the straight-backed chairs sits a thickset Sikh whose burly presence contrasts sharply with the interrogator's slim build. Hopkinson, having scanned the culprit's personal records thoroughly for any incriminating material, has latched onto one pertinent piece of information: the man, Mewa Singh, age 34 years, the same age as him, is originally from Lopoke in Amritsar, India.

In order to intimidate and to impress upon the culprit the hopelessness of his predicament, Hopkinson has had to rely on an old trick. He knows his unlettered victim will be easily impressed by any material manifestation of official bureaucracy, and the books and registers randomly gathered from a hallway bookshelf for court records have been hastily heaped onto the table for this purpose only.

Seeing the unresponsive man seated opposite him staring balefully back, Hopkinson pauses in mid-sentence, as he has seen court examiners do, and pretends to consult a certain page here, a record there, noisily rifling and shuffling through the records.

In the awkward silence of these first moments of their encounter, he stares at the face before him. He takes note that it is partially hidden behind the rim of the turban and the outlines of the folded beard. Hopkinson suddenly realizes that though both of them are apparently of the same age, the other has aged so very differently. The familiar lean and gaunt face that stares back at him in the mirror each morning has always been free of wrinkles or blotches, and other than the occasional outbreak of sun-related damage, he has seemed fairly youthful, almost boyish even in midlife. The face now confronting him has been etched by exposure to the sun and the wind, and its podgy folds scoured by fine lines. He notices that the pair of pupil-less eyes exploring him are as hostile as they are unsure, and that the man's breathing is uneasy and laboured.

"Mewa Singh, on 17th July, 1914, you were arrested by the provincial police in Abbottsford with 500 rounds of ammunition and two automatic revolvers purchased in the United States. You were returning from a trip to Sumas, Washington, accompanied by Bhag Singh, the president of the Vancouver Temple Society, and Balwant Singh, the *granthi* and scripture reader in the temple. We know that while in the USA, you bought several revolvers and boxes of shells in a hardware store. Is that correct so far?"

What Hopkinson and the immigration branch want to achieve from this staged interrogation of Mewa Singh is to obtain a statement that will implicate his companions in criminal or seditious activity, and perhaps then enrol Mewa as an informer.

Hopkinson consults an open page of one of the books scattered on the table. "According to Orders of the Council (Section 23 of the Immigration Act) Immigration Department dismissed their petition for habeas corpus. The intending immigrants appealed to the Supreme Court. Chief Justice Hunter accepted their contention and held both the Orders in the Council ultra vires of the Immigration Act, under which they were claimed to have been passed…."

He scans Mewa's face for signs that he has understood any of what has just been read out to him. There is as yet no sign of compromise and Hopkinson's glance only encounters a confused but hostile response. He decides to switch from English to Punjabi.

*"Tukk*, Mewa, if you make a statement now then we can let you off with a lesser charge. If you accept that these men were with you when you came across the border, then we can all work something out that will help you save face with your friends, and give us what we need. Otherwise, we can just as well leave you to rot here in jail."

Noting that there is still no response, Hopkinson launches into animated Hindi, gaining further confidence as the consonants roll off his tongue at just right tone, with the listener finally awakening from his dazed state.

*"Dekho*, Mewa, personally I would rather keep you locked up in here for your own safety. And, if you do not cooperate you could easily receive twenty years in jail. Your friends in the community are never

139

going to believe that you didn't sell them out. But, I also know perfectly well that you can be of greater help to your community out there rather than in here. We know that your compatriot, one Taraknath Das, helped you procure these weapons to smuggle them on to the Komagata Maru. However, once on the outside you can help the Canadian government in weeding out the ruffians who are disrupting your peaceful lives here in Vancouver, and not just in Canada but also throughout the entire American continent."

There is still no response from the impassive face before him, and Hopkinson awkwardly decides to switch back to his stilted Punjabi.

"*Tukk*, I want you to help us. Make a note of anything that seems to be out of place, or anything that doesn't sound right. And, you report directly to me. Not Bela, nor Baboo, but me. And I will see to it that you are handsomely rewarded. See our friend Bela? You may know him only as the person who brought Bhagwan Singh to your temple. But, see how he has managed to aid us in arresting so many of these thugs. And, like him, we are willing to offer you our full protection. And also reward you in the process! I have heard good things about you and I can persuade the judge that there were extenuating circumstances in your case."

Here Hopkinson pointedly consults another page from a book strewn across the table, before lifting his eyes and spreading his palms wide open.

"…And I could also put in a few good words that you have been of tremendous assistance to the police and the immigration departments. You have provided us with valuable information, and I am sure you will be allowed to go Scot-free. And no one in your community needs to know of what has transpired between you and me here. We can even make it seem that we did not have enough evidence against you."

Seeing the look of disdain beginning to spread across the other's wary face he watches the mouth pucker up beneath the whiskers and beard, and then begin to relax, the burning coals of his eyes lighting up briefly and then fading.

Hopkinson pretends to consult his notes once again.

"…And though you have been caught smuggling weapons, and ammunitions to pass onto other trouble-makers in British Columbia… we can see to it that there is no record of this messy business at Sumas ever actually having occurred, and that there is no evidence of you ever having been to Sumas or the U.S.A."

Finally, there is a softening of the cold stare that has held him contemptuously from the moment he began this inquest.

"Can you understand what I am offering you?" Hopkinson inquires, unable to contain his frustration. The sudden change in the tone of his voice momentarily jars Mewa from his apathy, and he looks up before stuttering into speech.

"I, … if I sign I walk out of jail?" Mewa asks incredulously.

"Yes," comes the reply. "Yes, my friend, you sign you walk out of here. And all charges against you will be dropped. You cooperate with us and you walk out of here a free man."

A summon is now hastily sent out for Gwyther to translate as Mewa reluctantly dictates his affidavit, confessing to all that the immigration and police have asked of him.

Hopkinson has expected more but is willing for now to let Mewa go; sure that other evidence would be forthcoming later. He has seen this occur time and time again: you spring someone from prison under whatever pretence and then sit back and reap the rewards.

The document that Mewa Singh will finally sign will make its way to the office of Malcolm R. J. Reid, Dominion Immigration Agent, who will submit it in court to stay the hearing into the Mewa case.

FRJR/FEN.

Immigration Branch
Department of the Interior
Canada
Vancouver, B. C. 8th., August, 1914

Sir,

With reference to the case of the Hindus detained at Sumas, Bhag Singh, Balwant Singh, and Hernam Singh is still under detention.

Yesterday the trial of Mewa Singh came up, for carrying concealed weapons. He was fined $50.00, or in default 60 days – Mr. W. H. D. Ladner prosecuting on behalf of the Customs – the Immigration staff being represented on behalf of the Customs – the immigration staff being represented by Inspector Hopkinson, stenographer, myself, and Bela Singh. At our request, an adjournment was granted for one week, until Thursday next, as Mewa Singh had intimated he would be willing to tell the correct story, which we thought may probably involve some of the local agitators among the Hindus. The story as given is not entirely satisfactory. He explains that he may give us still further information.

Encl.    I attach hereto, for your information, a copy of the statement referred to.

Your obedient servant,
Malcolm R. J. Reid
Dominion Immigration Agent.
W. D. Scott. Esq.
Superintendant of Immigration
Ottawa
Encl.                    ….This copy for the information:-
H. H. Stevens, ESQRE., M. P.
Vancouver, B. C.

Statement of Mewa Singh, son of Nund Singh, Village of Lopoke, District Amritsar, India.

On the 16th July, 1914, at about 10 a.m., they were present at a meeting of the basement of the Sikh Temple, Bhag Singh, Balwant Singh, and Rahim.

Bhag Singh and Balwant Singh met me at the Hindu store on Granville Street at about 12:45 p.m. I asked them where they were going to and Balwant Singh replied, to Abbottsford. I then said I would go with them. The three of them caught the 1PM Eburne car

142

at 4<sup>th</sup> Avenue, for New Westminster where we each purchased a ticket on the BC Electric for Abbottsford. We stopped in Abbottsford for a little while and then caught the next car to Huntingdon. On arrival at Huntingdon the three of us went to the Canadian immigration office where Balwant Singh told the immigration officer that we wanted to go to Sumas to meet somebody to arrange about a lot in Seattle. The Canadian officer told us we could go, and an officer of the Unites States who was there at the time took us to his office where Balwant Singh told the Inspector in Charge that we would like to meet Taraknath Das in Sumas and talk to him about some property, and he gave us permission for three or four hours to do so. We then went to the Swail Hotel where we found Taraknath Das waiting. A conversation took place regarding the transfer of certain properties and then we adjourned to a restaurant to have our meal. This was about 7 p.m., after which we retired to the hotel and slept there for the night. The following morning we had our breakfast and we all went into the town. Bhag Singh went back to the hotel and Balwant Singh, Das and myself walked around the town. The three of us then went into a hardware store where Balwant Singh purchased and paid for four revolvers. He also received a packet of ammunition for each. All the conversation took place in English and Das was the spokesman. Then we went to another hardware store where Das conversed with the salesman in the English language. I could not understand what was said. At this store I bought a pocketknife.

When the revolvers were bought I took one, and Das took the other three back to the hotel where we went with him. At the hotel the revolvers were put down and I told them I was returning to Canadian territory and picked up one of revolvers, and Balwant Singh told me to also take the ammunition and they would join me later. At this time Harnam Singh joined us at the hotel. I took my revolver and hid the same in my crotch, and also took three boxes of ammunition and put one box in the sock of my right foot and one in the left foot, and one in the inner vest pocket and left for Canadian territory. On arriving in Canada, I was arrested by the police and these things were found on me. I do not know what happened to the rest of the revolvers. As far as I am aware and from what I could understand it was the intention of those people to try and convey these to the Komagata Maru. I am very much afraid of any of this information being given out as I am likely to lose my life. At the store where we purchased the revolvers we first saw them exhibited in the window. Taraknath Das suggested going inside and we went, and Balwant Singh then asked the man in the store if he would sell the revolvers. The salesman said there was no objection and handed out a revolver to each of the three of us. I purchased one for $5.00. I made the money over to Balwant Singh and he paid the same over together with the amount for the other three revolvers. I have never been in the full confidence of these dealers and it was just by accident that I happened to come along with them to Sumas. There was another man with Taraknath Das who came with him from Seattle. I do not know the name of the man. When I left to come back they were all seated together. When I purchased my pocketknife I came out of the store and left Balwant Singh and Das there. I do not know what transpired. My expenses for my defense and a fine inflicted on me are being paid by the Sikh Temple committee.

Relieved to be stepping out of the police confines so easily, there is so much Mewa Singh Lopoke wants to tell the Immigration officer, even though he may not be able to articulate his thoughts so coherently.

I, Mewa Singh, Punjabi resident of Vancouver, gurduwara volunteer, part-time mill hand, farm worker, have witnessed every frustration of the passengers of the Komagata. I have been a part of the desperation of our Shore Committee's efforts in trying to rescue them. And, sadly, I have also witnessed doubt, strife and bloodshed in our holy temple.

Walk into any public place and you will hear someone declare 'I don't want to sit next to a fucking Hindoo'. Popular restaurants, bars and nightclub all have a separate section for the non-whites. Here, even film houses have a special segregated sections for those of colour.

You dared to cross these fault lines at your own peril, or you could, like almost everyone in the circumstances did, curl up and shrink into oneself and accept whatever was reserved as the second best even though the money charged was exactly the same as that for the privileged.

And on the street you faced such constant crushing belligerence you quickly learnt how to survive: by not confronting head on but finding it within yourself to continue by turning the other cheek, and by leading marginalized and invisible lives. You proved yourself through your work, hoping that it would be your salvation, and that sheer application and determination would allow you to rise above your circumstances. There was a glass ceiling in all social and economic circles and no matter what your accomplishments were you eventually encountered it unexpectedly at some point of your life.

Whether it was streetcar, or a bus, or being at close quarters with someone on the street or inside a cramped store, someone is sure to murmur: I don't want to stand next to that shifty-eyed fuckin' coon, wog, injun, raghead: carriers and peddlers, all!

Blacks, Indians and other immigrants all gravitate for work at the sawmills, as these are the only places that offer some form of compensation for brute work. You quickly learn to sit in the segregated section of the movie theatres, learn to move to the back of the streetcars, do not occupy vacant seats next to females, and enter respectable hotels only through the backdoor. In fact, barely five years ago when the first black world heavyweight-boxing champion, Jack Johnson, visited town and was looking for lodging, he was turned away by the St. Francis Hotel, Hotel Irving, and the Rainier Hotel, as well as the Astor Hotel at Cordova and Abbott Streets. He even inquired at the Metropole, where I have heard $2 got you a room with steam heat, electric lights and running water, and he was still refused admittance.

I, Mewa Singh, Punjabi resident of Vancouver, sometimes wonder if any blue-eyed person has ever been turned away from any of these establishments?

People see you one way only and that is the only one way they will ever see you; and what you do not see you will never be able to assimilate into your life. So, they act polite and look past you. There is no confrontation, no need to acknowledge the unpleasantness. You make it unpleasant and the victim will soon leave. In your marble courts you pass discriminative legislation and the outcomes are assured.

Hopkinson, you as a white man cannot fail in this society as the whole system is geared towards you. Yet, we the minorities eventually succeed in spite of all the obstacles you lay before us; like poured cement curing to concrete, obstacles only harden our resolve.

In this rough and tumble world a man is only defined by his work. When it came to wages, you knew the labour will be more strenuous and at a rate that is always a fraction of what others working alongside you are making. You learn to accept what is offered and then look the other way. Making $1.50 or $2.00 a day, you take fewer days off, you live frugally on a sparse but adequate diet and save most of what you earned. What you save you never bank but keep on your person, with the ultimate objective always to return to your village.

Employing fresh immigrants is so profitable that mill managers have worked out a system by which they will sound a whistle to warn the men of 'special visitors'. And, since the only visitors at the worksite are the immigration guys, *hide*. Distributed all over the lumberyards are hollow tree stumps equipped with blankets in which you hide yourself till the all-clear signal is given. Often, an entire day's work will be lost in between signals since the inspectors are paid to ferret out the illegal workers and know who they are dealing with.

And sometimes a season of work will unexpectedly be brought to an abrupt end - an unexplained and unjustified dismissal, an intransigence, a moment in between tasks in which you are caught sitting idle; or merely a refusal to pay deserved wages, or honour a commitment; and the worker is headed back to being idle all day, to relocating and establishing new contacts, to a demeaning existence of desperate scrounging.

And, I, Mewa Singh, Punjabi resident of Vancouver, confess that until the day I landed here, I had never seen a white man do any meaningful work with his hands. Each one of them seemed to have been born to give orders over whomever they happened to be governing at the time, and I used to wonder who did the real work, the lifting and carrying of the burden in their own world. It turns out it is people like me.

You, Hopkinson, had once shared with me the revelation that the real difference between the men in the Indian world is between those who are carried and those who carry. You had asked me: "Mewa, given a choice, which one are you going to be in *this* world?"

Given a choice! When were we ever given a choice?

On the occasional Sunday afternoon when families leisurely picnic on the nearby Stanley Park shores, the intermittent laughter of adults and the excitement of children's strident trilling carries over the water on the drifting wind. With these sounds the physical presence of the denied landscape then escapes the shores and invades our rolling decks. Sometimes, it is the smoke arising from picnic fires that carries with it the aroma of roasting chestnuts; other times it is dry twigs and leaves that drift in on the wind, or seeds of cottonwood and fragile dandelion will waft in to settle on our weather-beaten deck. And, over the noisy squabbling of seagulls will be heard the abrupt crack of a cricket ball being struck, horseshoes being pitched, croquet balls ricocheting off wooden mallets. The cheers of the participants will mingle with the dissonance riding the water and caroming off the buckled sides of our ship.

For a few fleeting moments, the distance between the shore and the ship's railings will then be bridged, and we are ashore again. It is such a delicious delusion.

There are other sounds that the wind also carries away from us. These notes travel all the way to the teeming wharfs at the foot of Granville and Burrard, catching the puzzled listeners unawares with its unfamiliar and exotic ululations. Harmonized, yet rough voices, have been raised in chanting, a harmonium and tabla is in accompaniment with the abrupt staccato bursts of the joy of human clapping. Sometimes, these are mingled into the strains of the *kirtan* and the *gurbani*; at other times it may even be a spontaneous outburst of homesickness in snatches of childhood lyrics:

> *Raba, raba, meen barsa*
> *Sadhe kothe daane paa*

I watch Gurdit strolling absent-mindedly over the sprawling deck, his passage marked by solitarily clucking seagulls, which part like well-behaved pedestrians, momentarily take wing and then alight as soon as he has passed through. With the final hope now abandoned of the court proceedings offering us any reprieve, and the province's Supreme Court quashing any hope of a favourable acquittal, the passengers have begun to improvise and make the best of their isolation. All our earnest plans have been dashed against an insurmountable wall of bureaucracy and the obstinate will of individuals with a peculiar and rigid interpretation of the law. After all, they have proclaimed self-righteously that ours is a lesser claim to theirs.

As Gurdit approaches closer to me I inquire after his health and then inevitably the conversation swings awkwardly towards thoughts of food and water. We peer at the sky in unison.

"Master-ji, no luck today." He offers, raising his open palms upwards.

In a bid to force our hand, the imperious though retired schoolmaster, has even taken it upon himself as a personal mission to ensure that no food or water is permitted to reach onboard.

And, as a direct response to this strategy we have gradually drifted into a daily onboard routine that relies on the passage of tides, and the availability of light and rainwater. As the days of waiting have dragged on, the sun has been setting later and later each day, so that at nine you can still sit on deck and read a newspaper. For the first time in my life I have learnt to sleep while it is still broad daylight outside and rise when the sun has been up for more than two hours.

Initially, since it had been raining at least once weekly we could obtain drinking water by stretching our tarps across the deck. But, lately there has not been enough of it to meet the daily needs of all on board, and it is also never sufficient to keep the boilers going to power the ship's generators. As the amount of rainfall has dwindled, we have quickly learnt to conserve every drop of water. Amidst the rising heat and humidity, the water levels in the boiler tanks and water barrels have continued to dwindle at an alarming rate. This, in spite of the fact that we have been routinely topping them up with rainwater gathered from canvases and oilcloths rigged strategically above the decks. We have continued in our naive belief that given a few hours notice we may be required to pick up enough steam to make it to the shore, not realizing that a tugboat could just as well perform this task when needed. And, more than once someone has wondered aloud: "Is this really the One-Couver where we have been told it never stops raining?"

Two weeks go by and not a drop falls from the sky. Then, a sudden downpour catches us unawares, dumping enough water into out barrels to last us for a month. But now the storm is followed by a heat wave and we consume a week's quota within a single afternoon.

Meanwhile, the Japanese crew and the captain have their own basic supplies delivered to them, or the captain personally ferries them in on his frequent visits ashore. We also know that these trips are carried out to keep the port authorities informed of our deteriorating conditions.

Overhead rigging or not, there is also no relief for us from the blistering sun reflecting off the water.

As we continue to obsessively scan the harbour and the hillsides for signs of life, we watch the far northern peaks shrouded by a roiling mass of cumulus clouds that are the colour of water. The sun, however, still has another hour of descent. A patrol boat is anchored at close range barely a hundred yards off and none of its usual sentinels are visible.

This peaceful scene is suddenly interrupted. I watch as a launch rapidly appears from around the eastern edge of Stanley Park and heads straight towards us, its deck crowded with about a dozen men. A few moments later another boat speeds simultaneously towards us from the west in what appears to be a concerted two-pronged attack. When the boat to our right is close enough for us to discern the colour of the turbans, the somnolent patrol boat comes to life, swiftly banking with a powerful menacing wake and then heading off to face the first of the attackers. I watch puffs of the steam pluming off both the launches as the sentinel boat cuts off their approach, with one boat reluctantly executing a U-turn on a stuttering engine and then drifting back into the distance. But this hasty retreat has been a diversion for the other launch to approach us broadside with the patrolmen in hot pursuit. A rider in a blue turban cups his hands to his mouth and shouts something to me, but his undecipherable words are instantly whipped away by the wind and the revving of engines.

These run-ins had been very common in the first few weeks but are now becoming infrequent as the opponents have tested and then learnt from each other's strengths. Like the seagulls, the patrolmen have also become inured to this frequent testing of our boundaries, and they now go about their business as a matter of daily routine, keeping a watchful eye when there are threats, or fishing and playing cards noisily when the marine traffic around them has died down. Sometimes, during the quiet nights, knowing that it will annoy us, they toy with the Sea Lion's steam whistle playing on it through randomly rising or descending scales.

During the night the distant hillsides still continue to glow with forest fires that we know can now only be doused during the next downpour. On some days, the smoke from these forest fires is so thick that it shrouds the city rooftops with an opaque blanket stretching all the way down to the water's edge, until it seems as if we were once again miraculously afloat at sea and the illusive land mass has finally vanished into thin air. Perhaps, it is just as well. Vancouverites can keep their precious city to themselves.

During one particular night, the lights above the northern horizon have flickered so brightly that Jeevan wants to know if these are the sky lights that we had been told to look out for. Some one immediately corrects him:

"Na, *yaar*, that is the east you are pointing at. These are not the northern lights? At this time of the year it can only be a distant forest fire."

Overhearing this exchange Gurdit ponders to himself: "If we

stay here long enough we may yet get to see these wondrous lights. And, perhaps, mercy towards unwelcome strangers at your doorstep will eventually allow us to step on land. And, if we stayed here long enough our problems will be resolved by themselves. Perhaps." Within the next instant he is left wondering bitterly: "How can this happen? Through divine intervention? Human meddling? Qismet running its course?"

Meanwhile, once again on deck we follow a formation of clouds wheel overhead and race towards the mountains. And with them our thoughts turn towards home where family, spouses, children, parents and lovers await a rumour of our fates. What was it that had possessed us so long ago at the other end of this world, a city and a shore whose invisible reach seemed to stretch across to our continent? What feverish madness had touched us all and altered our perception of the harsh reality of this world, and thus undermined our instincts for survival? Why had we expected that in a foreign land we would be treated any better than we had been in our homelands? What sane reason could there be for the inscrutable Englishman to behave any differently in Canada than they had in an enslaved India? Was the benevolence of a beguiling, beckoning shore an illusion, and a figment of our own imagination?

With the honeyed light bathing the backdrop of blue grey mountains, the air is noisy once again with seagulls and tugboat whistles, while smokestack plumes drift over the morning breeze. An occasional human voice, raised in alarm or laughter, traverses the water to dramatically shorten the distance between us. And, all morning curious onlookers have detoured the paths of their vessels to approach closer and stare up at us, only to be instructed to move away by the two patrol boats that have kept us company throughout the night.

With nowhere to go and nothing to break their monotony, some of the men have taken to collectively circling the ship's 300-foot long deck. To Gurdit, the scene is reminiscent of the circuitous prancing of captive animals and of those in traveling circus tents. He muses aloud to his Daljit: "Animals in captivity will chew the bars of their confinement, and in extreme circumstances even chew off a limb. What do you think this lot will do next?"

The sight of grown men pacing back and forth the length of the deck like caged animals has also become for the locals a sight that is worth the short journey from the shore. Launched in boats from their unwelcoming shore, these sinister, gawking men in trench coats appear clutching cameras and flashlights that are pointed up directly at us. They gesticulate for us to strike heroic postures, taunting and coaxing with exaggerated motions to elicit a reaction from us, any reaction, to justify their outing. And when we are not obliging enough they show their belligerence with threats.

"Go back home, you good for nothing louts!"

In the brief period of six weeks our uncompromising morale has been worn away into something that is as pathetic as the inhabitants of a floating zoo of performing animals, a floating prison that is exposed to one and all, and where every element of inclement weather contrives against us.

As we take turns to prowl the deck it becomes obvious to all that the area is no longer suited for uninterrupted walking. You can barely walk a dozen steps on the metal surface before having to step over piles of ropes and cables, and then circumvent the bridge house. You duck under diagonal ropes and rigging and the tangle of lowered mastheads, and then you learn to dodge the tarped-over lifeboats and pontoons. In addition, with most of the cooking being carried out in open hearths, the decks are strewn with random piles of heaped ash and garbage. Since we are not permitted to toss any of the refuse overboard as we would have done at sea, we burn what we can during the preparation of meals, salvaging inflammable materials from the bunkers, yet the ash heaps continue to grow. Beady-eyed rats with whiskers twitching nervously are becoming bolder daily, emerging out of nowhere alongside the seagulls to feed on this garbage. I once counted ten to a single pile until it seemed the refuse pile itself was quivering with life. Importune cockroaches feast until they are unable to scamper off or take wing. And during nighttime walking, there is the added satisfaction of hearing the crunch underfoot of a cockroach carapace, which momentarily startles the feeding rats to scatter in all directions.

We know we have overstayed our welcome when the seagulls refuse to take flight at our approach. One grumpy creature has chosen the aft railings as his domain and manages to all but shut out human intrusions by narrowing his irises and hissing menacingly at our every approach. Jeevan, who claims the creature's demeanour reminds him of the barking orders of his former quarter sergeant, and he is convinced it is a 'he', has even gone so far as to dub it 'Commander sahib'. He has taken to saluting it at every pass, or going to great lengths to avoid offending it in any way. But Harjeet, or '*Win/Lose*' as I have been calling him, is of the opinion that this is none other than the spirit of his late but vigilant mother-in-law who has returned to keep him out of mischief.

"I tell you, I am convinced she has followed me all the way from Punjab to haunt me here in Vancouver's harbour."

And, now yet another front has been opened up in our desperation to feed ourselves. Over the protests of Captain Yomamato, a handful of us have mastered the art of improvising seagull traps. A glob of flour has been proffered to entice the first emboldened victim, and the men are successful on their very first attempt. When the baffled, squawking, and, until very recently a confident and trusting creature, is overwhelmed, it is smothered with a rag, its precision beak tucked under the wing, and its neck swiftly wrung - the feathers are stripped off even before the feet have stopped twitching. The meagre ribcage with its ridiculous stubs of wingtips resembles a plump chicken.

Arjun is ecstatic. *"Yaaro,* hurry up. *Jaldi, jaldi!* Why restrict our efforts to just one. Lets capture a dozen of these, smother them in lard, skewer them onto metal shafts and then rake them over a bed of coals. Who needs the fish when we have a limitless supply of these creatures messing the deck all day and night?"

However, regrettably Arjun's advice is quickly quashed by an old hand: "Wait! I know it looks tempting now, but has anyone of you ever tasted one of these birds before. One bite and you will never stop retching again."

Jeevan now brings out a set of curved metal wires he has been fashioning all week into fishhooks. Optimistic and hefty morsels of pink seagull flesh is skewered onto each hook and dropped over the railing, each lumpy contraption disappearing into the murky water with an audible 'plop'. Over the next half hour there are excited cheers as the fishing lines begin to twitch and jump about. However, every time the hooks are yanked out of the water they come up empty.

Once again we have to rely on Jeevan's resourcefulness to figure out the problem.

"When I was no bigger than a *dholi* my *Chachaji* used to remind me on every fishing trip that in order to catch big one you have to think small. What you have to do, *mere yaaro,* is reduce the size of your bait. *Oi,* Puran, do you remember that bottomless pool we used fish at as boys back in Dhudike?"

Give these two an audience and you will never get them to shut up.

*"Hahn,"* Puran grunts, seemingly exhausted by their clowning. "Some of the best days of my childhood."

*"Hahn*! I suppose they were. Perhaps when we return we can catch that fat illusive bastard that tormented us for years. What beast could possibly resist my very special and secret bait?"

"What secret bait?" Jeevan can only grin back at him, knowing their routine is well on track.

"Come on, you know…"

"Well, you can spit on it all you want…"

"No, no! You know the other bait."

"Aw, you are sick, yaar. Do you still believe peeing over the bait will improve your odds? Well, then try it on yours, I am not letting you come close to mine."

Their clowning is interrupted by someone asking: "Now, if we could somehow coax a goat or a buffalo onboard. Do you think they have goats here in Canada? Do you think our night oarsman can arrange for that?"

"The question is not whether they have buffalos or goats here, what we do know is that they have cows. Now, it is up to the shore committee to find a way to sneak a cow onboard."

"By the way, has anyone noticed that there are two police patrol boats now running circles around us during the daytime also? Perhaps, the goras are getting desperate, or it may just be that they have nothing better to do.

"Or, after all this it may turn out that One-Couver is really a peaceable town, where the police have nothing better to do but to watch us fishing with pieces of stale roti and seagull meat."

"I wonder how long the seagull bait will keep in this heat. Well, never mind that. There's more where this came from."

"Why do you think the fish are not serious about seagull bait? Here's an opportunity for them to get back at their chief predator. And, look all they do is nibble and then run for cover."

"Here nice *dholis*, look what a tasty treat I have for you," murmurs Puran enticing the fish to bite.

"Do the stupid fish know any better?"

"By the way, did you see that funny looking flat fish that Jeevan caught yesterday? It had both its eyes on the same side of the face. Kind of like this, huh?" He rolls his eyes in mimicking an exaggerated squint.

"Sort of like your mother-in-law on a good day, huh?"

And, thus, momentarily we forget the reality surrounding us, as share our tall fishing tales, nostalgically recalling childhood verses and snippets of superstitions passed to us by our grandmothers. Their baggage of personal fears passed on to us by our elders in the faint hope that these would allow us to cope with every situation we would encounter later in life. We forget momentarily that we have now been cut loose and set adrift from the reassuring security of our shared childhood memories where jinns stalk fearless adventurers at every corner or challenge them with tasks of fortitude. Where the highpoint of every festival celebrating the life and deeds of a saint includes a battle between legendary wrestlers in the dust of fallow fields, and the koel is once again the harbinger summoning the monsoons. We recall how rowdy crowds would gather at the least excuse for a spectacle or celebration, or in their desperation to escape their boredom will fritter away their hard earned money on wagers on the most trivial phenomenon.

Whatever our collective memories can succour from other places we cling desperately to ward off this state of sudden disconnection, this wavering between melancholy and defiance, frustration and boredom, this sudden elation followed by bouts of depression.

Hometowns that once sustained and nourished our imaginations have now became our narratives, and are enmeshed in our life stories: Moga, Ferozepur, Bhatinda, Malout, Muktsar, Faridkot, Ludhiana... even the names are loosing their resonance. In the beginning we had effortlessly drifted into groups with common families or hometowns, or even districts. But, since then these distant boundaries have melted away leaving us only with a faded pride of where we first ventured out.

Someone states that his hometown of Ferozepur has several memorials dedicated to the freedom fighters of India. "At the nearby town on the Ferozepur- Moga road there is a place called Zira that has the beautiful Jain Swetembar Temple with its ancient icons and murals." Others mention Battinda's 1800 years old fort. Malout - an old mandi town, where produce from surrounding areas is brought for sale. Muktsar - linked to the victory of Sikh forces over the Mughal forces under the command of prophet Sri Guru Gobind Singh. Faridkot - the capital of erstwhile Phulkian state, famous for its forts and palaces, each with its extraordinary murals, mirror work and frescoes. Our hometown has marble-lined pools; ours has two thousand year old public gardens.

"And, ours has a dung stained pool in which the buffaloes take a daily dip," someone pipes in.

This time it is the reclusive Gurmukh of Lalton who brings a brooding touch to this outpouring of painful memories: "Near our village there is a hillock on the southern horizon where exotic and illusive migratory birds are said to nest. As you all know, I wasn't always this old man that you see before you. I was once young and agile like you. When after months of anticipation I did finally reach the hillside on a hot summer afternoon it turned out to be a total disappointment. A few scraggly chinars in which crows nested, a pair of curious and friendly squirrels that nibbled at the food held in my outstretched hands. And that was it. There were no other birds or animals to be seen. It may just as well have been the wrong time of the day or the wrong season. But whatever the reason, I did not return to the place to find out. I guess when we do land on shore, it is going to be different."

Someone asks Gurdit: "Bhai Bhagga, what did bhai Arjun mean by stating that in One-Couver the goras cross over to the other side of the street upon seeing us coming?"

"I know, but that would be true of any city in the Empire, even in India. Yet, you cannot continue to dwell on these matters at a time like this," Gurdit admonishes, suddenly edgy and churlish.

"What we are dealing with here is a struggle for life and death, and all you can worry about is how the goras will greet you on their streets. Why should we care what grows in their dark hearts. Somehow, we have to find means of getting out of here alive, and the world must now learn of how we have been treated here by this dominion. We are all British subjects. Surely that means something. Some of us have even fought for the vaunted glory of this Empire. An assurance was given to us that we as subjects of the King could move about freely within the Empire, and now that we are here at their doorsteps, they slam the gate shut on us merely on a minor technicality. I tell you, I will not rest until each one of us is safe and has been allowed to land, and I am allowed to conduct my business in peace, and provided compensation for all my losses."

The talk once again moves away from belligerence to the reassurances of familiar threads. We recall favourite songs and offer up half forgotten stanzas. There are candid revelations of a purely personal nature, and of frictions between extended families, for after all was not ours an open book culture of joint families that share every open courtyard.

Someone recalls the sweetness of the water from the village well.

"What I miss is the *Barfi* from the corner *halvai* shop."

"*Jalebis* dripping in syrup."

"Wedding *luddoos* with almond hearts, coated with gold leaf. As many as I can hold in my palm and cram into my mouth at one time."

"*Zarda!*" I offer, theatrically presenting the guests with my choice of dessert.

The image of the last of these delicacies is compelling enough for Gurdit to seize this as an opportunity and offer amends.

"Does anyone here know that saffron was once such a rare commodity that in earlier times it was worth its weight in gold? Today, I would gladly give away whatever I have left for the taste for a handful of caramelized golden rice. *Zarda!* What an evocative name for such an exquisite dish."

Another voice describes how in the early mornings the smoke from cooking fires would snake so close to the village grounds. Then the lingering aromas of cooking *parathas,* as the herds of buffalos head out to pasture with their fluted chorus of bells.

"Out in the fields my wife bringing me *saag todha* and *lassi* for lunch."

We sit long into the night and recall in vivid detail all those intense regrets, the highpoints of our half-finished lives now left far behind us. Here every character is flamboyant and extrovert, and the spirit is still untamed and unbowed, and nothing can be too private or too personal anymore to keep from the shared camaraderie.

As dew settles on the deck, the moorings creak with the ship straining at its anchor.

There are moments like this when the shore seems so close at hand even though I know it to be at least a 250 yards distance, this after our ship was nudged further from the shore as we were blocking the shipping channel. It is late in the evening and once again I am seated as close to the railing as I can get. There is nothing of interest left to observe on the opposite beach.

I realize this almost as an afterthought that if I were to cautiously slip between the railings and quietly enter the water, I could probably swim to the shore in less than fifteen minutes. But once more sanity prevails and I hastily put the thought aside.

With a breeze dimpling the surface of the water it now cool enough for me to duck below deck and grab my pullover, its abrasive wool briefly chafing against my neck. Even though the deck is deserted, the danger is not only from the patrol boats but also the distrusting crew and the two security men who have commandeered the bridge house as their quarters. I can see them snapping at mosquitoes and slapping each other's shoulders boisterously, their eyes intent on the card game. For some reason I keep expecting the ill-fated Nakajima to step up to me, confident that he would somehow manage to cover up for me if I were to make my escape.

To my south lies the nearest pier that is sealed off from all sides by floating log cabins and shacks crudely assembled from dislodged logs. Even in the dim light I can distinguish a miniature window and a low door in each cabin, a skiff tied loosely up front, and smoke rising from the chimneys. Some of these cabins are tilted so precariously towards the waterline that they seem ready to slip under the next wave. Behind these cabins is the gunmetal blue of the city slopes, crisscrossed at this hour with ghostly lights of what I presume are motorcars or horse carriages. And, what of the figures I can just barely discern moving about the harbour front? Could these be humans heading homewards so late in the evening?

A refrain from a popular Ghadar song comes to mind:
*We weary travelers have no home...*

Still, this patch of water directly below me continues to hold me spellbound. My position is such that it is located close enough to the stern to be protected form the direct view of the bridge house. Now, if I could somehow bring myself to ease into the water unnoticed, a mere twenty minutes or less is all it will take... if the determined Nakajima was once able to do it under such unfavourable circumstances, what is there to keep me from attempting to swim to this shore so tantalizingly close.

But returning to the deck I find that nearly a dozen men have occupied the spot of railing I have occupied all evening. In these fantasies of escape I have overlooked one minor detail of our imprisonment: the night deliveries.

On certain nights identified for us by the exchange of signal flags, a curious event takes place around midnight. About a dozen men begin to casually drift across the deck before congregating at a spot close to the stern. I can now see them bringing up bundles of their personal belongings, examining the deck and then settling down close to the railing. Their conversation flows easily yet in a tone low enough to pass unnoticed. They spread their belongings all around them, cautiously keeping an eye on the bridge house and the surface of the water.

About a month after Mr. Ried's imposition of the restrictions on food and water deliveries to us, we began the use of signalling flags from secluded spots on the ship. It was at this critical juncture that one of our onshore sympathizers, a local named Sorian Singh Meham, has stepped in to literally keep us alive. Unassuming, slim and lithe, our hero has been harassing the patrol boats during moonless nights, like a pesky mosquito come to relieve them of their monotony but also severely testing the patrolmen's tolerance. During the first week of his mission he began by testing the limits of how close the patrol boats would permit him to approach the ship. And, once that boundary had been defined, he began rapidly polishing his skills as a one-man delivery team.

Only once have the patrolmen threatened him with bodily harm, one jittery guard brazenly pointing his rifle directly at him and taking aim, whether to frighten or inflict damage he will not linger to discover before cautiously melting back into the night.

Moving closer to the shore, Sorian bhai has been experimenting with dipping his oars at certain angles that will allow him to perform the circuitous twist of the wrist, repeatedly, until the oar emerges effortlessly and clears the surface soundlessly with not a single drop to give away its motion. With the need to be invisible as well as silent, he tries out varied backgrounds against which he will be undetected during his nightly approaches; selecting only clothing that will blend into the backdrop such as that raggedy stand of conifers close to Brockton Point, or that shallow cliff facing Deadman's Isle. He tests various degrees of weight that the boat will safely bear before tipping over, and how much of the dead weight he can safely reduce before its maneuverability or speed becomes critical at that crucial moment of escape. Selecting various vegetables to deliver, he discovers that spuds are not easily bruised and are the easiest to cram into soaked gunnysacks that will quickly sink below the surface. He diligently oils every interacting metal part to silence its friction, coating all reflective surfaces and exposed metal parts with pitch, and discovering in the process that the pitch actually silences the movement of the oarlock and the oar.

He trusts no one with his venture, his delivery schedules guided by the phases of the moon, the wind patterns of waves under the night sky; often choosing moonless nights or waiting until the moon has set.

More than once he has been able to sail within a stone's throw of the snoozing patrolmen. Approaching the giant black mass filling his sight, there is the first cautious contact - at first a brief and gentle tap above the plimsole line, followed by three sharper knocks against the buckled steel plates towering over him; the eager onlookers having followed each step of his cautious approach are already deploying the line to trail in the water. The sunken sack of spuds lashed to the bottom of the boat is now unwound and then double-knotted to one edge of the line of knotted turbans deployed from above. The contraband is gingerly hoisted clear out of the water and not a word exchanged. By the time the sack has cleared the railing the boat has already melted back into the night, its owner plotting the next night's mission.

Sometimes, delivering the food packages is not enough. There maybe a letter carefully sealed in oilcloth and tied to the end of the turban. Perhaps, an urgent message addressed to the Shore Committee, and he must carefully untangle this before attaching his own package. The pleas have usually been for more food, or a particular medicine.

Only once has there been a request for a local newspaper.

# BASHIR'S PUNJAB SLEEPS

I have been drifting in and out of fitful dreams.

The land of *sufi, sadhu, sant, faqir*
The land of the poet
The lover and the madman
And all the great fallen warriors
All asleep
And the five rivers leisurely chasing each others tails
From the Himalayas to the seas
Pausing only to sing the land to sleep
And everywhere is sleep
Yet where shall we lay our weary heads?
We are laying our heads on the pillow and yet we are not sleeping.

My head is reeling from having read too much Tagore, Whitman, Rumi and Ghalib. I can even feel the grass blades beginning to stir beneath my feet. I can hear the wind keening off the water and over the hillside rocks. The familiar lines of ink in the handful of books I have chosen to accompany me on the voyage have become muddled strangers. After much deliberation over my well thumbed collection I had narrowed the selection down to the following eight choices: The Quran, Rumi, *Dewan-e-Ghalib*, Iqbal's 1905 publication of *Tarana-e-Hind (Song of India)*, Smith's *The Wealth of Nations*, *Das Kapital*, Tagore's *Gitanjali*, Fisher's *English Grammar* in case I forgot the differentiate the words 'Betwixt' and 'Between,' and finally a reluctant choice imposed upon me by professor-ji: Kipling's *Kim*.

In sleep I continue to dream of fires.

Fires that are still burning in the mountains and valleys.
This rusting metal bucket is on fire.
The fire consumes this pretend city called One-couver
And this pretentious dominion of Canada.
The fire also consumes the premature and stillborn world of one revolutionary named Kartar Singh, my hero, my alter-ego, the writer of *Ghadari* slogans and poetry.
It consumes my two loves: my Khadeeja and my Kausar.
Now where shall I lay my weary head? Their solace once sustained me. Where are they now that I so need them?

"Bashir, Bashir bhai?"

Far into the distance recedes the remembered land of lovers and madmen, the land of poets, of *sufis, sadhus, sants, faqirs* - all asleep, my land asleep, its horizons now lost to me forever, my childhood, my youth, my parents, my beloveds. Which beguiling spell, what maddening fevers, what conniving jinns had possessed me to abandon those morning dews that I shall never tread again. The arms that will never hold me or soothe my brow.

"Come on, come on hurry up, wake up you idiot!"

Puran's nagging voice is insistently shaking my shoulder.

"Hurry! Bhagga has summoned another meeting."

"What is it this time - another appeal to sanity? I ask wearily. Another jurisprudent tactic unveiled?"

"There is hope yet, Bashir bhai, in spite of your cynicism. Just you wait and see. Bhagga will get us out of this mess."

"Alive. I hope?"

"Stop being so melodramatic. You know what your problem is? You think too much. You lose yourself in those books and then you lose sight of what is real or fictional."

"As if I haven't been told that before."

"I hear a verdict has finally come down on Munshi's case. This could be our lucky day. This could be our ticket to One-Couver."

I wake to the sound of someone nearby reading extracts from the paper *Ghadar Ki Goonj* examining how the Russian revolution is close to succeeding and the Indian one has not yet materialized:

Unfairness of the English Rule

'The English are taking five million rupees to England yearly. That is the reason the Indians are so poor, their income being on the average only five pice a day.

Taxes are over 65 per cent.

Money spent on education is 77,500 rupees and 200,00 rupees only is spent on health, but 29,500,000 rupees are spent for the army and navy.

The English rule is deteriorating.

In ten years two million have died in India.

In sixteen years from plague alone eight million people have died, and the death roll in thirty years has increased from 24 to 50 per cent.

They are trying to force the law in such a way in the States as to put the Hindus against the Mohamedans, and vice versa.

If an English person were to ill-treat an East Indian woman or kill an East Indian, there is no redress for the East Indian.

Monetary help from the Hindus and Mohamedans is given to Christians.

The English rule is always trying to put some sense for disagreement between the Hindus and Mohamedans to keep them at enmity to each other.

The profits from the manufactures and industries are given to England.

With the money and lives of India the English help Afghanistan, Persia, Egypt, and Burmah.

It is fifty-six years ago since we last fought in India, and we would like to fight again.

The population in the native States of India is 70,000,000, and under English rule 240,000,000.

There are 79,614 English officers and men and 38,948 volunteers.

People are still talking about the mutiny they had in Russia, and even up to the present they have not got all that coming to them, but they are overcoming their oppressors. They have broken down the barriers. These results have been obtained within few years.

The difficulty is to start a mutiny, but once people begin to see it is successful all take up arms to help.

It is hard to wake a person asleep, but once awake it is not difficult to make him do anything.'

"Wake up. Bashir, you have fallen asleep again. I wanted to inform you that the Supreme Court has rejected Munshi Singh's final appeal. Now, we are doomed for sure."

*'Safar aur saqar mein sirf nuktay bhar ka farq hai'*
*Travel and Hell are separated by a single dot.*

While boarding the Komagata maru in the orient we had all been flung into close quarters with entire strangers, and we had naturally aligned ourselves into regional groups. I found myself lumped in with the rest of the Amristari Muslims. The *Doabis*, from the region of Indian Punjab surrounded by the rivers Beas and Sutlej, began by looking down at their northern neighbors from the hill regions, the *paharis*. The soft-spoken, eastern *Doabis* called *Brijwasis* complained about the uncouth western *Doabis* they were now being asked to share quarters with. And, the stern Pathans, never to be outdone by anyone else, expressed utter disdain for all Punjabis. But now, after having endured the challenges that our indisposed Canadian hosts had hurled at us, the regional bonds of the home regions had loosened, and all gatherings were now open to all.

Realizing that the core experience of a shared language allowed me to overcome social barriers, I kept myself endlessly entertained, slipping unself-consciously between one gathering of men after another, and letting the different dialects and dialogues wash over me. An overheard snippet of gossip here, a whispered secret shared between friends here. It was a lot like opening a book randomly, reading a few pages and then jumping ahead to the next chapter.

At one of these gatherings I overheard someone I did not yet know recalling his home life in India "… and, as my youngest I named him Rujoo. *Bas ruj gaye*, I said. Six already. It is enough! Now at five Rujoo cannot yet distinguish between men in uniform - to him a policeman is as good as a soldier - and will parade with his siblings tirelessly for hours on end in our courtyard: '*LeftRightLeftRight - LeftRightLeftRight – Thanedaar di bebe aayi.*' Already, I see a subedar in waiting, and it gladdens my heart."

There is another conversation taking place amongst a group of retired orderlies: "…I never really understood the pig-headedness of the sahibs and their memsahibs as they lorded it over their army of fawning servants. Why would they stodgily refuse to learn a smattering of useful phrases of our language? What they did instead was to adapt nonsensical English phrases to communicate phonetically with us. Occasionally, my memsahib would instruct me: '*there-was-a-cold-day-there.*' Can you guess what she was actually trying to say?" He pauses dramatically, waiting like all good talkers for us to provide the answer.

"*Darwaza khol do!* See. All she wanted was for me to open the door."

"And what did she say when she wanted the door closed?" someone asks.

"*There-was-a-banned-car. Darwaza band kar!* See. After a while you get the hang of it. Very resourceful in its priggish way.

"However, what baffled me most was the behaviour of the Indian ayahs working as the memsahib's wet nurses. In every instance they considered it a privilege to suckle the sahib's infant while their own progeny withered away. Somehow, an idea had been planted in their twisted minds that there was a greater dignity in suckling the sahib's pale baby rather than their own wheat coloured ones.

"So much for the *angrezi* women. Our colonel sahib never understood why every Indian orderly who retired from his service, never returned to see how everything he had left behind had prospered. This after having spent an entire adult life serving him and his family and having watched over the children as they grew up. Each one would leave for their hometowns and then never be heard from again."

This monologue is followed up by another retired army man:

"But why should the characteristically subservient and obsequious orderly ever want to come back? Hadn't he had enough of living vicariously?"

"Wait, wait. I have a good one about an orderly." The first speaker who is reluctant to see the audience moving away from him offers this. "A retiring orderly was once asked by his officer that if given a choice of roles in another lifetime, what would the man opt to return as: the commanding officer or the commanding officer's wife?

"That one is easy, sir, replies the orderly. The wife, of course."

"Why? Well, sir, for two reasons. First, I, too, would then get to sleep around all day and order everyone about. And secondly, you have been screwing me all my life. For once I'll get to enjoy it."

There is only one grumpy face in all this jocularity.

"Hold on a minute. What do you mean by saying the orderly is always subservient and obsequious? I will have you know that for over twenty years I was one, and I never…."

But, there were other conversations around the deck to distract me when such exchanges became awkward.

Next, I dropped in on a group of retired military men as they reminisced about past battles. One of them was running his fingers through his full beard while talking.

"A long time ago we had headed out of our villages as eager sixteen or seventeen year olds, lying about our ages or counting on the mercy of the recruiting agent – for during wartime everyman in uniform was already a hero. During my first month of training, when I had showed no interest whatsoever in the daily routines of military life, my subedar pulled me aside one day and lectured me: 'What kind of a military man are you - not caring either about payday or rations? Man, at least get your priorities right'.

"We were shipped off to unknown continents; bagpipes would lead us into distant battlefields. Four foot trenches zigzagging across rapidly denuded landscapes, the barbed wire held aloft by the first in the trio so the rest could slip through, a traverse then a shallow bay carved into the embankment, one man standing to mind the gun, one seated next to him on the ledge, always within touching distance so that if one collapsed the other would take up the slack, while the third rested in an eighteen inch wide ledge carved into the side of the trench. Our unit performed like clockwork, an oasis of sanity amidst all the devastation and desolation. And as for food, there was never enough of it. Desiccated biscuits, Canadian red cheddar, tinned jam, whatever meager rations there were went through so many sticky hands that there was little left by the time it reached us in the trenches. Initially, our trench was located within sight of a horse carcass that was crawling with rats and bored men took blind potshots at them. And all the time the six-inch howitzers firing salvo after salvo at unseen targets in the distant, the blast of compressed air striking you like a physical blow that worked its way through your entire body.

"We learnt to rub whale oil on our feet to prevent them from getting all wrinkly and moldy. And sometimes, with snow on the ground, the cold would be so severe the Enfields would not fire. This was well enough as both sides were confronted with the same problem. At the first break of light, and then later at dusk, we would raise up our periscopes to peer at the enemy, as these were the preferred times of attack. An observer could only risk being exposed for the first three seconds or so, as the other side would be equally alert and doing the same. I found that out the hard way on my fifteenth day in the field. I was the designated observer for the day. In a moment of bored numbness I peered over the edge. The next thing I remember was the stretcher-bearer retching and applying field dressings to my face. That was the end of this war for me. And, look, this is what they finally gave me for it, declaring me to be a hero."

The narrator extracts from his trouser pocket a shiny medal and shows it to the gathering, his mouth contorted into a grimace, and then noisily clearing his throat he hurls spit far onto the deck.

He returns to his narrative: "In the beginning when I returned I talked incessantly about my experience, and everyone made comforting noises. Then I began noticing that no one really understood what I was talking about, so after a while I fell silent. But having bottled it all up inside me it will not let me remain quiet anymore."

Gradually, he begins to relax, sitting cross-legged in the middle of his silenced companions, and resumes:

"The battles we once fought, yaaro, were never without a cause, even when we could not comprehend the underlying motives. And, even when the bigger picture remained clouded from us, there was always a dignity in the good fight. When we set forth from our homes and villages we were meant to seize our destiny in our two hands. As Sikhs we have always been firebrands, priding ourselves on our physical prowess, and leading protests against injustice. But this, this prolonged waiting and praying and then waiting again for a response... Where is the dignity in this?"

He rises stiffly, and before anyone can intervene, hurls the medal overboard.

Later on, there would be others who would perform similar acts of protest - former soldiers all - who, in an effort to fill up their boredom, would obsessively disturb the ghosts from past battles.

Seeing that for all practical purposes we were captives onboard, Gurdit-ji summarized it succinctly for us:

"*Gal paya tol wajana penda ay.* You have no choice but to beat the drum placed around your neck.

"The enemy this time, *jigro*, is not the *angrez*. It is these transplanted *goras* who think they own this conquered land they call Canada. It is not the British but the Canadians we are fighting for our rights. We seem to have picked the wrong enemy to fight our battles. Somehow, we have to take the initiative and gain control of our circumstances and take this battle back to India where it belongs."

Barely a week passed and Misters Reid and Hopkinson offered us one such opportunity that to their chagrin would play right into our hands and lift some of the gloom from our weary shoulders.

# GO BACK HOME

*'Few emigrant bands in history have come so far to be sent back. They are rejected not because they are an outland people, but because they come from a strange part of the world where men's skins are not only pigmented, but their hearts also. It is not the brown skins, but the brown mind that makes them unwelcome.'*

- Vancouver Sun, July 11, 1914

"GO BACK HOME! GO BACK WHERE YOU CAME FROM."

Ah, the shrill anthem of the cosy but indignant and self-righteous is being sounded again. And, marathon starboard/portside champion shouting matches have been regularly taking place over it. There no clear winners just yet.

"Go back," they all seem to yell. "Go back home while you still can or play out the roles that history, fate and your collective, misguided-idealism has cast you into."

They cup their hands around their mouths and shout till they are red in the face. There are about a dozen of these men standing tipsily on the flat deck of a scow. The policemen watch them languidly as the jeers become louder and louder as if the shouting was being coordinating at a sporting event. However, when the shore committee's launch appears on site it is promptly chased away with honks and blasts from the patrol boat. Instructions to move away are megaphoned and the police launch takes up a defensive position between them and us.

Meanwhile, the vessel with the goras has switched sides and is now astern. And the diligent watchmen are still drifting on the other side of the ship.

"Go back! Go back!" Someone on board the unsteady craft is shouting through hands cupped around his mouth.

"Go back where?" Jeevan responds boisterously.

"Go back to your country. We don't want you here," comes the reply.

"Why don't you go back to England? We don't want you here, either?" Jeevan is not to be outdone in this shouting match.

"This is not England. This is Canada. This is our home. And we don't want your lot here."

"This shall be our home too. It doesn't belong to you."

"Well, look around you. It does now."

"Why don't you goras get out of India and go back to *your*

homes?" Jeevan offers up this demand leaning perilously over the railing.

"What are you talking about?" Comes the response. "Are you men daft? This is Canada not India. Go back where you belong. We don't want you here."

"We don't want your like here," another assailant repeats.

"Go back home! Go back home!"

"Well, I will when the colonist camped in my India will crawl back to his own home instead of poking furtively around every corner of the globe? Is it not the presumptuous nature of the colonist to expect to be welcomed everywhere but to be reluctant to accept anyone else on their own shores?" Jeevan delivers his extended monologue.

Later in the night there is one final scene, when we are subjected to the curious spectacle of a boatload of men dressed in women's clothing, all jeering at us, with one man pointing a shotgun, while another holds up a noose. Other than the obvious intent to intimidate us, I am left wondering who these men are and what has been the significance of their dress and their rude pantomimed actions. What had we done to focus so much hatred as to compel so many to set out in the middle of the night to deliver their belligerent messages?

It will now be worth quoting one of Bhagwan Bhai's Punjabi poems entitled 'Kill or Die'; which translated in English it reads:

*'Let us kill the whites; kill the wicked and tyrannous Europeans. Do not leave any trace of them. Extirpate the whole nation. Show no mercy, whatever. Flay them alive so that they remember for ages. Fill the rivers with their dead bodies. We will even go to England shouting kill, kill, kill.'*

Such passion, and such bitterness were once meant to stir our hearts. But I have often wondered how effectively these words would deliver their message to the opponent's side? Perhaps, Bhagwan should have used the words of an English poet to get his message across. Perhaps, the words of Byron, whose anguished Cossack hero Mazeppa proclaims towards the end of his eventful journey:

> *'But time at last makes all things even,*
> *And if we do but watch the hour,*
> *There never yet was human power*
> *That could evade, if unforgiven,*
> *The patient hate and vigil long,*
> *Of those who treasure up a wrong.'*

However, my mind would continue to linger over Kartar Singh Sarabha's poem *'Who We Are'*. I found myself reciting it more often to myself than to others:

> *'If anyone asks who we are*
> *Tell him our name is rebel*
> *Our duty is to end the tyranny*
> *Our profession is to launch revolution*
> *That is our namaz, this is our sandhya*
> *Our puja, our worship*
> *This is our religion*
> *Our work*
> *This is our only Khuda, our only Rama.'*

I have committed several of his other lines to memory, too. This one has followed us halfway across the world:

> *'Serving one's country is very difficult*
> *It is so easy to talk*

*Anyone who walked on that path*
*Must endure millions of calamities.'*

Visionaries such as Barakat Ullah and Lala Hardayal had been the first of many to have aligned our attempted journey to the freedom struggle already taking place in India. But what the former had initially set out to do in mid-career was to imagine a nation that the Muslim brotherhood could call its own - a second flourishing of Islam's Golden Age across the globe. However, his pan-Islamic focus was creating a dichotomy of visions for India's freedom, one that was causing qualms for his followers and colleagues, including myself. Yet, we all knew that eventually Barakat Ullah's dedication to the cause of secularism would win out over his spiritual focus.

The rebellion that we had all been anticipating was already being called the Second Ghadar after the failed one of 1857, and its scope was being cast in a widening circle throughout the Pacific Northwest, South Asia, Middle East, and East Africa. As a logical corollary to this, it was only a matter of time before its seditious ripples would spread to every corner of the Empire.

Where I was to be relegated to the role of only a minor footnote in this history, it were these giants who foreshadowed the dream that would only become a reality if we were sufficiently dedicated in our efforts. We had to be ready to make every sacrifice at the crucial time. They had promised an altered world, dreaming the reality of its impossibilities. Through these protagonists I was learning that the Empire, though still continuing to expand, had already subjugated over 80 percent of the known world. Its children had sailed each of the earth's uncharted oceans and landed on every nook and cranny of the sleeping lands that lay in their path; uprooting, taming and transplanting countless native populations in the name of civilization.

My minor role in the Ghadar began with publications in the seditious papers of Lahore, my first heady exposure to the world of ideas that lay beyond my farmland and my hometown. To show our solidarity with the imprisoned revolutionary Bal Gangadhar Tilak, a few of my friends took to sleeping on the floor. For the two summers of 1912 and 1913, my verses were regularly being published in the *Rebellion* paper under the pseudonym of 'Kartar Singh'. The paper itself was clandestinely printed at the campus of Government College in Lahore. And, gratifyingly for me, I watched each well-thumbed copy of the paper pass like a particularly irresistible and delicious rumour through several pairs of hands and eyes, and eventually return back to the campus.

Sprinkled amidst my poems were articles that proclaimed that the much-suffering masses had finally had enough; each cover story blared the time had come for all Indians to stand up for themselves. The Russians had already led the way and were now showing us how to overthrow the entrenched, tired blood lines of those who ruled us, whether directly as local monarchs or as rapacious colonizers. I could feel a certain anxiety and anger in the air the way ordinary men and women were beginning to vent their frustrations with their limited lot in life. Rumours swept like firestorms through entire communities, and vigilante mobs began taking matters into their hands. We heard of bombs being tossed at government officials, and the identification of the houses of toadies and benefactors of the British. As a direct response to all this clandestine activity, folks began to disappear from their homes or were openly apprehended on flimsy premises. One night, my college mate, Sardar Cheema, who ran our underground paper, was cornered on the way home and so badly roughed up by a gang of thugs that he permanently lost sight from one eye, and could not hear for days.

"Bashir, have you finally had enough of your idealism?" Professor Puran-ji inquired of me as we sat sipping overly sweet chai at an Anarkali tea shop.

"These are heady times, professor-ji. I am glad to be living through them. No history book could have provided such an invigorating education for our generation."

But his solicitation had little to do with ascertaining my opinions than to caution me. Unknown to me the threats being voiced against me were becoming now urgent enough to require his intervention. And, as usual, couched in his cautionary words was a deeper and more personal concern.

"What am I going to tell your family if something were to happen to you? Enough of this hot-headed literature and reliving history for now. I want you to go immediately into hiding, and destroy your current identity.

"One can never be too careful these days," he warned. "The angrez will do anything to get their hands on you in order to gain access to the rest of us."


Within a day of this exchange I had burned nearly all my clothes, shaved off my neat and trim beard, sliced my false identity papers and then burnt every tiny sliver, tossing the ash into the river. Then I returned to my original village of Lopoke to take up my life as Bashir Ali, the farmer's son, college student home for holidays. And by the end of summer I was working as an elementary schoolteacher of English, Urdu, Farsi & Punjabi. But these were still dangerous times, and though I had been assured of my personal safety, I was getting uneasy hearing daily accounts of betrayals and of arrests throughout the surrounding regions.

It was around this time that I decided to relocate, once again. And massive as India was, its opposite shores had rapidly closed in.

And, all this was to eventually lead me on to a floating prison from which there was also no escape.

One morning, when I found myself all alone on the deck, several opportunistic ravens flew in and got busy stealing scraps from our piles of garbage. All this occurred under the watchful beaks of the seagulls. It suddenly occurred to me that I too was beginning to feel like a rogue raven that had somehow been deposited amidst a flock of prized pigeons. Perhaps, I was no longer the sleek pale-bibbed Indian crow, the original migrant worker heading out each morning to make a living and then beating a slow retreat at dusk. I had by now metamorphosed into the crow's wilier, unkempt northern cousin, endlessly resourceful, opportunistic and more ruthless, the raven.

I reminded myself that the peculiar inventive cruelty of humans is less dismaying when we look about ourselves. Violence is rampant in nature and what we were being threatened with was tame compared to what had already been done to us.

Where the rest of the Ghadarite poetry was full of slogans proclaimed from the rooftops, mine would now be an emotional response that was closer to the bone. Where they were literal and appealing directly to action, I would use the language of symbolism. Where they harkened to historical pasts, I would look to nature for inspiration.

And I would learn new idioms, and uncover fresh timbre. I would learn new skills, as Rumi had said while writing on how birds learn flight: *they fall from the sky and in falling learn to fly.* I had done enough of the falling, and now, I, too, would seek to soar.

However, so caught up was I in the moment of inspiration that I could not anticipate the reaction my newly uncovered idiom would elicit from friends. Arjun patiently sat through my first reading of the raven poems and wanted to know why I had chosen to write about ravens.

"Why can't you write about not the familiar crow?" I pointed wearily at the mountains and the ravens foraging before us amongst the clutter of the deck.

"We are here in Canada, and in case you haven't noticed, this is not a part of India. Do you see any Indian crows out here? How can a lowly Indian creature continue to inspire us here in Canada?"

"But we are seeking a revolution in India, not in Canada. Look around you. Does this look like India to you?" I knew he was saying this merely to turn the tables on me.

"I know all this, yaar. But, just in case you missed the obvious irony, the crow has now been transformed by his experiences into the local raven. How could what we have endured so far not transform us in some way? Are we so bull-headed that we cannot learn new trades?"

"That we'll all become ravens now instead of crows?" he had asked me.

"As usual, you are completely missing the point. I have had an important revelation and I want to share it with you, *mere yaar.*"

And so it ended. The first set of my Raven poems went unread and unappreciated. Arjun was not ready to give up his argument so easily, saying something that was as eloquent as it was troubling to me.

"Bashir bhai, if we forget where we have come from, and who we are, then we will soon enough learn to forget where we are headed."

I recall thinking that I had also read something along these lines.

# RAVEN CHANTING

The retreating rainstorm
Staggers unsteadily down the valley
Chuckling something to itself
In staccato lightning patterns
Carving the cracked eggshell
With its mock belligerence.

Raven descends onto his favorite perch
Stretching his disheveled wingtips
Gingerly testing their reach.

He finds himself gripped
By a sad fleeting profound compulsion
Echoed in the swelling of chest feathers
How must he offer his humble homage
For the chattering of streams
And the steaming hillsides
The sighing of foliage
Shrugging its stippled burden?

Priming his craw he proclaims
*Caw!*
The note sounds insincere befuddled
*Caw! Caw!*
Only the encouragement of the wind
*Caw! Caw! Caw!*
Alarm at his ragged voice
And the sudden ease of a stone being lifted
He makes a mental note
To repeat his hymn often
And returns to preening his feathers.

Gurdit, trying to fight back a bout of bitter disappointment at their setbacks, muses: "Given the magnitude of their own culpability in handling this affair I wonder how far the Canadians will really go to remove us from their sights.

"British subjects? Hah! There's a farce for you if I ever saw one. And now they expect us to mute our discomforting protests and quietly tuck our wings beneath us and fly off into the western horizon. They say we are breaking every law they have passed, and that we are an embarrassment to the entire Empire; that we have not only broken the laws of this dominion but the laws governing exit from our own homeland. And now even the fragile puppet that calls itself the Indian Government will not voice a whimper of protest in our support.

"In the discordant voices gathered at the increasingly rowdy and fractious meetings of the inner circle that is the Komagata Committee, no consensus has yet been arrived at. And I, as their formal arbiter must now step forward and boldly make the audacious resolution for them."

"We will not go down without a fight," it is none other than his secretary Daljit's voice. "Up till now, whenever we have been confronted with an obstacle that we could not surmount we have relied on our faiths and the force of our own collective wills. It is time now for us fight back. We came here to challenge those very same injustices that we are fighting back home. And leave if we must, we shall do so in the most dramatic manner so that our humiliation is made as universally public as possible. Our efforts cannot all have been in vain."

Surveying the gentle rise of the Vancouver cityscape, the surface of its shore waters becalmed as if a chador had been laid over it, Gurdit can see the ornate stone facades of buildings facing cobbled streets, and all is peaceful on this quiet sunny afternoon beneath the grating overhead of seagulls. Not a cloud in the sky. To him, this soporific city looks deceptively forbearing and magnanimous. Watching the humans scurrying across its paved streets, he is reminded of the hum of a fragile beehive, yet secretly animated in its inner workings as an anthill underfoot. Everywhere he looks, he sees timber - from the peripheral lands of the outskirts bristling with uncleared tree stumps, to the structures of buildings, abutments, and facades – they are all wooden structures. He realizes with a sudden insight how devastating a potential firestorm could become here. The Shore Committee has even offered just such a proposal, listing the woefully inadequate inventory of the local fire brigade.

Their urgent messages to him have claimed: "In the desperation of this moment we have the element of surprise on our side. There are men already roaming these streets who can carry out your word. A signal of some sort and Vancouver's three frenetic decades of hard-won achievements shall be wiped out in less than an hour."

But Gurdit has been reluctant to offer his acquiescence, pondering only on the fact that how soon we forget how difficult it is to build something and yet so easy to destroy. "This pretentious city," he muses, "is barely three decades old. Lahore, Bombay, Calcutta, Delhi, have all thrived for centuries, millennia even. Barely two months after its incorporation this entire city before me was once levelled by a firestorm within a mere twenty minutes. A blink of an eye in the scale of time. Yet, within a matter of days, I have heard it said that, out of these ashes the new city arose like a phoenix, on sturdier, firmer foundations built to last centuries. Yet all I see now is still made of timber. How would the new city hold up to another such firestorm this day? Would I go down in posterity as the man who out of personal frustrations gave the order for such a wanton conflagration? And how could this pan into achieving our undertaking?

"As for me, my personal mission is not yet over. We came here not only to challenge an empire but also to draw attention of the world to its hypocrisies and our plight in it. Now, after having achieved each of these goals, there is still work to be done. Just look, how these originally placid and unresponsive onboard comrades of mine have been transformed by their experiences here. How easily we have forgotten that our real battle is back in India, with Canada only a minor skirmish to it. And, once we return… once we return empty-handed and they hear how poorly we have been treated, surely it will give rise to a new rebellion.

"I may have been defeated in my first goal of landing on the American continent, but once we head for home we shall carry with us a new and furious determination that will eventually unleash a firestorm that is sure to drive the intruder out. Each of these 350 transformed men will return as one torch that has been lit from a single source and whose hearts share a common aspiration.

"I once set out to help my desperate brethren, and make a little money in the process and what have I wrought? They are all in a worse plight than before I met them. Would it have been better for them if I had not meddled with my good intentions? Who would have blamed me then or held me responsible, if I had done nothing and carried on with my existing enterprises? I would then have been a far richer man. Instead, I am now stuck here with this headmaster breathing down my neck, a two-headed monster watching my every move, and the security apparatus of three different countries out to foil all my schemes?

"If we leave now we could head for a more welcoming shore. What port could possibly be more unwelcoming than this one here?

"Perhaps we should head for Brazil. I have heard that it said that there is land there to be cleared, and the soil is rich, and fine timber is easily accessible. There is a profit to be made moving men into the forest and the trees back to East Asia. Fortunately, for us, there is still land at the other end of the known world that the British hand has not yet sullied, and where we can establish a foothold to welcome others who follow in our footsteps. There are already well-established Indian communities along the coast. The jungle will supply the raw materials for export; the towns will provide the labour and passengers for my Sri Guru Nanak fleet.

"This new plan of action seems real enough for now that I can smell the jungle rot carried over the sea breeze. Silt laden waters are rolling into the mangrove stands. There are miles and miles of all this stretching up and down the coast.

"Nearly fifty days and nights of standing still, anchored so tantalizingly close to a harbour. The anchor will finally be withdrawn from the water, and under a cloud of gathering steam my Guru Nanak Jahaz will finally swing its prow around, head east, round the park's headland and then head west. And once it has cleared the facing islands it will soar southwards beyond the California coast, beyond Mexico, and still further south than I have ever sailed, until it is warm once again and the tropical forested coastline will appear wavering like a mirage above the horizon. One stiflingly humid morning, Brazilia will rise out of the mists. We will settle there, free from persecution, and the curse of the Englishman… and this endless incarceration will seem but a moment's respite. I can already smell the jungle rot."

# HUNGER FOR EARTH

After the waters receded
Raven watched idly as men and beast of every ilk
Emerged
Basking in the sun
Celebrating each drying patch of land
While staking their claims.


Raven's territory
A rock a cave a tree branch here
Hollow tree trunk there
Mine he caws in pronouncing dominion
Seeking others of his tribe to bear witness
He counts none.

When there is no more land to fill the void
The emptiness grows and grows
Soon men begin gathering stones
Testing for heft and heave
They strip reachable branches
They light fires
Hone rough edges.

Raven flies deep into the remaining sky.

# BATTLE OF BURRARD

*Jaako raakhe saayian maar sake na koi*

One who is protected by God, cannot be killed by anyone

(Guru Nanak Devji)

Sunday, July 19, 1914

Minutes after midnight the alarm finally goes off.

Ever since we ran out of our last morsel of food we have been staving off hunger with bouts of frantic activity, the only available option for seizing control over our destinies. We knew that since the immigration officials wanted to starve us to death by forcing us to head back for Asia without an adequate supply of food or water, a confrontation of some sort was inevitable. With this possible scenario in mind, Gurdit has already sent out a note to the Shore Committee through his secretary Daljit Singh that the passengers were now ready to 'die and kill' if police were to forcibly try to come aboard.

We began our preparations by constructing wooden barricades across the deck, and stockpiling lumps of fire coal from the cargo holds to use as missiles. We hauled up driftwood from the Burrard Inlet and began honing these into weapons and projectiles. We practiced various scenarios of how we might be attacked, the military training of several of our men coming in handy.

As recently as yesterday, our captain had yet again abandoned his ship on some lame premise, and when he returned we decided not to let him back onboard. And, with the captain's departure had also gone the sycophantic, groveling, unctuous, importune Dr. Raghunath. This doctor who had been hired by Gurdit at the onset of our journey, had recently kept himself busy scribbling one incriminating letter after another in self-righteous protest, and fabricating lies against Gurdit, the Komagata Maru committee. In these efforts he had even named individual passengers so that he could foment and redirect official hostilities directly towards us.

We knew that our desperate act would not go unpunished for long, and we had done our best to prepare ourselves for what would be the opening gambit in the continuing tug-of-war between the passengers of the Komagata Maru and the Canadian Immigration authorities.

Now, out the enveloping dark our observers have located several boats loaded with militiamen heading towards us. Within minutes several hired boats crammed with security guards have begun circling us to gauge the best approach.

I notice that the Sea Lion has once again been engaged for this purpose. Seeing the scow's top deck crammed with crates of food supplies I can only surmise that this time it is on a delivery mission. In fact, it is ferrying provisions that Mr. Reid has deemed adequate to last us during the return Pacific crossing. For nearly two months this tower of logs has hounded us, ostensibly looking for suspicious activities on and around the ship, its searchlight playing on us at odd hours of the night. The Sea Lion has also come armed with an equally annoying piece of equipment, a steam whistle that operates on a sliding scale such that the bored crewmen have been able to tease us by playing short snippets of popular songs. Is that a snippet from the 'White Canada Forever' that they are now playing to goad us into action?

This delivery service is also accompanied by a boarding force of about a hundred odd armed men and dozens of specially deputized immigration officers, also armed with rifles. And, though the tugboat is a sizeable vessel, its deck is woefully crammed with men jostling for position amongst the crates of food.

This expeditionary force, we will learn later, is the result of a late evening meeting that took place yesterday. News of Mewa's arrest in possession of weapons was barely two days old and still fresh in their minds the police. They already suspected that we could now use some of these guns and ammunition if an attempt was made to openly storm the ship. And, Vancouver's pride, 'the peoples' dick', the parliamentary member, Harry Stevens, was able to lay out a detailed strategy for attack. His plans call for boarding our ship with men armed with open bayonets, and he has assured Vancouver's Police Chief McLennan that with the element of surprise on their side against a few hundred unarmed men with a pistol or two between them to deal with, this explosive situation can now be swiftly dealt with once and for all.

"This is just the opportunity we have been waiting for," he has assured the police chief, "and we can head them off out to open sea now and be rid of them forever. We have the strategic advantage of surprise working in our favor, while they are starving and sitting pretty in the open water. All we need do is mosey along with a few armed men and nudge these fakirs in the right direction. In fact, I am convinced that at this point in our negotiations all we need do is show up and put the message forcefully across to them. By early morning this sordid mess will all be behind us. What can possibly go wrong?"

Famous last words, these.

We watch silently as the Sea Lion cautiously approaches within hailing distance of our ship, its probing searchlight sweeping across the deck. The light reveals a line of fierce men leaning from the Komagata's railings, each person armed with all manner of spears, staves and swords that have been crudely fashioned out of wood and odd metal parts.

Moving the tug starboard to the ship's portside, the first move is made by the tug's captain as he hurls a grappling hook into the ship's railing. As the line holds it seems that all is going according to plan and the boarding will take place as scheduled. Other lines are hastily positioned to tie the Sea Lion securely to the ship.

At this point, the deck suddenly comes to life, erupting in a single united shriek as men use axes to swiftly chop down the tug's grappling lines. Others begin to hurl showers of coal, firebricks, clubs, iron bars, hatchets and other missiles onto the exposed and crowded tugboat deck. They manage to injure several of their adversaries in the very first few minutes of the engagement. A number of police helmets have tumbled into the water, and at least one police officer has been knocked down onto the deck. Others have been injured by blows to the head.

Someone on deck shouts that he has spotted the bowler hat of Harry Stevens and the gold braided cap of Hopkinson inside the pilothouse. In the confusion, impetuous Herman Singh, the only one onboard possessing a revolver, now rapidly fires four shots in the direction of the Sea Lion's pilothouse. No one is sure if he found his target. One of the policemen, seizing upon the urgency of the situation, draws his revolver and aims it at the mass of men pressed against the ship's railings. Harry Stevens swiftly cuts him off with the command: "You fool, don't you dare use your gun until the chief gives orders."

For nearly fifteen minutes the barrage of various odd missiles continues, with the tug seeming to be at the receiving end of a coal chute, while trying desperately to retreat but unable to do so as it is still tethered to the ship. The ship's passengers have by now succeeded in getting an upper hand and keeping the policemen at bay using nothing better than rock-coal and improvised staves. They also have the added advantage of towering ten feet over the tug. As the searchlight rakes wildly across the decks, a water spray propelled at high pressure from a hose is brought to play on the men. This momentarily halts the flight of hurled objects but the tug is still unable to tear itself free. A constable on the tug, who has been struck several times, finally picks up a cabbage from one of the crates and hurls it towards the ship's deck.

In the dim light, mistaking the cabbage for a bomb, an urgent warning spreads fast among the ship's men and they move en away masse from the railings. In the hiatus the constable now bravely leaps forward and using a hatchet manages to sever the remaining line, thus allowing the tug to move away slowly back into the night and head for shore. It retreats through the water surface now littered with police helmets and odd pieces of wood projectiles.

Seeing the tug retreating, the men onboard the ship let out a loud cheer, this one louder than the rallying cry of attack. Over the noise of the celebrations someone shouts triumphantly: "We will cut the hearts out of any dogs of the white race that come aboard the Komagata."

Thus concludes the first chapter of the Battle of Burrard in our favor. However, amidst the celebrations, we were all sure the second confrontation was not going to be nearly as one-sided.

Our jubilant mood did not last for long. By Monday morning, a mortified Stevens had used all his influence to summon one half of Canada's navy arsenal, the HMS Rainbow that was currently stationed at Esquimalt on the east coast of Vancouver Island. By Tuesday morning, it headed into the Georgia Strait, crossed the First Narrows passage and come to rest next to Komagata Maru. As an additional precaution two hundred members of the Irish Fusiliers and Sixth Regiment were also mobilized to effectively deal with the next looming confrontation. Once again the plan was to storm the ship by pulling up alongside and then sending soldiers with fixed bayonets over the gangplanks. But this time, the threat would be enforced by HMS Rainbow's array of two six-inch and six four-inch guns, four twelve pounders, as well as its fourteen-inch torpedoes. This impressive armament would have been no match against any other navy of the world, but against an unarmed junk trawler it could only prove to be an overwhelming menace.

But by then, seeing the suffering of the men onboard and the prospect of being pushed into the Pacific with no provisions, Gurdit, the onboard Komagata Committee and the Shore Committee, had already capitulated. A final meeting with the Shore Committee members was hastily arranged onboard the Komagata Maru to persuade those onboard to look upon these concessions favorably, and provisions for the homeward journey were negotiated with officials representing the Dominion. T h u r s d a y, July 23rd, dawns with a clear sky and a slight nip in the air, yet it will turn out to be one of the hottest days of the year. Even this early in the morning huge ra-ra crowds have returned to festoon the rooftops of the post office and every accessible waterfront building. Following a celebratory pattern established during the last few weeks, thousands of lawyers and office workers are now jockeying for position for a favourable view of the historic events unfolding in the Burrard Inlet. At the northern ends of Burrard and Howe streets thousands more are milling around and watching the activity on the water. A large number of spectators also crowd the shore above the Canadian Pacific Railways tracks looking down over the Coal Harbour.

As Iqbal Hundal, a young Southeast Asian boy watches the belligerent crowd milling around excitedly at Pender Street, he sees the familiar figure of a local mill worker Pratabh Singh baiting the restive crowds. Pratabh is so overcome with frustration and the jibes of the gathered crowd that he hurls out a rallying cry: *"One on one, anyone?"*

With the eyes of the world focused on his small-town Vancouver, Dilip Singh Uppal, a member of the Shore Committee has spent all his free time during the last two months collecting provisions for the Komagata passengers. He watches sullenly as the waterfront crowds briefly pick up the verses that have been bandied about throughout this historic week:

*We welcome as brothers*
*All white men still*
*But the shifty yellow race*
*Must find another place...*
*This is the voice of the west and its voice is*
*White Canada forever, one watchword ...'*

Unable to sustain their numbers and the volume required to keep the verses flowing the crowd is easily distracted.

A few minutes before sunrise at 5:10 a.m., with the Rainbow's exposed guns still pointed at it, the Komagata Maru with its 352 original passengers still on board lifts her anchor and sails eastwards. The Canadian sea pilot Barney Johnson, who had exactly two months earlier guided this ship into the inlet, now guides it around Brockton Point and out of view of the hundreds of spectators. For nearly two decades the Komagata Maru had carried tens of thousands of immigrants to Canada but had never before been turned back, in fact, it will now be known as the first ship bearing migrants to be turned away from a Canadian shore. Mercifully, the passengers are as yet not aware that before them is another anticipated port of call at which the Komagata Maru will be equally unwelcome.

The HMS Rainbow today accompanies the Komagata Maru as far as the three-mile boundary at the southern tip of Vancouver Island when the Canadian sea pilot is removed and Captain Yamamato returns to guide the ship back to Asia.

The HMS Rainbow then taps out one brief message to the Esquimalt station confirming completion of her mission:

*'Passed out, Komagata Maru, under Rainbow convoy.'*

## WEEKLY REPORT OF THE DIRECTOR OF CRIMINAL INTELLIGENCE, SIMLA, INDIA DATED 22ND SEPTEMBER 1914.

'The latest news of the Komagata Maru is that she is coming straight to Calcutta from Singapore and not via Colombo. Arrangements to meet her at Calcutta have been concerted between the Bengal and Punjab Governments and this Department. There is reason to believe that the attempts to smuggle arms on board were not altogether unsuccessful, as it is reported that during the fight with the police in Vancouver harbor two or three shots were fired from the ship.'

# HOPKINSON LECTURES
## 11 a.m. 20th October 1914

Attending: Constables Gordy, Eric, Seamus, Robbie, O'Riley, McCormick.

Clearing his throat nervously, Hopkinson erases from the blackboard the last vestiges of yesterday's lecture on the new rezoning of the police units. He is allergic to the milky swirls of chalk dust that his motions have launched into the shafts of sunlight. Characteristically reticent, being cast in the role of a lecturer does not come naturally to him, and he keeps his back turned to the men until he feels comfortable that the right moment has arrived. By then he has completed tracing a perfect oval the size of a human face.

There are six police constables gathered in the wide high-ceilinged barn-like room that has four large windows facing the sun. A flood of golden sunlight pours into the room through the five-foot high murky glass panes. A set of skylights is also positioned above these into the arched ceiling. This building had originally been built for use as a cannery, the large banks of windows designed to let in maximum light. Cigarette and pipe smoke now mingles with dust mites swirling in these shafts of bright light, thus making the air come alive. This creates the illusion of a transient solidity where even the unlit volumes of space have come alive with stormy whirlpools, and where even the slightest movement of the inhabitants sends the slices of light into a disarray of bustling chaos.

Squinting into the distant eastern horizon Hopkinson notices a vivid bank of clouds beginning to mass. The realization enters his conscious mind that with age he has become more sensitive to bright light. He raises a hand to his brow to shield himself from the light and to silence the rounds of gossip in the room.

Years of delivering training lectures have taught him to open the session with an anecdote. And, given his knack for retaining seemingly trivial and unconnected bits and pieces of information from his intelligence reports, there is never a paucity of appropriate accounts he can dredge up for the occasion.

"Does anyone of you men know why a group of German army generals spent most of last summer following a local circus from city to city across America?"

The audience is suddenly attentive and silenced.

"Sir, they may have been seeking an alternate line of work." This comes from a burly constable slouched in a seat close to the blackboard.

"I know, I know," pipes in another voice from within the cloud

185

of tobacco smoke. "They probably thought the army is a circus of sorts, so why not look at the circus for fresh recruits."

"Maybe, they should have been studying O'Riley's antics here instead of the circus," someone chips in.

Half-hearted laughter follows.

"Actually, they were hoping to understand how such a disjointed group of performers and props could cohesively and continuously perform at such peak levels." Hopkinson offers up the answer. "Often, at very short notices the circus is required to be able to dismantle a monstrously large complex of smoothly functioning structures - such as people, supplies, tents, facilities, booths, housing - and then ship all these out to set up shop at a new location within a matter of days. I ask you men, are armies on the move any different than relocating circuses?"

It is late in the morning and the men are restless, sucking at their cigarettes and pipes, anxious over the unlearning of their old ways, and then acquiring unfamiliar techniques. This one has been foisted upon them by their well meaning but idealistic chief of police, the forty-four year-old Malcolm MacLennan. The chief has insisted that the Vancouver police department step into the new century by adopting modern techniques of detection.

Barely a week ago by Reid had indicated to Hopkinson the reason he had been chosen for this training assignment. With his immigration staff of inspectors and translators all gathered in his sunlit office, he had pointed out to Hopkinson that the department an efficient method for separating large crowds into identifiable individuals.

"Your system of classifying individuals by their unique distinguishing marks will go a long way in this identification process and then holding each individual accountable for his actions," he had stressed.

"Any face can be quickly altered," Hopkinson now announces to his captive audience.

"Shave a man bald of all visible hair, then give him a moustache and a beard, and a pair of horn-rimmed spectacles, and not even his mother will recognize him. And, by the way, this is exactly what some despicable characters I encounter in my line of work have done.

"Now, what I ask you gentlemen, is the single most precise identifier of human features, even in the absence of identifiable facial hair?"

"The eyes?" someone attempts as an answer.

"… and yet how would you classify a particular pair of eyes, other than the obvious colour of the irises. Your honour, the criminal had blue eyes. So what?"

"A person's height," offers Eric, and Hopkinson dismisses it as unworthy of a response, offering only two words 'high heels'.

He follows this response with the drawing of a series of embedded whorls, circling them with an oval outline, and then tapping the board he announces:

"This is a typical human fingerprint. As far as we know today, it is the single most precise measurement of a person's identity. No two are identical in their pattern of whorls. Or, let's just say, contrary to all speculation, we have not discovered an identical one just yet. But before we talk about the uniqueness of the fingerprint, lets briefly talk about another method of identification of unique body parts, the Bertillion Method.

"Let just us say we were to take, oh, say fourteen different measurements of any visible body part of just one person."

He scribbles '14' at the top right-hand corner of the blackboard.

"Now, what would you say are the odds of finding another person with identical measurements for the similar body part?"

He peers expectantly at the drowsy and befuddled peacekeepers before him, not one of them now willing to risk his neck or venture a lucky guess. And then staring into the swirling mass of dust mites before him he mimes the act of making a complex mental calculation in mid-air. He turns around, and with only a moment's hesitation writes: '286,435,464' beneath the number '14'.

"Does anyone know how I arrived at this magical number?"

Seeing there are no responses, he continues: "I could just as well have written any other nine-digit figure and it would be valid for the sake of this discourse. The odds, no matter how you stack them up, of matching fourteen similar parts from two different individuals are astronomical. However, accurately measuring fourteen different body parts is impractical in the field.

"Now, to return to the fingerprint. Our very own Scotland Yard adopted the fingerprint classification system at the turn of the century. It was originally devised by one named Sir Edward Richard Henry. There you heard it right, three first names.

"Subsequent fingerprint classification systems are all generally an extension of Sir Henry's system. His 1892 book, 'Fingerprints', includes the first such classification system for fingerprints, and it firmly established the individuality and permanence of fingerprints...."

Midway through the lecture, Hopkinson is distracted by a sudden darkening before him of the skylights and the massed array of windowpanes. The effect has been so sudden that he imagines an electric switch being thrown or someone abruptly lowering shutters over the windowpanes. He swiftly moves to the pane closest to him, noticing that the banks of distant cumulus have now begun to block the sun.

For several moments he watches whole continents of cumulus being sloughed off like icebergs from their continental mass, and then begin to crowd the eastern horizon. These massed bulkheads are stippled with silvery blotches like a quivering salmon heading his way.

Hopkinson also notices that directly below his window, a street-cleaner is leaning on his broom, staring vacantly at the flow of streetcars, hansom cabs, motorbuses and cars, while pedestrians and fleet jitneys dodge in and out of traffic. Dark ribbons of drooping telegraph lines crisscross over the sidewalk, upon which a restless flock of starlings rises in unison and swirls through the air like a shoal of fish in a pool, as if it were collectively listening for some hidden signal to migrate, before settling back onto the wires.

Hopkinson returns to the lecture, barely able to pick up the lost thread of his narrative.

"By the way, has anyone of you noticed anything unusual lately around the False Creek area, a sudden dying of fish in the seasonal streams …?"

"Actually sir, this is quite a normal occurrence in that part of the city," a slim intent looking constable named Seamus remarks. "The industrial waste drains directly into these streams and the dying of fish in great numbers is a fairly common occurrence. Last summer, the whole area wreaked so heavily of dead fish that you could be smell it all over downtown. Even bears were spotted emerging out of the bush to scoop up the loot."

"No, no. This was at a different location. It was further upstream, closer to the Fairview," Hopkinson clarifies.

"Unless, you mean the end of the annual salmon migration... it occurs around this time, you know?"

"There was also a massive failure of the Coho run last year," O'Reilly offers helpfully. "However, I have heard this year's run has been a healthy one."

The salmon that hopkinson had seen littered around Wally's body, had all seemed to have uncharacteristically long, hooked snouts and sharp, canine-like teeth. He had noticed that as the fish lay dying, their bodies were mouldy and had already disintegrated partially. Several wild creatures were feeding directly on them, including several large raccoons, squirrels, even eagles.

Actually, it had been quite by accident that he had stumbled upon Wally's body and this phenomenon of the dying fish.

Ever curious about what nature tucks away from view, something unusual about the vegetation had caught his eye during an evening walk. He had glanced down an embankment to the water and was momentarily stunned. The water was teaming with scarlet salmon that were thrashing languidly in the shallow dappled, rippling stream. However, it was not the presence of so many brightly hued fish present in one place that had startled him, but their desperate state of exhaustion of their flopping, undulating bodies: each of the bright scarlet fish had vast patches of greenish fungus splattered across its flesh. Some individuals were missing whole chunks of their bodies as they lay panting for air through curved beaks, their bodies tangled amidst the rocks and fallen branches, the water sometimes pouring right through the missing flesh.

His first conclusion at the alarming sight had been that the stream must have been poisoned. But then, what could possibly account for the unhurried pace of the predators feeding off the hapless fish. No alarm had been sounded at his approach. The overfed birds were simply unable to launch themselves into air, and the marauding raccoons just barely shuffled out of his way.

Upon closer examination of the scene, he had noticed a human body draped on a fallen tree trunk that was submerged in a few inches of water. And he could easily recognize the cotton undershirt Wally wore during all seasons.

*Wally?* Upon his first arrival in Vancouver from India, Hopkinson had stayed for some time at a downtown boarding house. During that early time when he was still seeking out his bearings and work in a new city he had somehow befriended an elderly man, known to him simply as Wally. Over the ensuing months they had gone out on several fishing trips in exploring the west coast. Perhaps, it was, Hopkinson had been quick to notice, Wally's slightly asocial mannerisms that had allowed them to bond so easily. And, Wally's company had also filled a need in him that Hopkinson had not found easy to identify. Much later it would become easier to pass him off to his family as a long lost relative.

Hopkinson realizes that with so much of his personal history tied to the incident there will be no end to this digression and he cannot go on reliving it forever. There is a lecture still left to deliver and conclude.

"Stop grieving. Don't grieve for those who are not related," the comforting words come intriguingly to him in the voice of his father by way of his mother. Don't grieve. The old man is gone and is buried. Move on.

He clears his throat loudly to draw attention and to regain the lost momentum.

"Anyway, as I was saying, think of the amount of clay needed by a sculptor to construct a face. There is only so much fixed amount of material to redistribute; lighten the nose and the adjacent areas like the cheeks and forehead can now become heavier. You will obviously have seen that nature has its own laws for this distribution through inheritance, which is why abnormalities stand out so much and you can instinctively pick up on them.

"Now, if you take the average face of a man in the street and observe it over his lifetime, then it becomes quite another story. Time distorts most human features, and you come to realize that the face is like a squat statue viewed high up in a cathedral alcove. Did you know the figures in the alcove are deliberately distorted by foreshortening, the legs squat, the upper torso and heads elongated, so that when viewed from the ground level the figure is restored by the eye to the proportions of an average human being?"

He pauses briefly to see if this digression has made any sense to his listeners, and then taps the image he has been tracing. It looks like a standardized version of the face. Next, he erases and retraces the lines with a flurry of bold strokes, transforming the face from youth to dotage and then back. He tags on a beard before erasing it completely.

"Hey, Riley, isn't that your gramps?" This time it is Seamus with the cheeky remark. There are brief appreciative snickers from the audience.

"You see, how we have now stumbled upon a process by which time kneads the salient features of the face like heaps of pliant dough, relocating the geography of the face, and gradually eroding the resistance of cartilage, bone, tissue and muscle. Meanwhile, the skin has become looser and is scoured with blotches of liver spots; the ears and the nose have become elongated, thus shrinking and stretching the skin over this interior beehive lattice of bones. A dull, clouded ring now resides around the iris. Yet, miraculously, the essential ratios between our measurements remain constant. And this is the crux of the Bertillion System."

He is stumped again by an inner voice that points out that this face that he keeps redrawing is beginning to look familiar. "Is it Kartar?" he wonders to himself. "Well, maybe. But then there was another chap, a confused passenger we held captive for a while on the Sea Lion? A Muslim. Amar? Rahim? Did he not have these same features?"

Hopkinson returns absent-mindedly to the blackboard and worries the chalked image with the practiced eye of the taxidermist, teasing illusive details from the limiting material of opposing muscle....

But the inner voice will not be silenced just yet.

"It was something rhyming with '*baksheesh*'. Wait a minute. Wasn't it Bashir! Bashir from Lopoke. There, I have finally it figured out. The last piece of the puzzle that has remained unresolved for so long. First thing tomorrow morning I must wire the India Office and have him picked up immediately before he can do further damage. I wonder why I was not able to see this earlier?"

He returns his attention to the image on the board.

".... Incidental patterns of bone and muscle, like that of the top layer of skin, account for what we mistakenly come to associate as a distinct culture," he continues.

Though Hopkinson has resumed the lecture, a separate part of his mind that has been trained to perform just such a task, has now been set free by the resolved mystery, while another is held captive by the image of the dying fish. It continues to linger over the discovery of Wally's body. How long had the body lain there? What was Wally doing wading in a foot of water?

A distracted Hopkinson moves closer to his multiple reflections in the windowpanes and stares out at the riot of colour just below his line of sight. A boy is hawking newspapers, while another one stands by a street corner, smoking, and kicking a sardine can against the wall. The sweeper has moved further down the street. A blazing maple stands towering over a street corner, littering the pavement below with its extravagance. Miraculously, this flagrant tail end of a summer that refuses to end, is still pumping out vibrant sunny days, and holding the October rains at bay, rains that will eventually pelt the tattered grapevines and rotting pumpkins into submission. Between these final conflagrations of shortened afternoons, and the latticework of tumbled sunrays filtering through a waterfall of green tinted glass there are worlds colliding, and in between their collisions time freezes.

On a day off from work at the mill, the part-time *granthi*, Mewa Singh, is polishing the glass windowpanes of the temple with a rag in one hand. The mechanical repetitive motion sets his mind free to explore the scene outside the temple compound. How soon the summer comes to an end, he muses, while his free hand practices one motion repeatedly, the slide of polished metal across his palm, flexing his bicep in anticipation of its recoil, his palm beginning to blister in the places he has imagined it to be continually braised. He does this obsessively until boredom with the ritual sets in. A troubled part of his mind is unable to come to grips with the thought that no matter how he imagines the scene he cannot see the bullets leave his pistol. But he can always see a white shirt flash before him as it soaks up blood, the stain spreading at an impossibly rapid rate even though there is no visible wound. But the bullets have not left the pistol just yet. Mewa beseeches, over and over: "I haven't fired just yet. *Waheguru*, Am I able to kill with merely a thought? *Waheguru*, what is going on here? What am I doing wrong?"

## FIVE MEN GATHER ON A DESERTED STRETCH OF THE VANCOUVER WATERFRONT. 20th, October 1914

*Balwant Singh:* I have said this repeatedly but no one listens to me anymore. We need to hold our gurdwara meetings in a private and safe place. The minute a meeting is open to one and all, the rats get wind of our plans and then the whole world learns about it.

*Rahim Hussein:* But having closed meetings would undermine the very process of carrying out all our affairs in a transparent and responsible manner. As Sikhs, we hold open meetings so that everyone can share in the decision making process and have their say. Besides, our meetings are not attended by Sikhs only; Hindus and Mussalmans are present as well. A handful of duplicitous, misguided people cannot impact us so heavily that we forget who we are as a community.

*Sohan Lal:* No, if we are to survive here in Kanada and establish a foothold, we must first deal with these three men, Hopkinson, Reid and Stevens. These three are interlinked like bricks in a wall that we need to tear down. So far, they have both done far too much damage to our community. And, somehow, we need to negate them and limit their adverse impact upon us.

*Balwant Singh:* So, are you all with me on what I am proposing?
He looks around for affirmation.

*Natha Singh:* There are five of us. If each one of us sets out to do the needful thing, how many bullets do you think will they be able to dodge?

*Mewa:* Out of the three targets I would choose Reid as the easier one.

There are snickers all around.

*Sohan Lal:* Do we have the required guns and ammunition stashed away?

*Rahim Hussein:* Yes, but how do we determine who will strike first and whom? Shouldn't we draw straws?

*Mewa:* I will do it! There is no need for straws. I will do this alone. Masterji, *do-mui* and the *mimber*. I will do them all. *Saray de saray wadh daN ga!*

There is a brief moment of disbelief before Balwant approaches closer to Mewa and places a hand on his shoulder, embracing him in a bear hug.

*Balwant:* Mewa, *mera jatt veer,* Hopkins is enough for now. Get him and may the Gurus accept your *shahadat.* We are all equally capable and determined as you to carry this out. We all have equal reasons to rid this land of these vermin. But first Hopkins, then the others.

*Mewa:* No, no. This *qurbani* is for me alone, and I am ready for it. Besides, I also have a personal score to settle with the bastard.

Mewa looks around for acknowledgement from the others, finally receiving gentle taps on the shoulder from each one.

*Balwant:* How do you want to carry this out? Fire at him in a dark alley when he is returning home from work? No one will see you this way and you can make good your escape.

*Mewa:* No, no. I have to do this out in the open, and there have to be witnesses. I won't do it like a coward. He has to see my face before he dies.

*Balwant Singh:* Then where?

*Mewa:* I know what I have to do. Let us meet later when I have the pistols in my possession.

*Rahim Hussein:* Pistols. Are you going to need more than one?

*Mewa:* Yes. I need two good ones at least. Guns I know I can rely on. I have to make sure I complete the task.

*Sohan Lal:* Well, if this is settled then all we need to determine is what would be the best time to carry it out. There is no room for error. It has to be done now before the rat can testify on Bela's behalf and spring him from jail once again.

*Balwant Singh:* The deed must definitely be carried out before the Ghadar begins. It may seem today that mid-February is a long way off but we need to start preparing for it now. This is not the same rebellion as that of 1857, and this time with the Guru's blessing we shall not fail. And, be careful whom you talk to out there. All it takes is a single slip of the tongue, a whispered word at the wrong place and no Indian is going to be safe from the angrez's wrath, whether here in Kanada or in India.

The men quickly disperse in different directions.

Much later on this fateful day, many Vancouverites will recall that once the last traces of fog had dissipated, an immense and dazzling slice of the half moon had lingered over the peaks of Vancouver Island. With the sun rising feebly behind Mt. Baker, the half chewed wafer had gently slipped down to earth, disappearing into the Island's western peaks.

Vancouver's grand Victorian-style provincial court is a distinctive landmark, a monument of chiselled stone located at the northwest corner of Georgia and Howe Street. With imposing pillars propping up its striking front facade and a pair of sculpted stone lions guarding its entrance, it is home of the British Columbia Court of Appeal, British Columbia Supreme Court and the County Court for Vancouver. This late in the morning its antechambers, inquest rooms, and waiting benches have been swiftly occupied, and the court is already humming like the secret heart of a beehive.

During the course of this morning three men who are dispersed on the premises of this imposing monument to the British Columbian justice will see the course of their destinies unravel to fateful conclusions.

One of these men is an Immigration department's seasoned translator, the sulking Bela Singh, who for the moment waits nonchalantly to be lead up the spiral staircase into the middle of the courtroom. There he will be asked to wait for that critical moment when the defendant will request an immigration official to step up to the witness box and give testimony on the defendant's behalf and vouch for his impeccable character. He is familiar with the routine that is to be followed, and knows that the invaluable inside information that will be provided in his defence will assure one and all that Bela has indeed provided a vital service to the security of the Dominion. And, he hopes this should be sufficient to set him free. After all, the odd bits of valuable surveillance information he and his men have provided to the immigration and police authorities has been garnered at great personal peril.

But the self-doubts linger. There is this tiny niggling matter of the affair at the Sikh temple that continues to nag at him. The details of this 'tiny niggling matter' are that Bela had recently walked into a prayer meeting at the Kitsilano temple and opened fire on the priest and other worshippers. Half an hour later when Bela finally left the building, three men were already dead.

Bela has tried throughout his weeklong incarceration to not dwell on these details for he has been repeatedly assured that he need not fear any harm from these courts. More alarmingly, he has also been informed that about a hundred Sikhs have turned up for his hearing. Now he waits impatiently for the court to plough its way through the day's formalities of picking up the pieces from yesterday's proceedings, each petition and submission neatly filed within his lawyer's leather carrying case.

In a few minutes time, the defence will call upon Immigration Chief Inspector William Charles Hopkinson to vouch for Bela's unimpeachable character. This should then set in motion the formalities for Bela's release.

Hopkinson is late. Momentarily stepping outside his door to see what kind of a morning it is going to be, he retreats back into the house to leave his umbrella behind.

'Nellie's Brollies', indeed, he grins recalling an earlier conversation.

Barely a few feet from his doorstep, the first traces of an autumnal fog have completely blotted out the landscape. The fog is thickest near the waterfront, with wisps of it forming and reforming with the drifting inland breeze. He is glad to be setting out early.

The brief walk downhill from Fifth to Fourth Avenue takes barely a minute or two. Even at this early hour, the street is already busy with pedestrians heading off for work downtown. He passes horse carriages laden with produce, and a man on a bicycle, their passage briefly disturbing the muffled silence within the fog. There is still no sign of the streetcar that will take him downtown, and Hopkinson pulls out a pocket watch and studies its hands intently to check if it's still working. He absent-mindedly plots out the day's itinerary, calculating that at this pace he will probably be too early for the first appointment of his day in court.

He tucks away his personal frustration at Bela's lack of constraint, muttering to himself, "That rascal, I never should have trusted him. Just look at all the muck he is dragging us through."

After nearly ten minutes of patient waiting, and with no sign of his scheduled streetcar, an importune jitney approaches the stop. He signals and climbs aboard. The vehicle with its load of seven passengers and driver lurches unevenly up to Granville and then down to the water's edge, bumping onto the wooden bridge over False Creek.

In spite of his efforts not to do so he finds himself reading the blaring headlines from his newspaper. Buried among the political news are items of Russia's abolition of state sale of alcohol and Britain's reply to the manifesto of German professors. There is news from the war front that the critical heavy bombardment and assault has finally begun on the western front at Dixmude. Arras has also been heavily bombarded and attacked, and at the Argonne, the French have finally begun a recovery. On the Eastern Front, Germans have begun retreating from Warsaw, and Russia has annihilated the Germans who had crossed the Vistula.

Rattling noisily across the wooden trestles over the Granville sandbar, the driver notices a large crowd milling around a stalled streetcar at the opposite end of the bridge. This crowd is partially blocking their path. From his high vantage point in the raised backseat of the vehicle, Hopkinson can see that a farm wagon has tipped over sideways in front of the streetcar, and that several of the loaded metal canisters of milk now lie scattered by the roadside. Some of the milk has begun to pour down the wood trestles of the bridge.

Hopkinson can see directly below him a large pale discolouration spreading rapidly over the surface of the dark water.

Examining the dented front of the streetcar, he notices that it is the one he would have taken had it made its way across the bridge and then uphill to Fourth. The collision would also explain the delay.

As he continues to examine the scene, an air of urgency spreads through the massed throng of stretched necks and faces peering down at the ground. A welter of gesturing hands is holding each other back.

Hopkinson can see a pair of tawny hooves thrashing wildly in the air.

With the jitney coming to a standstill he hastily alights to see how he can resolve the situation. The crowd before them suddenly splits apart as urgent shouts of *"stand back, stand back everyone…"* ring out.

A moment later a single gunshot ricochets outwards from the scene of the accident, the blast sending a visible wave of response in the turmoil of stretched human necks and arms and open gesturing palms.

The jolt of the blast alarms a mixed flock of pigeons and seagulls into flight from a surrounding rooftop.

Several moments pass before the silence gently seeps back. The twitching body of the workhorse, now a jumble of limp legs and drooping head, is dragged to the side of the road; the passengers pile back into the jitney, and they finally manage to go round the obstruction and resume their trip.

Hopkinson once again glances briefly at his watch, tapping its dial and testing the tension on the windup knob to ensure it is still functioning, realizing with a sinking feeling that he will now definitely be late for his appointment. However, he also knows from experience that court routines always have a way of winding down endless paths in acquiring a life of their own, uncannily filling up any void they encounter. And, the trifling inconvenience of a delayed testimony will in no way adversely impact the day's proceedings.

Hastily alighting at the Robson crossing and briefly glancing at the shop windows already advertising winter's fashions, he makes his way west through the sidewalk crowds. He covers the block briskly until he is standing before the stairs leading up to the Roman columns of the British Columbia provincial courthouse.

It is nearly the end of October and there is yet no sign of the cold. Among the throngs gathered at the entrance of the court are men still dressed in light summer suits that flap in the cool breeze. A few dark weather-coats can also be seen.

Hopkinson notices that there is a throng of Indians gathered at the main entrance to the courthouse, awaiting their registration before entry. He can recognize a few of them from earlier proceedings in this case. He spots Basant Singh, Sohan Lal and Natha Singh shuffling into the line up, neither of them establishing eye contact with him. And, after Hopkinson has been ushered into the building, he makes his way up the stairway to the second floor entrance of the Assizes court to await his summons.

Minutes later, Hopkinson is seen slouching next to a wooden bench at the Barrister's entrance with both his hands in his trouser pockets. He glances anxiously at the wall clock opposite him as it marks the hour, the hands clicking audibly into position.

10:00 o'clock precisely.

This timepiece, like its several facsimiles scattered all over the building, is only a faceplate having no clockwork mechanism of its own. Instead, it is connected by miles of narrow copper tubing to an ingeniously designed master clock lodged in the main rotunda of the building. As each passing minute is accurately counted off, an invisible pulse of compressed air is launched to each of the clocks. Hopkinson watches as another minute is counted off.

10:01 a.m.

There is one other occupant seated next to him on the bench, waiting patiently for his turn to be called into the courtroom. And, a while later, when the man is finally called in, Hopkinson has enough time to examine his surroundings more closely.

This length of the corridor, though cut off from direct natural light, is dimly lit with electric lamps that are positioned at intermittent distances such that they create islands of diffused light. Brighter natural light spills out of the stairwell. The cast iron heating sideboard beside him hisses over its patch of marble floor. He becomes aware for the first time of the sumptuous and ornate marble arches and the heavy, dark polished wooden doors that surround him. The floor, he observes, is laid out in an odd pattern of alternating black and white square linoleum tiles laid diagonally. His survey of his surroundings is momentarily interrupted as a member of the clerical staff steps out of a room and begins to clumsily drag behind him a trolley overflowing with files and registers, and heads for the door to the courtroom. Recognizing Hopkinson near the door he waves wanly, intent on the task of getting the barrister's reference materials delivered on time. The wheels of the trolley produce an audible rhythm in rattling over the square tiles in passing from the dark to the lighter tiles. A heavy wooden door slams in the distance as muffled sounds of human exchange escape across the door. Into the silence that follows the clock ticks off another minute.

10:06 a.m.

The stillness of the rectangular passageway is suddenly interrupted as a head peers out from the stairway. Hopkinson instantly recognizes that it is none other than Mewa Singh. Alarmed to see Mewa in the corridor, Hopkinson rises to his feet and watches the man head straight towards him. It has been several months since their last exchange during the Komagata Maru crisis when Mewa had been arrested at Sumas while smuggling guns from the United States.

A monotonous droning of subdued voices drifts out of the courtrooms and mixes with the ambient layers of the hissing of the steam clock and the noise of the street traffic below. Mewa Singh's loud footsteps echo across the marble floor as he swiftly covers the distance separating him from Hopkinson.

When he is within a dozen feet of his victim, Mewa deftly withdraws a pocket, nickel-plated .32 calibre revolver and fires it in quick succession until realizing that the chambers have been emptied.

Caught completely off-guard by the unexpected brazenness of the attack, Hopkinson has had no time to react before the first shots strike him, his assailant having rapidly covered the distance separating them. he is now firing at point-blank range. As Hopkinson sinks to his knees, he grabs his assailant around the thigh.

Hopkinson hears a muffled popping crackle close to his ear. It is followed by a brief period of total silence, in which there is a sudden and unexpected frenzied quickening. There is the muffled sound of desperate shouts in the murky distance, and as he sinks to his knees through a fog of bewilderment, he hears another popping sound, this time from much further away. Clutching the assailant's trouser leg for support, he voicelessly mouths the words: *"You have the wrong man…"*

Having emptied the nickel-plated revolver, Mewa clubs Hopkinson over the head with it. He lets the empty gun drop to the ground, and tugs at his trouser leg to extract a snub-nosed revolver that has been strapped to his shin. He swiftly transfers it from the left hand to his right. The elation of the pent up emotions and tension finally break through to him and he leaps high into the air, each fresh bullet finding its mark.

Within a few seconds he has fired all six of his shots.

With both guns now emptied, Mewa looks down at the crumpled body before him, unable yet to comprehend that the deed has been done. He turns around to see if there have been witnesses to the deed.

Five minutes later William Charles Hopkinson's heart stops beating.

One floor below them, James McCann, the courthouse janitor, had been talking to two other men while standing at the base of the grand staircase. On hearing the firing they have all raced to the upper floor only to encounter a group of eight Hindus heading downstairs for the exit. They find Mewa standing over a slumped human body, a nervous smile on his face, mouthing the words that all the newspapers will carry the next day:

*"I shoot, I go to station."*

McCann rushes forward to prevent Mewa from escaping, seizing him in a viselike grip, even though the latter has offered no resistance.

By the time a doctor comes to his aid, Hopkinson has already been dead for several minutes. A post-mortem will later reveal that he has received six bullets in his body, one of these piercing the heart.


On the long wait inside the locked paddy wagon before the transfer to the police station, the manacled Mewa Singh finds himself dozing off, the elation of the action draining and numbing his entire body.

Seeing how shabbily we had been treated by the Empire at the eastern end of the world, I had been wondering throughout the return voyage why we were still gullible enough to believe that we would be treated any differently when we reached our Indian homes? Our Vancouver counselor had already warned us that we might run foul of the government of India's laws for having exited India illegally.

By the end of the voyage I had also fallen in with a group of men from the village of central Punjabi village of Dhudike. In the jovial company of Bagga Gill, Puran Gill and Jeevan Gill I realized that our pooled resources were barely sufficient for the return journey to Punjab. I think we were still a day or two away from our first port of call, Yokohama, when we first arrived at a consensus. There was no other option realistically available to us but to somehow travel back to the American continent. What we could not yet decide on was whether it would be direct sailing to Canada or America.

About this time Jeevan recalled that one of their neighbors had left a few years ago to settle in California. I had heard Gurdit speak several times of heading for Brazil, but this destination seemed too remote and unsettled a place to meet our needs. Instead, we settled for Mexico.

We had hoped throughout the voyage that once we touched land that was not sullied by the meddling of the British, and recited our travails to our compatriots, our plight would be on everyone's lips. Gurdit-ji even speculated that there would be a public outrage at our treatment, and that this would lead to protests and riots.

Instead, what we received upon reaching Yokohama was the sobering news that while we had been steadily making our westward Pacific crossing, the Europeans had become embroiled in a global confrontation and everyone else was also pre-occupied with the novelty of a world war. The sensational news of our arrival on the Asian coast was hastily brushed aside and went unmarked. There were no popular uprisings, no celebrations of our survival, and no one yet seemed willing to take up our cause for justice in the global court.

It did, however, feel wonderful after a period of nearly five months to finally have the firmness of land beneath our feet once again. Yet, our immediate plans were to set off all over again on an unpredictable path. The outcomes of this contemplated journey would be equally unpredictable as when we first set out on our bullock cart ride out of our villages, the week long train journey to Calcutta, the two-day voyage from there to Hong Kong, and then onto the doomed Komagata Maru.

Making inquiries onshore, Bagga located a small cargo trawler that was heading for Mexico within a day of our arrival. We settled on a passage using this vessel to make one last attempt at getting back into Canada. My father had always cautioned me: "When you wish to overcome an insurmountable hurdle you must approach it obliquely". Perhaps, Mexico, being as far from our Vancouver as we were prepared to get, would be a more hospitable alternative.

Incidentally, the Empress of Japan had also berthed opposite us, and as we watched we could see its Canadian passengers accompanying their baggage ashore.

While provisions were being lugged into the holds of Komagata, we took advantage of the ensuing confusion, and bidding our hasty farewells descended the gangway one final time with a few belongings. Gurdit himself waved at us wanly as we descended, perhaps already thankful that there were four less mouths to worry about. What lay ahead for them was still lost in the future, whereas we finally had the freedom to choose our own paths.

The enormity of what we had managed to achieve only began to sink in once our trawler began retracing the route of our first outbound passage. Somehow, these immense distances had now shrunk and become manageable. The Empire seemed a much smaller entity to challenge, perhaps, one that could, one day be taken on by a more united, smarter and better organized group of rebels. As for me, my days of rebellion seemed over for now. All I wanted was to claim my piece of land, earn a decent wage, and lead a quiet life.

A week into the journey we encountered the first squall, the water briefly turning the colour of chai, but the rest of the voyage proved uneventful.

Within twenty-five days we sailed into a Mexican harbour.

Mexico turned out be a pleasant surprise as the indian community there had already heard about the voyage and tragedy of the Komagata Maru. And, though their hospitality knew no bounds we were in hurry to get back to Vancouver before the onslaught of the proverbial Canadian winter. Our hosts were all Punjabi immigrants from Hoshiarpur, Jullundur, and Ludhiana districts of Punjab. In settling here they had initially found work on the Western Pacific Railways of Northern California. The men we noticed had mostly abandoned their beards in an attempt to fit in with rest of the locals. This community helped us reach the San Joaquin Valley of California, a location that was remarkably similar in climate and demography to the irrigated areas of the Punjab. It was here we met the remarkable, and magnanimous, Jawala Singh, the region's 'Potato King'.

While we stayed with him for a few days to prepare for the

journey ahead, he introduced us to the rest of the community with an account of their struggles to establish a foothold.

"When we came here initially a decade ago, we were able to establish ourselves quickly due to our familiarity with farming techniques," he told us in his commanding stentorian voice, "and that gave us an advantage over the American settlers of these newly irrigated areas of the San Joaquin valley. We made good money but soon found out that we were unable to buy respect. We were insulted, despised and discriminated against everywhere. So, when we heard of the publication of the Ghadar paper in San Francisco last year, my partners Wasakha, Santokh, Sohan Bhakna, Kesar, and Kanshi Ram and I were the first ones with offers to support it."

When Jawala bhai offered us assistance in our impending journey, he could not believe that we were attempting to cross the Canadian Rockies so late in the year.

But, he was able to reassure us. "I know just the man who can guide you in this enterprise but to meet him you will have to wait a while. For now make yourselves at home here." With these words he sent for our guide.

When Baba Udham Singh, arrived two days later, we were surprised to see that how elderly and handicapped he was. He suffered from such a severe limp that he could barely walk unaided, and had to be carried everywhere by two men. But, what we also noticed when he rose to his unsteady feet to greet us, was that his spirit was still as indomitable as his name.

For a few of the productive years in his life he had worked on building the Canadian Pacific Railway lines between Calgary and Vancouver, and he was now a patriarch of a large harmonious Mexican-Hindu community. Some of the men in his community had married Hispanic women; usually sisters or female relatives who married Punjabi business partners, thus forming joint households and raising families that took the best of both cultures and made one harmonious world out of it.

"I suppose you are all wondering how I am going to be able to guide you when I can barely walk by myself," he announced to us in a rasping and fluted singsong voice. "Put your minds at rest. I have no intention of making this foolhardy journey myself. If I didn't already know your history I would have asked you if someone else had set you up to this - crossing the Rockies on foot so close to winter? I wouldn't have made such an attempt even in my youth.

"There is now only one reason why I am willing to assist you in getting back to One-Couver. Down here they call us 'dirty Hindus' and even worse, 'half and halves'. Even though we were the first to introduce rice to this region making everyone who worked with it very rich, yet when the goras do not want to sell us the land we have to buy it in our women's names. Now there is talk of laws that will further deny the men, and even our Amriki wives, the rights to have deeds to their own land. Some of the women of our community who are from Yuba-Sutter, Fresno and Imperial Valley, will lose all they own. Our Memel Singh even stands to lose everything. Up until now we have gone around this dilemma by forming verbal partnerships with some of the Amrikis to hold the land for us. But I see a time coming when this will no longer work. I see your determination to help our communities establish a firmer foothold here in Amrika and Kanada, and wish I were twenty years younger."

And, with that clarification the matter was finally settled. Over the next two days as we fed ourselves silly on rotis that tasted like tortillas and corn tortillas that tasted like corn rotis, Babaji Udham prepared us for the arduous journey that lay ahead. I took copious notes, yet it was the singsong tone in which he recited the instructions that was to stay with me.

We were too polite, however, to ask about his leg until the day came to say our farewells.

He gave each one of us prolonged hugs. "In case you have been wondering about this leg," he began by tapping the wooden peg with his cane. "You will have heard of the Panama Canal that has opened recently. Well, everyone knows that it took ten years to complete, is fifty miles across and cost millions to build. But what no will admit to you is that there was a death for every mile that it saved in South American circumnavigation. Mine is just a small token of that adventure. Let the Amrikis chew on that.

"Remember, do not linger in the mountains and get out of there as fast as your legs will carry you.

"And, may the Gurus watch over each one of you."

"Remember the order in which they will appear: Calgary, Morley, Banff Hotspring, Canmore, Kicking Horse Pass. Here the Bow River flows southwards and the Columbia River northwards. Then a glacier, which will lead you to Selkrik and to a point at which the Columbia River will begin flowing southwards. Now watch out for the Eagle Pass in the Gold Mountains, which will lead you to Kamloops. From there you follow the tracks till you approach the North Thompson River. The Fraser River will begin flowing south at Lytton. Next you will come to Yale, Hope, New Westminster, and finally Vancouver.

"There! You are home."

Studying these notes I can still hear Babaji Udham's singsong delivery, confident that his advice would see us safely to Vancouver.

To get to Alberta's Calgary you will have to ride the trains through the American Midwest river canyons travelling north from California onwards through to Cascadia's Oregon and Washington states. Turn east to Spokane and then into Idaho followed by Montana, and finally crossing unobserved into Canada at southwest Alberta.

Branch off to the east into Montana before you come close to the BC border and only then head towards Calgary. This will allow you to skirt the south-eastern corner of British Columbia, and even though the temptation to head northwest directly to your destination will be strong, head instead for the north. Calgary is located at the beginning of the foothills of the Rockies and at the end of the eastern plains. Keep going till you come to the city.

At Kicking Horse Pass the switchbacks trace zigzags up the steep slopes. The railway tunnel disappears and reappears several times on the same slope. And, at every exit of the tunnel there is a steep path up the overhanging slope. After the first fortnight, you will have become acclimatized to the rare mountain air, and will become adept at scrambling up fairly precipitous slopes. It takes a cargo train a half hour to puff up a single mountainside. You should be able to do it in fifteen minutes.

While travelling by rail you will become shifting shadows on the compartment walls, unobtrusively sliding to the ground or scuttling off to the washroom to wait out the collector's attention; learning and uncovering the signs that signal a train's arrival at a station. Avoid all unsolicited close attention of fellow travelers.

Out of necessity walk closer together in the gloom of tunnels, wary of the telltale headlight of an approaching locomotive. Remember that the clearance between it and you at such close quarters will be slight and the rush of air can suck you in.

Wherever possible, hide and sleep during daylight hours and walk at night only so that anyone looking out for you will have less of a chance of spotting you. Always walk single file with each person five feet behind the other, and in the dark you must talk continuously to each other. Hum or shout out verses of hymns, folksongs, childhood rhymes, prayer chants, and poems, anything that will keep you awake and inform the others of your presence. When you have exhausted your repertoire, let the slogans of Ghadar sustain you. Look for creative ways to form a tether between one another.

While traversing the switchbacks near the Kicking Horse Pass look down for well-worn chutes that earlier travelers and workmen have carved out of the stony outcrops. Slide down these carefully at every opportunity. Wherever you walk you will find that the surrounding landscape is etched with pathways that take the shortest route between two points.

You only take from the land what you need to sustain yourselves, cautiously disguising your intrusions. And if forced to do so, bargain for your food. Towards dawn each day when you are at the end of your endurance stop by a stream and bathe one by one using the buckets you have lugged with you, then gather in prayer, eat and find a clearing located away from the railroad and pathways.

If you see a mountain lion then holler, and make a nuisance of yourself, stand on each other's shoulders so that you are made formidable. If you see a black bear then play dead and it may sniff at you or take a bite here or there but will leave you alone. And never look a bear in the eye, no matter what type it is. What you have to watch out for are the grizzlies. They are out to hunt and feed. And don't ever think of outracing one. Of course, going downhill will be a different story given that the bear has shorter front legs and racing downhill is always in the danger of tipping over.

A few days out of Calgary we watched a bear racing uphill and covering the entire slope faster than anything we had ever known possible. A day later we watched a grizzly family, a mother with two cubs, scampering down the opposite slope to the valley below us.

> Puran, rolling his eyes at Jeevan in ill-disguised fear:
> "Is it a *ritch*?"
> "Bear or grizzly?"
> "Do you see the V–shaped chest patch?"
> "Yes."
> "Then it is a grizzly. Run."
> "If I see a *ritch* I don't really have to outrace it; all I have to do is

outpace you - the rest will take care of itself."

"*Chal yaar*, what makes you think you can outrun me?"

"Hah, honestly, have you ever seen yourself wheezing up a mountainside? Ten steps and you are panting like an engine running out of steam. I am sure I can do better than you anytime."

'I suspect at this time of the year your greater concern should be for the cold for you will often find yourself shivering even in broad daylight at noon. It begins to snow early in those mountains. Sleet, ice, and the wind and the fear of freezing to death should keep you alert. It will be cold and wet, so always dress warm. Having to choose between the two, avoid getting wet. In rain, whenever you can, wear wool as the outermost garment for even when wet it will keep you naturally warm, but beware of cotton for when it is wet it can freeze to your skin. Cotton can kill you. A gun of any sort will be handy as you are traveling over hundreds of miles of inhospitable country.

You need to average 20 to 30 miles a day if you are to cross the Rockies before the onset of full winter. And wait no longer then mid October to get the hell out of the highlands.

Then follow the CPR rail tracks westwards

All the way to the eastern boundary of BC

You will know you have crossed into BC when the River Columbia after heading north snakes back on itself and begins to flow southwards.'

"How will we know which one is the Columbia and which one the Fraser?" I had inquired.

'The Columbia will be the first large river you will encounter flowing north and then curling back to the south

Next will appear the Thompson

And finally the Fraser which will take you to One-Couver

Stay out of sight as much as possible

Avoid drawing attention to yourselves

When passing through towns spread out

And never be seen traveling together as a group

Spread out thinly, unevenly

You will arouse less suspicion that way

If you see others walking the tracks, avoid them

Do not engage in idle conversation

And whenever you are out of sight of the others

Sing loudly enough for your companions to hear you

But not too loud

And travel only westwards

But be wary of the railway police
And other security personnel in the towns you pass
The locals will be less suspicious and cautious of you
They will not be unduly concerned if you show you do not intend to stay
And are only passing through
Do not show undue interest in the land or the farms and crops
Praise the Gurus and they will protect you
Talk to no one else outside your own trusted group
Sleep under the tarp whenever possible
Let Bashir bhai do the talking since his *angrezi* is better than the rest
Even though you are transients always look presentable
Highland winds, landslides, avalanches
Late summer rains and early autumn snows
These will challenge your ingenuity
Remember wind robs moisture swifter than the sun.'

Wherever the track follows an upward slope we encounter crude gravestones laid out in orderly grids between the stony ridges. However, there is no indication that the Chinese coolies were ever here even though thousands worked and died here. Marvelling at the sweat of the men that had hewed these precarious ledges out of tumbling unsteady rocks, we stumble upon a rectangular gravestone etched with the words: '*Here lies Edward C Burke, (1841-1842) CPR foreman. What I gave, I have; what I spent, I had; what I kept, I lost.*'

Once, after having traversed the steepest part of our journey we awoke to the distant sight of a blue ribbon of water, which appeared to be racing downhill and mercifully falling off to the west.

Or so we argued trying to reassure each other.

Somewhat further west we forged a stream that bifurcated into two tributaries that headed in opposite directions, one east and the other west. Puran promptly began to pee into this stream water, all the while chuckling to himself.

"Look at that, one half is going back to Calgary and the other half to One-Couver. Now, do you think we will get to One-Couver before it does?"

We had been told that we would enter British Columbia when the rivers began flowing west. This knowledge now adds elation to our step, thinking that it would all be downhill from here onwards. And, once we had safely crossed into B.C. we planned to fearlessly hop onto a train and make our way to the outskirts of Vancouver.

Gradually the rocky gravel and scrub gave way to orchards and then pastures where summer wheat stood waiting for harvest and we knew that we had achieved the impossible.

At this stage on the journey it was already getting unbearably warmer but a slight breeze kept things bearable for most days.

While talking to Babaji Udham, Bagga had been especially concerned about the risk of being struck by lightning.

"Of all the potential perils that will beset you along the railway tracks during late summer and early fall, is lightning. Very often waves of thunderstorms mark the end of a heat wave or a late summer such as the one we are having this year. You will have to learn to avoid these, and learn to decipher the signs that a thunderstorm is headed your way."

Jeevan had been sceptical about this. "Babaji, as usual you are exaggerating the peril. Have you ever known anyone who was struck by lightning? In fact, have you even been within miles of someone when they were struck by lightning?

"Well, neither have you, and you are already frightened shitless. See? In fact, I was once walking along a beach that lay parallel to the path of a thunderstorm that was still about six or seven miles across the water. As I watched, thunderbolts struck the water repeatedly. One of these bolts traveled the entire distance to the shore, and suddenly it seemed like midnight at noon. There was a fisherman casting his nets into the shallow water a few feet ahead of me. Within an instant he had collapsed and fallen head first into the water. When I dragged him out onto the sand I saw that his trouser cuffs were still smouldering, and his legs were badly burnt from the feet up to the knees. He never recovered from the shock. I have even heard of farmers being struck down in rice paddies during the monsoons.

"So, are you convinced now?"

We could smell the ocean long before catching the first glimpse of it from a hilltop, its moist warmth welcomed with every breath. Puran had been surveying the mountain view at the time.

"What do they call these hills, yaar?" He turns to ask Jeevan.

"The Rockies."

"Ha, the Rockies. By Rockies you mean small rocks." He spits on the ground with mock contempt.

"Now, if you wish to see the really big rocks then come to our *Himalaya*. We'll show you real big rocks." He picks up some pebbles and holds them up close to my eyes. "Look, the Rockies."

And that is the way it was going to be for the rest of our trip, with Puran belittling every salient feature of the land and recalling every trivial homesick detail of the world far removed from ours.

During one windless night the landscape is draped with a light dusting of snow. Seeing halos of feeble light magnified by the suspended flakes Jeevan imagines a giant hand somewhere up in the clouds flaying cotton wool.

Sleeping in the open air my breath freezes onto the blanket's edge that covers my face. And since the soil on the ground was soft, we cupped handfuls of it to make shallow depressions to fit our bodies, and then rolled some of the soil back on top. This technique worked whenever we slept on soft pliable ground.

And, as if we had not suffered enough, clouds of mosquitoes now began swarming maddeningly all over us, working their way into the nostrils, ears and mouths. We had been told to soak our shoulder cloths and to wind them tightly around our faces, but this only offered minor relief. Since Puran seemed to attract the most creatures, he was now able to boast: "*Waheguru*, look, even the humblest of creatures seeks out the wisest amongst us to bless."

On day twelve towards sunset a sudden freezing shower that we had been scanning for several hours, finally caught us in the open ground with no shelter nearby except for a small stand of young, spindly elms. We huddled together under the stretched canvas and watched the valleys below us disappear in the drenching, while flashes of lightning struck the peaks at regular intervals. The wind suddenly picked up and began flapping the canvas menacingly until we could stand it no longer and took out extra layers of clothing to cover ourselves. Yet our teeth continued to chatter. We were reluctant to move away from the safety of the overhead branches.

Finally, after an hour of pelting us with chilled rain, the storm moved westward and the sun finally peeked through, briefly lighting up the surrounding slopes.

We struggled out from under the tarp and lit a large bonfire to warm ourselves. We could see a gleaming ribbon of light in the far distant north.

"Water?"

"That must be the Fraser, observed Jeevan. Can you see which way is it headed?"

"I don't know it's too far to tell."

Since we were now routinely travelling by day and sleeping nights, we decided to continue to follow the tracks until light would force us to choose a shelter for the night. By then we were all convinced that the distant river that we had seen had indeed been flowing southwest, and that meant that we had already made it over the midpoint in our journey.

The next morning a chill wind rushes up from the valleys and tears at our clothes; once again our task seems too foolish to contemplate.

tears at our clothes; once again our task seems too foolish to contemplate. It is difficult even to stand up straight.

Bagga finally plants the germ of a new idea in our heads.

"Yaar, what dignity is there in living like this as vagabonds? There has to be an easier way to do this. I no longer care whether we are now in BC or not. Let's find a way to give our feet a well-deserved rest."

The decision to board the first passenger train headed west for the rest of the journey west, has been unanimous.

The hour of travel from Donald to Kamloops kept us preoccupied in juggling the two tickets we could afford to buy while the rest of us slouched on the floor, pretended to be asleep, or made long trips to the toilet. There were to be more than one close call with the railways police and several with our nervous fellow passengers before a porter would finally appear to announce that we were pulling into the Kamloops station.

At Kamloops, we had to wait two more hours in pouring rain for the next train to deliver us to Vancouver, and while waiting we took refuge against a sheltered wall of the platform. As I watched idly the platform gradually began to fill up with passengers again in anticipation of the next train's arrival. I found myself speculating how closely the railway platform resembled a stage-set and a three-ring circus rolled into one, the props rearranged before each arrival, with the stationmaster conducting the cast of outbound passengers onto the platform. The arrival of the train in clouds of smoke, and the sudden burst of frenetic energy in which all the props are set into motion until the final whistle blows amidst another cloud of steam. The platform is then cleared for the next show. Exit stage left.

From Lytton through Princeton and Hope and on to New Westminster, until finally, late on the afternoon of October 21st we alighted onto the poured concrete platform of Vancouver.

Freshly delivered to the Vancouver downtown station we descend eagerly to touch the ground that has eluded us for so long. As we pool our meager belongings we are nervous to see the platform crawling with so many belligerent folks, noting that we could not have picked a worse time to disembark. Vancouver's wary downtown is bristling with pressmen and officious looking in derbies and bulky overcoats with fur-lined collars even when the rest of the passengers continue to roam about in light garments. The policemen appear to be armed to their teeth even when their weapons as hidden form view. We could make sense of the presence of the militia at the station, after all this was a time of global wars, but the heightened security of the local police came as a total shock. Besides, everyone seemed to glare at us and I wonder aloud if it would have been safer to stay on the train instead of the platform.

alarm over our arrival?

Among the neat piles of massive, heavy-gauged steamship suitcases, delicate hat and shoe boxes, elegant tin, wicker and fine leather luggage lining the platform, our pathetic island of three tin buckets, four bundles of clothing tied in broadcloths and crammed into knotted jute sacks, four soiled blankets and a tarp, stand out in stark contrast. And standing still and befuddled amidst the swirl of surrounding activity we are becoming increasingly conspicuous by our inactivity. We finally gather our belongings and beat a hasty retreat off the platform to the safety of an isolated fence beyond the railway tracks.

Puran once again suggests we pause for a moment before setting out to explore Vancouver and try to locate someone from our community.

"Before we head out, why don't you all let me bake you some rotis and cook some *daal*. I am starving," he protests.

"But we just ate an hour ago at New Westminster," Jeevan points out in exasperation. "Where do you tuck away all this food?"

As a train pulls away from the facing platform it reveals more of our surroundings, and it takes us several minutes to get our bearings. I notice the outline of the faded blue mountains lining the horizon, and the large body of water stretching beneath them. In between the mountains and the water is a narrow strip of familiar land dotted with spindly trees. I should know this scene with my eyes closed. After all we have spent two months in isolation in front of it. Stanley Park! Miraculously, we have come full circle, grateful now once again for the solid ground beneath our feet.

Three loose bricks and some driftwood are hastily located and assembled, a fire is soon crackling under a griddle, and within moments the rotis are sizzling. I am concerned that the aroma of baking dough will drift across the multiple sets of tracks and on to the railway platform. And sure enough, here come two policemen, their nightsticks at ready.

"Oye, oye, what do you think you are doing here?" A policeman in a bulky overcoat is heading towards us, his beefy face livid.

"Oye, you ragheads. Don't you see the firewood lying close by? You will set the whole damn place on fire. Move on, don't you know you can't do this here."

After standing dumbfounded for a several moments we pick up our makeshift hearth and move out of sight. Every time the indignant cops order us to move on we relocate a few feet further away before settling down. By then another indignant man with a head locked tight inside a large bowler hat has joined the policemen. The two stand glaring down at us. Unlike the other, the new arrival has less patience with the preparation of our meal. He kicks at the hearth and rapidly demolishes it, the griddle toppling over, and the rotis going up in flames. He stomps the fire out with his giant shoes, all the while glaring and shouting at us to 'get out, get out'.

"Run along, now. You can't do this here. Go find a restaurant or a hotel. Go and do this in your temple."

Within minutes the area is deserted.

We are rescued by another voice summoning us in Punjabi from across the tracks. It never ceases to amaze me how easily one Indian will locate another even in the most remotest corner of the Empire. Into this milieu now steps a tall, slim hook-nosed youth who introduces himself as Moti Lal. Coming to our rescue, he hastily gathers our belongings and guides us away from the railway station.

"*Jaldi, mere saath chalo.* Your lives are in extreme danger here," he whispers through clenched teeth and an undisguised look of urgency. "Trust me and just follow me out of here. And, by the way, how long have you men been out in the woods? Your clothes and belongings stink."

He leads us to a horse drawn cart, hastily tumbling our luggage into it. We hurry alongside him and move further east along the waterfront.

"So, where are you men coming in from?"

"Calgary." I offer, unsure of how much we should reveal to this complete stranger, albeit one who claims to have saved our proverbial hides.

"Calgary? That's a long way off. Well you are now in One-Couver, and today happens to be your lucky day," he beams with his palms pressed together in a *namaste*. "Welcome friends to One-Couver where our community finally has an occasion to distribute sweets to total strangers."

"Why is it such a special day? Is it Diwali?" Puran squeals in delight.

"It is a sort of Diwali, Holi and Eid all rolled into one. Let's first reach somewhere safe. And, by the way, has any one of you men heard of the ship Komagata?"

"Heard of it, we were on it?"

He turns to look at me incredulously.

"You expect me to believe that you all came here on the Komagata and then left for Calgary? Impossible. I know each one of the lucky few who were allowed to land, and that includes Dr. Raghunath and his family. No one ever mentioned you folks."

He shakes his head in disbelief, unable to take us seriously.

"Well, never mind all that now. You are here and that is what matters most. Come on; let's get some food into you, and then maybe a change of clothes. First things first, right?"

change of clothes. First things first, right?"

We had meant to keep our arrival a secret but word of it spread rapidly throughout the Indian community. And soon enough, my friend Arjun arrives beaming from ear to ear, and shaking his head in disbelief, greeting us and rudely brushing off Moti Lal's inquiries.

"Look, what kind of fish is this? One moment you are out there leaning over the railings hauling sacks of potatoes and now you are here on solid ground. Are there more than one of you, tell me?"

"Sadly, given our last reception here no one else wanted to return," I reply joyously. "I swear never to set foot of my own free will on another ship, and shall make an honest life for myself only on solid ground."

"Well, you are the lucky ones in more ways than one. There was so much bloodshed on Komagata's arrival at Buj Buj. So many of the passengers are still missing. I hear there were some twenty deaths amongst the passengers. But let me get you some food and some new clothes first. You must be famished."

Moti Lal, who has continued to follow us, suggests Rattan's shack and we all head eastwards in a throng. "A little taste of home," he whispers. The shack is actually a dry goods store that is crammed with jute sacks and wrapped packages. It also appears to cater to several of the peripheral needs of our community. And tucked away from view is its tiny kitchen that is the size of a table to seat four.

As soon as are seated Arjun breaks out in a broad grin, repeatedly slapping my shoulder and chuckling to himself in repeating, "I knew it, I knew it. I knew somehow you would find a way to get back here. Tell me, how many others are out there? And why are you coming in from Calgary?"

I stretch my arms expansively into the air. "That, my friend, is a story that will have to wait. First there is something else I have to attend to urgently."

Following the warm meal, we stroll once again down to the waterfront, led there by an instinct to a spot closest to where we had been stranded at midstream. We spend the rest of the evening squatting on our heels as close to the water as we can get, lost in our individual thoughts in reminiscing about those distant days of deprivation barely two months ago, suddenly grateful for the food in our bellies and the firm land beneath our feet. I have the sudden urge to reach down and run my fingers through the water, to step knee-deep into it, to bathe in it and offer thanks. I feel the water rising between my toes, and I reach for it on the impulse to honour an elder by bending down and touching its feet.

"Well, we finally got him," Arjun blurts out. "*Waheguru*, how we holes in broad daylight. In full sight of everyone, right there under the judge's nose. And, then surrendered peacefully to the police. He has got rid of a monster that has been a thorn in the side of our community since the day he arrived here."

"By '*do-mui*' you mean Hopkinson, don't you?" I ask incredulously.

"Yes. The one and only Hopkinson. With their hero now dead the immigration police are suddenly suspicious of every Indian they see around them. They think each one of us is after their skin. After what he put you through, aren't you glad he is finally gone?"

# THE NARRATIVES OF MEWA

# THERE ARE NO WORDS IN MY LANGUAGE

As Victorian prisons go this one is less draconian with only the occasional garbled message echoing off the three stories of frozen walls. The imposing building's southwest walls face the Fraser as it races west, past the distant White Rock, a wisp on the southern horizon, and into the wild Pacific.

There is no means, should Mewa Singh wish to do so, of communicating with the rest of the inmates. However, a curtain has already been drawn between him and the affairs of the external world. There is a kerosene lamp in the cell, a patch of torn sky sectioned off by inch thick steel bars hung high from one wall, and a heart still beating. There are whimpers and occasional screams during the night. Men cough, spit and retch; there are whispers of beatings, and dark things happening during sunny days. A contraband still calms frayed nerves and flared tempers in full view of the guards armed with breech loading guns. Ice forms on the walls as tensions hover in the air like rusted wires being stretched taut. However, most of the time the monotonous routines of boredom remain unchanged, often stretching from days to months, and even years at a time.

Segregated for the last few days before the gallows are prepared, Mewa has been interred in solitary confinement since mid October. It is January now. He has gradually become immured within his homogenized drab and gray surroundings, where even the brief jaunts outside for fresh air fail to hold his attention.

And yet, he is discovering within himself a newborn grace, and acquiring a new skill for internalizing all his experiences and observations. It is only the infrequent visits by the temple priest Bhag Singh that brings him out of this apparent fog of apathy. Under the watchful eyes of the guards and wardens, hastily scribbled notes are exchanged while verses from the Granth Sahib are recited; their exchanges having fallen into familiar patterns. The *granthi* will begin by quoting the verses:

*Even Kings and emperors with heaps of wealth and vast dominion cannot compare...*

To which Mewa will respond:

*...with an ant filled with the love of God.*

*I am not the born...* recites the priest,

*... how can there be either birth or death for me,* replies Mewa.

Barely eight years ago during his baptism at the local gurdwara, Bhag Singh, as the temple priest, had reiterated to him to be flexible in his worship and avoid ritualism of all sorts.

"Remember only the core values you hold true. Remember, a Sikh is a lifelong learner.… Remember, the Sikh symbol of the double sword is your god's reminder that he is the Creator and the Destroyer. … And that the kirpan is worn on the left side so that in defence your right hand can reach it easily, … and the karha on your right wrist as a constant visual reminder of your commitment. Remember… remember…"

Now in a singsong tone they exchange the news of all that has transpired since their last meeting.

"Was it not in this manner," Bhag Singh asks with a twinkle in his eyes, "that we were once able to address the entire congregation and get past the watchful *do-mui* and his *chamchas,*" a reference to Hopkinson and Gwyther, the two unwelcome translators who were often present in their midst.

But these are only brief and rare moments of respite from the solemnity of their circumstances.

Before leaving, the priest reminds Mewa that we as humans are frail, and as conscious creatures we are confronted with a lifetime to endure the might of an unpredictable universe that appears to be massed against us. The only hope of resistance we can offer in response is our faith, our belief in a power that is mightier than not only ourselves but also the entire universe. We hold this flame above our heads and are emboldened by it as it banishes the dark, and makes the light and shadows of our days and nights slightly more bearable.

The brief notes that Mewa recites will be smuggled out beyond these prison walls and transcribed; portions of them will circling the globe within days and inspire others.

Mewa spends the few of his remaining days in mourning, for all the days and nights of his past life. In the beginning he grieves mostly for himself while examining the arc of his life, from early awareness of a child and the daily toils through the sunshine of his youth in Lopoke and central Punjab. Eventually, his mind returns to his arrival in Vancouver nearly eight years ago. A burning bitter bile rises in his throat as he chokes on the words: *there are no words in my language that can express…* but then he calms himself down, reminding himself that his personal welfare is not at stake here anymore. What he had once set out to achieve has been nothing less then epic in its historic scale and significance. There will be time for everything else later on.  In anticipating the planned Ghadar date he is reminded that the first rebellion had failed because of the deceit of the enemy and our sycophantic royalty. But this time there would be no such hurdles. The *angrez* now depends on their Sikh defenders for their own safety. This time ours is the hand that will seal their fate. Already the days have lengthened and the nights compressed. He watches his breath thaw the ice on the cell walls.

"I have seen the nodes on the branches begin to transform into buds. Already the sap is moving within the tree trunks. A few more weeks and this cold snap will end in the blooming all around us."

*Waheguru,* how fast February twenty-first already draws near when we shall triumph. I have spent a mere twelve weeks in here and another six weeks from now the revolt will begin from Agra, Khanpur, Allahabad, Lucknow and Meerut, and even from Lahore, and the time will come to seize back what is ours."

If there are doubts in his mind, he hastily pushes them aside. Yet, his reservations continue to gnaw at him through the fog of delirium. "Always in the past there have been traitors amongst us sniffing out opportunities for personal gain. The greatest rat of them all, Bela, is still at large, tucked away in some cell for his own safety from our wrath. How long will he evade the vengeance that will seek him out even in darkest night, with even with the king's security smothering him in their protective embrace? Is he not already turning into ash like his crony Mr. Hopkins? And his other rat companions, are they not already being picked out by us one by one. How long will they escape our wrath?"

"I have begun this mission and it is up to others to finish it," he whispers through clenched teeth to the priest, as if tasting for the first time the frustration gritting against his teeth.

At his inquest, his friend and confidant, Sohan Lal, had cautioned him: "Mewa, you must realize this that after this highpoint in your life everything else will be a let down, and nothing else, not even the gallows, will ever match the intensity and excitement of this moment."

Mewa has gradually begun to accept that all his life has been lived only for those few moments of his leaping triumphantly into the air after the firing; even the finality of the waiting scaffold can only be a let down.

However, in his state of delirium he hums to himself, switching between the easy comfort and re-assurance of the Punjabi lyrics recalled in snippets from childhood chants, and even the infrequent clumsy smatterings of English that out of necessity has been assimilated reluctantly into his lexicon and his consciousness. He is hesitant in these final moments, to be held back and contained within himself, as if the essence of his human life were being poured into another vessel. All he desires is to loose himself further in the familiar lilt of the kirtan and the words of the epic of scriptures and Gurus embroidered into the Granth Saab. These words are etched into his heart and consciousness, an unbroken chain that stretches five centuries before his time and yet the glow from each word is as alive and relevant to this day as it was when it was first issued through blessed lips; the message of every verse is deeply personal, and will come alive with every repetition to sooth and heal frayed minds.

In his feverish and disassociated state, he mutters repeatedly into the void, but more urgently to himself, "*Wahe Guru,* accept my sacrifice; and let me not be found wanting in any way.

> *O God, my mind is fascinated with*
> *Thy lotus feet as the bumblebee with the flower;*
> *Night and day I thirst for them.*
> *As fragrance abides in the flower*
> *As reflection is within the mirror,*
> *So does your Lord abide within you,*
> *Why search for him without?*
> *From its brilliancy everything is illuminated."*

By early January, after witnessing this delirious state and hearing Mewa's garbled verses, his defence lawyer makes a last desperate attempt by asking the court for clemency in the verdict. He declares that the defendant was of unsound mind when he committed the crime, and that this was a crime of passion and that he was instigated by others to carry out the deed. And as a direct response to this a medical examiner has already visited Mewa to perform a series of tests on him. But Mewa has anticipated the implications of such a move. He remains particularly alert and responsive during these examinations, realizing that he has not come this far to have his sacrifice snatched from him. He could just as well have taken a pot shot from a dark alley and completed his mission. No, it had to be done out in the open, for all to see that he had not been afraid and that he was out there to make a very public statement.

The lawyer continues to argue with him.

"Look, the deed is already done. The person you wanted to remove has been removed. There is no further need now for you to sacrifice your life also. What good will your death accomplish? Your well-wishers have also taken up the same theme, reasoning that the bigger battle is still not yet fought, and we need you in our midst; the Khalsa needs you. We need men like you who can inspire others to take up the cause against injustices everywhere."

But his imploring is spurned.

"I am a simple man who has led a simple life," Mewa tells him through a translator. "I have never before questioned the worth of my sweat or the impact of my deeds on the world around me. The Guru's world has always been bigger than all that I could comprehend. Only asking at the end to be rewarded for the day's toil. And mine has been a lone voice in the wilderness. I have lived amongst these unbelievers and never questioned my treatment at their hands. And yet, this man pretending to be my friend has done more damage to our community than the entire might of the Canadian government. He has mocked us, and taunted us with the witless impersonations. He has even been desperate enough to sneak into our midst, and still has the nerve to wag his tongue in anglicized Hindi into our ears; he has toyed with us like a god arbitrarily choosing toys to bless or punish. He is a shadow that stretches out of India to pursue our heels; pitilessly selecting those amongst us he cannot bear and returning them back to India or sending them off to Canadian cells. And we have suffered under the thumbs of his web of ruffians, each worse than the other and no one worse than Bela who openly taunts us, and soils the sanctity of our temple with blood and curses, boasting within its grounds that no one can touch him as long as he resides in George's dominions.

"In my native land I would effortlessly slip from one social gathering to another, able to arbitrarily join in on any conversation with easy social camaraderie. Here I am pushed to a peripheral role on the margins of a polite and pretentious society that chooses to look away rather than acknowledge my existence. They see through me as if they were looking through a glass pane. Yet little do they know how we are all like the breath fogging this windowpane."

The counsellor leaves shaking his head in frustration.

However, throughout that night bouts of frustrations and exultations wash over Mewa in intermittent waves, like a tide that ebbs and rises, a moon that waxes empty and fills again.

Towards the end there passes a brief hiatus in which mewa is alone and able to free his mind from his immediate surroundings and soar beyond the granite walls.

It is late in the afternoon. Staring idly out of a second story window at the southern horizon his eyes follow the shiny strip of the Fraser River as it sluices down from the surrounding slopes of farmland and flows into the sea.

He wonders if the tide will be moving upriver at this time of the day. All this sweet water flowing westwards, pouring into the salt-flecked waves and the mouth of a greedy beast that tears tirelessly at the frayed edges of this lush land. The sweet water then flows down into a maze of islands and further out into the ocean's open water that spans several days of sailing. The wind carries his mind till it arrives on the shores of the Japanese isles, and further still onto the Chinese shoreline and then Hong Kong and then over the Malaysian isthmus to a land called Hindustan. There it sweeps over the Deccan plains until you come onto an earth that is the shade of ripened grain, its patina deepened by the sluice of sunlight, mountain streams and the unburdening of clouds.

Out of the dark interior of a familiar hut there emerges an

ancient woman with a stooped back, staring up at the sky while shading her eyes with an arthritic hand; an equally ancient man heads out to the fields at the outskirts of the village; buffalos festooned with naked young boys wallow in a muddy pool.

Mewa recognizes this as the land he once nurtured with his sweat. But wait, what is this that he sees in the middle of his vast open field, this imposing bor tree with roots that are deeper than the stretch of its barren branches. And, each of its branches is laden with birds that have soiled the land beneath. As Mewa watches, the birds rise in flocks and come to settle on the ground, endless wave upon wave rising into the sky and settling across the entire countryside, and plundering its harvest. Outside the prison yard a sheltered snowdrift has survived against a north facing brick wall, and a handful of pale blue crocus buds have ploughed their way through it and now quiver in the chill breeze.

Three ravens, feathers ruffled, eyes gleaming, beaks at ready crash into the yard and begin to caw.

The final day dawns bitterly cold and wet.

Mewa has spent the night in prayer and meditation on the teachings enshrined in the Granth saab, teasing out the muted human voices behind the inflection of the holy lyrics; teasing out subtle implications tucked beneath the surface of the verses.

> 'Alone let him constantly meditate in solitude on that which is salutary for his soul, for he who meditates in solitude attains supreme bliss.'

The cadence of each verse gently falling in its allotted space like a leaf littering the moist earth, his subdued thoughts permeating the woven aesthetics of *gurbani*:

> 'Sing the songs of joy to the Lord, serve the Name of the Lord, and become the servant of His servants.'

But, by then Mewa's essence is lost in the one vivid recollection, this one act that has summoned every ounce of strength from him. Over and over and over he relives it. The light spilling through shards of tinted glass of the courthouse stairwell. His measured and determined approach to his prey. Where he had always been lethargic there is now an electrical charge propelling him forward, rapidly clearing the distance, rushing headlong, momentarily deaf, dumb and blind. His tingling fingers exploring the hard metal buried in his coat pocket, his shins stiffening under the unfamiliar weight of the other gun strapped there. He is now a mountain stream threading its wilful path downhill, he is a waterfall crashing earthwards, a locomotive hurtling through ridges and valleys, thundering beyond self.

*'There is but One God, His name is Truth, He is the Creator, He fears none, he is without hate, He never dies, He is beyond the cycle of births and death, He is self illuminated'*

In his mind he has had enough time to ponder how it came about that he would be placed upon this particular spot so many worlds removed from his, this refuge within a sea of hostility, this heart of solace within a tossed sea of turmoil, and the comforting trappings of his religion?

"*Waheguru,* your God's world stretches east and west and north and south beyond my limited imagination. How did this speck of dust borne by the waves and sea breezes happen to land here? How was this spot allotted to me, this moment assigned to me, these acts chosen for me to perform? How and why was I blessed out of the teeming *lakhs*? Why was it decreed that it would be *my* blood that would be spilled in your honour? And *my* sacrifice accepted? From a lifetime of sins which good deed was it that led to my salvation?"

"When I climb these fifteen steps I will be welcomed home."

## MEWA SINGH'S FINAL MESSAGE
San Francisco Chronicle, January 12, 1915

My religion does not teach me to bear enmity with anybody, no matter what class, creed or order he belongs to, nor had I any enmity with Hopkinson. I heard that he was oppressing my poor people very much. I made friendship with him through his best Hindu friend to find out the truth of what I heard. On finding out the fact I, being a staunch Sikh, could no longer bear to see the wrong done both to my innocent countrymen and the Dominion of Canada. This is what led me to take Hopkinson's life and sacrifice my own life in order to lay bare the oppression exercised upon my innocent people through his influence in the eyes of the whole world. And I, performing the duty of a true Sikh and remembering the name of God, will proceed towards the scaffold with the same amount of pleasure as the hungry baby does towards its mother. I shall gladly have the rope put around my neck thinking it to be a rosary of God's name. I am quite sure that God will take me into his blissful arms because I have not done this deed for my personal interest but to benefit both my people and the Canadian government.

At death, the clocks in the family home are stopped, the picture frames covered with cloth, and time forced to stand still.

Elsewhere a garland is placed around the portrait of the loved one.

Jean holds the hand of her younger sibling, looks up at a gossamer length of cotton stained the colour of the sky. It dangles from the topmost branch of a surviving hemlock whose exposed roots snake the length of their back garden.

She yells excitedly: "See, I knew it all along."

She brings Connie out to the backyard to point out the stain in her sky.

"See, I told you, I told you…" she repeats.

"… *yeth, injun lope tlick! injun lope tlick*," the younger one mimics gleefully, seeking and finding comfort in her sister's proffered hand.

After the cremation, the ash rises on an updraft of warm air and is wafted away. Its heat dissipating rapidly, it drifts back to earth. It settles onto the surface of the water where surface tension momentarily holds it suspended in defiance of gravity. Eventually, it breaks free and settles into the suspended nutrient soup that will now nourish and nurture other lives. Where-ever it settles on the land it mingles with the grass blades and weeds, the rotting fall leaves and fecund debris of extravagant summers, and is laced inextricably into the soil.

An extended lamentation rises from the Hopkinson household and goes unheard.

"Hopi, O my Hopi, all this vacant space and time stretching before me that you will never fill now with your presence, or with the comfort of your warmth; your silent absence rasping in my ear like an ache that makes my head spin.

"Your face in final repose appears knotted with an unfamiliar grimace. Faded now forever is that absent-minded and vacant expression you so often wore and that once so infuriated everyone who cared for you. You lived most of your life in an interior shadow world into which no one of was ever privileged to intrude; chasing after and teasing illusive creatures from your shadows, weaving recognizable patterns out of brief flashes of light that few of us had the ability to see".

The shadow of these times will continue to stretch into the rest of Nellie, Jean and Connie's days and nights. And, their abruptly re-arranged world will become a sharp, jagged place they will gingerly revisit many times; each such visit tinged with the bitter tears of regret and the heaviness of unanswered questions.

"In the face of the immense odds heaped against daily, our determination finally wavers and begins to whither. And, we attempt to fill the surrounding void with our feeble chants, the only response we can offer in a silent and hostile vacuity that greets all our efforts. And when we have exhausted ourselves and are finally spent, then we wait for a response, even if it is only to hear an echo of our own message. There has to be more to this existence than this unresponsive and silent void into which our chants are so hopefully launched. We are chickadees and infants chattering incessantly for attention in staking our claim to this existence.

"And, the universe returns back to us only the echo of our own hollow chirping, and all our chants are returned to us unacknowledged, our prayers unanswered. Are we chattering only to ourselves?

"...and still the crocuses push towards the light through the ice and snow and the dark dirt, and birds take wing into the open void, and incomprehensibly distant stars continue to flicker.

"The pale wisp of a half moon like an inked image flicked absent-mindedly onto rice paper, tumbles behind the impossibly blue hills at the far end of the horizon, and disappears as if it were another one of Hopi's confounding sleights of hand."

# BASHIR'S EPILOGUE

# UNEXPECTED VISITORS
## 13ᵗʰ November 1921

"What else did they say?" I ask searching the boy's confused face for clues, further testing his earnestness. He is a student in one of my classes and has also been assisting us in communicating with others in hiding.

"Nothing else, just this that you were to prepare a feast for some important guests. And to make sure that the *zarda* is properly caramelized."

"What?" I ask as perplexed as he is.

"He said that you are to make sure the *zarda* is well caramelized. I don't really know Masterji what he meant by that."

"Hah! How many did they say were coming, how many?" I ask impatiently.

"I think it was one or four. I really couldn't fully understand the instructions since the man's face was partially covered and it was already getting dark in the evening and I was late for my *Maghrib namaz* and…"

"Well, never mind all that now. When did he say the visitors would be arriving?"

"Around midnight, exactly a week from now." I stare at his solemn face and try to regain a semblance of control.

"And, what else did he have to say?"

"Only what I have already told you."

"But that doesn't make sense to me. Why should anyone else care whether the *zarda* is properly caramelized? Unless, of course, the message is from…" Seeing my mind thus pre-occupied, the boy begins to slink away. A few steps later he turns around unexpectedly.

"Oh, and he also said not to let anyone else know since this piece of information was meant solely for you."

And so it was that on seeing how troubled he was getting, I had to let it go at that. But as soon as I did so, he began chasing after me again, breathlessly muttering something inaudibly.

"The messenger also asked that you send your entire family away for the duration of the visit."

"You idiot, if I send my family away, who will prepare the feast?" I fire back unable to keep the exasperation out of my voice.

He looks down uneasily at the caked mud between his toes, until I place a reassuring hand on his shoulder to make amends for my rough manner. What else could I do? I had to be sure that what he was telling me was the entire truth and that it had been conveyed fully and accurately. One could hardly be too careful these days in which thuggies posing as subversives were always seeking out the gullible. A single slip here and someone in our neighborhood was bound to whisper, and I certainly had everything to loose by this.

About the coded clue regarding the dish of caramelized *zarda*, the sweet saffron rice - there was a time aboard the Komagata when we were beginning to get creative in staving off our hunger. Each of us had in turn prepared an imaginary dish of our favourite food. When I proffered caramelized saffron rice, Gurdit-ji had burst out laughing, claiming his mouth was already watering. Who else but Gurdit himself would send such a message? But a sixty-plus years old fugitive at large from the *gora paltan* with a reward of 40,000 Rupees on his head would never have shown up so brazenly at Lopoke.

As Kartar Singh, I have twice rejected sarkari hospitality and the clutches of a two-headed snake, and at the end of each escape I have reincarnated myself, phoenix-like into a different persona. Currently, I am Bashir Ali, the elementary schoolteacher who has returned from abroad to Lopoke, his ancestral home, to finally pick up the frayed threads of his life and weave them into a semblance of an outwardly normal life. And now, Mewa Singh has removed forever the singular threat that would have exposed me. Only one night in a Lopoke cell and a few hours of incarceration on a patrol launch in the Vancouver harbour are all it has taken for me to learn the value of my personal freedom. What had begun in the fever of my idealistic youth has now become a somewhat ambivalent passion. My shadowy double identity is kept hidden from even my closest family, and I have aided dozens, if not hundreds of determined and steadfast others like me.

In the past few months, I had even harboured an Ibrahim Ali Lopoke who stayed with me as my maternal uncle, when in reality I had never set eyes on him before. In addition, nearly every village in the district of Amritsar has had some form of covert activity within its confines; clandestine meetings have been held in the enclaves and *havelis*, all at great personal risk to our families and to our properties. We have organized training camps ranging in the use of firearms and homemade explosives, to the distribution of seditious literature, and acting as underground messengers.

The demand for my seditious literature has never flagged even though my output has decreased significantly.

Perhaps, this account will make up for it.

Our 'subversive' activities have often resulted in unexpected arrests, with many comrades exposed and taken away from their homes, never to be seen again. We have organized hunger strikes in protest against the inhuman treatment of prisoners, their poor conditions and substandard food, putting to test the Britisher's claim that they are moral and just administrators; the lie that what goes on behind closed doors is above the law.

Traveling by bullock-carts and third class compartments of trains, I have found myself increasingly drawn to the Red Flag under which we have been organizing Kisan Sabhas within the framework of the Punjabi Kisan movement for farmers to congregate and rouse other peasants with their common concerns. And, our movement has always known at heart that our real strength did not rest in the British-educated babus who run our political organizations and yet remain immune to the injustices around them. If our revolution is to continue it has to do so from the ground up, and in the question of Punjab, it has to be rooted in the soil and free from dialectic discourse and rhetoric. And, what frightens the authorities most is that ours is a movement rooted in the soil and not in abstract philosophies. When I examine myself closely, I, too, am a creature of this soil. It has nourished and sustained my forefathers for thousands of years, even as far as our human memory can stretch. Yet, within a single lifetime of the intruder finding shelter on our shores, I have been forced to turn my back on my land. What the tight clutches of the landlord and the sleazy moneylender's hand reaching into my pocket could not achieve, the Farangi has achieved within a few decades.

But enough of this idealistic talk of revolutions for now. All throughout my enforced bachelorhood while traveling or working in Vancouver, I have spent too much time in the company of men. This ascetic existence without the comfort of extended families that we Punjabi males have all grown up with has been most demanding. Surely grown men were never meant to live like this. There has been little time to contemplate lost loves, and seek new ones, and anticipate affairs in the future. It is time now for Khadeeja and Kausar to enter my narrative.

At this moment I have family matters to attend to. There has been no peace in our home since last week when the first message arrived. Khadeeja, my wife of four years, has been fussing all about the home tidying things up for the expected guests, and gathering all the ingredients for the scheduled feast. She has also sent word to her parents that she will be at their home by Friday night. We have argued back and forth whether she should stay behind and personally supervise the preparations and the servings, and by Friday morning with the cooking in full swing, she has reluctantly agreed to let Kausar stay behind. Kausar, the one I married barely a year ago, is to stay behind.

Kausar is to stay behind!

Catching me staring repeatedly out the door, Khadeeja pokes an elbow playfully into my side:

"Are you sure this is not just another ruse to get me out of the house?"

I smile back at her, wanly.

"All right then, have it your way. I know Kausar can take on this responsibility, but I still think I should stay instead of her. I have more experience than her. And, I understand your needs better."

Then, as if on cue, beguiling Kausar hurries past us to the smoke-filled kitchen. We watch her fussing about the open courtyard and attentive to the outdoor clay oven. She is wrapped in an air of newfound grace, authority and maturity, and firm in her instructs to the retinue of servants around her.

On the rare and fleeting occasions when Kausar and my fingers have brushed or when our fleeting glances have met she has nervously looked up at Khadeeja and hastily moved away, both of us aware that we must wait till after the feast is over and the guests have finally departed.

Late in the night, when I hear the sound of someone clearing his throat outside my door, I know that the guests have arrived.

Amazingly, it is bhai Gurdit Singh himself who first steps into the light, quickly drifting through the door and into the house, anxiously glancing back over his shoulder.

*"Ah, mere* Bashir *prah,"* he sighs, breathless from his exertions. We greet each other as if an age has passed since our last meeting, embracing and then he tapping my shoulder repeatedly and calling me *master-ji, master-ji.*

A young man who has guided him here slouches back into the shadow of an adjacent wall outside the door, well versed enough to keep guard and warn us. I am equally cautious that this meeting has the potential of just as easily resulting in my arrest for harboring one of the most sought after fugitives in India. But for such an honorable guest I am willing to take on this risk, excited at the prospect of this unanticipated re-union.

I am shocked to discover how much older he seems, a mere shadow of the man that I once knew. Seven years on the run had obviously taken their toll. He looks gaunt and tired, the straggly beard unkempt and completely white where it had been full and peppered with gray, the brow now heavily set in tension. But I can still recognize the crusty old fighter in him. When I first met him on the Komagata Maru, he had already been the eldest amongst us but the intervening seven years seemed to have aged him by twenty. I am relieved to discover that beneath the newly acquired web of lines, his eyes can still light up to accompany the crinkled grin that is now plastered across his broad face. His firm clasp in greeting me has a slight tremor, and I attribute it to over exertion.

It turns out there is to be only one visitor. The rest have been hastily dispersed to other hamlets and bhai sahib will not even reveal who or how many of them were there.

When I enquire about his recent sojourn in Sindh, he cackles in mirth like a boy being reprimanded of a prank. "Lets eat first and we'll talk about it later," he remarks.

"And what has become of your fourteen-year-old son, Balwant," I ask concerned as I had heard that the two had been separated at the fiasco at Buj Buj, but he hastily brushes this aside.

"Masterji, I had so desperately wanted it that Balwant should be educated in Canada or failing that at least in a Western environment. Clearly, I was not able accomplish this dream."

He turns to peer into the veranda and the dark courtyard lit by a solitary oil lamp. "Where are your children?" He asks with a withering look of surprise.

I shake my head in reply. "Allah has not chosen to bless us just yet."

We quickly move indoors, and seat ourselves cross-legged on the spread mats, and I leave momentarily to let Kausar know that there will now be only one guest and that we should begin to serve immediately. She fusses over the minute details of the presentation, sprinkling the garnish over the dishes, the crushed almonds and pistachio over the *gulab jamans* and *kheer*, and the sumptuous meal my household has been preparing for two days suddenly seems modest for such an esteemed guest.

Minutes later I invite Gurdit-ji's guide to come inside and join us in an enjoining room. And, when I lift the covering sheet from the dishes, a cloud of steam escapes with the scrumptious aromas filling the entire room. We first tackle a large circular tray of *pullao*, scooping up the steaming rice with our bare hands, our conversation interrupted every time a new dish is served, the memory of shared hungrier times stoking our appetites.

In between the muffled slurping of mouthfuls of rice, beef kebabs and goat meat stew, bhai Gurdit regales me with accounts of his time in hiding in Sindh.

"You know, how we Punjabis always love to poke fun at the expense of the Sindhis? Well, have you ever heard this one before: if you see a Sindhi and a snake in your path, first kill the Sindhi. Well, the Sindhis have a similar saying about us Punjabis."

"What if the snake is a two-pheaded one?" I ask joining in the mirth.

Our efforts to lighten the mood has its desired effect, and he rises stiffly to get a drink, the sound of the sloshing water drowning out all other sounds.

"Do you recall the time in the harbour in mid-June when our water rations were running low, and mercifully, we were not aware at the time that there was yet another month of this deprivation in store for us? Well, if it hadn't been for the daring efforts of that one man supply team, Sorain bhai, keeping us supplied with morsels of food right under the patrol boats and the immigrations officials' noses, we would not have been here to joke about it today.

"*Waheguru,* what an indomitable warrior, what guts. Perhaps, it was this one man's audacity that saved us all. Night after night, snaking his way to our ship, and not a telltale ripple from his oars in the stillness of the summer nights, he would surely have been shot right there had he been caught, and then no one would have been the wiser. I was never able to figure out how he lugged those heavy sacks of potatoes into the water by himself, unless, of course, he had onshore accomplices. Midnight, and our lookout would start scanning the distant water for patrol boats. What courage and what total disregard for his personal safety. What we had needed were a dozen such men and the Ghadar would already have been won.

"Throughout my life I have traveled to all corners of the globe and..." he drains the water from the bowl, and beaming expansively while wiping his mouth and beard with the back of his hand, remarks, "... nothing has ever tasted sweeter than this.

"Tell me, masterji, did your banished emperor Shah Zafar ever long thus for the water of his homeland?

"Dear friends, the weight and responsibility of once having challenged the empire has been a heavy one, but I will live one day to see this monstrosity brought to its knees".

In the uncomfortable silence that follows I notice that our mood has turned pensive. There are several ghosts with us attending the feast in this room.

"Perhaps, we should have come better prepared for the challenges ahead, and should have paid closer attention to *Giani* Bhagwan bhai's words when he came aboard to warn us. What a terrible waste of a noble human being to end up on the gallows at the Singapore garrison, the feel of the tightening noose around your neck the last sensation you will ever feel. So many of our brethren have gone that way. Surely, each of us is like an army of *sawa lakh*, but in *Giani's* case it has never been truer."

"Well, be that as it may, it sure beats being made cannon fodder like the others were." I add.

"Yes, I know. It's not all over just yet. There will be others. As for me, after tonight I have one more night of freedom left and then I, too, shall head off for Nankana Sahib," he announces unexpectedly.

"For a pilgrimage to Punjha Sahib?" I ask making the obvious assumptions.

"Well, I will make that pilgrimage, too, but I need to get to

Nankana Sahib next to attend Gandhiji's *satyagarha*. And at this prayer meeting, in the company of our families, Daljit and I shall finally surrender ourselves to the authorities."

He looks up at me to see my reaction and I am flattered that my opinion actually matters that much to him.

"I have been advised to do so by not only my closest companions but also Gandhiji himself. At this meeting the stage secretary, Master Sundar Singh Lyalpuri, will invite me onstage to address the Sikh assembly and to tell my story. I will then lead a procession to the police station.

"You know, I first met Gandhi-ji last year in Bombay through our Congress leader V. J. Patel. Since I was in disguise, when Gandhiji asked me my name I replied: 'I have no name; the one I have I cannot disclose here; if you still insist please allow me to speak with you privately for fifteen minutes.'

"Gandhiji replied that he had no time for this type of talk and that there was no need for privacy. I persisted by saying that all I really needed were five minutes, and he insisted that he really had no time. And that was the end of that meeting. Much later, when there was a challenge put up by Pundit Rambhuj Chowdhari to Motilal Nehru's accusation that 'the passengers at Buj Buj had lost their temper and violated the law'. Chowdhari defended us by saying that he had first-hand knowledge that 'the innocent passengers of the Komagata Maru were the aggrieved party'. And it was Chowdhari who persuaded me to set down my account of the Komagata voyage.

"I have lived a very interesting life over the past few years, and the fear of imminent arrest and internment has never been far from my mind. Such an arrest would then silence me from telling my story, yet throughout my seclusion I have been scribbling notes on my experiences. And that is the main reason I have come to see you. I now have the entire manuscript ready for you to publish. Before becoming a *sarkari mehman* I would like to hand this *amanat* to you."

He extracts with difficulty a large binder from beneath his vest and hands it to me.

"Here! Defend it the best way you know and let the world know what we went through for the sake of our people and our country."

The deed done, he seems to relax, as if the act had drained him of all his anxiety.

"I mentioned Gandhiji earlier on. Do you know what he said to me during a private meeting last month? Among other matters, his words to me were: '…the true soldier and servant of Guru Gobind Singh is one who will substitute his sword and kirpan by wielding the sword of non-violence. That will be the true consummation of the Guru's spirit. So long as one retains even one sword one has not attained true fearlessness, and no power on earth can subdue you when you are armed with the sword of ahimsa.'

"He also pointed out that the hero of the Komagata Maru should not have to live in such an undignified manner and constantly have to hide like a common criminal. Word must have finally reached his ear of my travails and predicament."

"But bhai sahib," I offer in empathy, "how long can they possibly keep you in there? One day you shall return to us and remind the world of your daring and your travails will inspire other generations. Why can you not stay in hiding a little longer until this manuscript is published?"

"There you go, four years as a teacher, and you are already beginning to lecture to your elders. Even though you were already more educated than any one of us, you were also the silent one amongst us. And I admired your self-restraint when everyone else so vociferously questioning my motives and lunging for my throat.

"When that day of freedom finally arrives, my friend, and they throw open the gates to set us free, perhaps our story will inspire other generations. Or perhaps not. Every generation has its priorities and ours may not be theirs, too. But you are right in questioning how long this state of affairs can possibly continue. Anyway, with their incorrigible cowardice at the Jallianwalla Bagh and incidents of bomb throwing making the news so fast beyond our borders, you can see how the *angrez* is now being challenged at every street corner. When they have nothing to attack them with the locals now toss garbage from their rooftops.

"We can already see a pattern developing here, and, the angrez must be getting extremely uneasy at having to resort to such increasingly desperate measures to maintain their hold on us. Surely, for every Englishman in our Hindustan there are a thousand of us. How long can this imbalance continue before it reaches its logical conclusion? 'The Great War to End All Wars', isn't that what they are calling it now, is over, but our war has not yet begun. Even the Russian revolution has succeeded whereas ours has sadly failed to materialize.

"Do you recall that after two months of Canadian 'hospitality' when a reporter asked me: 'Towards whom do you feel most unfriendly as a result of being forced to return to your own land?' I had replied: 'We had no cause to complain of the attitude and treatment accorded to us by the Canadian people. But we are most unfriendly towards our own Government in not being strong enough to see that Hindus as British subjects are not allowed to go to any place within the Empire.' The real battle we were engaged in was not only for those in North America, but also those who were back home. How can our people elsewhere live with dignity if our home country is still enslaved? The battles have not yet been won, and I am already in my dotage, still tied to the yoke, scrounging to eke a living. I, who once could challenge mighty empires and bring them to their knees, Guru, what have I come to?

"Masterji, it has been very lonely on this mission. And, our followers have often been fickle, for a mortal's personal resources are always limited at best. Yet, we continue consciously and repeatedly choosing to take on enemies a thousand fold mightier than ourselves.

"A while back you had asked me how my son was faring. The truth is that I myself do not know. My Balwant is as estranged from me as I am from him. Perhaps, it was foolhardy of me to take him along across the ocean so soon after the death of his mother. I should have left him with other relatives and not put him through dangers such that even a grown man learns to dread. And then at Buj Buj, when he disappeared from my side during the firing and the confusion of the chase that followed it, and then his remaining in hiding for almost a day, what father could forgive himself after that?

"Perhaps our failure was in trusting everyone else's enthusiasm for our cause and we should have had a better screening process in place. Just because someone could spout seditious slogans or proclaim *Down with the British,* and *Angrez murdabad,* we embraced them with open arms. Yet, who knows what men carry in the dark corners of their hearts? Throughout our history, at every turn of our struggle there have been those who have sold us out, and we have only uncovered their subterfuges long after the damage had been done. You see, not every traitor is as brazen as Bela who was able to blatantly mingle in our midst and yet proclaim his allegiance to his English king. When a man's true motivation for carrying out a deed is often clouded from even himself, how can we expect him to be pure and steadfast over any lengthy period when brutally challenged?

"But then how would such men stand up to the administration of the 'third degree'? Put anyone through that for hours at an end and how many of us will still remain dedicated to our cause. Masterji, human flesh is weak even when the spirit is unbending. A tiny blister on a finger or a slight toothache can keep you awake for nights. What chance does a mere mortal stand against the twisted machinations of one who is endlessly inventive in his means of torture, and who sees you as a wall that stands between him and his just reward, and is willing to go to any length to obtain it?

"Come, Bashir bhai, I have not come here to spill the poison of my melancholy into your blissful life. Let's get back to the feast for now, for tomorrow I shall have to rely on our government's hospitality.

"Now before I head out let me ask you one more thing. Do you still write your poetry for the Ghadar?"

I mention that after my hero Kartar Singh Sarabha's martyrdom,

I do not write a lot. I show him a few of my newer, shorter poems, and he pulls out a pair of wire-rimmed glasses and squints into them silently mouthing each word, his breath laboured.

"*Bhai ji*, I too have a question for you. For a long while I have been curious about Bela's fate. Is he still loyal to his distant king?"

We chuckle in unison at this.

"Bela! Haven't you heard, he now lives in his ancestral village heavily guarded and unsure of all those who surround him, mortally afraid of even his own family members."

Gurdit cackles in obvious delight at this morsel. "Well, how safe do you think he now feels in his majesty's mighty Empire? And where are his erstwhile saviours now, his Hopkinson and Reid and Stevens and that despicable Nawab Khan of Ludhiana, the British mole in all our Ghadar schemes, who once clandestinely spirited Bela out of Vancouver when we began turning up the heat?"

He remains silent for a few moments longer, before reaching for his shoulder cloth. His companion has quietly slipped out of the room and both of us are once again alone in the inner room.

"One other matter that has continued to bother me. Bashir, there were several things that I overlooked during the planning stage of our voyage, and the most critical and costliest error was not equipping the ship with a two-way radio. If not for that, we would have landed at Port Alberni, right under the immigration inspectors' noses and completed our mission. No one would even have heard of the doomed voyage of the Komagata, and you and I would only have been a footnote in the history books."

He seems troubled by this candid revelation.

"Yes," I concede. "But Hopkinson would then still be alive to carry on his rampage. And, others following in our wake would have been sure to run into the same trap that we did. Only, this time, instead of waiting for distant Ottawa to draft the necessary legislation the British Columbians would have created their own in-council regulations post haste."

We embrace one last time in preparation for his parting, and heading for the outer alcove. But then inexplicably Gurdit-ji returns to the inner room.

"Bashir, there is one other thought that has been bothering me. You have been an exemplary host and I owe you this. And, I do not want you to misunderstand my intentions for sharing this with you. It is also a matter that may have led me back to you." He pauses a moment for my response.

"I will not blame you if you do not want to reveal anything more about this matter to me."

"Anything for you, just ask, bhai sahib," I respond unsure of just what I was volunteering myself for, and at the same time wondering if Gurdit-ji had any lingering doubts about my sincerity and dedication?

He takes a while to compose his final words.

"Can you tell me what Hopkinson said to you on the Sea Lion, and why he kept you there for so long? There was apparently no reason why he should have held you there. What did he say to you in whisking you away with your head covered in a blanket and not even a word of farewell? You have not provided anyone with a satisfactory reason for this. Now, if you still do not want to share the reasons with me I will try to understand and forget this conversation ever happened."

"No, no." I stammer. "There is nothing sinister about my silence on this matter. It's embarrassing, that's all. I had no idea I would so easily end up grovelling like that. Actually, what Hopkinson said was this: that he suspected I was Kartar Singh whom he had once pursued in India. And that he thought I knew more than I was willing to reveal about the coming Ghadar. He kept on making these allegations about a killer setting out from Lopoke to untangle Hopkinson's web and to destroy him forever.

"Like you, bhai sahib, I, too, have often wondered why he was so fixated on Lopoke? Wasn't he originally from Lahore, and Lahore is in the same region as Lopoke, isn't it? So there may have been some imagined connection between the two places, but...?"

"*Waheguru!*" Gurdit suddenly exclaims, arriving simultaneously at the conclusion I was making. "I now know why he thought someone from Lopoke would come to kill him. Wasn't our *Shaheed* Mewa also from Lopoke?"

"Yes, but way back then in the summer of 1914 Hopkinson could not have known that his assassin would come at him from Lopoke. Even Mewa had no idea at the time that he would volunteer himself for this mission. Unless, of course, he had been planning it all along."

Gurdit looks at me intently, his face beginning to age before, all signs of the relaxed atmosphere of our recent exchanges removed. He sits down again. "But then would Mewa have confided in someone else? Perhaps someone from our midst was able to inform on him, even though the assassin was not apparently chosen until the last few days. How else could Hopkinson have made this connection five months before the assassination?"

We stare at the surroundings for several minutes, uneasy for the first time, our minds racing through various scenarios and imagined conspiracies, and seeing threats in every innocent exchange.

"I suppose it will remain a mystery for now," he finally says kindly as we embrace one final time. He drapes his shawl tightly around his shoulders, and walks warily into the unlit street. He has not revealed where or how he is going to team up with Daljit who has faithfully followed his every travail and will now join him in the final surrender.

I look for the guardian at our door but he has melted back into the shadows. I step back inside; continuing to be puzzled by the mystery, with an unidentifiable dread descending over me like a cowl and sending a chill down my spine that not even Kausar's presence by my side will allay.

It is almost dawn. The final quarter of the night. Once again the humpbacks are sounding off the west coast of Vancouver Island and the ship echoes in sympathetic resonance. There is a man eagerly scanning the horizon for an illusive shoreline, and searching a familiar constellation to guide him in to prayer.

However, this time I know that everything is exactly as it is ordained to be for I have been here before. I know the true direction of my *qibla*. This time I will make it a point to learn the names and natures of all the creatures I encounter, and be able to identify each species of wind-inclined spruce that marks our arrival. This time I shall arrive better prepared. This time I shall look into the depths of the dark hearts that greet us and be able to anticipate their every move.

This time I belong here as I belong everywhere.

And, this time I will not turn the other cheek.

## EATING CROW

When morning hunger pangs and errant winds
Buffet him afar
Raven finds beneath him an unfamiliar forest
Every feature white
As the all-blanketing snow
Even the ravens here are bleached
All pale feathers pupils beaks
Blending right back into their landscape.

Raven clips his ruffled wings
Crashing down
Hungering for a beakful of earth.

Seeing him thus approaching
A blot across their perfectly pale sky
An alarm is sounded
Flocks rise to intercept him in mid air.

Plummeting in self righteous fury
Raven concludes
There are only two colours
Black and Red
And White?

White is not even a colour!

# ACKNOWLEDGMENTS

A project of this scale could not have been undertaken without the generous contributions from several individuals who shared detailed accounts of their families' involvement in the Komagata Maru events. Some have chosen to remain anonymous. I owe an immense debt to each one of them.

I would especially like to acknowledge significant narrative assistance from the following:

Herb Singh Gill of Dhudike, for sharing the incredible and till now undocumented accounts of his grandfather, Jeevan Singh Gill, a passenger on the Komagata with family members Bagga alias Budd Singh Gill, Inder Singh Gill, Mewa Singh Gill and Puran Singh Gill, and their remarkable journey back from Yokohama to Mexico, and their record of walking the railway tracks from Calgary to Vancouver during the fall of 1914.

Jack Uppal, for his passionate recollection of his father Dilip Singh Uppal, a member of the Shore Committee during Komagata Maru's voyage. His enthusiastic and informed efforts have been instrumental in keeping the memory of the Komagata Maru alive.

Jaswinder Toor of Komagata Maru Heritage Society, for his notes on his maternal grandfather Puran Singh Jauhal of Janatpura's involvement in the Komagata Committee and the Ghadar activities.

I was privileged listening to Babaji Ghulam Mohamamed telling me about the life of his pioneer father Dan Ali. Sadly, Babaji, who had been the cornerstone of the extended family spanning four generations and living together, passed away a month after our last interview.

The late Hari Sharma who had been an ardent supporter of this project but sadly did not live to see it come to light.

And, finally, to the irrepressible seniors at Kerrisdale Community Centre in Vancouver, I say thank you all. You cherish extraordinarily vivid, long memories of your in a younger Vancouver. Of these, I am especially grateful to Patricia Fulton.

I extend my grateful acknowledgement to the Vancouver Public Library,

Vancouver City Archives and Burnaby Public Library for the extensive use of reference and archival material. Other material was accessed from the archives of The Vancouver Sun and The Province also at the Vancouver Public Library. A particular note of appreciation goes to Vancouver's Inter Library Loan services.

This novel could not have been written without the moral sustenance provided by my Nina and our children Farrah and Salman, and friends Sultan Somjee, Mick & Cheryl, Rasik & Melinda, Rashid Ahmed, Sadhu Binning, Sohan Lal Pooni, Ajmer Rode, and Baji Khalda Khatoon.

And, finally a note of thanks to Ashis Gupta and the folks at Bayeux Arts for their craft, care and patience.

The following valuable published sources were used extensively for research and incidental detail:

Hugh Johnston: *The Voyage of the Komagata Maru, The Sikh Challenge to Canada's Colour Bar*, Delhi: Oxford Press; and *The Surveillance of Indian Nationalists in North America, 1908-1918*, BC Studies, UBC; Kesar Singh: *Canadian Sikhs (Part One) and Komagata Maru Massacre*; Norman Buchignani & Indra Doreen, 1985. *Continuous Journey: A Social History of South Asians in Canada*. Toronto: McClelland & Stewart; *A White Man's Country – An Exercise in Canadian Prejudice*, Ted Ferguson, Doubleday Canada Ltd.; B. A. McKelvie: *Magic, Murder and Mystery*: S.W. Fallon: *A Dictionary of Hindustani Proverbs*, Asian Educational Services; Michael Kluckner: *Vancouver Remembered, Whitecap Books;* Jim Fairley: *The Way We Were: the story of the old Vancouver courthouse* (an excellent resource that curiously makes no mention of the Hopkinson murder); several web-based sources, including the Academy of the Punjab in North America (www.apnaorg.com) and Sikhipedia.

Though this novel is based on and inspired by the events surrounding the voyage of the Komagata Maru, I have tried my best to remain true to the original historical and personal accounts. Any chronological or historical errors or omissions of detail and any poetic license are entirely mine.

All comments are welcomed at: www.tariqmalik.net

North Vancouver, 23 May 2010